Surfing In Stilettos

By

Carol E. Wyer

Surfing In Stilettos

Published in 2012 by FeedARead Publishing

Copyright © Carol E. Wyer

British Library C.I.P.

A CIP catalogue record for this title is available from the British Library.

Web site: http://www.carolewyer.co.uk/

Acknowledgements

Being a blogger is a rewarding experience. I have made more friends since I began blogging as research for my debut novel, *Mini Skirts and Laughter Lines,* than I could possibly mention here. They have all been hugely supportive, and they are very special to me.

I would like to thank a few individuals who have helped me along the way, through their encouragement and positive posts on their own blogs: LindyLouMac, Dizzy C, Sylvia Massara, BaldyChaz, LG, Celia, Fran aka Fishducky, Melynda Fleury and the exceptional Ao, who has been a huge help from the off.

I would also like to extend special thanks to Pauline Barclay and Stephen Hise and their teams of fellow authors for allowing me to write features on their websites and providing me with excellent writing advice.

I must mention Andy, Kim, their children, and of course, wonderful Old Ted, who is probably the best behaved dog in the world. They kindly let me stay in their delightful gite in France and drink most of their wine while writing this book, and they were the inspiration for the characters Jeanette and Mark.

Grateful thanks to Judy Bullard for preparing the front cover and putting up with my indecisive nature. I still think the green would have looked nice. Or, maybe the pink...

Last, but certainly not least, I am completely indebted to Dannye Williamsen, who has patiently worked her way through this book several times, battling with both my use of slang expressions and French. Her input and expertise has been invaluable, and I can't thank her enough.

As Amanda's mother says: 'He who laughs…lasts!' May this book give you quite a few chuckles.

BLOG: Fortifying Your Fifties

Introduction

Welcome to the first post on this, my new blog—**Fortifying Your Fifties**. It is not, as the title may suggest, about drinking your way through your mature years, although I might be tempted to get Phil to stop off at various vineyards as we travel through France. When I mentioned that we'd have the chance to taste wines, he snorted rudely and said if I started doing that, I'd still be in Bordeaux by the end of the year, pickled at the bottom of a very large vat of wine.

No, this blog is for those of us who may be in our fifties but feel in our forties or even thirties—or in my mother's case, her teens. She has a brand new venture which is keeping her occupied–one that will surprise you all—but more about that later. She has also found out about Skype, so the weekly phone call from her has taken on a whole new dimension.

My newly discovered vigour for life is due in part to having finally shoved my son, Tom, out of the nest. Given we were having trouble convincing him to fly solo, we decided to jump first, so now we are the ones who have flown the nest, leaving Tom still in it.

I also put my new desire for life down to having enjoyed a steamy, online relationship with a hottie. It made me realise that maturing doesn't necessarily mean becoming old. "You don't stop laughing because you get old; you get old because you stop laughing." So why not follow my exploits and hopefully have a few laughs with me?

My grumpy—yes, he is still grumpy—hubby Phil and I are about to take off on a gap year to tour around Europe. I envisage a life of relaxation under moonlit skies, passion rekindled, and a lot of wine. There will be stylish shops to visit, places of interest, quaint cobbled streets, different cultures, vineyards, more shops, and hopefully, a lot more wine.

It should be fun, provided Phil cheers up. I hope we manage to enjoy ourselves and don't end up in the divorce courts or worse still, a prison cell, having been found guilty of murder on the Bürstner camper van. The way my life swerves about, I am sure I could end up at a completely different destination to the one planned. So climb on board and join the journey. *Tickets please...*

Posted by Facing50.Blog

5 Comments

SexyFitChick says...Love this new blog and the photo of you and Phil in the sidebar. He doesn't look half as miserable as you paint him to be, particularly in that woolly hat with all those badges on it and those roller skates. Why are you sitting on a giant, orange Space Hopper? I hope you intend posting some photos of the hunky foreign men you meet en route. Don't forget to hand the best-looking ones my business card. I'm counting on you. By the way, what do you mean you enjoyed a "steamy, online relationship with a hottie"? This is Todd we are talking about, I presume? *The* Todd Bradshaw. The Todd Bradshaw who lives near me here in Sydney and is often to be seen with a young girl on his arm. The dirty rat, cheating, lying ex-boyfriend hottie...

Facing50 says...Hello SexyFitChick. Thank you for the compliment. I have all your cards and will do my best to promote you! I'll explain about the Space Hopper in my next post. Maybe I exaggerated about Todd a little, but he was pretty good-looking in his day and certainly *hot*. Can't stay online long. Phil (not a *hottie*) is cooking baked beans on the gas stove outside, and judging by the grunts he is making, I think the food is ready. How romantic.

PhillyFilly says…Glad you are blogging again. I missed you. I spent the last few weeks getting some essential surgery. I had a bun lift. I guess you'd call it a bottom lift. I look like J-Lo, but I'm having difficulty sitting down. I keep sliding off the chair. The neighbor whistled at me yesterday. My daughter said he was whistling for his dog, but I don't believe her; it had to be my sexy new ass he was admiring. I saw him; he couldn't take his eyes off it. I'm looking forward to hearing about your trip. I'd love to be on it. Are you going to Switzerland? There are some great clinics there. I'll send you the addresses in case you fancy a quick refresh while you are there.

TheMerryDivorcee says…I'd love to be on a European Tour, too. I went to Venice with ex-husband number six to try and patch up a few differences we were having at that time. It was going quite well until we took a gondola ride, and I ended up in a bar with the Venetian Gondola boatman, who, funnily enough, became husband number seven. Those Italians sure know how to treat a lady. You can't blame a girl—not when a guy sings so beautifully to her.

YoungFreeSingleandSane says…I'm so happy for you. I hope you don't fall out though. Being confined in one space with someone 24/7 can cause huge problems. Just living in the same flat as Jonathan drove me mad. He had some dreadful habits. He even used to pick his toenails while we watched television!

Gypsynesters2 says…We can highly recommend this life. We left our kids behind two years ago and have been traveling around the States ever since. Should have left them years ago. Don't worry about being in the same space all the time. We fought to start with, but then it all settled down. Maybe that was because I left my nagging wife behind at a service station and picked up a gorgeous hitchhiker, who has been with me ever since. Good luck. ☺

OneFlewOverTheEmptyNest says…What a great idea. Our kids keep coming back like boomerangs. Every time we think they have gone, one or another of them returns, needing our help. Enjoy yourselves and don't drink too much wine.

Chapter One

Todd Bradshaw lay exhausted in bed. The sheets were jumbled together on the floor. Sunlight streamed through his condominium window, which had an enviable view overlooking the coast at Hawk's Bay. He had rediscovered paradise. In his arms lay his first true love, Amanda Wilson. He had not been this blissful since the last time he had held her. Admittedly, she was older. There were some lines around her eyes, and her body was softer and a fraction rounder, but that made her even more delectable.

He recalled the afternoon of passion they had just savoured. Age had had an agreeable effect on her. She had matured in many ways and was far more confident about her body than she had been all those years ago when he had first known her. *Where had she learned to do that thing with an ice cube?*

Amanda opened a sleepy eye and smiled up at him. The laughter lines accentuated a little, making her look even more appealing and full of mischief.

"What are you staring at?" she asked huskily.

"You," replied Todd, tenderly tucking a stray hair back behind her ear and admiring the gleam that shone in her green eyes. "Shall I go and get some more ice cubes?" he asked.

She placed her hand behind his head and guided him towards her, kissing him fervently. She still had that power over him. Thirty years and more than double that number of women had been and gone from his bed since he had last been with her, but it seemed as if the years hadn't passed at all. What a fool he had been to wait this long to reclaim her.

Reawakened with desire, he ran his hands over her soft, smooth skin. His hands travelled past her firm, round buttocks and onto the tops of her legs. She panted hard. That wasn't right. In fact, the more he thought about it, the more he realised none of this was right. Her skin wasn't very smooth at all. Actually, it was quite hairy. *Gosh, she had really let herself go! Had she stopped waxing her legs?* The panting was getting more urgent and louder in his right ear. His ardour receded rapidly. *Yuck! Was that slobber?*

Todd Bradshaw woke with a jolt. The television was still showing the same football match he had started to watch half an hour ago when he had dozed off. Digit, his cattle dog, was asleep next to him, panting and drooling in his ear. Todd shrugged the heavy dog off and stared at the figures running about on the screen. What was the matter with him? In recent weeks he had been dreaming nightly about Amanda, but now the fantasies were spilling over into the day.

He really should forget her.

He blew his first opportunity decades before when he left her for a meaningless relationship with a diplomat's daughter. They had been a solid item before that, and Todd had even considered asking Amanda to marry him. They had met in the romantic city of Casablanca, where they had both worked. Their relationship had been intense, fuelled by the heat of the orange sun that set magnificently each evening in front of their apartment; long walks along pale, golden, sandy beaches with only the sound of the waves to accompany them; and the heady aroma of cinnamon and other exotic spices that rose from the bakery below them each morning. There was no doubt that living abroad in the dazzling country of Morocco had helped cement their passionate relationship, and both had fallen heavily in love, especially Amanda. Scared by the thought of becoming trapped in a more permanent relationship when he still believed the world was waiting to be explored, Todd had felt the walls closing in on him. When his contract in Morocco expired, he had immediately applied for a position in Kuwait, knowing Amanda would be unable to get work there. It would allow him a little breathing space before committing fully to the delicious Amanda.

The money was excellent, and Todd had just about decided to propose to Amanda when one fatal night, he went to a party at the local diplomat's house and was approached by Vanessa, the diplomat's twenty-year-old daughter. She fell for Todd's bronzed, good looks and suave manner in a flash. Todd, being Todd, couldn't help himself; after all, the girl practically threw herself at him. If he were honest, she reminded him of his Mandy in looks—his Mandy who was far away in the UK, teaching in a private school in the Midlands. Todd caved in and had his fling with Vanessa. Feeling guilty, he told Amanda about it. Amanda's reaction had been one of utter disbelief and dismay. They had split up, not to be reconnected again until Todd found her on Facebook.

He ruined his second opportunity last year. Amanda had been going through a crisis with her husband, and Todd knew she was on the brink of leaving him. He only had to persuade her that he was the one with whom she should be. He had been invited to his nephew's wedding in the UK and so decided to use the trip as an opportunity to woo Amanda. He arranged to meet her the day after his nephew's wedding. Convinced he would be able to win her round, he had far too much champagne at the wedding. Weaving his way back to his room, he became distracted by the beautiful young Australian bridesmaid who had cornered him by the bar and spent a long time chatting to him. She was extremely interested in him. Her being thirty years younger than he was, Todd was flattered by the attention. That fact, combined with several more glasses of champagne, resulted in his spending the night, pretending he was still twenty-five years old himself. The girl was a gymnast and wrung every ounce of energy he possessed out of him. He slept all morning the next day and awoke sometime in the afternoon with an appalling hangover. The girl in question wasn't about to let him escape and leapt on him as soon as he woke. Several hours later, Todd felt his age and older. The girl left him to recover along with her phone number written on a pair of her tiny, lace panties. He threw them away.

He had missed his meeting with Amanda. He had messed it up yet again. She had kept him as a friend on Facebook, but they no longer chatted or played Lust Scrabble. Habit made him look at the computer. He sighed. *Blast!* There she was. The little green light illuminated next to her name indicated she was online and was available to chat. He stood up and paused in front of the computer keyboard. Should he?

Something was seriously wrong. He hadn't chatted up a single woman since that wedding episode. Last night at the local bar, he had refused the advances of a delightful Swedish girl with baby blue eyes, long eyelashes, and legs to die for. She'd made it obvious that she found him attractive and had felt his muscular thighs, fit from years of cycling, in a highly suggestive manner. He'd made his excuses and returned home to watch television. God, how he wished it had been Amanda who'd been feeling his leg.

He clicked onto her page and read her latest status updates: *En route to La Belle France—watch out vineyard owners!*

There were various good luck messages under the last status. She and her husband Phil were off on a gap year, touring around Europe. Todd rubbed Digit's head affectionately, musing on what might have been. If only he hadn't got drunk and ended up with that bland blonde. Instead of making him feel youthful, she had only served to make him realise he was a fifty-six-year-old man—a man who currently had hair growing out of his ears and who had recently bought a nasal trimmer.

He sighed again, more heavily, and decided to turn in for the night. He had an early start cycling in the morning. He needed to train for the next Veteran's race in a few weeks. Ha! That just about summed him up—a veteran. The adrenaline produced in such a race used to give him a tremendous buzz. He always thought it was better than sex, unless, of course, the sex was with Amanda Wilson. Now, nothing seemed to excite him. He was starting to feel his age, and worse than that, he was starting to feel lonely.

The small green light next to her name flickered tantalisingly. It would be so easy to type *hello*. Maybe she'd respond. Maybe they could start afresh…

Digit emitted a loud fart and turned over, his tongue hanging comically out of his mouth.

"You're probably right, old friend," laughed Todd, pulling the plug on the computer. "Not this time."

Chapter Two

At the same time as Todd switched off the computer and went off to dream about her, Amanda Wilson was heaving the contents of her stomach into a bush, her face ashen grey with bits of something rather nasty stuck to her chin. Phil was sitting in the driver's seat of the Bürstner camper van, listening to the radio, his face devoid of expression. Amanda retched one last time. There was nothing left. Her stomach was finally empty. She felt utterly drained.

Clambering back into the camper van, Phil stared coldly at her.

"Feeling better now?" he asked querulously. He turned the key in the ignition as she buckled up. He was going to suggest stopping at the next cafe for a fry up but thought better of it, although he could almost smell the aroma of the eggs, bacon, sausage, grilled tomatoes, baked beans, fried bread, and maybe even some potato cakes.

"Yes, I think so. I don't know why I feel so bad."

"No, you probably can't remember," retorted Phil. "I wonder what could have made you feel so bad? Maybe it was the two bottles of homemade wine you downed as soon as we arrived, or it could have been the half bottle of Kahlua you quaffed after that—" He didn't finish. Amanda had shoved the door open and was hurtling back to the bush to be sick again. Phil harrumphed, turned off the engine, and turned up the radio.

Surveying her pasty face and her hair encrusted with bits of what looked like carrots when she eventually returned to the camper van, Phil felt marginally less annoyed with her. It wasn't really her fault. She had just been trying to be friendly. That was her nature. She always wanted to please people, like an over-exuberant puppy. She would do almost anything to make someone happy. It was the Wicked Witch of The South West who had caused Amanda to be so ill this morning. Thanks to her, they had missed their ferry and would now have to wait to join one tomorrow. He drummed his fingers against the steering wheel while Amanda fiddled about with her seatbelt, getting tangled up in it due to a lack of coordination.

It was her mother who had plied her with alcohol all night and kept her up talking so that by the time she finally fell into bed, it was time to get up. It was her mother who had clambered into the attic at three o'clock in the morning and insisted on dragging down a whole pile of Amanda's toys she had played with during the 1970s. It was also her mother's fault that there was now a huge, orange face staring at him in the rearview mirror. The Space Hopper was grinning stupidly at him from the back seat where it was strapped in with a seatbelt. He bet she had sent it to watch his every move.

God knows how her mother could keep up that energetic pace, but she did. It was completely unfair that, to cap it all, her mother had got up this morning after one hour's sleep, fresh-faced, cheerful, and displaying no trace of a hangover. *How on earth did she do it?*

They had stopped off to visit Amanda's mother before they departed on their gap year. Amanda and she had only recently buried the hatchet and had become friends. The Old Boot had been effusive in her welcome, but Phil had known she would soon show her true colours—after all, this was Amanda's mother, the scourge of the Twister mat, Queen of karaoke, she who could outdrink a sailor on shore leave.

Amanda and her mother had a lot of catching up to do, and Phil knew they needed time together. He excused himself early on in the evening to sleep in the camper van, glad he did not have to suffer any more of his mother-in-law's attempts to ply them with alcohol to get them into a party mood. Her homemade wine was more potent than bootleg Russian vodka. He rubbed his tongue against his upper palate, letting the tip brush the back of his teeth. He was positive her hooch had dissolved a layer of enamel from his teeth.

Amanda was turning grey again. He revved the engine and attempted to distract her. "Why is there an inflated orange Space Hopper sitting behind us?"

"Ah, I remember that part of the night, or was it morning by then? Mum had been on a trip down memory lane. She was reminiscing about evenings we spent together when Dad was away on exercise. He was often away abroad for months on end. We used to spend quite a lot of time together when I was younger. Anyway, she got quite nostalgic at one point. She kept rabbiting on about board games we used to play to while away the hours— MouseTrap, Buccanneer, Monopoly. She mentioned loads of games I couldn't recall so she went to find them.

"Can you believe it? She'd kept every single one of my old toys and all of my school reports? Oh Lord! The school reports..." Amanda recalled hazily how her mother had gone through the pile of reports the night before. Talking to her as if she were fifteen, she had reprimanded her again for being juvenile in chemistry and not taking German seriously. Amanda's alcohol-dazed mind had wondered how German could be taken seriously with a teacher named Herr Cutts, who marched around the classroom with a cane under his arm.

Her mother had reminded Amanda about her appalling handwriting and how she had disappointed her teacher in physical education class by constantly turning up with notes to be excused from various sports. The notes had, in fact, been forged by Amanda, who hated all physical activity, particularly netball during the winter months when they were forced to go outside in sub-zero conditions, wearing nothing more than a tee-shirt and a tiny gym skirt. Too tipsy to care about the reprimand, Amanda had giggled like a fifteen-year-old at her mother's attempt to reproach her while thinking to herself, *My handwriting may have been poor, but I was an ace forger.*

"Anyway, she got all teary at one point and said how she wished I hadn't grown up. Then she gave me some of the toys to remind me of the good years. My roller skates are in that box over there, and if we get bored, there is a great game called Frustration that we can have a go at."

Phil concentrated on the road. Honestly, there were times when he wished Amanda would act her age and behave more maturely. If she took after her mother, however, then she probably never would. What a dreadful thought!

BLOG: Fortifying Your Fifties

Day 3—July

Finally, we have landed in France. We've been together in this camper van for 48 hours, and I already have a strong desire to hit Phil over the head with something heavy—probably the Le Creuset pan I used to be sick in. He spent the entire trip here on the ferry asking me repeatedly if I fancied bacon and eggs with a nice, greasy slice of fried bread and then laughing.

"Sick?" I hear you cry. Yes, sick. I am ashamed to admit that it was self-inflicted. My mother is partly to blame, but I have known her for years (all my life in fact), and I really should have known better than to stay up drinking with her all night. Lord knows how her septuagenarian friends do it.

We visited her en route to the ferry port. I hadn't seen her for several years, not since my father died. It's only recently that we have decided to start afresh.

As Phil and I pulled up in the camper van or camping-car or motor home, which I've named 'Bertie the *Bürstner*', a giant Weeble came rushing out of the front door. On closer inspection, I realized it wasn't a Weeble, but my mother. She is now as wide as she is high. She had a cigarette in one hand and a smile the size of Wales spread across her face. She hugged me and then hugged Phil, who looked very uncomfortable. He has always been wary of her. We'd hardly got through the door before she shoved a can of lager into Phil's hand and poured me a huge vodka and lemonade. I didn't have the heart to tell her I stopped drinking vodka in the eighties.

Crafty old Phil made his excuses straight after dinner and took himself off to bed in Bertie, claiming he had a long drive the next day and needed to be adequately rested. He left me in the clutches of my mother, who gleefully declared, "Great! Now that Old Stuffy Drawers has cleared off, we can have some fun." She proceeded to drag out a couple of demi-johns from her brewing cupboard, which is really just a cupboard under the stairs that houses all her home-brewed wine.

"This is my special brew," she announced, dragging out a cloudy bottle. The stuff smelled evil and had a kick like a mule, but after a few glasses, I was too busy floating in an alcoholic haze to worry any more.

I think we reminisced, or my mother did. My mouth didn't seem to want to work. My lips had gone numb by then. She showed me how to link up to Skype. She set it up on my laptop so we can chat face to face while I am abroad. I really wish I had been sober enough to have prevented her from doing that. Regular Sunday telephone calls were bad enough, but now she'll see me, and I won't be able to put down the phone and make a coffee while she rabbits on anymore. She'll see if I am yawning or pulling faces at her. It'll be like being at an interview.

At some point, when my legs had joined my lips in the numb department and my brain was barely functioning, she magically produced a pile of toys and games I used to have. She'd saved them for me.

"I couldn't bring myself to part with them," she declared unpacking a game of Ker-Plunk and a pair of roller skates. Before I knew it, we were sitting on the floor playing the darn games. I remember laughing nonstop because the marbles kept falling down. At the time it had seemed so hilarious.

At one point I tried to leave to get some sleep or at least a glass of water, but Mum explained it wasn't really worth going to bed as it was nearly time to get up, which made sense at the time. She fetched me another glass of wine. I think I may have tried to bounce around the room on a Space Hopper, but things really did go out of focus at that point, and I believe I dozed off on a chair.

The next thing I remember was Phil shouting that it was time to get a move on or we'd miss the ferry. I had to go to the bathroom. I think you know why. Yes, I was sick. Eventually, I was ready and said goodbye to Mum, who seemed remarkably cheerful. Just as we were about to leave for the ninth time, she disappeared into the house, only to reappear five minutes later with an armful of games. She hugged me goodbye again and whispered in my ear, "You may want to play some of these while you are shut away together. Remember, you don't stop playing because you get old. You get old because you stop playing."

She then insisted on our posing for a silly-looking photograph before we set off on our big adventure.

"Say cheese! Come on, Phil. Make an effort! Think of something that makes you happy! That's better. Goodness gracious—you actually look quite nice when you smile." She took the photo which you can see at the top of this post.

"Now, you already look like you are enjoying yourselves. Remember, have fun! Talk to you soon, Amanda."

As she waved goodbye and we pulled away, I asked Phil what "happy" thing he had managed to conjure up that made him smile for the photograph.

"Not seeing your mother for an entire year," he replied.

My stomach rebelled all the way to Dover, and we had to keep stopping for me to relieve myself. I hope the trip gets better. Needless to say, we missed the ferry that day.

By the way, my mother seems to have sneaked the Space Hopper on board Bertie. Phil is not impressed. I have a feeling he might shove a large nail or pin into it before much longer.

Posted by Facing50.Blog

8 Comments:

Madasahatter says…I am so glad I found your blog. I really needed a laugh today, and that photograph is one of the funniest I have ever seen. Your green face looks great against the orange of the Space Hopper. I always thought Space Hoppers were very large, but now they seem so small. I had a game of Ker-Plunk, too, but my brother kept shoving the marbles up his nose so my mother got rid of it. Anyhow, seeing you both in the photo has made me seek out an old hula hoop. I shall go into the garden now and practice with it. Your mother is right—we need to find our inner child again and release it from time to time.

Facing50 says…I would like to release my inner child, but it is being restricted by my seat belt at the moment, which seems to be stuck. I can't seem to release it anyway. Phil has gone to the toilet at the services, and I am taking advantage of a few minutes to say hello to you all. I might have to get off the iPhone though and try to release myself before he gets back, or he'll be even moodier than usual.

SexyFitChick says…I think the rollers skates Phil was wearing were a bit tight because his smile is more of a grimace. He's in quite good shape for his age, isn't he? He'd be in better shape, though, if he actually used those roller skates. Maybe for his next birthday, you should buy him a proper pair of blades like the ones I have. You could both go zooming off down the Promenade des Anglais in Nice on them. I like the way he rolled up his trousers to show off his knees and to give the impression he was wearing shorts.

Well done, Phil, for being game. By the way, you really do look sick in that photograph. Your mother should get that rocket fuel of hers licensed and sent to Russia. She'd make a fortune. Skype! Way to go. I'm Sexy.1 on Skype. We should try to hook up, too.

Facing50 says…Don't remind me. I don't know what she uses in it, but I think it could be used as a deadly weapon if administered in the right doses. Yes, Phil is okay for his age. He doesn't think so, though, and keeps moaning about how he is getting flabby. He should worry—all my top bits now are sagging to meet the bottom bits. I should have a go at blading. I might just try my old skates first, though. My balance isn't what it used to be. As for the rolled-up trousers, that was my mother's idea. Phil was very cross that he had creases in them after rolling them up and spent some time in Dover trying to iron them back out. I'll add you to my Skype list and see if we can chat, although it could be awkward with Phil breathing down my neck all the time.

YoungFreeSingleandSane says…Hope it all gets better. Jonathan said I was too childish for him. That can't be right, can it? I agree with your Mum. We should always try to be a little youthful. Of course, compared to Jonathan, I am childish—he is twenty-seven years older than me!

TheMerryDivorcee says…Great photo. That Space Hopper looks like huge fun—its smile reminds me of my current husband. Actually, he's a similar color, too, after going to the tanning salon. Sorry to hear you were sick. Your Mom is a great old bird, isn't she? Message to YoungFreeSingleandSane: I bet he felt younger when he was with you. He'll probably miss your youth and vitality. Keep looking. As they say, there are plenty more monkeys in the forest.

Gypsynesters2 says…Hello from Mexico. It's fabulously hot here, and we are about to go skinny dipping in the ocean. Hope the trip heats up for you. We'll raise a couple of glasses of tequila to you both. We are on Skype, too. It's marvelous. We can check up on all the family back home and then shut the internet off and enjoy ourselves.

Facing50 says…Thank you all for your comments. I have managed to get out of the seat belt now, and Phil is squirting it with WD-40. I tried out the skates while he was busy, but I think I've lost the knack. They kept sticking. I'll get Phil to put some WD-40 on them, too, and see if that helps. Stay tuned for the next post.

Chapter Three

Bibi Chevalier gazed out of the pigeonnier window onto the courtyard below and sighed heavily as her husband's brand new black Peugeot CRZ disappeared down the gravel driveway, wheels spinning, gravel spitting dramatically into the hedges. Honestly, you would think the man was thirty. It was like watching an old episode of *Starsky and Hutch*. Bibi knew about Paul Michael Glaser and David Soul. She had watched all the series and, in fact, had learned almost all her English from television dramas. She used to love *Dallas* and hugely admired Sue Ellen with her massive shoulder pads. Nowadays, it was *Desperate Housewives* and old reruns of *Friends* that kept her vocabulary up to date.

The car was ridiculous. It looked like a pimp's car in her opinion, especially with those blacked-out windows. It was far too young for Didier. Still, it wasn't her he was out to impress, was it?

She stood in front of the mock Louis XIV mirror, staring at her reflection, wondering just how she should handle this latest problem. She didn't have long to consider it, though, because within a minute of the car departing, she could hear the faint ringing of a brass bell, signalling that she was needed. She patted her deep-brown hair back into its neat chignon and examined her elegant nails. She really should make another appointment at the salon. Her Chanel Red polish was beginning to look a little chipped. She mustn't let her standards slip; her mother had brought her up with the mantra that a woman should always try her very best to stay glamorous and youthful.

The bell rang again, shrilly and continually, as Bibi navigated the aged, wooden stairs into the main part of the

25

very large farmhouse where she found her mother-in-law sitting upright in her usual position in front of the log burner with that wretched bell in her hand.

"Finally," she complained. "Did you not hear me ringing? Has Didier gone? I wanted to wish him luck for this important meeting. Now, my coffee. It is cold. I would like another, a hotter one."

Bibi dutifully collected the cup and the tray it sat on and without a word, headed toward the kitchen where she slammed the tray with all her force onto the kitchen top. *Blasted woman! She knows as well as I do that Didier has not gone away on an important meeting. Or is she completely blinkered to her son's philandering?* she thought.

She snatched the kettle from the stove and refilled it. Didier had obviously made some attempt to grab some breakfast because a half drunk cup of coffee had been dumped by the sink next to a pile of croissant crumbs. He was in too much of a rush to meet up with his latest conquest to consider tidying up behind himself. She spooned the freshly ground coffee into the pot. It seemed to be the same routine every day. Didier would shoot off to work early and leave her to look after his cantankerous old mother, whose demands were increasing by the day.

Mathilde Chevalier was well into her eighties but was by no means an old lady. Her keen eyes missed nothing. Her brain was sharp, and she regularly beat her friends at their regular afternoon session of bridge. However, she had decided that she wanted to be looked after. So when her husband had died, she had convinced Didier, her only son, that his enormous, beautifully restored farmhouse could easily accommodate his ageing mother, who was approaching her twilight years. As for his wife, Bibi, well, she had plenty of time on her hands to help look after poor, old Mathilde, who wouldn't be much of a burden for too much longer.

Bibi had had no choice in the matter. Frenchmen were expected to look after their parents in this rural community. As far as his mother was concerned, Didier thought she could no wrong. He fussed after her, insisted she take the largest bedroom in the house, and told Bibi she would have to spend a little time each day with her while he was at work.

Bibi was furious. She had spent months orchestrating the house's renovations, then furnishing and decorating the rooms herself. The bedroom was to have been theirs, and she had lavished a huge amount of effort into making it just so.

"It won't be forever," Didier had promised. "She is very old and frail. She confided to me that the doctor has told her she needs to take great care now, and I would much rather she was here should anything happen to her."

Bibi had understood his concerns and had graciously accepted Mathilde into their home in the belief that it would only be for a short time. That had been ten years ago, and Mathilde showed no sign of deteriorating or departing. Bibi had looked after the old lady more out of loyalty to Didier than affection for Mathilde. The woman had shown little gratitude and seemed to expect her daughter-in-law to wait upon her like a servant. Up until recently, Bibi had accepted her lot, but Didier's latest adventure was just one too many, and Bibi was ready to rebel.

She wondered if it would have been different if she and Didier had had children. Smoothing her hand over her enviously flat stomach, she wished dearly that she could swap it for the middle-aged, flabbier stomach that women of her age often had. At least it would have meant she would have had someone to love: a child or children or now even grandchildren. She could have had children who, like Didier, would still love their mother even when they were grown up. If they had managed to have children, Didier might not have felt the constant need to replace her with a string of younger models.

Bibi had been brought up to understand that men would have affairs, but it was her duty to stand by her man regardless. She ensured that she always looked glamorous, slim, and well kept. She had regular appointments at both the beautician's and manicurist's salons. She had her hair done professionally every Friday and still had the same figure she had had when she first met Didier.

She knew she was still attractive. She was clever. She could speak three languages, enjoyed a whole range of cultural activities, and was amusing in company. So why was Didier spending a preposterous amount of time with his latest lover, a twenty-seven-year-old girl from Marseille, who had recently taken up employment as his secretary?

Bibi recognised the signs. This girl was by no means the first. If Bibi's memory served her correctly, she was the eleventh girl in the last three years. Didier normally tired of them after a few weeks. Bibi always knew when the affair was over because Didier would suddenly become attentive, shower her with expensive gifts, or whisk her away for a long weekend to Rome or Paris or even London.

Bibi loved London. Of all the places she had visited, London was her favourite. She adored the vibrancy, the bustling streets, and the cosmopolitan atmosphere. She squirmed in delight at the thought of having afternoon tea at the Ritz with patterned plates of dainty sandwiches and a list of teas so varied that it read like a novel.

In truth, Bibi would have actually preferred to be British rather than French. She could already speak English well, and she loved reading or hearing about the Royal

Family. She even had a small photo of Lady Di (Princess Diana) which she kept in her writing room.

Lost in memories that seemed to fade each day, she recalled how she had first met Didier, unaware that the water was now ready. A Parisian by birth, Bibi had been working at the Embassy when she met the confident and striking Didier Chevalier. Knocking into him in a corridor, she had dropped a pile of documents, and he had bent down to help her collect them. Their eyes had met. It was a *coup de foudre,* which had led to dinner, a walk by the Seine in the moonlight, further meetings, and soon after, a request from Didier to join him at his country home near Toulouse where he worked for Airbus.

Bibi gave up her social whirlwind of a life, trading it for the rural tranquillity of South West France, hoping to fill her life with making pots of jam, shopping at the local market, tending vegetable gardens, and watching over lots of little Didiers and Bibis.

Several years later, there were still no children, but each year they had hoped afresh, spending endless hours in each other's arms and enjoying each other's company. Then Mathilde had arrived. Almost immediately after that, Didier was promoted, and work became his life. He came home less frequently and travelled abroad often.

Bibi filled her days with Mathilde, the house, and the garden. She took up photography and art and often went out into the countryside to sit quietly and paint. Life here was not by any means unpleasant, but one tended to become reclusive.

This corner of France offered endless open fields, charming stone houses, fascinating gorges, and ancient cobble-stoned villages where shutters remained closed. There was not much evidence of life until the weekly market when the places would bustle with wizened-faced, old couples, all keen to chat to their neighbours and catch up on the weekly gossip.

She had never been accepted by the community because she was from Paris. Parisians were regarded as foreigners. Had she had children, she might have made friends with other mothers, but they, too, ostracized her. She was a threat to them in her elegant, figure-hugging, designer clothes. She had no one to talk to and no company, not even a pet dog, because Didier was allergic to their fur.

None of this had mattered though. It hadn't mattered until Didier became evasive and started to spend more and more time at work. It hadn't mattered until Didier started to wear cologne to the office. It hadn't mattered until she discovered receipts in his suit pocket for meals for two at expensive restaurants when he was supposed to have been at the office working so hard he could not come home to eat with her and Mathilde. It hadn't mattered until the day she received a phone call from the five-star deluxe Hotel Negrepelisse in Nice. Didier had gone there on a conference. The desk clerk had been very polite, asking for Madame Chevalier and informing her that she had left an earring behind when she had been staying there with Monsieur. The chambermaid had found it when she was making the bed, and would she like it posted back to her? Then it had mattered.

Bibi was not, however, going to give up without a fight. This philandering had to stop. She had an idea of how to sort him out once and for all and have him return begging for her forgiveness. She would wait until Mathilde took her afternoon nap to get started on her plan.

The pot now filled, cups ready on the tray, Bibi composed her face, and grace personified, she sashayed back into Mathilde's room. Oh yes, by the time she was finished, Didier would never dare stray again.

Chapter Four

At the same time Bibi was wishing she had had children, Amanda Wilson was wishing she had not. Phil was already in a stinking mood. He hadn't spoken to her for over an hour, and when she had put the radio on to break the silence, he had snapped it off with determination.

They had bickered almost nonstop ever since they had set off. She regretted they had ever had this stupid idea to travel around Europe. They should have known it couldn't possibly work.

Struggling to get up the hill, the camper van sounded strange as Amanda tried to read the text that had just come in. Without her glasses, it was a blur. Ferreting about in her bag to find them only irritated Phil further, and he huffed in annoyance.

Glasses on at last, she read: *Hi Mum. Hope u r havin gud time. Washin machine broke. Wot shud I do?*

Get repairman, she texted.

She took off her specs. Phil looked at her crossly.

"Who was that?"

"Um, Tom."

"What does that useless lump want now? Can't he manage without us?"

"Nothing. He's fine. Just sending his love and seeing if we are okay," she lied. She didn't want Phil to start on again about Tom. She had hoped leaving him to get on with his life would help him to grow up and become independent. It didn't seem to be working very well. Phil and Tom's relationship had been badly damaged the year before, and it needed some careful handling on her part to ensure they stayed friends.

Phil harrumphed and nursed the camper van to the top of the hill where the view was spectacular. They could see fields and hills for miles and miles. She felt the tension ease as Phil took in the green fields filled with healthy, brown cows, As they drove by, the cows gazed up at them with soft eyes, chewing, carefree in the warmth of the afternoon.

The phone beeped again. She rustled in her bag for her glasses, which had tumbled to the bottom.

The text message read: *Wots repairman's number?*

She replied: *I don't know. Look up on internet or in phone book. I am too far away to sort it.*

"Is Tom texting again to wish us a nice day?"

"No, just a query."

His attention caught by the strange noise in the engine again, Phil let the conversation drop. "This bloody vehicle is going to play up again," Phil snapped, slapping the wheel hard with the palm of his hand.

Amanda fervently hoped it would not. She was beginning to have serious misgivings about this whole gap year thing. It was supposed to bring the two of them together and be fun; so far, it was driving a wedge between them. Being cooped up all day in a cabin with a grumpy, frustrated Phil was exhausting. At least at home she could hide in her room and go on the internet to chat to her friends. Here, she had to share the same space with Phil all day and could only access her friends surreptitiously on the phone when they stopped for a rest. If things didn't improve, they wouldn't get through the first month, let alone a whole year.

So far, Bertie had broken down twice. Each time, Phil had lifted the bonnet and glowered at it, trying to will it into submission. Each time, he had failed. On the first occasion, they had been in the north of France. A tow truck had towed them to a garage or what was supposed to be a

garage. The forecourt was littered with vehicles, some with doors, and some without—all looking like they had been cannibalised for spare parts.

A grubby-faced man had emerged from under a bonnet of a Renault 4, wiping his hands on an equally grubby cloth. He had taken one look at the Bürstner and sucked in his cheeks in a display of despair. While he lifted the bonnet and listened, Phil had attempted to describe in pidgin French the noise he had heard before the camper van ground to a halt. Then a weird game evolved. Phil made clunking noises. The mechanic made another type of noise and clunked, too, only in a higher tone. Phil nodded. They both looked under the bonnet as only men can do. The mechanic fetched a spanner. At this point, Amanda had wandered off to sit under a tree and check her emails.

By the time she had read all her emails, posted a status on Facebook, and started writing a blog post, Phil and the man were by her side.

"Translate, please," barked Phil. Amanda's French was passable, having studied it at university. She could hold a conversation with people if they were talking about day-to-day things of interest, such as restaurant menus, shopping, or the weather, but mechanics and engine talk were not her forte.

"Um, he says the thingamajig that makes the whatchamacallit work...the sort of head, no, not head, um, brain...is kaput, broken. It is sick. No, it is ill. No, not ill, it is blocked. He does not have another thingamajig, and we need one. It needs two weeks for the thingamajig to arrive, and it is very expensive. He suggests we let him clean its bowels, no, not bowels...um, leads?"

"Well, just how much is a thingamajig?" asked Phil.

Amanda had translated. Phil had spluttered in disbelief. "There is no way it can cost that. Are you sure?"

Amanda checked. The mechanic had sucked in his cheeks again, nodding furiously as he rubbed his thumb and fingers together in the universal sign for expensive while proclaiming, "*Cher, cher!*"

"Expensive, expensive!" reiterated Amanda.

"Tell him to clean the bowels. Are you sure you took a degree in French? You don't seem to be able to speak much."

Amanda had winced at the barbed comment. Phil went with the mechanic to get an idea of what he intended to do, and with much pointing and nodding, he had seemed to comprehend the situation better.

"It's the ECU."

Amanda had looked confused.

"The Electrical Control Unit," Phil had explained. "Oh, never mind. It's the brain of the engine. It can't work because there's some corrosion. It needs cleaning out. He says we can have the camper van back tomorrow so we need to stay in a hotel. There's one down the road."

The hotel was pleasant enough, but costly. Phil had handed over his credit card begrudgingly because having the van was supposed to save on accommodation expenses. That evening they were the sole diners in a dingy dining room where, even with glasses, Amanda could not read the menu. At least Phil's complaining hadn't disturbed anyone else. The television in their room only offered French television. Finally, both had gone to sleep in a huff. Phil's mood hadn't improved when the mechanic handed him a bill for the tow truck and his labour the next day.

"Three hundred and fifty euros!" Phil exploded.

Amanda checked the bill. They had been charged almost two hundred euros for the breakdown truck. "At least we can get on our way now. We'll just have to not spend too much on food now. Maybe we should not buy any more

pains aux raisins for breakfast." Phil had glowered darkly at her. He adored *pains aux raisins*.

The phone call couldn't have come at a worse time. The ringtone "Don't Worry, Be Happy" rang out cheerfully. Phil flinched.

"Hi, Mum! How are you? Are you having a good time?"

"Tom, don't waste time with idle chitchat. What do you want?" hissed Amanda, trying not to let Phil hear what was being said by talking quietly and turning her head to one side.

"I can't hear you, Mum. Speak up. Can you hear me?"

"Yes," said Amanda sharply. Phil was bristling.

"What can I do for you?" she asked in a lighter tone, pretending nothing of importance was happening.

"I looked under *repair*, and I can't find anyone. If I type in *repair*, I get car, body shop, windscreens, Jaguar, or computer repairs. Anyway, I don't think anyone could help. The blasted machine won't work at all, and I think I may have broken the front door off trying to open it to get the washing out."

Amanda groaned.

"I don't know why it broke. It wasn't my fault," continued Tom. "It was fine when I washed the clothes. I only put in my duvet—"

"What?"

"My duvet. I needed to wash my duvet. It had chocolate on it and some chicken curry."

"Curry and chocolate? What were you doing in bed—having a tea party?"

Phil almost drove into the kerb and glowered at Amanda. She mouthed, "It's okay" and went back to the conversation.

"I can't understand what's wrong with the stupid machine. Is it old?" continued Tom.

"Did it not cross your mind that the duvet would be too heavy for the machine?"

"It didn't feel heavy at all when I put it in. It fitted in all right. It was a bit tight, I'll admit."

"Tom, a king-sized duvet weighs much, much, much more when it is wet. The drum is probably broken. Look under *washing machine repairs* and find someone to fix it or go to Mr Bubbles, the launderette, for the rest of the year with your washing." Amanda was exasperated beyond belief. "We can't afford to buy a new one, so sort it out and don't put duvets in it again. Text me when it is mended and try to not break anything else."

Phil was about to interject, but she snapped off the phone before he could say anything. Honestly, you would think Tom could look after things better than this. He had already texted her that the vacuum cleaner had broken. Apparently, he had managed to hoover up a plastic bag, which melted and clogged the cleaner. He had borrowed an old vacuum cleaner from his girlfriend's mother to last him until they returned. Leaving him to his own devices had apparently not been such a good idea. The way he was going, the house would be empty when they returned. He seemed to be breaking everything in sight.

She had fielded all the messages and kept them from Phil. The last thing she needed was a lecture from him about how useless Tom was. In his father's eyes, Tom still had a long way to go to prove himself after last year's shenanigans.

"The washing machine played up. I think Tom will sort it out," she explained, keeping her eyes fixed on the road. She could feel Phil's eyes burning into her.

"That's not how it sounded to me," retorted Phil. Unfortunately, or rather fortunately for Amanda, the Bürstner camper van coughed at that precise moment, then spluttered, grinding to a shuddering halt on the D926, just outside the perched village of Caylus.

Phil rested his head on the wheel and groaned loudly. Amanda took in a deep breath. This was a crisis point—not only could it be the end of their gap year, but it could also be a pivotal moment in their fragile relationship.

Chapter Five

The hairdresser was fussing over Bibi's hair, snipping away artistically with his scissors and staring intently at his creation. Jean-Claude was a perfectionist, and Bibi knew she was safe in his expert hands. She would not emerge from the salon unless she resembled a sleek, catwalk model. She flicked through the copy of *Allo*, the French equivalent of *Hello* magazine, and familiarised herself with the socialites.

It was whilst she was gazing at the photograph of Prince William and his new bride, Kate, that she felt the stirrings of an idea. Didier may no longer be interested in her, even though she was still in remarkably good shape for a woman of her years, but she should be able to regain his attention and have some fun at the same time.

She needed to find a lover—not just any old lover, a lover who would encourage Didier to exit the soft arms of his latest amour with all the haste of a cruise missile. She would make him wild with jealousy, and then he would become obsessed with her again. Ah yes, she knew his mind. He would want her if he thought she was madly in love with someone else. But just who? The local farmers were a no-no. They were only interested in their herds of cows and their fields or rusty old tractors. Besides, she couldn't imagine herself jumping into a clapped out 2CV with a grubby-faced farmer, dressed in the traditional blue trousers with a bib, which passed for sartorial elegance in these parts. Anyway, they all spoke that weird dialect, Occitan, so she couldn't understand them even when they deigned to speak to her.

No, she needed someone who would impress. Someone who would make Didier go crazy with passionate envy. There were no grand businessmen here in rural France.

There were no jet set actors or musicians. She needed someone good-looking. She needed someone young. What she needed, she decided as she continued to stare at the happy couple's photograph, was a young Englishman.

Didier loathed the English—something to do with the Hundred Years' War, or Agincourt, or football, or something. He had never really elaborated as to why he detested the British so much. All she knew was that he had no time for them. Whenever he found himself stuck behind a caravan slowly meandering its way up a winding hill with a trail of French cars behind it, he would point out the GB sticker on the back as he finally raced past it, tooting his horn in frustration, and declare that GB stood for Gross Brutes. He snickered wildly at the thought of their eating a large meal for breakfast. "Whoever heard of eating sausages and bacon for *le petit dej*?" As for their dress sense, well, Didier would drape his pullover carefully over his shoulders or wear a scarf at the merest hint of a windy day and scoff at the Brits, who continued to plod around the town dressed in shorts and sandals on a cool September day.

He may have hated them, but Didier was also somewhat fascinated by them. They had come to this remote area in France, renovated the tumbledown barns and houses, turning them into chic abodes with pretty rose gardens. They had started up cricket clubs and bingo games and didn't give a monkey's about the French culture. They spoke loudly in English or very bad French. Their children went to the local schools, teaching the French children rude English words and encouraging them, *sacrebleu*, to frequent the new McDonald's, which had opened in the nearby town of Caussade, instead of eating sensible French food at home with their parents as they had done for many decades.

In Didier's old-fashioned view, the precious French culture was in danger of dying out. If he was honest with himself, however, Didier was a little in awe of the British settlers with their confident air, cheerful dispositions, and their English fish and chip vans, which had started to roll up to the weekly market.

There were lots of British people in the area, but they were either married with young families or married and rather elderly. If Didier caught Bibi with a red-faced, puffed out, old gent, she would hardly provoke French rage and passion. No, she needed younger blood, preferably with a touch of the aristocratic about them. That would sufficiently rile Didier, and he would drop his floozy like a hot *patate*. Even though only slightly fascinated by Brits in general, posh Brits completely over-awed him. All she needed to do was track down a suitable candidate and lure him with her French feminine charms. How? She could only think of one way—the internet. There were hundreds of men and women on the internet who would be interested in being her friend. Social networking was all the rage. She wouldn't actually have to have a physical affair. She could have an online relationship; that would be sufficient to bring out the Frenchman in Didier.

Jean-Claude had finished and was standing back admiring his handiwork. Bibi smiled at his refection in the mirror. He had worked his usual magic. It was certainly worth the trip to Toulouse; the local salons in her area were more used to dealing with elderly ladies, not Parisian women on a mission. Satisfied that she had the makings of a plan, she headed off to the stylish shops to buy some new outfits. After all, one had to stay looking one's best.

Several hours later, hurrying to get back to Mathilde, who would, no doubt, be ringing her bell in annoyance, Bibi passed a curious sight. She did not realise it at the time, but her life was about to change. As she steamed up the road in her MG, she passed a camper van, which had obviously broken down. She noticed it because it had a large GB sticker on its bumper. She slowed as she passed it, took in the backside of a male, who was obviously trying to fix it, and couldn't help but notice a strange woman in shabby jeans and a faded tee-shirt. Nothing odd in that you may think, but she seemed to be bouncing about on a large, orange balloon. Bibi smiled to herself. How she loved the English and their eccentricities.

BLOG: Fortifying Your Fifties

Day 7

The sun is out. The sky is blue. France is beautiful. Just as well because I think we could be here for some time yet. I must say I thought Phil would blow up in sympathy with Bertie yesterday when we broke down yet again. We were stuck on the side of the road overlooking one of those fabulous perched villages nestled into the hillside. I took a couple of photos with my phone, but Phil caught me doing it and went a bit mental, shouting that we had real problems and why couldn't I take anything seriously. He takes things seriously enough for both of us. I don't see why I should waste any more effort.

I had to phone a garage again. There was one a few kilometres away. You see, Phil, sometimes you need a laptop to find out these things. Not only am I the only one who seems to know how to use a search engine, I am also the designated French speaker; so I put in the call while Phil glared at me. It rang for a while, and then a Monsieur Renard answered. I could barely understand him. There was a lot of banging and rustling going on. It took several attempts to get some sense out of him. Phil kept interrupting, saying things like "Tell him it's urgent. Tell him it's the camper van." Did he really think I was going to say, "Yes, a week next Friday will be perfectly all right, Monsieur Renard!"

Have you ever tried to have a conversation on the phone with someone while the person in the room with you keeps shouting out things? Well, it's impossible when you not only have to speak in French to one and English to the other, but you actually can't understand the mumblings of the person at the other end of the phone. Finally, I ascertained that Monsieur Renard would come out, but he couldn't come out for a while because it was Monday. He was shooting in a forest and would try and get to us as soon as he had finished. I told Phil.

"What?" he spluttered. "Can't come out because it's Monday? Is the man a half wit? Try another garage."

I dutifully tried every garage in the area. The phone rang out at all but the last one where I got the answer phone explaining it was Monday, that they were closed and to try again on Tuesday. I had one of those eureka moments that occasionally hit me.

"It's Monday," I explained to Phil, who thought I had joined the band of lunatic French. "Most provincial towns shut down on a Monday in France. They treat it like a Sunday." Phil was open-mouthed in disbelief.

"We can probably get someone in Toulouse. It's a city, so they are bound to be open, unlike rural France."

"Toulouse is a good hour away. It'll cost hundreds of euros to get towed there. We'd better wait for Monsieur What-ever-his-name-is."

The afternoon dragged on. Phil sulked terribly and kept stuffing his head under the bonnet in the hope he could encourage Bertie to start up again. I haven't said anything to him, but I think Bertie is a dud. When he wasn't kicking Bertie, he was complaining about the French. I pointed out it might be politic to keep his opinions to himself when Monsieur Renard turned up. We didn't want the Entente Cordiale being ruined by one man and his camper van, did we?

It's incredibly boring being stuck on the side of a French road. I suggested a game of Eye Spy, but that was a nonstarter, and I received a withering look for my efforts. I only saw three cars all afternoon. There was an English sports car at one point. I tried to cheer Phil up by pointing it out, since he likes old cars. He was half interested in it. He was cheered more by the stunning Frenchwoman driving it. She looked like Audrey Hepburn in her youth. She even smiled at me. Mind you, I was at that point trying to get some exercise by bouncing about on the Space Hopper. She probably thought I was a basket case.

Monsieur Renard turned up at dusk. We knew he was on his way even before we saw him. An approaching, chugging noise in the distance and acrid smoke alerted us to his arrival. An ancient Renault truck with a top speed of ten kilometres an hour rumbled up the slope. Phil commented that if that was the rescue truck, then we were all in trouble. It was. Monsieur tumbled out of the truck with a stinking Gauloise cigarette in his mouth. He extended a grubby hand and said something along the lines of "Allo. I am zee garage man. I am verrey sorry, but I 'av been 'unting, and I cannot drive." At this, he made the universal sign for his having been drinking. Goodness knows how many animals or, indeed, people he had shot today, and judging by his gait, I would think nothing was safe, not even if it had worn a high visibility jacket.

It transpired that he had asked his neighbour to assist since he had been "on the pop" all day. Another man appeared. He was English. Phil looked as if he had just won the EuroMillions Lottery jackpot. Hands were shaken, and Phil got into another manly huddle with the pair. Mark, who was English, was able to translate for Phil, leaving me free to check Facebook and send my mother a lengthy text message. Eventually, Bertie was hauled up onto the truck and ready to go to town.

We had to leave Bertie again, and the prognosis is not good. Mark is wonderful. He has a cottage that he is not letting out at the moment, and we are staying there until we can get back on the road.

There will be more about Mark, his family, and Ted, whom you will all love, another time. Now, I must leave you and try to deal with my mother, who has sent a message saying she wants a chat on Skype. Wish me luck.

Posted by Facing50.Blog

8 Comments

PhillyFilly says…You poor thing. At least you have broken down in France, and French women are very good at looking after themselves. You'll be able to get some nice facials and treatments to take your mind off the traumas. Must go—it's time for my seaweed wrap.

Gypsynesters2 says…We broke down on Route 66. We were quite fortunate, though, and didn't have to hang around too long before we got picked up by that nice group Aerosmith, who were en route to a gig.

Madasahatter says…S'ppose you could always try the roller skates as a mode of transport while you are stuck. Or the Space Hopper!

MiaFerrari says…You better hope it's not an Italian van. The factories are all shut for the summer holidays. You'll be stuck for at least a month! Still, I can think of worse places to be stuck than sunny France. They have wonderful food and wines.

Hippyhappyhoppy says…Sounds like lots of fun. Have a nice day!

DonnaKBab says…Cool that your Mom will be on Skype—she's such a hoot.

SexyFitChick says…Do I detect all is not well in paradise? Hot French chicks = bad news.

DizzyC says…I would gladly swap our lousy rain for some French sunshine. Enjoy it while you can.

Chapter Six

The bright winter sun glinted down onto the pavements. A large crowd of enthusiasts had gathered near the harbour and were beginning to applaud as Todd Bradshaw approached them with the iconic Opera House finally in sight after forty-five kilometres of gruelling cycling. The adrenaline coursing through his veins made him feel more alive than he had felt in some time.

Face gleaming with sweat and in the zone, Todd Bradshaw pounded the pedals. Having left the safety of the middle of the pack a few kilometres before, he was intent on winning this race. He always won.

His new bike that he had purchased on eBay was a dream. He had considered buying the well-known and desired Trek Madone like the one Armstrong and Contador rode, but he had settled for an Italian filly—a Colnago, which was infinitely cooler. Todd liked *cool*. The carbon frame was designed to "pass through the air unnoticed", resulting in faster speeds. This was definitely the case. Todd felt like he was flying, almost hovering above the road and hugging the bends.

He had the leader in his sights. It was all a matter of timing. He had guessed that Hartley Fischer, who had led the race from the start, would wait until five kilometres before the finish and then break away from the pack. Todd waited to make his move, gradually edging into position in preparation for the break. Only those with stamina and speed would have a chance. Todd had both and more; he had determination.

The streets of Sydney were a blur. This had been a tough road race, very fast-paced, and there had been little room for error. He had cycled this route several times, but this was the first time he had raced it.

In New South Wales there were fantastic routes and circuits for all types of cycle enthusiasts. Todd particularly enjoyed the hilly challenges. His favourite training route was to Akuna Bay via Wakehurst Parkway and Church Point. In the way of circuits or challenges, there wasn't much that he hadn't attempted, including criterium circuit races with multiple laps around a short track, time trials, and multi–stages like the Tour de France event, which consisted of multiple one-day events. Todd was partial to road races, preferably on an arduous course with hills, fast descents, and long flats like in Calga. As long as there were a few beers at the end of the day and a convivial spirit with teammates, he always enjoyed it.

Nothing gave him such a buzz as cycling. The indefinable sense of speed, the feeling of being on the edge but in control was phenomenal. He was a proficient, qualified diver and an excellent footballer, but cycling had rapidly become his passion. At the moment, Todd's focus was entirely on Hartley, and like a crouched tiger, he waited for the sign that it was time to pull out and head for the finish.

The pack had been very tight in this race. At one point, Todd had wondered if he would be able to navigate his way to his favourite position—fifth in the pack—where he could bide his time, appearing as a non-threat. His opportunity came just as he had forecast. Directly behind Cameron Cortez, a veteran racer of standing, Todd had waited until he sensed Cameron was weakening. Too eager to win and lacking strategy, Cameron occasionally burned out too soon. Todd knew his opponents; he had trained with some of them and raced with others. As he stepped up the pace, Cameron fell behind. Todd took up his position and waited to pick off the next competitor in front of him. He had patience. He would wait for his chance—just like he could wait for another chance to win Amanda Wilson.

Last night he had dreamt about her again, waking in a sweat even though it was a cool morning. He had stayed in bed a little longer, trying to return to the dream in which Amanda had been sunbathing naked beside him on a hot beach. The sun had been beating down, and the warmth had stirred an urge in him. He looked at her as she peacefully rested her head on her elbows and the sunlight glinted on the golden streaks in her hair. He began rubbing oil methodically into her shoulders, caressing her as he did so. She wriggled appreciatively under his strong hands.

With soft, circular movements, his hands had descended her back to rest lightly on the swell of her buttocks. He had rubbed more intensely, the oil shining in the sunlight. Amanda moaned softly. Todd had become aroused in an instant. Moistening his hands with more coconut oil, he was preparing to rub down her buttocks and in-between her legs, but his progress had been abruptly halted by the radio alarm clock on full volume. The disc jockey had cheerfully announced that it was another bracing day in Sydney while the torturous words of "If You Want My Body" by Rod Stewart played in the background.

Todd always worked out his frustrations, physically and mentally, by challenging himself in cycling, which had led to his being a formidable opponent, despite his short time in the sport. Originally, he had taken up cycling to stay fit and meet some tasty women. There were still plenty of fit women in the sport, but his appetite for them had waned. Maybe it was his age, or maybe it was because he had one woman on his mind.

A vision of Amanda in tight cycling shorts popped into his head. Just as he began to imagine her curves through the tight Lycra top, his opponent started to break away. Todd pressed all his weight and strength onto the pedals and pumped his legs hard. This was it. They would slug it out to the finish, and Todd would win. He knew he would win.

Hartley was directly in front of him, pumping harder and harder on the pedals. They and two other hopefuls had left the other cyclists some distance behind. The other two quickly began trailing behind. The contest was now purely between Hartley and Todd.

Todd was aware of the crowd cheering as they neared the finish, their faces a blur as Todd belted past them. Television crews were filming the race. Todd would no doubt be on national television again tonight. Not far to go now. Todd had the strength, and he knew Hartley was beginning to flag. He could take him. Preparing to pass him, Todd accelerated into position for pulling out to overtake him.

Then for some bizarre reason, Hartley's backside metamorphosed into Amanda's backside, moving suggestively from side to side in tight Lycra. Confused, Todd momentarily lost concentration. Fatal.

No one watching was quite sure what had happened in the last moments of the race. Some said Hartley's tyre had burst; others said his chain had snapped. They were all sure of one thing, however—Todd and Hartley had unfortunately touched wheels. None suspected the real reason Todd Bradshaw found himself flying over the front bars of his bike onto the street where he lay unconscious and bleeding as his beautiful, Italian cycle slid dramatically along the road and was crushed under the front wheels of the television crew's van.

Chapter Seven

The gentle ringing of church bells woke Amanda. It was coming from a village some distance away. Phil was asleep, mouth open, drooling slightly. Poor Phil. At least he had slept peacefully for once. She was tempted to wake him, but once awake, he would no doubt turn into Mr Grumpy again, and it was nice just to see him looking content for once.

The room was bathed in half light that shone in-between the slats on the shutters. She could make out the ancient French dresser in one corner and a wooden chair. Phil had attempted to drape his trousers on it when they had come to bed and missed, so they lay crumpled on the floor. He'd no doubt moan about that when he got up. He hated creased clothes. Sneaking out of bed, she arranged the trousers so they hung over the back of the chair.

Thank goodness for the Delfonts—Mark and Jeanette. Mark had been their knight in shining armour. After Bertie had conked out, Mark had driven them, along with Monsieur Renard, to a grubby, old garage, behind which was an enormous shed filled with broken-down cars, trucks and spare parts for every French car imaginable. In the corner was a rusty 2CV, housing hens who clucked nonstop as Monsieur Renard examined the camper van. Mark had acted as translator for Phil much to Amanda's relief as Monsieur Renard didn't speak French—well, not any French she recognised. He spoke Occitan, she later learned, which was accompanied by a twanging accent with lots of nasal sounds. In Monsieur Renard's case, they were particularly nasal, perhaps because he had an awful habit of snorting violently like a pig after a truffle.

Renard had spent considerable time under Bertie's bonnet. Wiping his hands on his oily rag, he had sucked in his cheeks. The prognosis was not good. Bertie was, for some unfathomable reason, very sick. It was a complete mystery to Monsieur Renard, who had insisted that the Bürstner was one of the best camper vans in the world, coming from Germany as it did.

"I wish we had broken down in Germany. This would be fixed in an instant," muttered Phil when Monsieur Renard went to his desk to thumb through a dirty, grey manual in the hope it would provide an answer. "The Germans are very efficient. I expect half of the problem is that every car in this country is French; they don't know how to fix any other make."

He was probably right. When they had first landed in France, they had played a game which they called "Spot the Non-French Car Game". It had largely consisted of yelling out the make of the car which was overtaking them. The first person to spot a car that wasn't a Peugeot, Renault, or Citroen won. It took thirty-four kilometres before Amanda had screeched, "Dacia, Dacia! Look, it isn't a French car!" only to discover that Dacia is owned by Renault and so didn't count.

"Well, at least Bertie isn't an Italian camper van," she had added brightly.

"And what, pray, is the significance of that comment?" Phil had asked, looking over at Monsieur Renard who was shaking his head in misery.

"All the factories in Italy shut for the month, and you wouldn't be able to get any parts for it until September," she had explained.

"Amanda, sometimes I wonder what goes on in that brain of yours," Phil had declared in frustration.

As it happened, they wouldn't be going anywhere for a while. Whilst the body of the camper van was indeed German-built, robust and luxurious, on further examination, it transpired that the chassis was in fact Fiat and therefore, Italian. Upon hearing that news, Amanda wished she hadn't opened her mouth. Monsieur Renard had puffed his cheeks out several times and shrugged his shoulders so much that she thought he might overstretch his rhomboids and be permanently hunched, like a huge, hungry vulture.

Bertie, or maybe it should now be called Bertoli, was going to have to wait in Monsieur Renard's garage among the rusty relics and chickens until the fun-loving Italians finished their annual leave and decided to send the necessary parts. Monsieur Renard said he would see if he could get them sooner and promised to talk to his cousin who lived near Nice, close to Italy. Maybe he could help out. Amanda and Phil would have to stay put in this region for a couple of weeks at least, maybe for the rest of August.

Renard pulled out three grubby glasses and a bottle of Ricard, offering one to Phil in commiseration. Pretty soon, Phil was feeling less miserable; in fact, he was considerably cheered. After a couple more glasses, Mark proposed that he take them both back to his newly-renovated gite for the night. After all, where else would they sleep?

The gite was one of those adorable stone cottages on the edge of the hamlet. It was next to Mark's house, a tumbledown farm in need of considerable repair. The gite should have been let out over the summer, but work on it hadn't been completed in time, and they had missed this season's trade. They weren't overanxious about it, though. Life here had made him and his wife, Jeanette, much calmer.

Over a few glasses of wine, Amanda and Phil learned that Mark had once worked in the city. Phil's eyes lit up. "A trader," he slurred, now in awe of Mark. Phil managed all their financial affairs and loved talking about stocks and shares, the economy, the global economy, or anything to do with finances. Mark, however, was reluctant to be drawn into that conversation. He had escaped the rat race, swapping his high salary, lack of sleep, and horrendous drive to work each day for a kind of Utopia in France. Here, by and large, he did little other than help renovate properties and spend time with his young family. Photographs of two small children were scattered about the ramshackle kitchen.

"I wouldn't have had any children if I had stayed in the UK," he announced. "Who wants to bring up children there? Here, they can enjoy life. We go out all the time—walking, cycling, swimming, or fishing. Over there they would be parked in front of a game console or the television, and I wouldn't see them anyway because I'd be at work all the time."

"Children are a complete waste of time," grumbled Phil as he dozed off in the faded armchair, head lolling to one side.

"You got any kids then?" Mark asked Amanda.

"Yes, just the one. He's still going through those awkward years."

"What, the teenage years?"

"Yes, something like that—only they seem to have stretched into his twenties," replied a jaded Amanda. On cue, the phone bleeped.

"Someone's ears must be burning," laughed Mark.

"Hmm, not his ears," she said, reading the text message: *Hi Mum. Got small prob. Not my fault. Dave was cookin and burnt pan. Also burnt curtins he put on pan to put out fire. Do you want new curtins? Dave sed he will pay. Dave sed soz.*

Amanda deleted the message. She'd deal with it the next day. She couldn't even think about what sort of curtains

Tom would choose if given the task. He'd just have to do without for a while. How had Dave, who was supposed to be a chef by trade, managed to set fire to the pan?

Mark and Jeanette were outside with the children when Amanda and Phil finally emerged that morning. Phil blinked and squinted as the lunchtime sun, reflecting from the patio, made his head ache even more. They were all having lunch. It was the perfect family picture. Invited to join them, Amanda and Phil sat down on the plastic chairs and before long, were relaxing in the quiet ambiance. They chatted and laughed. Time rolled by. Phil managed to get up and play a little football with the children for ten minutes until he puffed himself out. The children squealed with pleasure and ran around the garden chasing each other. Mark offered to jump in the swimming pool with them. Peals of laughter were echoing around the garden. It was a far cry from the lunchtimes she had spent with Tom, just the two of them sitting at the kitchen table colouring because Phil was trapped in the office. Mark returned with a giggling toddler wrapped in a towel.

"Listen, I know this is a weird request, and we don't know each other very well, but could you do us a huge favour? Jeanette got a call from her sister's husband yesterday. Her sister isn't very well, and we would like to go and visit her back in Ireland to make sure she isn't too poorly. He's got five children, so he could really do with some help and support or an industrial-sized bottle of Valium." Mark chuckled. "We can get a flight, but the problem is Old Ted. We need someone to look after him. He can't possibly go with us, and he will be really miserable if he has to go and stay somewhere that's unfamiliar to him. He likes the security of his own place, and at his age, it could prove too much to move him out even for a short time.

57

"He isn't demanding at all. Really he isn't. He only likes to sleep and go out occasionally. He doesn't even eat much. I don't suppose we could ask you to watch after him? You can stay in the gite for free in return. You can borrow our car, too, while you are here. I don't suppose your camper van will be ready for a while yet, so why not take advantage of staying here in the sunshine with the pool? It's almost like you were meant to arrive here on our doorstep."

"Um, well, that all sounds wonderful, and we'd really love to help you out, but well...I'm not very good with old people," stammered Amanda.

Mark and Jeanette burst out laughing. "Old Ted isn't an old person, are you, Ted?" asked Jeannette as a grey-faced dog, who had been hidden under the table, shoved his nose out, looked up at Amanda hopefully, and wagged his tail.

BLOG: Fortifying Your Fifties

Day 10

You can usually tell when my mother is not in Cyprus. When she is back in the UK, she rarely gets up to mischief and is often to be found in her flower-filled garden. She doesn't go out and behaves pretty much like an elderly lady might.

When she isn't in her garden, you can find her pottering out to the shops, terrifying a few people en route, driving as she does in an elderly and erratic fashion. She invariably rips off wing mirrors from parked cars as she squeezes by too close to them. You'll always find a lengthy queue of traffic behind her as she navigates the lanes at 20 mph. Because she usually parks as closely as possible to the next car in the car park, she almost always opens her door into the side of the other car, denting it.

All was arranged yesterday for our first-ever Skype call. Mum's Skype name is, of all things, Playgirl.77. Why she couldn't have chosen a sensible name like MamaHen1, I don't know. She said it makes her sound youthful, and 77 is her age. I am Amanda.Wilson228. Apparently, there are a lot of Amanda Wilsons in the world so that is why I am number 228. I hope they are not all like me.

We are now staying in Mark's cottage in France. I'll explain about that next time I post. Anyway, I told Phil, who was sunning himself on the veranda that I was going to speak to my mother. He really hasn't grasped this Skype idea and thinks that it is just like a phone call. Sure enough, as promised, the icon with my mother's name flashed to "online", and a sound like a phone shrilled on my laptop. Phil chose that moment to come inside to get a drink and was greeted by the sight of my mother with a cigarette in her mouth, adjusting her screen as he walked in. He shrieked like a girl, thinking for one terrible moment that my mother was sitting in the room, and zipped back outside at high speed.

My mother guffawed and then started coughing horribly. It's bad enough listening to her, but watching her face turn purple *and* listening was just awful. Eventually, she grabbed a glass of dark red liquid and slugged it.

"Hello, Mum. How are you?"

"Oh, very well, thank you. How's the trip going?"

"It's going well. We are still in France, but we are staying in a lovely cottage in a hamlet. I'll move to one side so you can see the beams and the log burner. So, what about you? Have you been up to anything interesting?"

"Oh, that's a nice log burner I can see behind you. Don't suppose you need that on at the moment. Um, not a lot. I went to the races last week."

There was a pause while I checked that I had just heard correctly.

"Races?"

"Yes, the gee-gees, the nags, the horses. Went to the races with a group of friends. Had a ball!" she said emphatically, nodding her head and shaking her cigarette to death. And so began her latest tale of fun and frolics.

Last week a few of the local ladies in their seventies and eighties decided they would go to the racecourse. They booked a minibus and got dressed up in appropriate Ladies' Day attire, which meant hats, matching handbags, and dresses. Betty and Ilsa turned up early in the morning to collect my mother.

A fashion parade then ensued as they admired my mother in her hat and outfit, and they all had a celebratory glass of wine before going on to collect Dotty. At Dotty's, they had another couple of glasses of wine and then went on to Maisy's house. You're getting the idea now, aren't you? There were twelve of them, so by the time they had finally collected Rosemary and grabbed a bottle of wine from her kitchen for the remainder of the journey, the minibus driver had his hands full with a bunch of cackling, old dears.

"He was a bit of all right, too," said my mother as she told me the tale. "Very buff." (Where she has learned this sort of language is anybody's guess.) Guffawing, she said, "Rosemary sat next to him and showed him a bit of leg when her skirt rode up as she clambered in. A bit of leg and a lot of bloomers!"

The "girls" had arrived at the race course and stumbled out of the minibus. Finding their way to the nearest bar, they had set themselves up with sandwiches and wine. "Young girls today just don't know how to do it properly," commented my mother. "They don't seem to eat at all, and they certainly don't know how to enjoy themselves. They were dressed in flimsy dresses with enormous platform shoes and heels. They couldn't walk properly and spent all their time complaining about their feet. They should have done the same as us—brought spare shoes."

Having consumed another bottle of wine, the dear old souls then made their way to the bookies beside the racecourse. They organised themselves. Pooling their money, they decided my mother would be the chief picker of horses as the rest of them were far too drunk to even read the names of the horses. Mum has a special system that she has never revealed to me. Many years ago, she used to pick racehorses from the *Racing Post* with her father, and I believe they had quite a lot of luck.

They had all agreed on Mum's first choice: Come On Eileen. They placed their bet—a few pounds only. After all, they are all pensioners. Then they chatted up the businessmen nearby. Two of the men had fetched them some folding deck chairs to sit on. Dotty had attempted to take photographs of them to put in her album and label them her "toy boys", but by all accounts, she managed to chop off their heads in the photo. Then they had cheered and yelled at the horses as they started to run. There was a huge overhead screen showing the race, but the wily bunch had managed to bag themselves a ringside position beside the finish line.

Betty and Isla did a ridiculous dance as their horse romped home in first place. They had won £10. The men who had gotten them folding chairs now volunteered to buy them champagne. They were on a roll, and by the fourth race, they had managed as a group to ratchet up four wins of a few pounds each race and were on to win the tote (jackpot).

The final race was the one that would decide all. Dotty wanted to choose Lucky Lady in the final race because they were all doing so well and were themselves lucky ladies. Isla agreed, and so my mother's choice, Get Out Of The Way, was dismissed. They put their bets on. The businessmen had decided to choose the same horses as the women since they were clearly enjoying good fortune. With bated breath, they watched the last race on the screen.

The commentary was piped through the tannoy system as everyone watched eagerly. It went something like this (although I have changed the horses' names to protect their identities! In truth, I just forgot their names).

"And they're off...it's Lucky Lady on the inside...followed by What a Day and Who's The Daddy...It's Lucky Lady, Who's The Daddy, and Bouncing Billy on the outside just ahead of What a Day. Approaching the first bend...Lucky Lady is still in the lead, followed by Bouncing Billy and Get Out of My Way...round the bend...and it's Lucky Lady, followed by Get Out of My Way with Bouncing Billy now trailing in third place…down the straight and it's Lucky Lady…Get Out of My Way is edging forward… Lucky Lady is clinging to her lead, but Get Out Of My Way is advancing on the inside…and it's Lucky Lady pursued by Get Out Of My Way as they head towards the finish line, and it's…Get Out Of My Way who takes the final race today and wins the prestigious Tatler Stakes."

The women groaned. The businessmen groaned. They went off to commiserate at the bar before seeking out their minibus for the return journey. Finally, they made it back onto the bus although what Betty had done with her pink straw hat was a mystery until they saw one of the businessmen wearing it as he got into a taxi. They were still in hearty spirits, though, because they had had a great day.

"What a shame," I said to my mother. She was swigging at her wine glass again. The ash from her cigarette had burnt right down to the stub and was now defying gravity as it clung in a thin grey line to the end of the cigarette. "If you had won the final race, you would have been in for a big prize."

"Yes," she replied in a way that suggested she wasn't at all upset. I recognised that look in her twinkling eyes.

"You placed a bet on the side, didn't you?"

"Of course, I did. I didn't fancy Lucky Lady's chances. The turf was 'good to firm'—much better for my choice. If only they had read the *Racing Post*, they would have known."

"So, what are you going to do with your winnings?"

"I think I'll put it towards next year's trip. We're going again. I think I'll supply the wine this time. It should pay for a few nice bottles." She paused to fill her glass from a box of wine, which was next to her on the table, and to light another cigarette. Smoke curled from the ashtray in front of her, which was filled to the brim with cigarette butts.

"I might even treat Betty to a new hat," she added, grinning wickedly.

She then insisted on fetching her outfit to show me how she had looked. I was treated to all of her ensemble and several more cigarettes, more coughing fits, and a couple of refills before she decided to call it a day.

After a good three quarters of an hour, she said she had to go. Allowed back into the house, Phil looked around suspiciously. "I'm sure I can smell smoke," he said. "Is it possible to passively smoke via Skype? Next time you decide to talk to the Old Dragon, give me fair warning, will you? I don't need too many shocks like that. My heart can't take it. I'm not as young as I used to be."

No, he isn't, but judging by my mother's antics, age is apparently not an insurmountable barrier to having fun. I hope a few days here will sort him out.

Posted by Facing50.Blog

8 Comments

QuiteContrary says…Does your mother have a gambling habit? Only joking. I hope I haven't offended.

Hippyhappyhoppy says…Your Mom and her friends sound like so much fun. Have a lovely day. Hugs x

Gypsynesters2 says…We went to the races last week. Oh sorry, you are talking about horses. We went to the Nascar races. We even got a ride around the track with our favorite driver. This gypsy life is brilliant. How's France?

TheMerryDivorcee says…Got rid of number 2 because he gambled. He played poker and bet our house on a game one night. It's okay. I won the house back and a shiny Porsche to go with it. What a donut!

MiaFerrari says…Your mother sounds amazing. How's the French food? I love Italian food, but I'd settle for Canard à l'Orange if I had to!

Facing50 says…Thanks everyone for your comments. My mother is getting more and more juvenile as she gets older. So are all her friends. I think she's a bad influence on them, though. However, I wish Phil was half as lively as my mother. I can't work out why he seems to be getting gloomier even though it is so pretty and sunny here.

SexyFitChick says…I'm not being rude but I think he might be having hormone problems of his own. Google male menopause. In the meantime, here is something to cheer you up: What do you call a man who is irritable, moody, and bad tempered? Normal! LOL

Facing50 says…Thank you. That has cheered me hugely. I checked out male menopause, btw, and I think you could be right.

Chapter Eight

This whole idea was certainly wild, but the more Bibi investigated it, the less crazy it seemed to be. Where else would she meet eligible men but on the internet? It was safer this way, too. She could filter out those who didn't interest her and just converse with those who showed potential. First, of course, she had to find a suitable candidate.

She looked at Twitter, which afforded her anonymity and the ability to follow total strangers, but it wouldn't give her what she needed. She wanted to be able to chat with men. She wasn't entirely sure how the process would work, but in her mind, it seemed reasonable that she should be able to track down a suitable male, have conversations with him, and then work out how to use this person to rile Didier. Her plan was hazy at this stage, but Bibi was confident she could get it to work. First step was to get online and see how it went.

She had given much thought to her online name. She could call herself Femme Fatale, but that sounded too whorish. Desiree was no good, nor was La Belle. They sounded like false names. Clearly, she couldn't use her own name. Perhaps the men she wanted to attract wouldn't like a French woman; she should pretend to be English. If that were the case, she would need an English name, something ordinary, yet with a hint of class.

The new Princess who married Prince William last year was called Kate, a name that was both simple and classy. That was what she needed. What was the name of that funny woman who had just arrived in Beaulieu, the nearby hamlet? She was staying at the recently renovated cottage next to the farm. Bibi had admired the window boxes only the other day as she drove past. The garden had the flavour of an English garden with multi-coloured roses climbing the stone walls and grass cut in neat green stripes.

Bibi was certain it was the same woman she had seen sitting on a large, orange balloon by the side of the road. Her name had been mentioned in the village, too, where there was talk about the English couple who were renting locally. What was it? Angela? Anne? Amanda. Yes, that was it. Amanda, Amanda Wilson. Bibi pondered for a while. She said the name out loud a few times. Amanda was a name that could conjure up an upper class woman with a desire for adventure. She would borrow it. She would add an extra *l* in Wilson just to make it different. The real Amanda surely wouldn't mind or, indeed, know.

She prepared a fictitious profile using her new name, Amanda Willson. Yes, it was simple, elegant, and very English. Next, she had to produce a profile picture which could be seen by everyone on Facebook. Obviously, she could not use her own face. Remembering a wonderful photo she had taken of an Aston Martin DBS when she had last been in Monaco, she decided it was just the right touch of British meets French. She would display that. The car was posed in front of the Hotel de Paris next to the famous Casino. That should attract the right sort of people. She uploaded the photograph.

She had to fill in a few details about herself so she mentioned that she spoke both English and French. She also mentioned that she had been educated in the UK and at the Sorbonne. A whopper of a lie but, nevertheless, it would make her sound intelligent and ensure she attracted the right sort of person.

She posted a message, known as a status, on her personal page: *Fresh challenges should never faze you and should be embraced. Please join me here on my journey to discover a new, virtual world.*

Now, how could she attract attention and make virtual friends? She could not invite anyone she actually knew to become her friend. Besides, she knew very few people. She preferred her own company. She only wanted to converse with intelligent and stimulating people. She asked the search engine how to make friends on Facebook. It was not difficult at all. You put words into the Facebook search box of activities or hobbies that interest you. She typed in *Matisse*, clicked the Like button for that subject, and then read comments that other members of the page had left. When she saw a comment that appealed to her, she clicked on the name of the person who had left it. This allowed her to send them a direct message or a friend request. She found one or two who looked suitable and sent a request.

She searched for various reading groups. There were so many to choose from. She discovered one that might appeal to men with literary tastes. The F. Scott Fitzgerald site had attracted 80,593 people to it. She became member 80,594 and posted a comment about *The Great Gatsby,* which she had read in her youth.

There were plenty of car groups with large followings so she "liked" an MG page since she owned an MG and then found a site entitled *Cars*, which had 2,153,357 Likes. She sent various requests to people who seemed fascinated by classic British cars. She left a comment asking if anyone knew where there was a good, classic MG garage in France.

She spent a further hour leaving her calling card on various sites where she hoped interesting males would discover it and request she become their virtual friend.

"Amanda Willson" was now ready to act as bait. All she needed were some curious fish.

BLOG: Fortifying Your Fifties

Day 17

Like a lot of middle-aged women, I have a weight—or maybe that should read "size"—problem. No matter what I do or eat, I seem to be spreading girth-wise. Although I'm a similar weight to several years ago, gravity intervened at some stage, and the weight all seems to have distributed itself around my midriff, and my bottom has fallen to somewhere behind my knees.

As we quaffed wine with Mark and Jeanette the night before they left, I was complaining about my weight problem. "Maybe walking the dog will help," I suggested.

They roared with laughter. "Ted won't go walking, will you, you lazy old thing?" cooed Jeanette. Ted the dog looked up from his basket and thumped his tail. "He used to go for miles and miles, but since we had the children, he prefers to lie in his basket. If you take him out, he turns around and heads home." She scratched his ears.

"Help yourself to the gym while we're away. There's a cross trainer and weights," Jeanette generously offered, switching back to my original topic. She is a fitness instructor and has her own well-equipped gym and studio, so looking after dear old Ted the dog is turning out to be a really good thing.

Our instructions for Ted were simple. "He eats only one cup of biscuits a day, nothing else, or he'll put weight on. He'll tell you if he needs anything," explained his owners.

"Tell me?"

"Oh yes, you'll soon understand him. He is very intelligent."

Ted looked out from his basket with a pained look as the youngest child, only one-and-a-half years old, pulled his ears enthusiastically. Goodbyes were said, and Ted managed to not burst into tears at the departure of Mum, Dad, and the two extremely noisy children. Within an hour or two of their leaving, we were beginning to understand just how intelligent Ted was. If he needed to go out, he sat right in front of you until he got your attention, and then plonked himself by the door, tail wagging furiously. Likewise, if he wanted food, he'd sit next to the fridge, nose pressed to the door. If he wanted to go for a walk, he'd first attract your attention by making a keening noise and then sit on your shoes with much tail wagging.

"Oh, look! He wants to go for a short walk," exclaimed Phil as Ted sat on my boots, tail swishing. Ted leapt up and down like a two-year-old dog while we put on our shoes, clearly delighted that we understood him. Door open, Ted belted off like a puppy.

"Wow! Look at him go. Given that he is 84 in human years, he has a lot of energy. I hope I'm like that when I'm 84," said Phil.

"I wish you were like that now," I replied as Ted joyfully careered around the bushes, sniffing and grinning with tail wagging like mad. Well, Ted didn't turn around. He kept going and going, and several miles later, having all enjoyed the warmth of summer and the myriad of colours that festooned the hedgerows, we ended up back home. Ted went for a siesta. Two hours later, he was up and ready for another walk. And so it went on. I put on my pedometer the next day and discovered we were covering almost 7 miles. Three days later, Ted had eaten his ration of biscuits and was staring at the fridge with his nose pressed against the door. We guessed he was hungry. We couldn't let him fade away so he joined us for our food.

Ted was completely rejuvenated within four days and couldn't wait to go out. It was so gorgeous outside that we, too, enjoyed it. We all took to walking briskly around the many lanes and over the fields, admiring the multi-coloured butterflies, the huge bales of hay that farmers had cut and left out to dry, and the golden sunflowers that grew in abundance in this area. Ted sniffed each bush and flower as if he'd never seen it before—tongue out, tail twirling like a majorette's baton. He was impeccably behaved and didn't run off, not even when he spotted a group of deer in the fields. He just woofed playfully and pointed them out to us. The walks became longer and longer, and we soon clocked up 12 miles a day over three or four walks. Ted would wait each morning and bounce with all four feet in the air as if on springs when we went down to him. Then he would herd us up, barking furiously to encourage us to hurry up.

Each day he became younger and more puppy-like. His appetite increased, too, with all the fresh air and exercise. He scoffed his way through two huge Toulouse sausages, half a family-sized lasagne, six beef burgers, half a turkey roulade, veal, chicken Provencal, lamb, pizza, and seven croissants with a smear of jam, as well as his biscuits. Each evening he would take up position near us on the carpet and fall fast asleep every night smiling, probably dreaming of the rabbits he had seen running in the fields.

At the end of the fortnight when Mark and Jeanette returned, their arrival announced by loud screams from one of the children and ensuing wailing, Ted headed for his bed rapidly and laid low. "Oh, look at you two! You look amazing. You've lost quite a lot of weight and look so fit. You must have worked out hard every day in the gym," squealed Jeanette when she saw us. "But not you, you old lazy mutt," she murmured affectionately to Ted, who rolled on his back in his bed and thumped his tail. She bent down to tickle his tummy. "I bet you've stayed in that bed snoring since we left. It's a good thing your stepparents here didn't give you too much food or you'd be like a big barrel," she continued. Ted looked up at us as she rubbed his belly, and we are both certain he winked at us.

So dogs, just like humans, may appear more aged on the outside, but when the conditions are right, they are surprisingly youthful on the inside. As for me, I've clearly discovered the way to lose weight, get a pert bottom and increase my energy while also drinking copious amounts of wine—borrow a dog for a fortnight, preferably in France, and go walking.

Posted by Facing50.Blog

12 Comments:

Lillian says…What a great post. My father is 99 years old and goes walking 2-3 miles every day. I agree completely with your philosophy.

Hippyhappyhoppy says…Your posts are always so cheerful. Have a wonderful day. Hugs

DonnaKBab says…I hear you. I am on my way out now for a long walk. My butt needs raising for sure.

SexyFitChick says…All that exercise last year did nothing for you. Two weeks in France, and you are a new woman. I think you should live there. How does Phil like your new bottom?

Facing50 says…Hello Lillian - Thank you for your comment. I have to admire your father though. That is quite an age to still be so active. Hippyhoppyhappy - Thank you. You seem cheerful, too. DonnaKBab - Go for it. I feel far more energetic than before Ted. SexyFitChick – Like Ted,

Phil falls asleep as soon as his head hits the pillow these days. I don't think he has noticed any change in me at all.

Gypsynesters2 says…We are planning to hike up Machu Picchu next month. Now that is a walk. We are taking altitude pills at the moment in preparation for the big event. Hope you get on the move soon. You must be getting fed up with France by now.

Des says…Hi! I live in South Africa and love your blog which I have just discovered. We have four dogs, all of whom need walking. It is the best form of exercise. Your positive approach to ageing is refreshing. I shall be following your progress with interest.

Facing50 says…Gypsynesters2 – Gosh, your lives are so full. You must have a tremendous camper van to get to all the wonderful places you are visiting. Good luck with the walk. I am most envious. Des – Thank you for following my blog. South Africa has always sounded fabulous. I would love to visit it one day. The Drakensburg Mountains look phenomenal, and Cape Town is a place I would love to see.

FairieQueene says…Cooee! Hello, my dear. I didn't know you had started a new blog. Shall I keep quiet about it? You don't want your mother following it again, do you?

Facing50 says…FairieQueene – Spencer! How are you? I thought you had given up blogging when you started up a business with Grego. No, please don't tell my mother about this blog. She isn't aware of its existence. I see enough of her on Skype without her joining in here, too. I'll email you as soon as I can. Love to Grego. x

SexyFitChick says…Hi Spencer aka FairieQueene. Nice to see you back online. You haven't fallen out with Grego yet, have you? Don't you dare tell Amanda's Ma about her blog.

You don't want an Aussie chick breathing down your neck, do you?

FairieQueene says…Ha ha! Mum's the word! Sorry, I couldn't resist writing that. Hope Phil is enjoying the gap year with you, Amanda.

Facing50 says…What is there not to enjoy? Tom is slowly destroying our house, and the camper van has broken down!

Chapter Nine

The internet highways are always busy. Hundreds of thousands of people at any given time are interacting with others online. Amanda was one of them. She perched the laptop on the ancient kitchen table and waited for PlayGirl.77 to get in touch. Her last blog post was attracting attention and several comments had been left. She hadn't been entirely truthful, though, because Ted's owners had not, in fact, returned.

Ted, however, was indeed rejuvenated. His coat was glossy, his eyes shone, and each time he thought he was about to go for a walk, he would indeed run all over their shoes and proceed to bounce high in front of them, emitting whimpers of excitement. He certainly didn't seem like an aged dog now. They had walked miles, and both Phil and Amanda had lost some weight. After ten days of looking after Ted, they had received a phone call from an anxious Mark

"This is a heck of a favour, but Jeanette's sister is very poorly indeed. She's going to need surgery. Obviously, Jeanette wants to stay around and help Mickey with the kids, and I really don't want to leave Jeanette and the boys. Is there any way at all you could stay in the gite and continue to look after old Ted?"

"No problem," Phil had replied. "The van is off the road until the first week of September, and Ted is doing us both a world of good. He's like our own personal trainer. We've covered miles and are both a lot fitter, thanks to him."

"He's been walking? Miles? I don't understand. He usually lies under my desk and snores all day. You must be good for him," Mark had chuckled.

After a lengthy conversation, Amanda and Phil had agreed to be Ted's stepparents until further notice. As a reward, they had been told where to find the keys to the cellar where Mark kept his collection of red wine.

The computer rang, and PlayGirl.77 came into view. "Bonjour, Amanda," said her mother, her face filling the entire screen.

Amanda automatically backed away. There was something in her mother's voice that made her anxious. She was up to something, or she was going to tell Amanda off for some reason. Oh no, maybe she had found out about the blog and would want to know why Amanda had kept it secret from her. Amanda always experienced guilt when she knew she was hiding something from her mother. It stemmed back to her teenage years when no matter how much she thought she had covered her tracks, her mother would know what mischief she was concocting.

Her mother always knew when she was being dishonest. She had a canny instinct that had undoubtedly been passed down from generation to generation. Amanda understood now how mothers always knew what their offspring were thinking or doing. She was a mother, too, and she always knew when Tom was hiding something. *Blast!* She had forgotten to text the wretched boy. She needed to do it before Phil found out about the curtains. She'd do it after she spoke to her mother.

Her mother gave her *that look*. Amanda had never really understood its significance, but she had seen it on many occasions. She recalled one episode when her mother had been waiting at home for her, arms folded with that look on her face.

Amanda had bowled through the door to be immediately reproached. "I understand you bunked off your study period at college this afternoon and went to the new coffee shop in town instead," her mother had said in a steely tone.

How she had discovered this was as much a mystery to Amanda today as it was then. As far as she knew, no one had seen either her or her friend. The coffee shop had been empty, and her mother had been miles away at work. Even now, as grown up as she was, she worried that her mother would discover her misdemeanours. If she got a parking ticket, she worried that her mother would find out and chastise her. She could imagine the conversation. "Amanda, I just heard that you got a fine for parking your car in a *drop off only* zone. I am very disappointed in you. I didn't bring you up to get parking fines."

Amanda was brought back to reality by her mother moving away from the screen. Goodness, she wasn't wearing a blouse. Amanda could see her neck and the top of her voluminous cleavage. Oh Lord, the woman was topless. Maybe she was beginning to lose the plot. Amanda had heard that people of a certain age started to forget things. Maybe her mother had forgotten to get dressed. Amanda froze, unable to comment.

"I have someone here who wants to say hello," her mother announced.

A face appeared on the screen, and Amanda was dazzled by shining white teeth.

"Grego," she exclaimed. "What are you doing there?"

"Cooee!" said another voice.

"Spencer! Is that you?"

Her mother's face reappeared, beaming.

"Isn't it lovely? The boys are here to keep me company. It's so much fun. We've been sorting out some designs for Grego's new collection. We thought you might like to see them first." With that, she pushed back from the screen to reveal her ample figure squashed into a sparkling, sequined boob tube. Amanda's mouth fell open. Well, at least she wasn't flashing her wares as Amanda had first thought.

Before she could recover, Grego came into view. Someone, presumably her mother, had put on some catwalk music. Grego strutted forward and twirled. He was sporting what could only be described as a beret, along with a multi-coloured striped tank top. Mouth agape, Amanda was first reminded of Frank Spencer from the old, seventies comedy *Some Mothers do 'Av 'Em*; then the small boy who used to appear in the Hovis Bread commercials popped into her head; finally, she decided that she was watching the sixth member of the pop group The Village People. He strode away in time to the beat, passing Spencer who swaggered up to the screen. Spencer was sporting a flamboyant waistcoat with no shirt underneath, revealing muscular arms and shoulders. He blew her a kiss.

Amanda was in an episode of the *Twilight Zone*. Clearly aliens had landed and taken over these people's bodies. She sat agog as her mother paraded towards her in the sequined top, pouted, and then twirled dramatically, which resulted in an offstage coughing fit. Puffs of smoke filtered across the screen as Grego and Spencer continued to do their funky catwalk in time to the song "I'm Too Sexy".

Mercifully, the entire surreal episode came to a close, and Amanda was coaxed back to reality by the three gabbling voices.

"What do you think? I thought I carried off the boob tube rather well," her mother's voice entreated.

"Do you like the waistcoat? I embroidered it myself," Spencer announced.

"Should I wear the tank top without a shirt underneath to show it off more?" inquired Grego.

Three eager faces grinned at her. Her mother looked delighted. It was thanks to her that Grego and Spencer had even met. She had arranged a blind date, knowing they would hit it off. Now they were not only an item, but Spencer had also moved to Cyprus to help Grego with his fashion business.

"Grego has been invited to put together a new collection for a big fashion house. Of course, the first thing he did was come and see me for advice," explained her mother smugly.

"I couldn't do it without you, dah-ling," replied Grego.

"I have all my old patterns from the seventies when I used to sew; so we thought we would use those ideas and do a Retro collection. The seventies are due a revival," continued her mother, dragging on a cigarette. "The sixties have been done time after time, and I think leg warmers, tank tops, and flat caps should all be brought back. The boys have asked me to help them with this, and now that you are off gallivanting around the world, I thought I might like to give it a go. I'll be mostly in a supervisory capacity, though. I think my modelling days are over," she chortled, shaking herself back into the stretched boob tube.

"Wow! Gosh…uh…what can I say? You'll make a formidable team. Will you be staying in the UK or travelling back to Cyprus?"

Smoke fogged up the front of the computer creating a misty image of her mother's face behind it. For a moment, Amanda had the ominous sensation that her mother was fading away as she watched. Then the cigarette was stubbed out, and the screen cleared, bringing her mother into sharp focus again.

"I think I'll hop back with the boys for a few weeks. I can always Skype you from there, too, and the weather will be much better for me. This constant grey here, even in the summer, gets me down. Besides, Grego's father is having a huge party for his birthday next week, and I wouldn't want to miss that, would I? Now, do you want a quick chat with Grego and Spencer? They've been dying to know how you are getting on, and I need to get ready to go out. We're off to Giovanni's for dinner, and I think I might just scare the waiter if I show up wearing this. Take care, Amanda. Speak soon." She hesitated as if debating whether to add a more personal note; then she quickly kissed her fingers and placed them lightly on the screen for Amanda before vacating the chair to let the boys chat with her.

The conversation was enjoyable—full of what they had been doing over the last few weeks. Grego and Spencer were hilarious together and quite adorable. As they recounted events and stories for Amanda, they were habitually finishing each other's sentences, and without even realizing it, each was constantly making affectionate gestures toward the other.

Their enthusiasm for life and each other left Amanda feeling disheartened as she shut down the laptop. The boys were so much in love it hurt to watch them. Phil had not touched her since they left home. Not even being in this wonderfully romantic hamlet had pulled them together. The night before, Phil had ignored her when she tried to rub his shoulder. Turning his back to her, he had fallen asleep without even saying goodnight. She thought they were over that, but now the distance between them seemed even greater than before.

Maybe it was just her stupid hormones playing up again. She seemed to feel increasingly sad and sometimes teary for no good reason. This wasn't how she should be. What kind of role model was she for someone who wrote a blog called *Fortifying Your Fifties*?

She took a deep breath in preparation to exit with a cheerful smile on her face and regale her conversation to Phil. However, haunted by the image of her mother fading in front of her eyes, she couldn't shake off the nagging feeling that it was a sign—a sign that time was rapidly running out for her and her mother.

Chapter Ten

This was most bizarre! For some reason Todd was flying—well, not actually flying, more like floating. No, it wasn't floating; it was more like swimming—swimming not in the ocean, but in the vast blue sea of the sky. He turned onto his back and did a few effortless backstrokes. Wow, that was cool! Hang on a minute, how had he managed to become so huge? He must be at least the size of a blue whale. Checking himself over, he realised that he had, in fact, turned into a gigantic whale—one that in spite of all logic, could swim or float in the sky. It was very peculiar. Nevertheless, it was a wonderful sensation. His body was completely weightless, and considering he was such an enormous whale, he moved with effortless grace. He swam for a while longer, getting a kick out of the feeling it gave him. He was free and oh, so comfortable. He had never felt so comfortable. This was truly amazing!

He drifted about for a while, marvelling at how high he was. The world below him was far away, but he could see everything below with absolute clarity. He was currently somewhere over the Royal Botanic gardens and could view The Opera House and the harbour, If he screwed up his eyes, he could even make out the Quay Restaurant at The Rocks where he normally ate on a Friday. He continued to float lightly over the coast, drifting effortlessly over the Northern Beaches at the entrance to Sydney Harbour. There were so many beaches in Sydney. You were spoilt for choice. Some of the ones here were fantastic for surfing. He'd had a go at body bashing—Aussie for body surfing—a few times here. It was thrilling to dive into the waves and feel their immense strength as you navigated your way, travelling with them to shore. The thrill diminished the day he was turned over and over as the wave that had trapped him, kept him tumbling like washing in a spin dryer. He'd been thrown a considerable distance down the coast before the wave spat him out, shaken and weak. From then on, he had stuck to swimming and diving.

From his high vantage point, he squinted at some figures below, who were playing a game of volleyball. He moved onto his voluminous stomach and looked down at the individuals more closely. He knew that group. It was Doug and a few of the lads from football. He tried to call down to them but could only make a muffled, mooing noise. He attempted to wave, but of course, being a giant whale, he had no arms.

How had this happened? He strained to clear his mind. If he were a giant whale in the sky, wouldn't someone notice him? It wasn't normal for whales to swim about above people's heads. The whole experience puzzled him. Whales swam in the sea. He wasn't in the sea; he was in the sky. Yes, an enormous whale in the sky would attract attention and probably terrify everyone below. Yet, no one was terrified of him. Doug had looked up, shielding his eyes from the bright winter sunlight, but if he saw him, he had not seemed either surprised or perturbed by what he saw.

Everything was fuzzy, but fumbling in his brain to make sense of what had happened to him, Todd gradually realized that he wasn't an actual whale. He was an enormous cloud that was shaped like a whale. *A cloud? How had he become a cloud?* Drifting again, his body as light as air, a sense of calm rushed over him. Of course! He knew what had happened. He was dead. He had died, and his energy had left him to reform into another part of the cosmos. He had been transformed into a cloud. Todd was comfortable with this idea. He had visited India many times and liked the idea of reincarnation. He could be happy as a cloud.

Maybe he could change shape if he thought about it. He could become a dog, like Digit, his cattle dog, or a house, or an elephant. He liked elephants. Amanda liked elephants. It had been her dream to work with orphaned elephants. When he was trying to think of places to visit last year, he remembered her talking about it. So he went to Thailand in the hope that he could get Amanda to join him, but she was going through some kind of crisis at home and had refused his invitation. Perhaps if he had made it a more formal invite…

The keepers had been completely dedicated to the elephants, even sleeping with them at night to keep them company. Todd had helped with recreational activities, some feeding, washing them, and of course, playing football with them. They were great footballers. England would do well to sign up a few of those little "ellies" for their squad. Amanda would have adored the elephants.

Amanda. His Amanda, whom he affectionately called Mandy. No one else called her by that name. She would never let anyone else call her Mandy. He would never be able to see her again, not even a photo of her on her Facebook page. As he reflected on his present situation, he realized that, although it was comfortable, he didn't want to be a cloud anymore. He'd rather be at home working out ways to get back into Amanda's good books. He'd had a fantastic plan, one that would help him see her again and maybe even win her over. After all, that idiot she lived with clearly didn't appreciate her.

He began to change shape again. No, he didn't want to be a cloud. He didn't want to be dead. He wanted to be Todd.

Pain seared through head, and Todd Bradshaw woke up in the hospital bed. A nurse, who was checking his stats, looked up. "Ah, there you are, Mr Bradshaw! How are you feeling? You might be woozy for a while, but that's just the drugs working. So don't worry about that. Now, I'll go fetch the doctor, and we'll need to check you over properly. You were very lucky you weren't more seriously injured."

He struggled to comprehend her words, but his world was becoming fuzzy again. His knee was immobile, and his shoulder hurt like crazy. As he tried to communicate, the nurse was fading from view, her outline all that was left as he began to lose consciousness. He knew he couldn't give up. He had to come up with another way of winning Amanda's heart; after all, it was probably the thought of her that had pulled him back toward life. He had to make one last effort to earn both her trust and her love. Smiling at the thought of her lying next to him, her leg thrown over his, and her gentle breath warming his neck, Todd Bradshaw began to float once again. The nurse wondered about the smile on his face before racing off to find a doctor.

BLOG: Fortifying Your Fifties

Day 24

I'm sure as you get older you become more juvenile. After several days in France looking after dear old Ted the dog, Phil decided we should do something enjoyable and French—as if drinking wine in the sun isn't enjoyable enough. So we agreed on a kayak trip down the river Aveyron, a stunning river that descends past the 12th century picturesque village of St-Antonin-Noble-Val, where you can collect a canoe or kayak. Then the river heads down toward the ruined castle of Penne and beyond, snaking through some of the most phenomenal gorges I have ever seen. As yesterday was a bright sunny day, we thought we would take advantage and drift quietly downstream to Cazals, some 12 kilometres away. We planned to meander gently downstream, maybe stop at points to admire the view or have a drink, and then be collected at Cazals by the minibus, which would bring us back to the starting point.

We arrived on time, only to discover that we were setting off in a convoy of three kayaks. There was another family—Pierre, a Frenchman, and his wife, Denise, a sound woman from Yorkshire, along with their eleven-year-old twins, Thomas (you don't pronounce the *s* at the end) and Charlotte. We all got on nicely, and Phil and I chatted to them as we waited for a couple of burly chaps smoking ghastly Gauloise cigarettes to get the kayaks ready and sort out life jackets from the messy pile lying on the floor. The family lived in the area and had decided to have a family day out. Pierre spoke minimal English so I took advantage by practising my reasonable French on him while Phil chatted to Denise, who was glad of the opportunity to speak her native language instead of conversing in French. Mum and daughter were in one canoe and Papa and son in the other. We took the third.

Phil and I have never kayaked before. He sat proudly in the front, and I sat subserviently behind. We were advised to all stay together and travel at the same pace so that we could all be collected at the same time— approximately four hours later at Cazals. We were pushed off. Off went Pierre and Thomas in a steady fashion with Denise and Charlotte following, and off we went—round and round in circles.

"You're paddling too strongly," chuntered Phil crossly. I lessened my stroke. We continued to go around in a circle. "Ease off," he yelled. I eased off. Around we went. "You're doing it all wrong," he snapped. I sulked and took my paddle out of the water. He got angry and started telling me I was useless. I told him it was his fault, and he should let me paddle. We were squabbling like children. Looking anxious, Pierre and Denise had stopped their kayaks. Our kayak was drifting downstream in circles as we bickered.

Pierre and Denise had a quick chat before coming to our rescue. They suggested we change the configuration of the canoes. I'd go with Pierre so we could converse in French; Phil and Denise would go together in the second kayak; and the twins, who had kayaked a few times before, would take the third. There was some chaos as we all changed over, but eventually we were settled with Phil and I glaring at each other across the kayaks.

"Allez!" shouted Pierre.

"Off we go!" chorused Denise, and we began our journey.

It was breathtakingly beautiful. Pierre was confident and competent, and we soon adopted a steady rhythm cutting through the water smoothly. After a poor start with Phil, who managed to make Denise's kayak go around in circles, too, Denise exchanged places with him, seating him at the rear and got him to paddle correctly. We all kept in a steady line over the weirs and along the river. The rhythmical strokes of the oars and the rushing of the river had a calming effect, and even Phil looked much more cheerful. The gorges were indeed magnificent. The banks were a colourful display of reds, oranges, and yellows—truly wonderful.

All was going well until Thomas shouted in French to his father, "It's like a race: France versus England, Papa. Look, England is winning!" Pierre's back suddenly straightened. Denise and Phil were ahead in their kayak. He visibly bristled and swished his paddle through the water a little quicker to catch up with the other kayak.

"Ha, ha! Allez, Papa!" squealed Thomas in pleasure.

"Aha! Ship ahoy! Hoist the main brace," shouted Phil gamely to Denise as he spotted us approaching. They quickened their pace, too. Now, I'm a highly competitive person, and I was still feeling a tad cross with Phil's reproach earlier, so I put my back into it. Before much longer, Pierre and I edged ahead. Phil and Denise decided that the gauntlet had been thrown, and with the children's shrieks of delight echoing in our ears, we all thundered down the river, no longer admiring the view.

"Allez, Papa!" squeaked Charlotte.

"Go, Mum!" yelled Thomas.

"Vive La France!" shouted Charlotte.

Pierre started singing the French national anthem. I joined in: "Allez enfants de la Patrie..." we sang loudly.

"Rule Britannia, Britannia rules the waves..." rang out from the other boat.

"Marchons, marchons," we screeched.

"Britons never, never, never will be slaves!" howled hubby and Denise, lengthening their strokes.

We hurtled along. Pierre was determined not to let down the French, and we went careering down the river at top speed, descending the small weirs at a fair lick. It was exhilarating, and soon we were steaming ahead. I turned around and waved at Hubby, who was clearly exasperated that we were advancing so well. He dug his paddle in with even more determination but to no avail. Faster and faster we coursed through the water, gaining in confidence with each stroke and each bend. Even after we had put quite a distance between us and the other kayaks, we continued to race down the river, whooping in delight, adrenaline coursing through our veins.

Shooting round a sharp bend, we suddenly found ourselves headed rapidly towards our greatest challenge. It was a particularly deep weir with an enormous protruding rock jutting out beside it which required careful navigation. There were several people on the top of the rock enjoying a picnic.

"Pierre, attention!" I shrieked as we rounded the bend and faced it.

He stuck his paddle in upright to slow us without much effect.

"Ooooooh!" squealed all the people on the rock, dropping their baguettes and cheese to watch our approach at rocket speed. Amazingly, we navigated the weir expertly, but alas, we ran smack bang into the edge of the rock where we capsized magnificently. Living up to his name, Pierre immediately sank like a "stone" in spite of his life jacket, which seemed somewhat deflated, and he had to be pulled spluttering from the waters by the picnicking people, some of whom applauded us for the entertainment.

I floated better than Pierre but still had to embrace the embarrassment of being rescued by a crowd of giggling Frenchmen. Miraculously unhurt, clutching our paddles, which had never left our sides, but very bedraggled and with egos dented, we sat on the edge of the rock and watched the twins, followed by Denise and Phil carefully navigate the weir and wave gaily as they disappeared into the distance singing "Row, row, row your boat, gently down the stream."

Our kayak ended up further downstream where some more people caught it and waited for us to collect it from them. We dragged it back into the water, thanked the people, and headed back downstream much more cautiously.

Pierre shrugged in a Gaelic manner. "Ah well," he reflected, "we may not have won the race, but we were by far the better team, no?" I agreed with him. "And we had the most fun. There is no point in being old and boring," he concluded. "One must always have joie de vivre. Without it, what is life?"

The others were sitting contentedly, and perhaps a little smugly, on the riverbank eating ice creams when we arrived. We had to wait there for two and a half hours for the minibus to pick us up; after all, we'd arrived at our destination far too early. It gave us plenty of time to reflect upon the incident and how fortunate we were not to have come off badly. It certainly hadn't been boring, but maybe sometimes I should try and act my age, not my shoe size.

Posted By Facing50.Blog

15 Comments

Gypsynesters2 says…We took a trip over Niagara Falls last year. It was thrilling. Hope you find lots of other exciting things to do. When are you leaving France?

Facing50 says…You guys are incredible! I didn't think people could go over the falls, just under them. Wow! Not sure when we will be moving on. Hope Bertie gets fixed soon.

YoungFreeSingleandSane says…I might have been tempted to capsize the kayak when I was going round and round in circles with Phil. Well done on keeping calm. Sorry you lost the race, but boy, what a great story!

SexyFitChick says…What can I say? You must have the DOMS now. Bet your shoulder muscles ache like crazy. Well done, girl. You nearly showed them.

Facing50 says…SFC - what's the DOMS?

SexyFitChick says…Delayed Onset of Muscle Soreness due to not using your muscles for a while. I expect Phil will experience something similar if he ever gets back in the saddle!

Hippyhappyhoppy says…You do have such a lot of fun. Hugs xx

PhillyFilly says…You won't get me in one of those things. They are very unstable. Great story. I was with you all the way— until you fell in. Hope you got all the dirty water out of your hair.

Madasahatter says…Bwah! I can just imagine all those French people, staring open-mouthed and dropping their baguettes. Hope you've dried out now. Thanks for the laugh.

Facing50 says…Thanks everyone. I'm all dried out, thanks, but now my shoes squeak when I put them on. I think they've had it. I won't be going again, that's a fact. It was a once-in-a-lifetime experience.

FairieQueene says…I am SO tempted to tell your Mum about this. She will love this story. Go on, let me. Please!

Facing50 says…Don't you dare!! If you do, I'll tell Grego about your secret desire for lime green jelly and marshmallows.

Chapter Eleven

It was dusk when Amanda put the finishing touches to her latest post about the trip down the river and staying young. Truth be told, it hadn't been at all hilarious. In fact, she and Phil had argued quite badly on the trip, and although, in essence, the story was true, it didn't have a happy ending.

She craved fun and light-heartedness. She wanted to make people smile. Writing the blog was important to her, and getting positive feedback from those who read it was the only thing keeping her spirits afloat at the moment. Life with Phil was becoming unbearable—so much for their gap year and starting the next phase of their lives.

She appreciated that it was difficult, particularly for Phil. Here they were in a foreign country with nothing to do. It was bad enough back in the UK, but at least when he was there, Phil could mess about with his car, do the garden, and go out to the usual haunts. Here he didn't even have the luxury of familiarity. He still didn't know in which drawer he would find spoons or plates; the bed felt alien; and there was nothing of their own around the place.

He was all right during the day if they went out to explore the pretty towns or go for a long walk with Ted, but the second he returned to the cottage, he became restless. He wouldn't settle with a book to read, or look at the internet or, indeed, even chat with Amanda. He was currently flicking through all the channels on the television in an attempt to find something to watch.

"Seven hundred channels, and they're all full of crap," he complained when she sat down on the sofa opposite his. He jabbed at the control button without settling on any station until he reached *Bloomberg*. Red and green share prices traversed the bottom of the screen while some presenter sat above them talking about the global economy and how the future looked bleak for the euro.

Amanda detested *Bloomberg,* but it kept Phil quiet for a while. The businessman in him was still interested in shares, stocks, and business news. She took the opportunity to muse about her blog. She had received an interesting email today. Someone wanted to put it onto a large database and suggested it was so well-written that she should turn it into a book. The idea appealed. Nothing pleased her more than making people feel positive or laugh. It was just a shame she couldn't spread her cheer in Phil's direction. He had thrown the control down onto the table separating them and was glued to some item about capping high earners' salaries.

There were endless possibilities for fun or interest if you just looked. Phil had been unable to get beyond his world of work. Ever since he had retired, he had been a lost soul. In spite of all her efforts to interest him in hobbies, sports, or activities, he had remained fiercely stubborn and refused to enjoy any of her suggestions. She had checked online and discovered that Phil was not alone; he was most likely suffering from a combination of factors: feeling worthless now that he had no occupation and the male menopause. She had learned that men, too, could suffer from a drop in their hormone levels, which made them irritable and lack enthusiasm for anything. The subject was quite interesting and helped her be a little more understanding towards Phil. She knew too well how awful you could feel some days. One website had recommended that she try to help him by giving him back rubs. She had snorted at that piece of advice. There was no way Phil would accept her giving him a rub of any sort at the moment.

This trip had been his idea—one that she realised they were now both regretting. They had only been away for four weeks, and it already felt like fourteen months. Bertie was still not fixed, and the novelty of living in rural France was waning, particularly for Phil. He was so fed up he had even taken to mowing Mark's garden for him while he was away. He had put neat little stripes in it like he used to with his own garden. He had tied up all the roses and swept the patio. Amanda had praised his efforts telling him how smart it all looked, but Phil had only gazed into the distance—no doubt thinking about what state his garden at home would now be in, given that Tom was in charge of it.

Tom was another huge problem, and Phil didn't even know the half of it. Amanda had been convinced that Tom would handle living on his own quite well. After all, he had Alice as his girlfriend, and she was a very sensible girl, so sensible in fact that she had received a promotion at work and now was not at home during the week. This meant Tom was solely in charge of cleaning and caring for the house, and Tom still had a long way to go.

So far she had fielded all of his text messages, but Phil must be aware of some of the catastrophes that were beginning to befall the house. Tom needed to learn responsibility, but perhaps looking after the house was too much to expect from him.

The latest text message had her very concerned, so concerned that she phoned him up.

"What's all this about a broken front door?"

"Ah, well, it wasn't my fault," began Tom.

"Don't you dare start with the usual excuses. I've heard them all before. I have just about had it up to here with you," she began, then realised that Tom couldn't see her or her hand which was below her chin. "The broken washing machine, I could understand. That was just carelessness. The curtains—well, I'm jolly annoyed about Dave grabbing them to use as a fire blanket. He shouldn't have been in the kitchen in the first place."

"He was cooking my dinner for me," interjected Tom.

Amanda ignored him. "Losing the shed key was plain stupid. By the way, have you got the padlock off it yet?"

'Um, I was going to do it this weekend.'

"If the shed is locked up, how on earth are you cutting the grass? The mower is locked in there. Your dad will go ballistic if you don't keep the garden tidy."

"Oh, that's sorted. Alice's dad has been cutting it for me until I can sort out the shed."

Amanda rolled her eyes. How could she have produced such a hopeless case? "Okay, that's good. At least I can tell your father his garden is being looked after. Now, what exactly happened to the door?"

There was a pause. She could picture Tom now, trying to conjure up a plausible excuse that would be based on some truth but would also vindicate him from the actual crime.

"I had a sort of housewarming party for a few friends: Dave, Brian, Nick, Steve…you know, the lads from the football team." Apart from Dave, Amanda had never heard mention of these friends before.

"They're really good lads," continued Tom, which indicated that they were probably anything other than "really good lads".

"I only invited a few of them, you know. I wanted to be responsible. Alice was at her Gran's. We all sat about chilling, you know, watching a film and eating pizza. Then we ran out of bevvies so I went to get some more beer from the off-licence, and when I got back, there were loads more of their friends, whom I didn't know, in the house. They had already had a bit too much to drink at the pub and decided to have a rugby match in the kitchen, and it sort of spilled out into the hallway. I tried to stop them," he whined. "But, well, you know, they were quite drunk, and there were lots of them. So, they decided to have a friendly scrum down, but it got out of hand. Brian hurt his nose. Someone stood on his face. I think Nick was involved, too, but I can't remember. Anyway, the door got bashed. I think someone shouldered it like a battering ram or something," he mumbled. "The wood made a crunching sound, and it just shattered. It must have been rotten, or it wouldn't have just broken." His voice trailed off, and he waited for the silence at the other end of the phone to be filled.

After a long pause while she digested this latest episode, Amanda announced, "Okay, this is what you are going to do. You are going to phone a joiner first thing tomorrow morning and get him to repair it. You will then text me to say it is repaired. If you don't, we shall come home immediately, and you will have to put up with living with us again until we think you are old enough to leave home. Judging by the way you have been behaving, that could be when you are about fifty-four years old. Am I making myself clear? If we have to come back to the UK because of your exploits, you are going to regret it for a very…very long time. This is your last chance. Finally, when the door has been replaced or repaired—at your expense by the way—you will get it painted. The paint is Dulux paint—sage green Dulux paint. Make sure this is all done before your father finds out, or you may find yourself in your own private scrum with him, and I wouldn't fancy your chances."

Once the conversation was over, Amanda felt saddened. She hated telling Tom off. If only he could behave more sensibly, then she wouldn't have to chastise him. She didn't want to be labelled a nag. Tom was her only child, and she didn't want to damage that particular relationship. Look what a falling out had done to her relationship with her own mother. They had missed out on friendly chats and hadn't experienced any closeness, thanks to a rift caused by one of them being a nag.

She couldn't help it though. She just couldn't trust Tom to resolve problems without her interference. If she didn't sort him out, then Phil would, and that might result in losing Tom altogether. It was best if she fielded the texts and calls. She didn't want Phil provoked. He seemed to have enough problems without adding to them.

She looked at him as he stared at the television. Dear Phil, where had all his happiness gone? Was there any way she could help him find it?

Phil caught her looking at him.

"What are you gawping at?"

"I wasn't gawping," Amanda retorted, feeling prickly at his tone and choice of verb. "I was just looking at you affectionately."

"Well don't. Don't waste your time."

Chapter Twelve

Richard Montagu-Forbes sat back in his leather chair with a large mug of coffee and sifted through the latest list of gullible fools who had sent friend requests to him on Facebook. He clicked lazily on each name to learn a little about them. There were seventy-nine requests today. It was quite ridiculous. He didn't know any of these people. They didn't know him. They knew nothing about him, what he did, who he was, or indeed, what he looked like. They only knew what he had told them, and of course, he hadn't told them the truth.

His profile photograph was that of a puppy that he had copied from the internet. In fact, it was a picture of a Labrador from the Guide Dog website. Honestly, these people were crazy. Where else would you befriend a total stranger and tell them all sorts of things about yourself other than on the internet? He kept getting endless messages telling him how adorable his puppy was, and even worse, messages about their own damn animals. What was it with women and animals? He wasn't at all interested in their cats or dogs. He was after something else.

So far he had attracted over three hundred "friends", further requests to join other groups, and had even had two job offers. Mugs! Still, what should he expect? His profile indicated he was a writer, currently residing on the French Riviera in Nice, who enjoyed films, animals, and art. Wasn't that what women looked for in a man? He couldn't fail with a profile like that.

You didn't need to find real friends on Facebook, people who actually knew you. You could join various groups and societies where people who wanted to be noticed would try and befriend you. Writers and artists were the most gregarious. He had signed up to quite a few artist and author groups. All you had to do was type in *writing group* or something similar in the search box, find a page that seemed to have a lot of fans, and then click the box marked Like. You were then automatically part of that community, and the chances were that if you sent a friend request to another member of the same community, they would respond positively on the basis that they felt they knew you.

He had started his quest several months earlier. After much research, he had composed an interesting profile which told anyone who clicked on to his page that he was a widowed man writing his first novel about life in France and which also introduced the fictitious dog, Ben. Before the first day was out, he had thirty-five requests to be a friend.

It was simple to sign up and create a profile on Facebook. After all, who would check to see if you existed? Befriending random people was incredibly easy. Who wouldn't trust a person who had over three hundred followers and a sweet puppy as his profile picture?

Richard Montagu-Forbes was particular about who he befriended, though. He was only after a certain sort. To date he had a few possibles. He had made friends with men so it wasn't obvious that he was singling out women. He had a list of potential subjects but felt none of them were quite right.

He had better post a status. What waffle should he concoct today? Status posts about the fictitious dog usually did the trick: *Ben, the little beast, has just run off with my slipper and buried it in the garden. He then looked at me with those adoring eyes. You just can't get cross at a naughty puppy, can you?*

There that should do it. He'd no doubt get lots of soppy messages again, but at least it made him look human. It should make the ladies think he had a heart, which, of course, he didn't. Richard Montagu-Forbes clicked haphazardly on names of people whom Facebook suggested he might befriend, but who in reality he had never met. Maybe one of them would be ideal for what he had in mind.

Tanya Basingstoke? What was she sucking in her profile picture? No, she was a definite no. Izzy Walton? No, she lived in New Zealand, which was hardly around the corner. Her About Me section said she loved hiking, nature, and sailing. No, definitely not what he was after. She was far too clean living and wholesome. Amanda Willson? Yes, she sounded promising. Amanda lived in France. That was interesting, too. She hadn't written much yet about herself, but what he read was intriguing. She was obviously new to Facebook and had rather foolishly made her profile public so anyone could read it. She should have blocked it so only friends could see it. This was becoming more and more promising. She spoke English and French. She had been educated at the Sorbonne. Well, well, well. She loved art and literature and had "liked" a couple of the same groups he had. This was getting better and better. Under the About Me section, she had also written that she liked "fast cars, adrenaline fuelled days, exotic wines, and passionate nights".

Richard read it again. She had only put up one status so far, something about "fresh challenges" and her "journey to discover a new, virtual world". On further investigation, he discovered she was part of the same car group as he was and had posted a question about MG garages.

Richard liked MGs. There was something very British about them. She could be the one he had been looking for. He would try her out. He clicked the friend request box, smiled briefly at the profile photograph of an Aston Martin outside the Casino in Monaco—what a coincidence. He knew the Casino very well. Now, he just needed her to befriend him, and he could move on to phase two at last.

Chapter Thirteen

Amanda was working on her posts for her blog, which were beginning to gel together nicely, even forming a cohesive story. She was engrossed with it all and often found herself thinking about posts and stories, rather than concentrating on what she should be doing. Last night she had put a pizza in the oven and forgotten about it because she wanted to jot down some notes on some characters she had invented. The squealing of the smoke alarm had quickly brought her out of her absorption with her blog to discover that the pizza was a lost cause.

She found Ted sitting next to the back door, desperate to escape the high-pitched squealing, and let him out. When all was quiet and the last of the stench had evaporated into the air, Ted still hadn't returned. Phil had sent her out to look for him in the dark. After all, it had been her fault he had bolted. It had taken an hour of calling him before she found him hiding in the outside laundry room.

Regardless of the collateral damage, the idea of the book was very exciting. She believed she had something here that people would enjoy—something that could prove to be very successful. What if she managed to get it published with a well-known publishing house like Random House? Her thoughts transported her into a world of fantasy. She might even become a household name, featured in magazines, interviewed on the television; maybe she could make it big in the States.

"Today on the Jay Leno Show we have a phenomenal success story: Amanda Wilson, who has shot to fame with her debut novel, which has recently become a box office success. Amanda, welcome to the show. Let me start by asking you, did you ever imagine when you were in your

little village in Staffordshire that you would become an international star?"

"Hello, Jay. It's a pleasure to be here. No, this has all happened so quickly. I am amazed at it all. Little did I know when I was writing about my life that it would be so interesting to people."

"What was the catalyst for all of this?"

"Well, Jay, I suppose it all began a number of months ago when my husband decided we would take a gap year and go around Europe in a camper van. I wanted to share the adventure with others so I started a blog called Fortifying Your Fifties. I wrote about all the fun things we were doing. Then, one day, I was approached by an online writing group, who said they had found my blog and were thoroughly enjoying my posts. They suggested that I turn them into a novel. I did. It became a best-seller and ranked number one on the Amazon charts for two entire months, even winning several awards. Peter Cattaneo, who directed the sequel to "Bridget Jones's Dairy" and "The Full Monty", heard about it and sent a letter to my publisher, and the rest is history. I am delighted, of course, that it has been nominated for several Oscars—"

"Amanda?"

Amanda was pulled from her warm, comfortable daydream by Phil's angry tone.

"Amanda, for goodness sake, can't you leave that bloody computer alone for five minutes? I thought you'd eased off on blogging and all that stupid networking nonsense. What is the attraction of talking to a bunch of sad people who don't have proper lives? I'm going to take Ted out. Are you coming, or are you going to waste a beautiful day on that," he grumbled, pointing at the laptop.

"Hm, well…Mum is supposed to be on Skype in a few moments so—" She didn't finish. Phil turned his back to her and stomped out of the house, slamming the door so hard the wooden shutters on the windows rattled.

She was just reflecting on how Phil may have a point when the computer rang. PlayGirl.77 was ready to chat.

"Hello Mum," she began. "Are you wearing lipstick?"

"Yes, I thought I should make the effort. One is never too old to make the best of oneself. Do you like the shade? It's *Hot Passion*."

"Er, very nice, but you do seem to have a lot on your teeth," replied Amanda.

"It wouldn't hurt you to put some makeup on, Amanda. You're looking very peaky. I thought it was sunny in France. You aren't very suntanned," she retorted, rubbing lipstick from her teeth and checking her appearance in the screen. She picked up her packet of cigarettes and tapped one out onto the top.

"For someone who is supposed to be on holiday, you look pretty dreadful," she continued, sticking the cigarette into her mouth and lighting it. She inhaled deeply and stared hard at Amanda. "I think you might be going through the change. You've got spots, and your hair looks greasy."

"Thanks, Mum! I feel so much better now I have spoken to you."

"There's no need to get shirty. I am just saying, and I am concerned about you."

"Sorry, I'm just a bit tired. I slept badly last night because I made Phil angry. I forgot that I had put the pizza in the oven and got carried away doing something else. It burnt, and we had to have tuna again for tea. I have greasy hair because I couldn't see the label on the bottle in the bathroom, and I put body lotion on my hair instead of conditioner. I thought it wasn't making my hair smooth. I only found out after I dried my hair and checked the bottle with my specs on."

Amanda's mother nodded wisely. "Ah yes, you start to notice it when your eyes get old. Still, at least you can't see your wrinkles in the mirror any more when your eyesight fails." She winked at Amanda. "You're going to be noticing some other changes soon, too. Sounds like you've reached that time of your life. Well, it's all downhill from here, my girl. You wait till you start forgetting other, more important things. I did a classic this week," she continued without missing a beat. "I had to go to town on Saturday to buy some hair dye. You remember the last time?"

Amanda nodded. The last time her mother had picked the wrong box of hair dye from the shelf in the shop, an easy mistake given the boxes all looked similar. She had blithely coloured her hair, and it was only when she rinsed it off that she realised she had gone electric blue instead of caramel blonde. She had loved it though and shown it off to all her friends, laughing about how bad her eyes had become. Her mother was coughing now. Amanda waited, trying not to watch her mother's face go bright red from exertion. At last she stopped her hacking.

"I had just closed the back door when I remembered I didn't have my library book that I needed to return. I went to retrieve the key from my handbag, but it wasn't there! I tipped the contents of my bag out and searched through them: library card, phone, indigestion tablets, purse, bus pass, diary, an old birthday card that you sent me, which I carry around because it makes me smile, photos of the kids (Tom and his girlfriend, Alice) but blow me over, no key. I had rushed out to catch the bus, somehow left the key inside the house, and pulled the door to without thinking. You may remember that the door locks automatically when you shut it, and I was now stuck outside."

"Did you get a locksmith to break open the door?"

"Ah, no, I wasn't going to ruin a perfectly good lock. Besides, those locksmiths charge a fortune. No, luckily the little window to the left of the door was fractionally ajar. I tried to get my hand in to reach the back door lock and release it, but my arms are too short, and I couldn't reach so I used my initiative. I went around the neighbours to find a small child who could crawl through the window and open the door. You managed it years ago when you were a teenager, and you weren't that tiny," she added.

"The first two neighbours were horrified that I wanted to use their precious children. You'd have thought I'd asked if I could borrow one to shove up my chimney. Anyway, the third house understood my plight and lent me Toby. He's about eight years old and just the right size. His dad came, too. Well, they don't make children like they used to. He snivelled and trembled and said he didn't want to do it. Not even for £5.00. His father had to take him home crying.

"Luckily, the commotion had attracted a few other neighbours, and Grant was sent over from Number 14. He never misses a chance to earn some money, that one. He's a bit tubby, but with some heaving and pushing, his mother and I got him in the house. I directed him to the lock at the back of the door and instructed him to turn it clockwise. That confused him. He turned it a few times left and right, and finally it unlatched. I gave him his fiver and a bag of crisps. He was very pleased and said that any time I locked myself out, he'd be happy to help.

I dropped my bag on the top and looked for the wretched keys to the back door. They weren't in the usual place. They weren't in the jar. They weren't anywhere. You can imagine that I was perplexed by now. When I am trying to concentrate, I find that a Polo mint always helps. I had a tube of them in my coat pocket. I got them out, and hey, presto, the back door key tumbled out, too! It had been in my coat pocket all the time!

"So, thought you might like to know that today it's pizza; tomorrow it'll be your keys; and..." she added, cackling like an old witch, "and finally, it'll be your marbles. Welcome to old age."

Amanda smiled in spite of herself. Her mother was pretty amusing some days. Soon they were chortling together, and her mother was telling her about how she had managed to put fly spray on her hair and rubber solution on the curtains instead of fabric freshener. It was good to chat. Amanda felt better when she waved goodbye to her mother. Her mother kissed her fingers and put them on the screen.

"Amanda, don't worry about Phil. He'll get over it. Stay happy and enjoy life. It has an expiry date."

Amanda nodded. Her mother now gone, she stared at the screen a little longer before calling up her documents. Stuff Phil! She would continue with her writing. It was fun—which was more than you could say about him at the moment.

Chapter Fourteen

The sky was blue, not its usual azure blue but a deep cobalt blue. Phil stared up at it, admiring the intensity of colour, unaffected by pollution. He was lying on top of a huge hay bale he had found in a field. Old Ted was running about, following a trail, tail high and wagging in pleasure. The only sounds came from cicadas chirping in the trees. Warmth from the evening sun flooded the field and enveloped him. Phil was reflecting on life.

Ever since he had sold his business and retired, he had felt alienated from the world he used to inhabit. In short, he was lost—lost in a world he no longer understood. He had no friends or acquaintances with which to communicate—not that he had been a huge communicator. He was a doer, a man who wanted results, and his communication was more often than not to do with business. He had an old-fashioned approach to things. It seemed to him that the second he walked away from the warehouse for the last time, he had been dropped by colleagues and people he had considered friends. He was now a dinosaur, a has-been. He had received his payoff, and the new managers were changing everything so that he had become no more than a vague memory, even to those people he had employed for decades.

The world outside was daunting. While he had been getting on with his business, a whole new world had somehow evolved. Everyone outside used mobile phones, laptops, those funny things for emails—what were they? Raspberries? Technology confused him. He was used to talking to people, not texting them or emailing them. He was used to looking at maps to find his way to a destination, not listening to some disembodied voice telling him to "take the next exit on the right". Even cameras no longer had viewfinders. There was no skill left in taking a photograph. Nowadays, if you took a picture and didn't like it, you embellished it with some software from the internet. Phil detested the internet. As a matter of face, Phil loathed most of the comforts that modern life had to offer. He hankered after the old days.

Life was mad. Things had not become better. They were, in fact, worse in his opinion. He no longer fitted in. He was adrift in a world that had become grey and uninviting. He was too old to be of use any more. The day he left work was the day he had ceased to be. He had no desire to do anything or achieve anything now. It didn't matter what hobby or activity Amanda suggested; he really couldn't find the enthusiasm to enjoy it. He didn't enjoy it. In fact, he enjoyed very little any more.

Amanda meant well, but she was irritating him. She spent all her flipping time online. Phil was bored. Worse still, he felt unproductive, ineffectual; he was no more than scrap. There was little to keep him occupied. He had read all the books that were in the cottage that were of interest to him. He had walked Ted so frequently that he was surprised the dog still had legs or that he hadn't worn them down to tiny stumps. He had even watered the garden, weeded it, and mown the grass just for something to do, even though the garden didn't need much attention. He had repaired the dishwasher. He had painted a small shutter that had blistered in the heat of the sun. He had filled in a couple of holes that had appeared in the stone walls with cement to help prevent mice from entering. He had visited Monsieur Renard so often that he almost felt like part of the garage.

The old boy was quite charming in his gruff way. He sympathised with Phil's plight. He shook his head at him every day when he wandered in to see if the parts the camper van had arrived and always tried to pour him a glass of that dreadful stuff he had served up the first evening they had arrived. Phil had learned his lesson, though, and abstained.

Phil knew he should feel better than he did. His attention was drawn to some blue butterflies that had gathered in a gentle, pale blue cloud above some cornflowers in the field and then wafted away. How he envied them; they had no worries. Phil wasn't so jaded that he couldn't recognize the paradisiacal qualities of this place, but he still envied the butterflies and even Ted, who seemed so content with his world.

Ted was now sitting under a hedge with his tongue out, appreciating the warmth of the evening sun, eyes half closed. The evening was calm, yet inside, Phil was in turmoil. He was even more unfulfilled here in France than he had been at home. If he were honest with himself, it wouldn't matter where he was in the world, he would still feel defeated.

The gap year had been a jolly bad idea. Being cooped up with Amanda had been dreadful. They had quarrelled far more than usual. The camper van, he now realised, had offered no privacy, and when he had wanted to be quiet for a while to reflect, she filled the silences with chatter. Even if they hadn't broken down in France and were now driving around Spain or Italy, he would have been forced to realise that he was actually sick of it all. The thought of twenty-four hours a day, seven days a week in a camper van with Amanda now filled him with dread.

He had to also admit that hour after hour of driving not only made him tired, but also stopped him from enjoying the scenery. One field looked very much like another field after a while, and one motorway resembled another. It was a good thing they had broken down, and he had been given the opportunity to think it through properly. They would have to go back home when the camper van was fixed, but what would he do when he returned?

He felt so useless and unimportant now. He used to be someone. His days were full of business meetings, decisions, activities, colleagues, and the rush! How he missed the cut and thrust of the business. He loved the haggling. He thrived on opportunities, and now what did he have? Nothing. He would be sixty this year and what did he have to show for his life? His business was in someone else's hands.

He didn't even know the names of other distributors anymore because those businesses had also changed hands and fellow directors had, like him, retired. Some had left the shores to go and play golf in Spain or Portugal; others had just disappeared off the radar; and some had died.

He supposed that was all he had to look forward to now—death. Although his heart problems were under control, recently he had developed some dreadful stomach problems. Every time he ate, he had awful cramps and pains in his abdomen. He was even losing sleep. Almost every night without fail, his stomach would wake him up, grumbling and hurting and swollen. This must be old age catching up with him.

The shadows were lengthening, and Phil decided to return to the cottage. Amanda would probably be worried about him by now. That woman was always fretting about him. To be fair to her, he hadn't been the greatest company in the world, and he had dragged her off on this daft trip. She needed some interaction with others, so he shouldn't be too hard on her. If she wanted to spend some time on the computer, then he should let her. The problem was his. He was the one who was lacking. The trouble was he just couldn't see how to resolve it.

Sliding off the hay bale, he whistled for Ted, who obediently slipped beside him to accompany him home. What a shame he couldn't be content with this life. What was wrong with him? He and Ted meandered along the track as they plodded back. Not a soul noticed them.

Chapter Fifteen

The annual pétanque match was quite an event. No local missed it. It had started several years ago when the first Brits who had adopted this beautiful region in France and decided to make it their home, also decided to become more French than the French. It was completely normal for an Englishman and his family to cross the Channel in their Volvo Estate, unload their furniture, then suddenly transform from roast-beef-eating Brits to croissant-consuming French, who gladly glugged wine with every meal and frequented every French market possible, swinging their wicker baskets and shouting "Bonjewer" to every person they met.

They also took to French pastimes like canards to water, and many had learned the national sport of boules or a more local variety of the game, pétanque. Unlike the French, who would spend hours in the shade of the village squares on specially prepared areas, perfecting the art of throwing, the Brits would buy heavy plastic, coloured balls or *boules* from the local supermarkets and chuck them about the garden with gay abandon while simultaneously consuming vast quantities of wine. A group of the first settlers had taken the sport to heart and had set up a British team. They had challenged the local French team and before long, a new tradition had been established—the Annual Pétanque match.

Every local in the vicinity, French or British, came along to support the match. There was some rivalry and yet also camaraderie between them. Often, by the end of each long event, the two teams, together with their supporters, would be found in huddles on the green in the local hamlet, attempting communication. One thing the Brits hadn't quite mastered was the art of speaking French, and even if they could converse in passable French, the locals would deliberately switch to the dialect of Occitan to confuse them.

Mathilde adored the event, and every year since it had begun, Bibi had prepared a picnic while Didier dragged out a couple of bottles of his finest wines from the cellar, and they all drove along to the hamlet to chat to neighbours and old friends and of course, to laugh at the Brits. Bibi usually kept herself hidden under the trees that shaded the area with her sketchbook. It meant she didn't have to converse with the locals, who still felt she was as much a foreigner as the British people playing in the match.

It was clear to Bibi that Didier's mind was not on the match this year. Ordinarily, he would have been in high spirits. He loved it when the Brits lost, which they inevitably did. She had to admire their spirit though because year after year, they took up the challenge again, returning with hopes of actually winning. Bibi noticed that Didier had been furtively checking his Blackberry for emails all morning, and at one point, he had been in the laundry whispering to someone on the other end of the phone. He had ended the call as soon as he saw her, pecked her on the cheek, and told her she looked lovely. That made Bibi even more suspicious. Didier disappeared ten minutes before they were due to leave and didn't reappear for half an hour. Mathilde was querulous and anxious. She didn't want to miss the match. What she really didn't want to miss was the opportunity to have a few glasses of Marie Brizard and a cackle with her friends. Bibi was sure Didier was on the phone again but couldn't find him. He appeared eventually from the far end of the garden and hustled them all into the car as if nothing out the norm had happened.

It soon became obvious that Didier was up to no good. He seemed distracted as they drove to the hamlet. There were no spaces nearby. Didier circumnavigated the crowd and stopped the old Peugeot in front of the bakery. The Peugeot was used for such occasions because it didn't attract attention, and it wouldn't hurt if it got a few more dings to add to the collection it already sported. Mathilde bustled out with the enthusiasm of a child where she was immediately greeted by the aged crowd like a long-lost relative. Didier attempted to return to the vehicle but was halted several times by handshakes, kisses and greetings. Bibi observed from the safety of the car.

It was an exceptionally large gathering this year. Small tables of food and aperitifs had been set up around the pétanque arena. This was a rare event. People had come from twenty miles away to watch. There was some excited commotion because Old Garrou had come out of retirement to play. He was a champion at this sport. The Brits wouldn't stand much chance today. Bibi noticed him in a huddle with his fellow players. Mathilde was now seated with her cronies. Didier shook hands with yet another ruddy-faced farmer, and with a wave to some others, he eased himself back into the car and took off at speed to park. After several attempts to find a space, he managed to squeeze the car in between all the other badly parked cars. The space was some distance along the road that led to the ancient church dominating the hill. The match was to be played in the pétanque arena immediately in front of the church. Checking his watch, Didier told Bibi to hurry up.

Walking back to the noisy crowd clutching the basket of food and her sketchbook, Bibi noticed the woman who had been sitting on the large orange balloon. She was talking to one of the members of the British team, and it seemed her husband was playing in the match. He was holding a ball as if it were made of gold, perspiration already forming on his brow. Of course, Mark had gone back to the UK. She had heard the gardener telling Mathilde that this couple was staying at Mark's cottage and looking after the dog. Mark was a nice man. She often saw his wife walking with their two children in the village. It made her heart ache. If only she had been fortunate enough to have two lovely children like hers.

The British woman was laughing. She certainly seemed cheerful. There should be more people like that in the world. Too many people were very serious, especially the people here. She didn't have time for any of them. She caught the eye of one or two of the crowd and nodded brusquely. She could at least show she could be civil. She had no desire to offer more than civility though. Leaving Didier to hang out with a group of middle-aged males who had gathered near the bakery, she took up her usual position near the church so she could observe and sketch the quaint houses which lined the route leading from the village square. The match had begun. It became quiet, and Bibi soon got lost in her own world. When she next looked up, she noticed the English woman was seated next to a donkey. She really was quite a case. Bibi should sketch her sitting there, face animated, with the old dog asleep by her side.

She looked about. Mathilde was dozing, too. Obviously, she'd had too much Marie Brizard. She looked for Didier in the crowd, but there was no sign. Her antennae pricked up. She scanned every face. There was no sign of him.

Without drawing attention to herself, she made her way back to the car. As she had suspected, there was now a space where the car had been parked. Damn him! He had disappeared to see that trollop. He had probably decided that he could nip off and be back before the end of the match, and no one would miss him. Bibi cursed him some more as she made her way back to the tree where she spent the remainder of the match staring at her sketchbook and wishing she had a very heavy metal boule to throw at Didier.

Chapter Sixteen

Amanda was writing a funny post about the Pétanque match that had taken place earlier in the week. Phil had been roped in to make up the numbers. She thought it had been good fun and that Phil would have enjoyed it, but it hadn't quite turned out the way they had expected. Still, it made excellent material for her blog. The camper van would be repaired soon. Monsieur Renard had phoned to say that he had the necessary parts and would begin work on it the next day. They could continue their journey.

Having been in France for the duration of August, Amanda was now reluctant to leave the hamlet and the life here. It was comfortable, and they had become familiar with the area now. She wasn't keen to get back in Bertie and continue the journey. Phil wasn't likely to cheer up just because they were travelling through Italy or Germany or Turkey. He was once again stuck under his own personal gloom cloud, and when he was there, she could not get him out from under it.

The phone rang. *Let Phil get it,* she thought. It continued to ring. Clearly, Phil wasn't back yet. Irritated that her concentration was being broken, she raced downstairs to take the call.

"Hello Mum," said a sombre voice.

"Hi, Tom, how's it going?"

"I need to talk to Dad."

"He isn't here. Can't you tell me?"

"No, I need Dad. I really need Dad," continued Tom shakily.

"Is your car all right?" asked Amanda, changing tack to try and establish the problem.

"The car is fine."

"Is Alice okay?"

"Yes, she's fine, too. Mum, I need Dad. I can't talk to you about this. Sorry. Could you tell him I called and I'll call again in half an hour?"

"Tom, don't go. Please tell me what the problem is. I'll only worry about you—"

The door was shoved open by Ted, who came in with tail wagging. He headed straight for the drinking bowl and lapped noisily.

"It's okay. Dad's here. I'll pass you over."

"Let me get my flaming shoes off first," growled Phil, who was bringing up the rear.

Amanda covered the mouthpiece up.

"It's Tom. I think he's in trouble. He only wants to talk to you. He refuses to tell me what it is. It must be serious."

Phil snatched the phone and took it outside so Amanda couldn't hear the conversation. She stared out of the window and watched Phil pace up and down. He shook his head, and she could tell from his demeanour that whatever Tom was saying, it was grave. *Whatever could it be?* She tried to see if Phil was shouting. No, he seemed to be deep in conversation with Tom. It couldn't be too awful. If it were, Phil would be yelling and ranting. He always ranted and yelled at Tom.

Anxious minutes later, Phil returned.

"Well?" she asked.

"Let me get in, will you? I need to think. Give me five minutes."

Five minutes became ten, which in turn became twenty. Ted had flopped down in his bed and was now asleep. Finally, Amanda heard creaking on the stairs, and Phil descended.

"I have to go back to the UK. There has been a break-in at the house. They got in through the front door."

Amanda gulped. Tom clearly hadn't told his father about the door breaking episode. The stupid boy hadn't got the door repaired, and these people had just marched in. What a complete buffoon he was. She groaned inwardly. She had told him to text her when the door was repaired, and he hadn't. She'd forgotten to chase it up, assuming Tom wouldn't be dumb enough to leave a front door broken. She should have checked instead of messing about writing stories for a book. She mentally cursed herself; then, she cursed Tom some more.

"The problem is that the people who broke in are camped out there. They are squatting, and Tom can't get back into the house at the moment. I shall have to go over and sort it out. Tom is staying at Alice's house now. I need you to book me a flight back to the UK as soon as possible. Don't look at me like that. I'm going alone. You can't come. I'd rather you stayed here. You'll just get in a lather. It doesn't need two of us, and Ted still needs looking after," he added. "Besides, it'll give you a chance to do some writing. Take your mind off it. Don't worry. Trust me. I am good at sorting out problems. We had gypsies camped on the land next to the warehouse a couple of years ago, and I got them off just through talking to them and appealing to their better nature. There'll be a way to remove these guys, too."

Amanda couldn't believe what she was hearing. There were complete strangers in her house. They were living in her home. They were sitting on her chairs, eating from her crockery with her knives and forks, and using all her things; they'd go through the drawers and cupboards. It was a good thing that most of their clothes were with them in the van. She'd hate the thought of someone going through her underwear drawers. Images kept passing through her mind like a slideshow: these strangers sitting on their settee, watching their television, and sleeping in their bed on their sheets. She felt sick. This was too horrendous to contemplate.

She knew, however, that she could count on Phil to take charge and resolve it. When the chips were down, you could always rely on Phil. He thrived on challenges, and this certainly would test him. When he was determined to do something, nothing could thwart him. Yes, it would be all right. When he'd got the rotten squatters out, she'd go back, and they'd refit the place. She'd get the carpets and settee cleaned professionally and the place disinfected. It could do with new decor and curtains anyway. She'd buy a brand new bed for them and new sheets.

Satisfied with her plan, she spent the evening with Phil, sorting out a flight for him and arranging a taxi to get him to the airport the next day. He phoned Tom again to make further arrangements.

Much later, when arrangements were made, they sat outside. It was pleasantly warm even though it was now September. Moths kept flying into the outside light until Phil took pity on them and turned it off. So now they sat beside the table, lit only by the bright full moon, which threw its beams onto the veranda.

"I'm surprised you are not furious about this. You seem remarkably calm," Amanda remarked.

"There's no point in losing my rag with Tom. It's not his fault that this has happened. He tries hard to be adult and to reach my expectations of him. He'll make mistakes as he goes along life's path, but he'll get there in the end." He paused for a while. The chirping of evening insects filled the silence. "He must have been beside himself when it happened. It was brave of him to face up to me, though, and tell me. He sounded miserable when we spoke and blamed himself entirely. It wasn't his fault. It's not like he left the door wide open with a sign hanging on it saying 'come in', now is it?"

Amanda thought it wise to keep quiet about Tom's part in all of it. She'd tackle him later. At the moment, he needed his father. His relationship with Phil at best could be described as fragile. Phil had high standards, and Tom did not usually measure up to them. Discovering that he was to blame for the break-in could fracture their relationship permanently. Yes, it was probably for the best if she kept her knowledge to herself.

Phil pushed back the chair and announced he was going to attempt to get some sleep before his early start. Wide awake and with no hope of becoming sleepy, she went into the far bedroom where she typed the finishing touches to the pétanque post and worried about her invaded home.

BLOG: Fortifying Your Fifties

Day ??… feels like day 100

There is always something special and olde worlde about France. The small hamlet or tiny village where we are staying is situated smack bang in tranquil countryside. Fields of sunflowers surround the hamlet of stone-shuttered houses, which are perched high on a hill. This in turn is reached by a 1:6 incline in either direction. Great for walks and for improving leg and bottom tone so we strode out each day with the dog. How we love France!

What always surprises me is that no matter where you go or what time you travel in Southern France, every village or hamlet appears to be shut. Shutters are closed tight, and there is no life to be seen or heard. Such is the case in the hamlet where we are staying. The only clue to the fact that there are any inhabitants in the twenty houses that are scattered about on the hill top is the abundance of pots of geraniums and periodically, the aroma of cooking.

Whatever time we go out, we see no one. Even the small church is permanently shut. The baker has a sign in her window indicating she is out on deliveries, and should we require any bread, a return trip at about four o'clock might find her there. We tried that, and although we could see smoke curling up from behind the bakery, there was no one present in the shop as we peered through the window.

We have been enjoying the warm days of summer. Nothing disturbs us but the sound of bird songs, bees buzzing lazily, and the occasional donkey braying in the distance. That was until the third morning when we awoke to the sound of the dog barking, alerting us to the presence of visitors.

"Morning!" yelled an English voice through the railings. "Hope we're not disturbing you," continued the voice of someone from up North in the UK.

We opened the gate to be greeted by two red-faced expats, who held a bottle of local red wine in their hands. Phil looked at the wine, bewildered since it was early morning.

"Well, this is France, and it's only three hours until lunch," said the first by way of explanation.

"There's another reason for the wine," continued the shorter of the two men. His accent smacked of Yorkshire. "We need your help."

With the wine opened and all of us sitting on the veranda, they explained the problem. Mark has gone away, forgetting completely that it was the annual Concours de Pétanque in the hamlet this week. It is only for people residing in and around the hamlet. He is an essential part of the team and without him, the men knew they would be well and truly thrashed by the local French team who took great pride in their prowess at playing pétanque. In their wisdom, they had decided that since we were temporarily living in the hamlet, then we qualified as residents. Thus, they hoped that Phil would agree to act as substitute.

For those of you unsure of the game of pétanque, it is similar to boules, the national French sport. Groups of people, mostly men, spend hours perfecting the art of throwing or rolling metal balls in a game similar to our sport of bowls. Medium-sized, shiny balls are rolled towards a small ball or as it is known in French, a *cochonette*. The person whose ball is closest to the cochonette wins. There is a lot of skill involved as well as a huge amount of pride. Rather than rolling the balls, Pétanque requires a particular way of throwing the balls. Although after several glasses of red wine, Phil and I were even more confused about the rules than before.

Phil reluctantly agreed to stand in and be the fourth British team member; after all, how difficult could it be to throw a ball at another ball? Delighted to have a full complement of Brits to enter the competition, the men weaved out of the door and into an old Renault 5, which wheezed down the road in the direction of the nearest town—no doubt to celebrate at the local bar. I highly suspect that the local red hadn't been their first bottle of wine that morning.

The big day dawned bright and sunny. Brightly-coloured bunting had mysteriously appeared around the hamlet overnight, and several dozen cats had gathered in the streets to no doubt watch the spectacle. They hung about on walls and steps watching through half open eyes. Large signs hung from the church announcing the "21ieme Concours de Pétanque". Still, no one was visible. Painted shutters remained closed. The baker's shop had a sign up, announcing she was shut due to the special Fête Pétanque.

At 12 o'clock on the dot, the church bells rang out, loud and long. Shutters magically flew open, and aged French men and women appeared from nowhere, making their way to the square where the competition was to be held. We knew they were French because they shook hands with all their friends or kissed them on each cheek several times, and as if that wasn't clue enough, they all sported blue berets.

Quite a crowd was forming. Aged men, carrying small cases which obviously contained the precious boules, scurried to the meeting place. A smell of aniseed filled the air. The cats seemed to club together silently. There were certainly more people here than the occupants of the twenty houses of the hamlet. Women were getting out freshly-purchased baguettes and laying out ham and cheese on tablecloths by the side of the road. Plastic bidons of red wine soon joined them. These were followed by large bottles of that aniseed-smelling drink, Ricard.

The women cackled into their aprons and brandished dried sausages animatedly as they chatted. Chickens began to gather in front of the church to join the melee, having been let out of their yards. Mme Fou-Fou La Folle arrived on the back of her donkey, carrying more baguettes like a bizarre Don Quixote. It was, in short, a sight to behold.

The air was ripe with good humour. People who had probably lived in the same hamlet for decades were greeting each other as if they hadn't seen each other for months. Suddenly, there was a frisson of tension. Up the road trundled an aging car, horn honking, fumes belching from the exhaust. "Les Anglais" had arrived. The same men we had met earlier that week tumbled out of the Renault 5, having gone into town for a livener and greeted the French with loud and hearty "bonjours" and handshakes. The French grunted gruff replies, but these men were no longer their friends and neighbours. Oh no, these men were now the opposition—enemies

Everyone was gathered in front of the church situated at the very top of the hill in the sweet hamlet. A couple of small lengths of flattened gravel had been created overnight, and a large crowd swelled under the tree that shaded the spot. This was the sacred Pétanque square— although, in truth, it resembled an oblong rather than a square.

The British team had just emerged from their old jalopy of a car and were in high spirits. Phil was called over for a team talk and to discuss tactics. Stan was busy explaining about his precious boules, which were his "champion boules", given to him by his grandchildren. He cherished these balls and only used them once a year. He was, however willing to lend them to Phil, who, of course, did not own a set. Phil assured him that he would take great care of them.

I sat on the ground with our stepdog, next to Mme Fou-Fou la Folle's donkey, which by now had a nosebag and was happily distracted. Everyone from a fifty-mile radius had gathered. This was a big day.

Tactics discussed, the men took up position with the other teams to be read the rules by the local Mayor, who was wearing his uniform and medals for such an important day. He was also on one of the teams. Phil's teammates, consisting of Eric, Stan, and Dick listened with glazed expressions. Obviously, the pre-match livener was wearing off by now.

Everyone huddled into groups. Boules were extracted from cases and polished methodically. Suddenly a loud rattling noise could be heard coming from afar, and up the hill chugged a large, orange, rusty tractor. Phil's team gave a collective groan. The opposition looked triumphant.

"Sneaky frogs," whispered Stan, "they've brought out Le Vieux Garrou from retirement."

The tractor and clanking trailer advanced slowly. The gnarled, walnut-coloured, weather-beaten face of an old farmer, hunched over the wheel with determination written all over his face, could finally be seen as he inched up the steep slope. He arrived in a smelly cloud of red diesel fumes and parked outside the bakery. Fumes belched over the crowd gathered there, but they didn't mind because this was their hero—Old Garrou, regional champion of pétanque, who lived in the farm in the valley and thus was a member of the hamlet. Even the donkey stopped eating and viewed him with awe. He patted a small dog on the head as he creaked his way down to the pétanque area. I half-expected people to chant: "Vive Le Garrou".

Stan was distraught. He explained all to Phil.

"Okay, this makes it harder. You really have to watch old Garrou. You just do what we say, and we'll be okay. Well, I hope so because I had a bet with Albert and Bernard that the Brits would win the match this year."

The game began. Glasses of wine were poured for the participants. The first Frenchman stood up to the line and bent his knees dramatically. He raised himself and lowered himself in an effort to limber up, then threw the small cochonette into the gravel further down. The crowd applauded. The first boule was lifted in a limp-wristed stance and flicked beautifully, to land neatly with an appropriate *thunk* noise near the cochonette. The crowd applauded. And thus it continued. Tape measures were pulled out, much gum sucking went on, and distances from the cochonette were measured with care. After a while, I decided the donkey was much more interesting than the match. However, I was apparently the only one, as everyone else was glued to it— everyone apart from the stepdog, who had wisely gone to sleep.

Eventually, having won their rounds, Phil, Stan, Eric, and Dick were through to the final match. Several bottles of Ricard and wine had been consumed by now, and they were all rather excited at having made it this far. It was hot. Some of the crowd were chattering to each other by now. The chickens had found their way into someone's vegetable patch and were helping themselves to some ripening tomatoes and peas. The cats had dozed off.

The Brits were doing well. Sid threw a super shot, his bowl landing very close to the cochonette. The French team had a few words in a huddled group. Bernard threw next. He took a measured look at the situation and throwing high, glanced a blow against Sid's boule which knocked it away from the cochonette, which now lay to the left of the pitch.

Phil was next to throw. He bent down and up again in fluid movements. Sid licked his lips. Phil aimed for Bernard's boule so he could get closest to the cochonette, and yes, he knocked it away, making the cochonette move further to the left.

Old Garrou cackled and came up to the line. He didn't need to practise. With one expert twist of the wrist, he flung the boule high in the air. It propelled from his hand like a missile and with a tremendous clack, walloped into Phil's boule, which leapt into the air due to the force. Old Garrou's boule stopped dead, right next to the cochonette. Phil's boule however, did not; it shot off the pitch.

As I have already mentioned, the hamlet is perched on the top of a hill with a 1:6 incline. Phil's boule erupted from the pitch and was propelled with velocity towards the church where it appeared to slow. It gradually came to a halt and teetered for a split second on the edge of the car park, and then suddenly lurched forward down the gradient, gaining in speed down the slope.

"My boule!" yelled Stan and started after it, followed immediately by Eric and Dick and of course, Phil. Like an old black and white Keystone Cop movie, the quartet ran down the slope, chasing after Stan's precious boule. Back on the square, the French watched, amused by the antics of the English, and then applauded as Le Vieux Garrou and his team collected the cup for winning the 21ieme Concours de Pétanque.

Garrou cheerily sent one of his sons down in the tractor with the trailer to collect the team, who, having finally caught up with the boule, were hot and bothered. They were brought back up the hill where they were cordially invited to share in a post-match feast, which, of course, involved much red wine and, I believe, a settling up of a debt.

Phil however, has declared that to be his first and last pétanque match. It turned out to be far more effort than he intended. Also a valuable lesson was learned—never take on the French at their national sport. Eric, Stan, and Dick, however, have a cunning plan; they are challenging the French to a game of cricket next month. Luckily, I don't think Phil will be there to participate.

Posted by Facing50.Blog

14 Comments:

Hippyhappyhoppy says…Oh what fun! You do have such a fun approach to life. Hugs x

Lillian says…Hilarious story. My father enjoyed it very much.

MaDGras says…Very funny. It reminded me of my childhood in Canada. We played a game like that.

PhillyFilly says…I loved that you sat next to a donkey. Great image. Cricket is an amazing English sport. You would whip those Frenchies at it. Does Phil not want to play because he's a spoilsport?

HighHeeledLife says…We have that game here in Canada, too. You brought back some lovely childhood memories of my father playing it. Thank you.

DonnaKBab says…I laughed so much at this that I snorted tea onto my computer screen.

TheMerryDivorcee says…Hubs # 3 was obsessed with playing baseball – I think you Brits call it Rounders. He was always out practicing. I took in a few matches now and then and then took off with the coach–Hubs # 4.

QuiteContrary says…What a ridiculous game. Over here we play Crown Bowls, which is far more accurate and sensible. We even have a proper white uniform to play in. This sounds like a child's game. Hope I haven't offended.

MiaFerrari says…My father used to play the Italian equivalent to this. It's called Bocce, and the little wooden ball you throw first is called a *baby*. There was still plenty of rivalry among the players though and a lot of drinking. If you get back on the road, don't forget to head over to Italy. We are not that far away from you.

YoungFreeSingleandSane says…Jonathan used to play Crown Bowls. It was exceedingly dull. At least this sounds light-hearted and spirited. I can just imagine you there on your sunny hill. I am out bowling with Kevin tonight. It won't be quite as crazy as *pétanque*. Thanks for the laugh today. Hope all is well.

Gypsynesters2 says…Greetings from Argentina. How's the trip going? I see you are still in France. It must be nice if you are still there. Just off to do some bareback horse riding. Adios Amigos.

SexyFitChick says…I can't imagine Phil playing any games at all. He must have looked incredibly fed up the whole time. Please tell me you took some photographs. It all sounds a bit tame to me. I would have preferred it if they had thrown the balls at each other and run around a lot more. Still, I suppose they ran quite a bit down the road.

PhillyFilly says…I realized halfway through the post that you were talking about lawn bowls. What a super picture you conjured up. I found myself almost laughing. I would have laughed properly if I hadn't had so much botox last week. My face looks like Cher's. Hope she isn't reading this. She might sue me.

Facing50 says…Lovely to hear from you all. I had thought when I wrote this that we would be back on the road next month which was why I said Phil wouldn't be here to play cricket. It's just as well because he can't play any sports. Things have changed a bit since I typed the post. I'll explain another time. I've been trying to keep the blog light-hearted and don't want to burden you with any woes. After all, the blog is called *Fortifying Your Fifties,* not *Listen to Amanda Moan*.

SexyFitChick says…Amanda, this is urgent. We need to talk. Skype isn't working for me so I can't get you that way. I'm not sure how often you check your emails, but I've sent more details to you. I saw an item in the local newspaper that will be of interest, if that is the right word, to you. There was a cycling incident during a race. It involved a certain hottie that you know well. I think he's badly injured. I wouldn't normally encourage you to check on him, but I thought this might be important.

Chapter Seventeen

The taxi had left at an unearthly hour. Phil would be waiting for his flight at Toulouse airport by now. Tom was to pick him up when he arrived back in the UK. Phil had promised to text her as soon as he landed. He had left specific instructions for her not to worry and to make the most of the peace and quiet to get some writing done.

Having a project, even a horrendous one like getting squatters out of the house, seemed to have instantly made him more focussed. He was like the Phil of old, almost relishing the thought of a head-to-head with these awful people. Overnight, he had turned from a grouchy, bored old man into someone more youthful, someone with purpose. He had even kissed her briefly on the cheek before he left and wished her luck with the writing.

Ted had been lying mournfully in his bed ever since Phil left. His best friend had just abandoned him. First his parents leave him and then his friends.

"Don't be sad, Ted. I'll look after you. I won't go until your family comes back. What about a slice of ham?" That cheered him instantly.

Amanda pulled on her shoes to take him out. A walk would help clear her head. Ted raced off as usual to explore the smells of the hedgerows, and Amanda was left to her thoughts. The solitude was very therapeutic, and soon she was conjuring up stories that would fill her book.

Passing a field of neatly rolled hay bales, she noticed the same hay bale Phil had sat upon the day before. It seemed inviting so she decided to climb on it, which proved to be somewhat of a challenge. She couldn't quite get on top of it. Apparently, she was the wrong shape because her curves proved to be her undoing. Each time she jumped up and grabbed the bindings to haul herself up, her lower body would slide down the bale, forcing her to let go and slide with it. Thinking it was a game, Ted barked joyfully, racing around her ankles each time she fell. He wasn't helping. One futile attempt followed another until she finally flopped back onto the ground, and Ted launched himself onto her stomach, making her giggle. She pushed him off, and they had a silly game of human and dog tag. After several further attempts to leap onto the hay bale and much puffing, she slithered down it for the last time before plopping onto the grass. She heard soft laughter coming from the hedge, and narrowing her eyes from the shafts of morning sunlight impeding her view, she noticed an elegant woman seated on a small stool with an easel in front of her.

"I am so sorry to laugh at you. I do not want to be rude, but you were very funny," said the stranger, standing up and coming towards her. Ted bounced up to her, and she knelt down to pat him.

"This dog is adorable, too. What is it called?"

"This is Ted, a ferocious guard dog, who will lead you to the house safe and lick your face as you rob it," explained Amanda. "I'm Amanda, and you…you speak very good English. How did you know I was English?"

"It was just a guess. French women would not exert themselves trying to get on top of a scratchy haystack at this time of the morning. Thank you for the compliment. I learned to speak English many years ago. I am Beatrice, but my friends call me Bibi. *Enchantée*," she added, extending a perfectly manicured hand.

Bibi took in Amanda's dishevelled appearance. It dawned on her immediately that this was the same woman she had seen bouncing on the orange balloon at the side of the road. She was the one who had been sitting next to a donkey at the local *pétanque* match, laughing merrily. Bibi liked her instantly. She exuded vitality even though she was not young and had dancing, green eyes.

"I was just painting," explained Bibi, showing Amanda the small watercolour on which she had been working. "I often come out to the fields to capture the light."

"Gosh! This is beautiful. Do you sell your paintings? I'd love to buy this for my husband as a thank you. He'd really like it."

"Thank you for what? Has he been kind?"

For no reason other than pent up frustration, Amanda found herself unburdening to this complete stranger. As Ted chased around the field in ever-increasing circles, she told Bibi all about the gap year, the camper van, Tom, the broken door, and even the squatters.

Her earnest nature and obvious loneliness touched Bibi. Besides, she had always had a fondness for the British. This one was feisty and funny in equal measures. She felt guilty that she had borrowed Amanda's identity for her internet project, and although she had no intention of removing it because she had already started to attract followers, she felt she should take this particular scruffy bird under her wing. It would give her a project. Besides, from what Amanda had said, as soon as the squatters left her house, she would return to the UK. There could be no harm in being friends with this woman.

They parted some time later, having made arrangements to meet in the nearby town of Caylus for coffee the next day. Amanda raced Ted home. Ted won by several minutes and was already on his bed with his tongue out, laughing at her, by the time she entered the house. It was weird without Phil. The house was remarkably quiet. She checked her phone. No text. Phil was more than likely on the flight. She logged onto Skype and sent a message to PlayGirl.77 to say she was online if she fancied a chat.

141

Ted dozed off. A fly buzzed around the room. Amanda poured a glass of red wine that she found in the cellar. It tasted of liquorice and red berry fruit. Even with her glasses, she couldn't read the label because it was so faded. She made out the word *Château* and something beginning with P. She slugged at the wine again and let it roll around her mouth to get the flavours. She decided that it must be a local wine, Château Plonk, and rather nice it was, too. She got comfortable in front of the computer. At least she had company here. She logged onto her blog to read the latest comments.

The last comment from SexyFitChick set her heart racing. No, this couldn't be! She knew SexyFitChick lived in Sydney, too, but this must be a mistake. SexyFitChick must have misread the article. She tried to get to her email box, but in her haste typed the wrong password three times. Her fingers had transformed into giant sausages, and she couldn't type properly.

At last, her inbox messages came up. SexyFitChick had sent her a lengthy email containing a newspaper clipping from a week ago.

> It was reported today that Todd Bradshaw is still in critical condition after colliding with a fellow cyclist during the prestigious Scarberry Trophy Race. The incident occurred in the final stages of the race as the contestants were approaching the finish line. No one is quite sure what happened, but it appeared that as Bradshaw was pulling out to overtake Hartley Fischer, their tyres touched, resulting in the two competitors spinning out of control. Fischer was later released with only a broken collarbone. Bradshaw remains in Intensive Care at Sydney Hospital.

She read it through again. Any hopes that it was a different Todd Bradshaw were quashed by the accompanying email from her Australian friend, who informed Amanda that this Todd really was *the* Todd—the Todd who had been her first love and with whom she had flirted all last year online. She had contemplated starting a new life with him the previous year when she and Phil had been going through a bad patch but had thought better of it at the last minute. Now he was in hospital, fighting for his life.

She went immediately onto Facebook. Todd was still one of her friends there. She hadn't had the heart to block him after they had decided to cool their relationship. She clicked onto his Facebook page, and sure enough, there were several messages wishing him a speedy recovery and good wishes. He might never read the message, but she had to leave one. It was the only way she could contact him.

Just heard about your accident. Hurry up and get better. I shall be waiting by the Scrabble Board for you to return. Love, Amanda xxx

Perhaps someone would read it to him and let him know that people cared about him. He might have been a bit of a cad, but she desperately hoped he would recover. What if he recovered and was unable to walk or do normal things? The thought was unbearable. Life always managed to take you by surprise. Her mother was right; you should try and enjoy it while you can. She desperately hoped Todd would be able to enjoy life again. After all, he was the most adventurous, thrill-seeking person she knew.

The phone flashed. It was the text she had been expecting. Tom was as apologetic as ever: *Dad here. Will text when we have news. So sorry Mum. Really I am. x*

She stared at the mobile and felt less angry with her son. Life is sometimes too short to get overly worked up about people's mistakes.

Chapter Eighteen

"Bibi, I want a bath. Will you run it for me? It is too much for me to keep going up and down these stairs. Don't make it too hot like you did last time. I was almost burnt to a crisp."

"Yes, of course, Mathilde. I shall run it as soon as I have finished shelling these peas," replied Bibi, splitting open each pod with a sharp knife to ensure she didn't damage her perfectly painted nails. Mathilde was a pain, but she was elderly, and Bibi, like many French women, respected her elders, especially elderly relatives. However, she didn't have much respect for her husband at the moment.

Didier had phoned an hour ago to say he would not be home for dinner again. He was full of apologies and promises. He would be very late and might even stay over in town because he did not want to disturb her by coming home so late. He had to see the accountant about some pressing tax issues.

Bibi made the right noises and assured him that it was fine. Begging him to come home was not an option, and above everything, she had her pride and dignity. She wished him a good night and, as a last minute thought, told him that she would be going out with a friend the following evening so could he ensure he got home to look after Mathilde? She could tell he was curious about this new friend. To his knowledge, Bibi kept herself to herself and had no friends. He didn't question her, though. He had too much to hide to start asking too many questions about her life. She momentarily sensed a minor victory.

She knew his excuse was a lie because Gerard Dubois, who was the company accountant and lived in nearby Septfonds, was on holiday in South Africa. She had heard two women from the village discussing it at the chemist while she had been waiting to get a prescription for Mathilde. The pharmacist, who knew everyone in the village and the surrounding area, had been chatting to the woman at the front of the queue about Mme Dubois having been in to collect malaria tablets for the trip.

"I can't understand why people travel so far," she had babbled. "We have everything we need here in France. We have sea, we have mountains, and we have sunshine. Why would you want to go abroad? They don't have proper food there either," she had continued.

Bibi had switched off at that point. Once the locals here started talking about food, you would be waiting forever. She spent the time looking at bottles of bath oils, which were stacked by the window. That was the problem with living in a small community—everyone knew your business. It was a good thing Didier worked in Toulouse and had his affairs there. No one in the village would travel that far, so he was unlikely to be discovered. As for her, the locals still kept their distance. It suited Bibi well enough. The last thing she wanted was for her marriage to be the subject of village gossip. Mathilde made sure, too, that everyone believed her son to be a saint.

"That man puts in every hour of the day at work just to look after his old Maman and his wife," she would say to her friends when they dropped round to play cards. They were undoubtedly sick of hearing about wonderful Didier. Still, at least they wouldn't know what a lousy husband he had become.

She filled up the enamel bath tub with warm water for Mathilde. With her out of the way for a while, Bibi could check on the internet and see how "Amanda" was getting along. Mathilde was now massacring an Édith Piaf song in the bedroom as she got ready for her bath. She would be soaking for ages.

Leaving a large fluffy towel on the towel rail for Mathilde, she went to the office and logged on. To her surprise, she had quite a few friend requests from Facebook. They were artists and writers and people from the groups she had joined. She scrolled through the list of new people and her eyes alighted upon an aristocratic sounding name—Richard Montagu-Forbes.

She could picture him now—distinguished, a man of importance, a man who had presence. He probably lived in an old manor house with some hunting dogs. She clicked onto his page. Oh, what a sweet puppy! Gosh, he sounded perfect. He liked art, films, and animals. He even lived in France. What could be better? Maybe she should find out more about him. She didn't really want to meet him, but if she could just forge an online relationship with him, she could convince Didier that she had taken a lover. It was early days yet, though.

Eagerly, she clicked on the Accept Request button. Now, she needed to send him a message to encourage him to contact her further. Should she mention his gorgeous dog? No, she was supposed to be an exciting, go-getting woman. A woman like that would not ask about his dog. She was sophisticated. He lived in a vibrant, cosmopolitan part of France. Looking at the groups he had liked, he seemed to appreciate French films. She would check to see what was on at the cinema via the internet and mention it. There must be some classy art film.

It was no good checking to see what was on at the local cinema in St-Antonin-Noble-Val. It was the only cinema in the area, and although they had a reasonable selection of films, an arty type film would take a few weeks to reach the provinces. The cinema was very quaint. It consisted of one large room with a large screen and comfortable maroon seats. It was surprisingly popular, though, and when a blockbuster movie arrived which would be shown all week in English with French subtitles, every night would be fully booked. Bibi occasionally dropped in to watch a film in English. They catered well to the British population there, and Bibi could sit hidden in the shadows among the foreigners and improve her vocabulary. She hadn't been for some time, though, so she wasn't sure what was on at the cinema here or anywhere.

She browsed through the search engines and got up all the cinema screen showings in Nice. Perfect! They were showing *The Beloved,* which had closed the 2011 Cannes Film Festival. It was set in the 1960s and 1990s in Paris, Prague, and London. It also starred one of Bibi's favourite actresses, Catherine Deneuve, and her daughter Chiara Mastroianni. She would use this information and try to come across as sophisticated, a little tantalising, and yet, aloof.

She opted for a direct message rather than write on his "wall" where anyone could see what she had posted. *I am delighted to meet you, Richard. Were you, by chance, the distinguished man seated near me at the showing of 'The Beloved' at Cannes this year? I was the lady in red.* She hoped that would intrigue him. Even if he hadn't seen the film, he might wonder about her.

The ringing of the bell alerted her that Mathilde was out of the bath and requiring some assistance. She took the damn thing everywhere so she could summon Bibi whenever she needed her. Bibi wished she could drown it under the bubbles in the bath. She clicked off and went to see what Mathilde wanted this time.

Chapter Nineteen

"Come on Mr Bradshaw. Let's see if we can get you up."

Todd glanced up at the nurse who looked as if she should have been a champion wrestler. He wasn't going to argue with her. She clearly would take no nonsense from him. Besides, he was too woozy to argue. The nurse helped him out of the bed, ensuring he didn't knock his shoulder or damage his leg any further. He was hoping to be discharged in a couple of days. He'd had his shoulder pinned together in an operation. It had hurt like mad, but the drugs they had put him on for the pain were doing their job; now all his days were comfortable, if not fuzzy, ones.

Seated in a wide, padded chair, Todd asked for his laptop. A friend had brought in clothes and his computer the day before. The same friend was making sure that Digit, his cattle dog, was being looked after and had plenty of food.

"Your dog is going feral," Jezza had said. "Bloody animal sits on the roof of his kennel and howls every night. I think he's attempting to contact his wolf ancestors. You better hurry up and get back. He's scaring the neighbours. And by the way, he stole your neighbour's salmon straight off the barbecue yesterday. He charged off with it when they were chatting to friends. He left the burgers though. At least he knows how to eat healthily."

Todd grinned. His dog had lots of character. He took after his master with a penchant for bicycles, females, and grilled salmon.

It was time to try and get back to his old life, fuzzy or not. He clicked on to his emails and read them through. Not much to worry about. There were a couple of emails about some funds he was holding. They could wait. There wasn't much else. That was the trouble; he didn't have anyone in his life who would be too concerned about him. All his close family lived in the UK and would have no idea of what had befallen him. That was partly his fault, too, because apart from the odd message on Facebook, Todd didn't keep in touch with his family. There had been some articles in the local newspaper in Sydney, but no one back in Old Blighty would have seen those. Jezza had brought the clippings in, saying he might want to keep them for posterity and to remind himself of how close he came to croaking.

He had no girlfriend or wife, and his friends, well…they were just mates he had met through cycling or sports. One or two had dropped by the hospital to check he was okay after the accident, including Hartley, who had caused the accident. He'd been pretty shaken up about the whole affair though, and Todd felt sorry for him. Being blokes, and Aussie blokes at that, once they'd ascertained that he wasn't going to die, they just gave him manly punches on his good arm and said they'd see him soon. Male testosterone—it prevented you from feeling much in the way of emotion.

He checked the news sites and then logged onto Facebook. There were a few old school friends on there along with his nephew and niece. He'd see if anyone had missed him. Surprisingly, there were more messages than he expected. Lenny, an old school pal had said he'd heard about it from another friend. Tony had heard about it from reading Lenny's post, and so on. He scrolled down the page, reading the get-well messages. After a few they began to go hazy. That last lot of drugs was kicking in. They must be really strong because it looked like that next message was from Amanda. He checked again. It *was* from Mandy. How had she found out about the accident? She was supposed to be making her way through Europe. Reading the message, Todd felt she was obviously concerned about him. She must still have some feelings for him to even leave a message. *What was this?* She was waiting to play Scrabble with him again.

Leaning back in the chair, Todd recalled how much he had loved playing Scrabble with her. They had their own special version which they called "Lust Scrabble". In their version, you had to get as many suggestive words down on the board as possible. It was more about the words than the actual score. The person who succeeded in placing the most suggestive words was the winner.

He remembered her playing the word *stocking* on one occasion. That had conjured up such images that he hadn't been able to play for a few minutes. Plus, if his memory served him correctly through its current drug-induced haze, he had enjoyed many a titillating dream after that.

He looked at her message one more time. If that wasn't an open invitation, Todd didn't know what was. He sent a message to her: *The thought of playing Scrabble with you is the only thing that is keeping me alive. Set the board up. I'm back from the brink!*

Chapter Twenty

Amanda was trying to get some sense out of her mother, which was turning out to be an impossible task at the moment. She had obviously been out and had a skinful because she was not only incoherent, but she also had two cigarettes on the go at the same time, and she didn't seem to notice.

"So he said, why not? And I thought it seemed a good idea. After all, there's not much to keep me here, is there? By the way, do you like my nail varnish? Spencer painted my nails for me. I haven't had them painted for years. He's done my toes, too. Would you like to see them?"

Amanda couldn't think of anything worse than her mother waving toes at her via the internet.

"No, it's okay. I can imagine they are the same colour. What colour is that exactly?"

Amanda's mother looked at her hand for a moment, puzzled. She had a cigarette in it and one in the other hand, too. She took a quick inhalation from one, then bemused, lifted the other to her lips and took a deeper puff.

"Stereo cigarettes," she chuckled, waving them about. "Um, some funny name for green," she replied. "Vertigo or verdures—something foreign."

Amanda rolled her eyes. Her mother had stubbed out one cigarette and replaced it with a brandy glass.

"So, as I was saying. I shall give it a go and see what happens."

"Mum, I have no idea at all what you are talking about. What are you going to give a go?"

"Didn't I say? Oh dear, it's all that wine we had at lunch. Grego and Spencer want me to go back to Cyprus with them and help with the designs. They have a big fashion show coming up and would like me to be part of it. Don't worry. We'll still be able to have our little chats. I have bought this—"

She leaned off into the distance and hiccoughed loudly. She rummaged about for few minutes and then held up an object in front of the screen. Amanda squinted as the object was moved in and out of focus by her weaving mother.

"What's that?"

"It's an iPad. Spencer helped me choose it. It's ever so light, and I can use Skype on it. It's better than the computer because you can carry it around and show the other person what is in the room or what is going on. It's got these great things on it called apps. I spent all morning on Bubble Shooter. It's huge fun and very addictive. I have completed nearly all the levels now and will have to go Premium soon. Grego can't beat my score on levels nineteen to thirty and is quite frustrated. You can get all sorts of apps. There is a Karaoke Glee app. I must try that. Of course, my favourite is Space Inversion. You have to shoot little coloured aliens as they go across the screen like small crabs trying to blow up your bases with their bombs. If you are lucky and hit a space ship, which comes over occasionally, you score extra points. I can't put it down. You should get one. Shall I show you?"

"No, it's okay. I get the idea. I used to play Space Invaders, which sounds similar when I was at university. It was a great game."

"I thought you were supposed to be studying French at university. That explains a lot. No wonder you only got a 2:2 honours degree. You were too busy blowing up green and red aliens all the time."

"So, when are you going to Cyprus?"

"Tomorrow morning. Grego has treated me, and we are going to hang out—see, I know all the trendy words—in the Business Class lounge at the airport. I'm going to be a member of the fashion industry now, so only the best will do," she chortled. "I suppose I'd better get packed. The boys are getting ready, so I must, too. Talk to you soon." She waved merrily at Amanda and the screen went back to the home page.

Just when did her mother become so youthful?

Amanda sat outside for a while. It was incredibly tranquil. There was a faint humming of bees as they gathered round the lavender bushes, which still had flowers even at this time of year. Their scent perfumed the air as the bees brushed past the tiny lilac-coloured blooms on the dark, woody stems. It was almost perfect. It would have been more perfect if Phil had been there and had been enjoying himself, sharing this wonderful day. She reflected again on their relationship. It was probably a good idea for Phil to have a little time away from her. They needed a gap year all right—one from each other. Ever since he had taken early retirement, they had been together every hour of the day, and it was definitely taking its toll on them.

If only she could come up with a solution, but try as she might, she had not so far been able to help Phil. He needed to help himself. All she could do was wait for him to find whatever it was that he was searching for. Besides, she had enough of her own problems. Last night she had woken up in a dreadful sweat that was not related to the weather. She had had trouble catching her breath and thought she was having a heart attack. Further investigation on the internet this morning had pointed to the fact that she was probably having a panic attack—one that was, without doubt, related to her turbulent hormones. This ageing process was no fun at all. What did she have left to look forward to? Phil probably felt the same. Still, being miserable about it wouldn't help. She needed to focus her mind on more positive thoughts. She should get on and do some writing. One could always find something funny to write about.

Her thoughts reluctantly returned to Phil, and she wondered what would happen when he had dealt with the squatter problem. Would he come back to France and would they continue their trip? Deep in her heart she felt emptiness. She knew that they wouldn't. They would just drift back to the life they had pre-gap year, and that held no charm whatsoever. Maybe he could take up some form of charity work, which would give him a feeling of worth. She would have to look into that possibility. She couldn't face another year of his moping about the house. Besides, she now had her own project. She was busy writing and couldn't spend all her time trying to find activities to amuse Phil.

The peace was interrupted by tyre squealing, which announced the arrival of her new friend, Bibi. Ted looked up from his basket but made no effort to move, that was until Bibi wafted into the courtyard in a cloud of Chanel No. 5. Then he propelled himself towards her with the velocity of a speeding bullet, leaping up and woofing joyfully.

"Bonjour, Ted," she murmured, fondling his ears gently. He fell onto his back and in a swoon, waited for her to rub his stomach.

"You tart, Ted." muttered Amanda fondly. "Bibi, he adores you. He hardly knows you, and he has fallen for your seductive French charm."

Bibi smiled. "I wish I had that effect on all men. I thought you would like a trip out, away from this dead hamlet—somewhere more exciting. I shall take you to Toulouse. Maybe we could do some shopping?" suggested

Bibi, looking pointedly at Amanda's giant, baggy tee-shirt, which completely hid her body.

The idea appealed. She had too much on her mind, what with the situation at home and her mad mother, to get any writing done. What woman wouldn't enjoy some retail therapy? Besides, she suddenly had the urge to act a little younger, too.

BLOG: Fortifying Your Fifties

Day… I think it might be a Thursday

I used to adore speed—and I don't mean the sort you take as a drug. When I was younger, I drove everywhere at top speed. I hugged corners and used the road. I enjoyed the thrill of driving. The roads in the UK were quite good in those days for an exciting drive. That was before the advent of speed cameras and potholes. However, even then, no road was quite as exhilarating as the roads in France.

You can really zoom down those well-maintained lanes in rural France, and I do. Admittedly, Mark's 2CV is elderly and doesn't have a great deal of speed, but for an old lady, it can race along enough for me. You never meet anyone coming in the opposite direction, and you can pretend you are at Le Mans.

One person who delights in driving at breakneck speed, even more than me, is Bibi. Bibi's husband is the proud owner of an MG. It is his pride and joy. He keeps it for special occasions. Bibi also adores the MG, finding it very "cool" and constantly pesters her husband to let her borrow it. He always refuses on the grounds that he knows what her driving is like, and he isn't sure his precious motor will be able to cope with her stamping on the brakes and walloping it up the gears in her aggressive fashion.

Yesterday, we decided to go to town for a shopping spree and a little lunch. Bibi was in the MG. I have a sneaky feeling that Didier had no idea she had borrowed it.

A squeal of tyres and a screech of brakes alerted me to her arrival. She tooted the horn, and I exited to find Bibi dressed up very fashionably in a headscarf and wearing oversized sunglasses, looking like Princess Grace of Monaco. She certainly suited the car.

"Viens, 'urry up. I want to see 'ow 'zis leetle car performs on zee motorway," she shouted. No sooner had I got in, than we were off, tyres spinning on the gravel. There was no doubt about it—Bibi should have been a racing driver.

We sped off down the motorway towards Toulouse, charging past every car on the road, with Bibi giving the car the workout of its life. We stopped at the motorway station, not to freshen up, but to ensure that our ticket which we had collected at the toll gate, did not let on how fast we were going when we checked off the motorway.

The day was delightful. We parked the car on the kerb beside a café where it attracted much attention, since it wasn't a Peugeot or a Renault. Bibi and I sat opposite it in the sunshine, where she also attracted equal admiration. We had a thoroughly agreeable time. Finally, we decided to return and headed home.

Bibi drove like a demon, overtaking everything in sight. Old farmers in clapped-out old vans sat open-mouthed as she zoomed by them. We felt young. We were having fun. Just as we left the motorway and entered our *departement*, Bibi finally managed to overtake a BMW, which she had had in her sights for a few kilometres.

"Haha! Vive zee MG!" she shouted triumphantly, only to follow it with "Merde!" A policeman from the Municipal Police stood with a radar gun pointed directly at the MG. "Merde, merde, merde!" she said again and checked her lipstick in the rear view mirror.

"Les poulets," she explained. Our slang word for them in the UK is pigs, but in France, policemen are referred to as chickens. No, I don't understand why, but they are. Further ahead was a lay-by in which was a police car. The radar holder had obviously alerted him to the MG's speed, and the policeman was waving for us to pull into the lay-by.

"Say nussing. You are French. Just smile and stick your boosoms out," hissed Bibi and hitched her skirt up a few notches to reveal her long legs. She pulled in and wound down her window, pouting in a seductive fashion at the policeman.

"Madame, do you know how fast you were going?" he asked (in French, obviously).

"Oh, officer, I am so sorry. We were in such a hurry. Our mother is very sick, and we were trying to get to zee 'ospital. Zis is not my car. I 'av just borrowed it, and it iz a leetle powerfool, no?" She smiled engagingly. The policeman wasn't won over.

"Maybe your maman would like you to arrive alive, Mesdames. You are no good to her if you have an accident, no?"

"Yes, we were a leetle foolish," continued Bibi, fluttering her lengthy eyelashes. "But we were worried, and zee roads, zey are not too busy." She looked dolefully at him. He coughed uncomfortably and put his hand out for her papers. Bibi wiggled about, her skirt riding higher up her legs as she pretended to look for the papers. The officer looked more uncomfortable but continued to wait for her paperwork.

With much pouting, eyelash fluttering, and lip trembling, she handed over her licence. In France they take off points, unlike in the UK where we add points to a licence when you commit an offence. If Bibi got a conviction for speeding, she would be out of points and therefore banned. Didier would be furious.

"Monsieur Gendarme," she asked politely. "I 'av been a leetle naughty in my past, but, well…you know?' She pouted again and gave that 'pfft' noise that the French do. "I must not get into trouble again. My 'usband will be so angry wiz me, and my leetle children will not be able to go to school if I cannot drive zem."

The policeman must have had a heart of stone. He was definitely going to give her a fine. He got out his pad and asked her to join him in the waiting vehicle to be issued with the ticket. She rolled her eyes at me and reached for her insurance documents.

"I suppose, Monsieur, you will need to see zis."

The officer cast a casual look at her insurance papers and then looked again. His eyes opened wide in amusement. He folded all the paperwork back up and handed it back to her with a smile playing on his lips.

"Maybe Madame, you would like to have a warning this time. I hope your maman gets better soon." He saluted and waved us off.

"What on earth was that all about?" I asked as we chugged away carefully with Bibi waving at the policeman, who saluted again.

"Insurance. It always pays to 'av insurance," replied Bibi.

"I still don't get it."

"Take a look at my insurance documents."

I opened up the papers to discover a photograph. It was a picture of the local mayor dressed in a frilly pinafore, holding a feather duster and wearing nothing but a smile.

"No! How did you get this?"

"Ah, I got it from 'is wife. She gave it to me one day when she was at the house. Mathilde gave her too much wine and she became verreey friendly. She said if ever I really needed to use it, it would 'elp. It makes zee poulets 'appy to see zee boss, 'ow you say—off duty? See you must always 'av zee insurance. Now let's see 'ow fast we can get 'ome."

Posted by Facing50.Blog

10 Comments:

Gypsynesters2 says…The French police sound more fun than those in Turkey. We got pulled over on one of our trips there and had to bribe them. Luckily, we had a large packet of chewing gum and plenty of Turkish Lira, or we might have ended up in jail.

Facing50 says…Wow! Good thing you had some gum.

Hippyhappyhoppy says…Sooooo funny. Hugs x

Facing50 says…Thanks x

SexyFitChick says…This new friend of yours sounds like the sort of person I should meet. She will do you good my friend. Stay youthful and get those roller blades on for some fitness.

Facing50 says…Thank you, SFC. She seems to be a lot of fun. She is certainly more fun than Phil. The roller blades are too old. I shall stick to walking Old Ted.

TheMerryDivorcee says…I would love an MG. So far I have collected four Mercedes convertibles, a Chevrolet, three Fords, a Mustang, a Dodge Viper, and a pickup truck as part of my settlements. I guess I should try for an Englishman next time and get an MG.

Facing50 says…If you married Phil, you'd get a broken camper van so don't count on it!

MiaFerrari says…Can't beat a Ferrari—sorry, girls!

Facing50 says…MiaFerrari ,we give in. You are right, but the MG is still good fun.

Chapter Twenty-One

"It wasn't nearly as bad as we expected," explained Phil when he could finally get a word in. Amanda had fired so many questions at him when he phoned that he felt like putting the phone down. She could be so irritating at times, and besides, it was costing him a fortune to phone her mobile. "I went to the Citizen's Advice Bureau first thing this morning. What a nightmare that was. It was stuffed full of people, so I had to wait for ages before anyone could even deal with me. It's a pretty complicated procedure, but if you are the occupier, you need a statement or certificate as required by section 12A of the Criminal Law Act 1977 that shows you are the rightful occupier."

"Phil, I really don't understand all that gobbledygook stuff. Could you just make it simple for me?"

Phil sighed. "The bureau told me I needed various certificates and would have to apply for an interim possession order to get the property back. It takes a few days. Anyway," he added as Amanda began to interject again. "I decided I couldn't wait for all of that so I went to the local police station and told them about the squatters. I explained that they must have broken down the front door to get into the house because when I drove past, it looked all smashed in, which is a criminal act in itself so they were very helpful. They sent a car round to the house almost immediately. I think they were going to arrest the group, but the second the squatters saw the police car arrive, they jumped out of the windows at the back of the house and legged it over the fields."

"Did they make any mess or cause any damage in the house?"

"Not too bad at all. It looks like it always does when Tom is at home: untidy, pongs a bit, clothes thrown in a pile on the floor, toothpaste on the bathroom mirror, crumbs on the kitchen top, but that is all."

"Is Tom back in the house then?"

"Yes, he was pretty shaken up about it all, but he's okay now. He and I have talked at length about it. He even seems very glad to have me back. He's changed quite a bit in a short time. Dare I say it? He's more grown up and more willing to listen to advice. We are going out for a beer in a while at the local pub. He wants to talk to me about his job. He's not told us much about it before, has he?"

Goodness, Phil and Tom bonding in the pub—that would be a first. They rarely managed more than a few grunts at each other. Amanda hoped that Tom didn't get drunk and confess to the broken door. If Phil discovered he was partly to blame for the episode, there would be hell to pay.

"So, when will you be returning to France? Bertie is ready, and we can carry on with the trip whenever you want. I think Mark is happy to come home. Jeanette's sister is making a good recovery, and Jeanette is not so anxious now. She'll not need Mark to stay with her.''

She detected a hesitation in his voice.

"Yes. Um, soon. I bumped into Richard when I was in town. You know Richard; he's one of the members of the management team that bought out my company. He asked if he could see me tomorrow, something to do with the business. I thought I'd drop by and see what he wants. It'll seem strange to be there but not be in charge any more. I wonder if it is very different. I might hang about for a few days."

"Phil, do you want me to come back there and join you?"

"No. Stay there. Get some writing done. Enjoy the sunshine. It's quite mild here for September. I might cut the grass tomorrow, too, now that I am here. There's no point in letting the place go wild. I'd better go. The phone bill will be astronomical. Hope Ted is well. Night-night!"

Amanda couldn't breathe again. Her chest tightened as she felt the familiar fear. The distance that was growing between them was more than the mere miles that separated them. She needed to think.

"Ted, do you want to go for a w—?" Ted was by the back door standing on her shoes before she finished the sentence.

The sky was studded with twinkling stars. There were hundreds, no thousands; maybe hundreds of thousands of them. It was a breathtaking sight. A particularly bright star suddenly dropped and flashed across the sky as she stared upwards, filling her with wonder. The world was such a beautiful place. What a pity that you couldn't always enjoy and appreciate it. Gradually, it all seemed to matter less. Standing beneath the firmament, Amanda felt that her home and indeed, her life in the UK was becoming a distant memory. She would love to stay here, away from it all forever. There were no pressures, no worries about husbands or children.

Ted beat her home again and was waiting outside the door for her. She patted him and filled his bowl with fresh water. He wagged his tail in appreciation. It was a shame, too, that people weren't more like dogs. Every day is exciting to a dog, every meal enjoyable, and every time they see you they are ecstatic.

She logged onto the internet to check emails and messages. A red mark over the envelope symbol alerted her to a new message on Facebook. She clicked on it. It was from Todd. He was all right. He was still recovering from the ghastly accident, but there he was, as cheerful and enthusiastic as ever. Her heart lifted, and pouring a large glass of Château Plonk, she logged onto Scrabble where Todd's icon flashed mischievously, and he had played the word *panting*. In the message area he had written: *I am panting in anticipation of a sexy game of Scrabble with you. Thanks for being there.*

She looked at her letters. The old feelings of flirtatious amusement were rekindled, and she put down the word *pecker*.

Had to keep your pecker up somehow, she wrote and grinned at Ted, who appeared to wink back at her.

Chapter Twenty-Two

The lady in red—how very mysterious, he thought. Thank goodness she didn't ask about his bloody, nonexistent dog. She had just earned herself another brownie point for that.

No, sadly, I was not the distinguished gentleman because I am sure I would have noticed you and would most certainly have spoken to you. The Beloved, however, was excellent. I see you have a fondness for art. Are you an artist? France is such an inspirational place to paint. I am currently trying to capture Matisse's fondness for colour in some stained glass windows that I am painting. Do you have a particular favourite artist?

Richard Montagu-Forbes sent his message and clicked off the Wikipedia page he had been using to acquaint himself with Matisse. He knew nothing about art. Still, in this day and age of the internet, you could convince anyone of anything, given the opportunity.

Bibi received her message almost immediately. She had been checking to see if Richard had been in touch when it came up. She had just been reading his status. Ben, his puppy, was up to mischief yet again. It would be so nice to have a dog. Even dear old Ted was a sweet, faithful companion. Didier wouldn't allow her to have an animal because he had an allergy to their fur. Didier! The wretched man had told her he would be home for dinner this evening so she was ensuring she looked fabulous. There was no way he was going to get away with his affairs. *How dare he carry on like this?* She would play him at his own game, and because she was much more intelligent than him, she would win.

169

She had spent considerable time on her appearance in preparation for tonight. Her eyes were outlined in smoky charcoal, making them look sultry. She was wearing a sleeveless, figure-hugging dress that accentuated her curves, and she had teamed it up with high-heeled, fashionable shoes. It wasn't for Didier, though. No, Bibi was deliberately dressed to kill, and she had every intention of disappearing the moment her husband returned. She would tell him that she was meeting Amanda but would do so in such a way that it would suggest that she was certainly not meeting Amanda, that she was making up a cover story. She, too, could play at duplicity and be far more convincing than Didier. Didier, being naturally suspicious, would immediately draw the wrong conclusions and believe she was meeting a man. She would encourage his suspicions by leaving a note next to the computer on which would be written *Richard – Cannes?*

Richard was definitely an interesting man. He liked Matisse—Matisse who spent his later years near Nice, an area favoured by many artists for its light. Bibi adored Matisse, particularly his later paintings, and also loved Stravinksy and Picasso. She had visited Picasso's house in Paris several times when she had lived there. She had seen Matisse's *French Window at Collioure* at the Centre Georges Pompidou when she had lived in Paris, but much of Matisse's work was in the Hermitage Museum in St Petersburg. Now, that would be a wonderful place to visit.

Before she got caught up too much in a daydream about visiting Russia and meandering around art galleries with a dashing Englishman, she typed back a quick message to Richard: *How wonderful to hear from you. Hopefully, I shall see you at the next film festival at Cannes. I dabble with watercolours, but I am not a professional artist. There are so many superb paintings that it is difficult to chose one sole artist, but those who use bold colour always appeal to me. They seem to be more daring. I hope you will share your stained-glass windows with us. Forgive me, but I must go now as I have an important meeting with my stockbroker in Toulouse.*

She pressed the Send button and turned the computer off. Her eyes glowed darkly as she checked the mirror again. Her hair was thick and glossy. Her lips were a deep, crimson red. She was ready. On cue, the pimpmobile screeched to a halt on the gravel, and she heard Mathilde calling out peevishly.

She picked up her soft leather jacket, laid it gently across her arm and gracefully walked to the door just as it was opening. Didier took in her appearance. She gazed at him, eyes widening, feigning surprise.

"Chérie, you look wonderful," he began and then noticed her jacket. "But, you are not staying?"

"No," she hesitated, letting her lips open slightly to reveal their fullness and pouted gently. "I have a rendezvous." She deliberately refused eye contact with him to ensure he suspected her of lying. She hesitated further as if attempting to think of an excuse. "I must meet…the English lady who is on her own. She is…" She looked away again. "She is lonely. I am going to take her out to cheer her up."

"Aren't you a little overdressed for the local village?"

She shrugged and pouted again. "One must make an effort," she offered with a shrug, kissed him lightly on the cheek, and brushed past him, ensuring her breasts rubbed into his chest as she moved by. "Don't wait up. I might be late. By the way, your Maman is calling."

Didier watched as she swung her legs gracefully into the car and shot off into the night without glancing back.

"Bibi, are you there? I need another glass of blackcurrant. I have a sore throat, and I am coming down with a cold," yelled his mother.

Amanda was sitting outside on the terrace, once again lost in thoughts. She was convinced that Phil would remain in the UK, and she had to decide what she wanted to do. Since the parts for the camper van had arrived earlier, Monsieur Renard had assured them that Bertie, the camper van, would be repaired in the next day or two without fail. Mark had assured her that he would come back home as soon as she told him she was leaving, but she wasn't sure she wanted to go back to her old life. There had to be something else. If only fate could throw her a lifeline.

She could hear Bibi arriving long before she saw her. She drove up to the front of the house and emerged smiling from the MG. How did that woman manage it? She was dressed for a gathering for social elites in Paris, not to eat a light supper with a scruffy friend in a stone cottage in an almost deserted hamlet and watch a DVD of *Sex and the City*.

Chapter Twenty-Three

"I prefer the culottes with the hippy beads," argued Grego wafting his hands about in true Italian fashion.

"I think you should add a shawl over one shoulder for extra effect," drawled Amanda's mother, cigarette dangling from the side of her mouth. The silver grey smoke curled around her head. "I'd better turn in for the night. I'm feeling a tad tired. It must be all the excitement of the travelling and then the party at Doreen's place."

"I don't know how you all do it," commented Amanda as she stared at the screen in front of her, watching the trio pouring over the sketches.

They had spent the last half an hour showing Amanda what they intended showing to the fashion house. Amanda couldn't believe how animated her mother became when discussing fashion. She recalled that she had always loved to sew, and as a youngster, she had many memories of her mother at her old Singer machine, humming while she made an outfit for herself or for Amanda. Her mother had even made some rather dapper clothes for her father, come to think of it. She remembered a very smart waistcoat on one occasion that her mother had made as a present. It was funny how she had forgotten about all of that. Somehow, once she became a teenager, she hadn't been interested in her mother's fashion tips, preferring to emulate her contemporaries rather than listen to her mother's advice. At one stage she had completely rebelled and had taken to marching around in a pair of scruffy jeans and an army jacket, thinking she looked very chic. She cringed at the memory. Her mother still had style. She was wearing a soft purple silk blouse and skirt complete with a bolero jacket this evening. In fact, she looked very elegant. Someone had

173

painted her nails again to match the outfit—must have been Spencer. He loved fussing around her.

She looked at her own nails, which needed a good file. She was letting herself go. She didn't need to worry here. No one was interested in her except for Bibi, who kept nagging her to get a haircut and tidy herself up. There was no way she could match up to that stylish creature. You either had it, or you didn't have it, and Amanda didn't!

Bibi had dropped by again yesterday. This time husband Didier had dropped her off while he ran an errand. Amanda had been typing when the MG pulled up and was surprised to see a handsome man about Phil's age driving the car. He had deep chestnut eyes, thick, dark hair, and an authoritative air about him. He politely introduced himself as Bibi's husband and asked if they had had a nice meal at the restaurant the night before.

"No, we didn't go to the restaurant—" began Amanda and then out of the corner of her eye caught Bibi shaking her head at her. She stopped abruptly and changed the subject clumsily. "Would you like an aperitif?" Didier declined the offer, saying he had to get to the store. He wished them a *bon après-midi*, grabbed Bibi, and gave her a passionate kiss that made Amanda's eyes open in surprise. Bibi had it all: looks, a gorgeous hunky French husband, and obviously a fantastic sex life. What a lucky woman! Bibi, however, hadn't looked too pleased about it.

Amanda had quizzed her about it later, and Bibi had given her some excellent advice on how to keep your man. She had used it in her latest post which she was just about to put up when Facebook beckoned.

You can't play titty, she wrote. *It isn't a proper word.*

You played booby.

Yes, but it is actually the name of a bird as well as being suggestive, countered Amanda

Blast! I was proud of that titty too. I'm sure there's a titty bird here in Australia.

Idiot. Have you taken your medicine today? Amanda couldn't help smiling.

Yes, but you are better than any medicine. You have lifted my spirits. I would have been very lonely without these games to keep me going. Digit is useless at Scrabble.

Before typing a response, Amanda took a deep breath, trying to center herself. *Can't have you lonely, can we? Shouldn't you be in bed? It must be late there.*

It's about one in the morning. I'm not very tired. Well, only a little. I'll go to bed after the next word.

The word *yearn* appeared.

It's not sexy, but I yearn for your company here. I would love to hold you and have you next to me. It's not likely, but I can still yearn for it. Thank you again for cheering me up. I think the shoulder is feeling better today. I shall go and get some rest. Hopefully, we can continue the game tomorrow. Night, Mandy. Sweet dreams.

You, too.

Amanda stared at the screen for a long time, half hoping he would return. He was so vulnerable at the moment. The accident had changed him. He was more gentle and appreciative. What a pity he hadn't been like this last year. She might just have left with him and gone to Australia. Still, she had chosen Phil, and Phil was the right man for her, wasn't he? Looking at the screen, she wondered if her "you, too" had just been a goodnight, or had she been trying to let him know that she yearned for his touch as well?

Yesterday, Bibi had marched upstairs the second Didier had dropped her off. Her little plan was beginning to

175

work, it would seem. Amanda had unwittingly assisted in duping the fool by starting to tell him that she and Bibi had not gone to the restaurant and then stopping when she caught Bibi's look. Bibi hadn't wanted her to divulge the fact that they had really spent the night watching DVDs until the early hours.

When she had returned home at three in the morning, Didier had pretended to be asleep, but she could sense he was awake, wondering what she had been up to. Luckily, Amanda had not said too much. In fact, by changing the subject as she had, Didier's flames of passion had been fanned. Of course, she would keep him in check. He would soon lose interest in her if he thought she could be persuaded by one kiss.

She ran the shower. Mathilde had collared Didier the moment he had walked in, and he was unable to get away from her. By the time he had escaped his mother and leapt up the stairs to pounce on Bibi, she had dressed for dinner and was carefully applying her makeup in front of the mirror. She had smiled benevolently at him.

"I had better go and prepare the evening meal, and then I have to play cards with your mother tonight."

Didier had nodded and gone to his office where he had spent the evening drinking wine and sending emails to his mistress.

BLOG: Fortifying Your Fifties

Day…I can't remember. They've all merged into one long day.

Due to popular demand, I am going to write today about the secrets that French women have kept to themselves for centuries. Now that I am almost a French woman, living as I am in La Belle France, my dear friend Bibi has been kind enough to impart her knowledge to me. Today I have a corker to share with you—how to make your man desire you.

Bibi was sitting in my garden eating strawberries. Her husband, Didier, had dropped her off and kissed her goodbye passionately. Such ardour made me inquisitive.

"How do you do it?" I asked, shoving an extra large strawberry into my mouth.

"Do what?"

"Arouse such passion in your man that he kisses you hungrily, even though he is only going to the DIY store to buy some picture hooks and will be back in an hour?"

"Does not your 'usband do zis?"

"No, he doesn't. Maybe it's because he's English."

"Did you learn nussing when you were younger about zis?"

"Now, let me see…algebra, history, physics, how to seduce men, math, German…no, I must have been off school that day and missed that particular lesson."

"Oh, you are tres amusante, ma chérie. Maybe you can seduce your 'usband by your 'umour."

"No, but I certainly make him laugh in bed," I concluded, thinking how unsexy I was.

"You need to learn zee art of seduction."

"Oh, I have my seduction kit already," I replied.

Bibi insisted on seeing it. We went to the bedroom and from the back of my bedside drawer, I pulled out my sexy underwear—for emergency use only.

"What in nom de Dieu iz zis?" she asked, holding my lacy, black thong balanced on the very tip of a perfectly manicured nail. She held it up for inspection, eyebrows raised in either horror or surprise.

"My sex kitten outfit."

"More like a sex 'ippopotamoose," she replied, not unkindly. "Zis is not sexy. Zis string will make you 'av a gigantic derriere. Zis 'orrible string is not sexy for anyone. You must get zee silk culottes. Zey hug zee derriere and are very nice to touch. Zey 'int at what is zere, not let it all fall out. Zis is non, non, non. You must get some Lejaby. You must buy some proper, sexy underwear. Zen you must make 'im want you."

Bibi then proceeded to impart further French secrets. Please get your pens ready. This is hot stuff...

"You must make your man want you."

I had a good guffaw at that one. "And how do I do that— crumble Viagra pills into his night-time cocoa?"

"Ha ha, you always make me smile, my leetle 'ippopotamoose," she replied, getting into guru mode. "Non, silly. I try different ways. Sometimes I wait until Didier 'as had a very busy day at work. I wait until 'e is very, very tired. I put on my silk brassiere and silk blouse and let zee top buttons undo. Zen 'e gets a leetle look at me, but e 'as no energy and has to go to bed because tomorrow 'e must be up early for a meeting. 'E zinks zat in zee morning I'll be, 'ow you say it, up for it? In zee morning, however, merde, I am in zee kitchen very early before 'e awakes. I am in a leetle, silky robe and 'av made 'im breakfast. Ha ha, 'e is not able to 'av 'is way. Now 'e is dressed for work and 'as put on 'is tie, suit and 'as 'is briefcase. I pout a leetle, I look at 'im longingly and drop my robe. I am wearing my sexy underwear. I tell 'im I am going for a shower and squeeze past 'im to zee bathroom. 'E can do nussing as 'e must go to work. 'E becomes mad for me."

She paused for a dramatic eyebrow raise and shrug of the Gaelic shoulders.

"In zee evening 'e comes 'ome ready to grab me. 'E is panting for me. 'E rushes into zee kitchen to grab me in passion. He finds me looking sexy and 'ot in a very short, tight skirt and stockings, bent over zee kitchen sink, but merde, I am talking to his maman who is waiting for 'er dinner and 'as, for some strange reason, 'ad too much to drink and so will stay up late talking." Bibi paused for another suggestive raise of her eyebrow.

"Finally, at night, 'e leaps into bed. I kiss 'im very gently on the cheek and say, 'so sorry, chou, chou, but I 'av a dreadful headache. Your maman was very tiring today. Tomorrow, I promise...and we shall make a night of it. Zen I turn over and go to sleep. Men always want what zey cannot 'av. Of course, sometimes we must give zem it and be zee naughty schoolgirls."

"I take it that Didier's mother was a little drunk last night and kept Didier up until very late then?"

"Absolutement, Chérie, and tonight I shall fan zee flames of amour."

At that precise moment Didier returned with a flamboyant squeal of his brakes to collect Bibi. He held her arm and led her to the car like a gentleman, giving her a kiss on the cheek. Bibi gave an imperceptible wink in my direction. I waved them off and went back inside where I chucked my thong in the bin. From now on it would be Lejaby silk for me.

Posted by Facing50.Blog

7 Comments:

SexyFitChick says… And we all know who would love to see you in Lejaby silk—or you could just spell Lejaby on the Scrabble Board and fan his flames of desire.

Facing50 says…I would score quite well if I played that word, especially on a triple.

Hippyhoppyhappy says…I loved the 'ippopotamoose comment—so funny. Hugs x

Facing50 says…Yes, she's quite the wit, especially since she is French, and I thought they had no sense of humour.

PhillyFilly says… I always thought thongs looked great, especially since I had my buns done. I like them on men, too.

Facing50 says… Just had an awful thought—Phil in a thong—yeurgh!

FairieQueene says…PhillyFilly, that is the grossest image. I now can't eat my salad. The thought of a man wearing a thong. Ouch! …Love your new friend's advice. I hope you heed it. Your Mum is having a ball, by the way. I won't mention I was here.

Chapter Twenty-Four

"The new signage on the warehouse is incredible. It makes the place look fresh and vibrant," explained Phil, which was exactly how he sounded, thought Amanda, fresh and vibrant.

"You could have knocked me down with a feather when they asked me to become a consultant for the business," he repeated for the fourth time.

Phil had phoned over half an hour ago with his exciting news. Judging by the amount of time he had spent on the phone, he was no longer worried about the cost of calls to France. Amanda had known before he even opened his mouth what he was going to say. You could just tell by the tone of his voice.

"Hello! How's France? How's the writing? How's Ted? You won't believe what happened. I've got a job—well, a sort of job. I'm going to be a consultant for my old company. They thought no one could assist them better than me; after all, I set up and started the business. Although there have been quite a few changes since I left, they want me to help with their expansion programme. We had a jolly long talk about it all, and I think it's a golden opportunity for me. I won't have to work nine 'til five. I'll have my own office, and I'll deal mostly with the management team who bought me out. I can't believe it. They'll pay me a whacking great salary, and I only have to give them my expertise. It's incredible! Did I tell you about the new signage?"

Phil had been transformed overnight into an animated human being. He was no longer the miserable curmudgeon she had been living with the last year. Part of her was immensely relieved. Another part was wary. He might be skipping about like a spring lamb at the moment, but this was only putting off the inevitable. At some point, when they no longer required his input, he would once again be facing unemployment and would have to face up to the challenges of retirement and old age. Retirement had not suited him, and had this opportunity not come along, heavens only knows what he would be like or, indeed, what they would have done.

"Where will you live? Will you move back home with Tom?"

"Ah, no. I had a long chat with him about that. He really needs to learn to be independent. When we set off for our trip, we told him he could have the house for a year, and he shouldn't have his plans spoiled just because our plans have changed. I am going to stay in the company flat in town for a while. I'll be doing some travelling, so it will suit me to be based there. There's another guy in it, too, at the moment—Gareth. He's just going through a messy divorce, so we'll be flat-sharing until he gets a new place of his own. He's looking to be promoted to one of the new sites so he might even accompany me on some of the trips. We're going to expand into the South East. I've already earmarked a few areas that I think we should consider."

"Phil, what about me? Don't you want me to return and be with you?"

"I didn't think for one minute that you would want to come back here just yet. You'd be bored rigid with me out all of the time or working on projects. You seem to love it in France. I'm sure Mark and Jeanette will let you stay in the cottage when they get back, or you could camp out in the camper van. You have got it back, haven't you?"

"Yes, it's parked in one of the barns behind the big farm house."

"Go on; have an adventure. You are always telling me life is for living. Here's an opportunity for you to live it. Use your time to write your blog or book or whatever. Besides, I doubt you would want to stay in the flat with Gareth and me. You'll be better off in France. Come back in a few months. See how you go. You could stay for six months if you like. You can come back whenever you want. I can come over to France in December for a couple of weeks and again at Easter. Let's just take it as it comes. It'll do us both good to do what we fancy for a while. You've spent over a year trying to keep me entertained. It's time for you to do all those things you wrote down—the bucket list wishes."

The thought was very appealing. She could actually have some time to herself after all the trauma of the last year or so. Phil would be completely ensconced in work. She knew him well enough to know that work was what he needed. It would save him from this awful depression that was beginning to take over his life and consequently, would allow her to have some fun.

She had Bibi, Ted, and enough bottles of Château Plonk to see her through her time in France, and if she got fed up, she could always take Bertie for a drive somewhere. She could travel to Italy or camp out by the sea. Her mother would tell her to embrace life—carpe diem and all that. This was probably just what they both needed.

"You have yourself a deal as long as you promise to come back in December. Ted misses you."

"Deal. I'm really looking forward to getting back behind the reins, so to speak. I'm taking Tom and Alice out for a celebratory meal tonight. We can afford it now that I'll be getting a salary again. Use your credit card and go out, too, with that new friend of yours. I'll pay the bill. Give Ted a slobbery kiss from me. Bye, Amanda. Good luck with the writing. Take care."

So, that had been the answer all the time: keep Phil in employment. He sounded like a new man, a younger man. Maybe men shouldn't ever retire. It was probably better for them to stay in work and feel useful. It certainly seemed to be the case for Phil. She sent a text message to Mark to let him know she would be at the cottage for however long they needed a Ted-sitter and then poured a large glass of wine.

"To Phil and his new job and to me and my adventurous, fun-filled gap year." She tipped the glass and let the wine flow easily down her throat as she wondered what lay ahead for her.

Chapter Twenty-Five

The message read: *There are a few garages in France for your wonderful MG, but one of the best is situated near me at Impasse Florian Cannes 06400 France. I can recommend the garagiste, who works on all sorts of vintage cars and can get any part you need for yours. Should you need an appointment, I would be delighted to make one for you and of course, should you decide to come down, I would love to take you out for lunch.*

What a super result. It hadn't taken many messages before Richard had invited her to lunch. He had seen her post on the Cars page and had offered to assist. They had been communicating for a couple of weeks. She had told him about her life—her fictitious life, at least.

They had had several conversations about travelling, art, music, and literature. They had such a lot in common. Richard enjoyed all the same things she did. He really was a find. It was a shame she wasn't looking for a substitute for Didier because this man seemed to be nothing short of perfect.

She had been enjoying the pretence and had become a little carried away with her own character. Her last message suggested that she was planning to take time out to travel through Europe, in her MG, of course. She had created a marvellous legend as the spies call them. She had, by alluding to certain funds and shares, given the impression that she, Amanda Willson, was a wealthy woman with a substantial share portfolio. Still, it didn't matter because although Richard was clearly interested in this exciting woman, who needed no man to support her and who was open to new adventures, he was never going to meet her. Even if he did decide to seek her out, he would not find

Amanda Willson, because the real Amanda with one *l* would be back in the UK or in her camper van with Phil.

Mathilde was playing belotte, an extremely popular national card game, with her friends. The four of them always played on a Wednesday afternoon. Bibi had left them to it. Mathilde and her partner Giselle usually won. They were as sharp as scissors and missed nothing. She drove the old family Peugeot down to St Antonin where she was meeting Amanda. It was more inconspicuous than the MG.

Amanda was already sitting in the shade on Place des Tilleuls when she pulled up. She couldn't wait for Bibi to climb out of the car. Even with her good command of English, Bibi struggled to comprehend what her friend was telling her. After manoeuvring her to a table at the cafe and ordering two Perrier waters, she ascertained that Amanda was going to stay in France for a few months longer and that her husband was going to remain in the UK.

"Mon Dieu, are you divorcing?"

"No, not at all. This will probably save our marriage," chuckled Amanda. "He is completely occupied with work, and I am free to enjoy some time in this beautiful country. I'm going to practise my French, write a book, and learn to paint like you. Will you give me some lessons?"

Bibi was amused by Amanda's vivacity. This grown woman acted like a child some days, but her enthusiasm was infectious. She agreed to give Amanda some art lessons. She set a challenge for Amanda to paint a rural French country scene for Phil. First they would sort out some materials for her, and then Bibi would start her off on some small sketches.

The cool air descended quickly in the valley this time of year, and although sunlight still played on the treetops, it began to get colder. It was time to return home. Bibi had no desire to go back to the large farmhouse. If

186

Didier could be bothered to go home this evening, she would rather he found her absent. Her attempts to rouse him were failing. He had not noticed the provocative underwear that she had deliberately left on the bedroom floor. He had not blinked one eyelid when he walked into the bedroom to find her receiving a phone call from a secret admirer. She had acted the part so well, too. Listening for Didier's footsteps on the stairs, she had waited for him to come into the bedroom. She was seated on the bed, back to the door, laughing suggestively into the phone.

"You naughty man," she whispered huskily to the dialling tone. She then stiffened, turned to face Didier, and looking horrified, had abruptly ended the call.

Her acting talents were completely wasted.

"Have you seen my blue socks, Bibi? These have holes in them," he asked, scrabbling about in his drawer, oblivious to the fact she was even on the telephone.

"These blue socks?" she asked, leaning in front of him and withdrawing the items.

"Thank you," he replied, bending down to change into them. "I might be back late again tonight. I have a pile of correspondence to get through, which can't wait until tomorrow. I'll get something to eat in town so don't worry about leaving any soup for me." He threw the holey socks into the bin, grabbed his jacket, and left her fuming.

Richard Montagu-Forbes was indeed extremely interested in Amanda Willson. She was exactly what he had hoped for when he started this quest. She was intelligent, adventurous, free, and most important of all, wealthy. Richard was confident that he could win this woman over easily. He knew her sort; after all, he had been with women like her before. They had all been enchanted by his charm and impeccable manners. They had all been vulnerable, gullible, and so very easy to dupe.

That was why he was now living on the French Riviera. His last victim had been a wealthy American. Recently widowed, she had been worth a mint. She was unsure of life as a single woman and had been very grateful to the attentive new neighbour, who had, at first, popped round to assist her with household inconveniences. He had recently moved into the area and was renting the house next door until he could find an appropriate property to purchase.

He took her rubbish, or as she called it "trash" out for her; he helped mend the garage door that had mysteriously broken (thanks to the removal of a few screws while she was in bed). He popped around to have coffee with her and provided endless sympathy and a shoulder to cry on when she complained about the cleaner damaging an expensive vase or the gardener not planting the right colour roses. He fixed her car when it refused to start one morning. She was running late for her salon appointment and was getting most exasperated about it. Richard had appeared at exactly the right moment, asked her if she had a problem, and lifted the bonnet to resolve it. It took only a few minutes to put back the lead he had succeeded in removing an hour before while she was getting ready to go out.

He watched ghastly, soppy chick flicks with her and even shed a tear at some of them, dabbing his eyes with tissues from a box they shared between them on the sofa. Elsie had no idea how much he despised her. She disgusted him, but that did not thwart him. He listened to her whining, comforted her, ate meals with her, and generally made himself indispensable.

Finally, when the time was right, he proclaimed his love for her. She was bowled over and ecstatic to have found such a compassionate man so soon after her dear Lionel had passed away. Richard wasn't Richard then. He was calling himself Brett Sinclair after one of the characters in a series called *The Persuaders*, starring Roger Moore and Tony Curtis. He played it cool, assuring Elsie that he did not want to rush her into anything, understanding that she would need time to grieve Lionel. He kept her dangling, providing just enough carrot to keep her interested in him. Then one day, he staggered over to her house, tears in his eyes, and between sobs explained how a business venture was going sour, and if he could not come up with some money in time, his company would have to go into liquidation. It was a disaster because not only would this venture work, given a few more weeks, but he also had another venture lined up, which was an absolute winner. Still, he couldn't finance it now that the squeeze was on him. He would be forced into returning to the UK if that happened as he could not afford to stay in the States.

Elsie, an intelligent woman, who really should have known better, was distraught at the thought of losing him. Without probing the issue, she insisted on giving him the necessary $750,000 he needed to save this venture and to use towards his next project, which would bail him out of difficulties.

Richard fell to his knees and kissed her palms gratefully. He thanked her profusely and hugged her, telling her she was the sweetest woman in the world. He would return every penny or, indeed, every dollar to her because he could only take it if it was considered a loan. He would not let her down. His next venture was going to be a huge success and bring in much more money than she had lent him. He told her that all of this had made him realise how much she meant to him and how, if she could bear to replace such a wonderful husband as Lionel, he would love to make her his wife.

Elsie went pink with excitement. Her heart had been well and truly captured by this Englishman. They made plans to go shopping for an engagement ring the following weekend. Richard explained that he would be out of town for the next few days, sorting out this deal. Elsie waved him off the next morning. He blew her a kiss and drove directly to the bank where he deposited the money. He then headed to the airport, boarded a flight to Paris, and that was the last Elsie ever saw of him or of her money. She waited all weekend for him. He didn't return. On the following Monday a sign went up at the house next door. It was to let again. Richard had disappeared without a trace, along with her money.

Richard Montagu-Forbes had been living the high life in Nice since then. He was currently renting an apartment which cost him a fortune each month. What with that, his proximity to Monaco with its irresistible casinos, and his flamboyant lifestyle, he needed another mark soon.

Amanda Willson would make an excellent victim. He could sense that she had warmed to him and that she was clearly missing the company of a sophisticated, amusing, male companion. He could fill that void. However, he didn't really want to entertain her in Nice on his patch; after all, he had a reputation to maintain here. One could not, as the saying went, make a mess on one's own front door mat. Besides, he liked living here. He was well known in the casinos here, and Riviera life suited him well. Of course, here he was not known as Richard Montagu-Forbes. That would be folly, so he would have to find out exactly where she lived without alarming her. He needed to display Richard's charm in person.

Chapter Twenty-Six

"It was probably the single most exciting experience I have ever had!" Phil declared before continuing on effusively, "It was idyllic up there. Gareth let me take the controls for a while, and I was completely hooked. As soon as we landed, I knew I wanted to sign up for a flying course. If I took lessons, I could go to the flying school with Gareth at weekends. It's even possible that I could get my pilot's licence before you return, and then I'd be able to take you up for a flight. I'm looking into it. You train on a Cessna 152. It's only a two-seater craft, but that should get me started.

"There are some beauties at the airfield…aircraft, I mean, beautiful aircraft, before you start to worry that I'm chasing women. I can't believe we have lived so close to that airfield for years, and I have never thought to have a go at flying before. If I get my licence, Gareth says we could go on a trip to Amsterdam or Jersey in his aeroplane. He's in a syndicate with two other chaps. They have shares in a slightly larger plane. This could be the start of something great."

Phil had never sounded so positive or animated. Amanda could have danced with joy. Not only was he exuberant about working again, but he had quite possibly discovered a hobby he could relish and had made some male friends in the bargain. It had only taken Gareth two weeks to transform the old grump into a fun-loving, youthful person again. She could kiss Gareth.

"So, how's France?"

"Lovely, as always. I've been writing every day, and I'm about half-way through my book. I don't know what to call it yet, but I'll wait for an idea to strike."

"How about calling it *Fifty Not Out*?"

"It's a novel about enjoying life no matter how old you are, not a cricket manual."

"Point taken. I suppose I'd better let you chose a title then. Well, I had better go now. I have to prepare a report for tomorrow's meeting, and I have no idea what the hell PowerPoint is. I'm going to write down a few points on paper, the good old-fashioned way, and they can lump it."

"Good luck then. Oh, and well done on the flying. I'm genuinely pleased you've found something to get your teeth into. You're not ready for the knackers yard just yet!"

"No, there's still some life left in the old dog. Talking of dogs, give Ted a hug for me."

"Will do. He's not at home at the moment. He'll be in soon. I have a large packet of ham, so he won't want to miss out on that. Night, Phil."

"Night, Amanda. Speak to you soon."

The call had cheered her. She sat down to tackle her novel with vengeance, only to hear the familiar ring announcing the fact that PlayGirl.77 was wanting to chat.

"Hello Pet," wheezed her mother, stubbing out a cigarette. "I thought I'd see how you were getting on without Old Misery Guts. How long do you think you might be staying in France?"

"Hi Mum. I'm not really sure. It depends on a few things. I'm going to take some time out and write a book—"

"Ooh, a book. Can I be in it? I've got just the story for it to start you off. Hang on. Let me light up."

Amanda watched as her mother tapped a cigarette expertly from the packet with one hand while the other sought out her lighter. She lit it with precision, inhaled deeply, and began.

"I was reading an item in the newspaper about an old lady in a home. It was her 100th birthday, and her family wanted to know how to celebrate her birthday.

"Do you want a cake?" asked her granddaughter.

"No, I don't want a cake."

"Would you like a family portrait painted?"

"No, no portrait."

"How about a huge party? We'll invite all the family and all your friends"

"No."

"Well, what do you want? We must do something to celebrate your special birthday."

The old lady thought for a while. "Can I have anything I want?" she asked.

"Yes, anything."

"Anything at all?"

"Anything within reason. It will depend on the budget."

"'I'd like to go and see *The Chippendales* at their next strip show," she replied.

Amanda's mother began to chuckle.

"That's a very amusing tale, but I don't see how I could use it in my book or how it involves you."

She caught the twinkle in her mother's eyes.

"No, you're not...?"

"You're becoming sharper, aren't you Amanda? No, I'm not going to go and see *The Chippendales,* but I am having an early birthday party here. I'm planning an event at the local tavern for all my friends, mostly female friends, and we're having a group of male strippers called *The Fuller Monty.*" She chuckled at the image it conjured. "Anyway, it's something I've not experienced before, and I thought, why not? So, I'll use my mobile phone and capture most of the action for you if you like, or I could just show you the photos when we next talk. I'm sure you could use that in your book."

Amanda shook her head in disbelief. Her mother turned her head and spoke to someone behind her. A woman of about fifty waved shyly at Amanda.

"That's Roseanne. We're going down to the bar to meet up with some other friends. Roseanne has just started pole dancing classes."

Amanda gasped.

"It's very good exercise apparently, so take that look off your face. Yes, that prudish look. It would do you good to loosen up a little and have a go at something more adventurous. Roseanne's love life has taken on new dimensions since she started, isn't that so, Roseanne?"

The shy woman giggled slightly and nodded.

"See, try a class yourself, and Old Misery Guts will soon be more cheerful. Sorry love, I shall have to leave you. Oh, there's a black dog sitting beside you."

Amanda looked down. Ted had biffed the front door open with his head and come in. He was now sitting obediently next to Amanda in the hope that she would give him some of that tasty ham she kept in the large magic white box in the kitchen.

'This is Ted. He's my stepdog. He's very obedient."

"Hello Ted! Hasn't he got intelligent eyes? He looks as if he's listening to every word I'm saying. I think you should train him to chase Phil and nip at his ankles when he misbehaves." She guffawed. "Must go now. Bye, Ted. Bye, Sweetheart."

Ted looked up at Amanda. "You wouldn't bite Phil, would you? He's your friend. You're more likely to jump on him and lick him to death."

Ted looked at her blankly. He'd clearly forgotten who Phil was. If she stayed here too long, so would she.

She couldn't settle with her writing so she checked the Scrabble board where she was rewarded with a message from Todd: *I'm feeling so much better, and it is all thanks to you. You have seen me through one of the darkest periods of my life. I owe you more than thanks. I'm starting with a new physiotherapist tomorrow. She's supposed to be one of the best. I want to get my fitness levels back, but my leg is pretty weak at the moment. I am determined to get back to racing, and my new goal is to walk Machu Picchu. Wish me luck. By the way, I couldn't play a dirty word, but here's what I could make out of my letters...'*

She looked at the word flashing on the board. He had played it on a double—the word was *grateful*.

Feelings she couldn't comprehend washed over her as she responded to him. *Good luck tomorrow, although by the time you read this, it'll be today. I'll be thinking of you. x*

It seemed everyone she knew was facing new challenges. It was a sign that she should get on with her own life, too. First thing tomorrow she would sign up for some yoga classes being advertised at the local fitness centre, and then she would buy some artist crayons.

BLOG: Fortifying Your Fifties

Day…don't know, but pretty sure it's October

I stared surreptitiously at the group of slim women in the waiting room. None of them weighed more than my left leg. They all looked serene, which was more than I felt. I stared down the hallway at the small group of chattering women in tight exercise clothes, waving bottles of water about and carrying towels, prepared for a great workout in the kickboxing class.

I used to attend a kickboxing class, but a few years ago, I was banned from it. I was also banned from spinning class, not to mention high impact aerobics, boxercise, body pump, and step classes. No, I wasn't misbehaving in them. I adore them. I was completely addicted to them and knew all the movements. I could always be found at the front of the class. I had boundless energy. No one could bounce as high as me or kick as hard. If someone couldn't see the instructor, they would follow my movements, knowing I would know the routine by heart. I knew all the instructors, too, as I went every single day. No, I was banned because the surgeon who operated on my leg for the second time told me I couldn't take part in any more high impact classes. I was not to do anything overly energetic and get my heart rate up too high; so I could no longer attend my daily exercise classes. He warned me that I was to slow down.

That's easier said than done. After a tedious struggle with back problems and surgery in my youth and into my thirties, I finally took up exercise in an effort to take control of my health. It started in front of the television with a DVD of some famous American woman in a leotard. She shouted out instructions, and I danced along in my front room with the curtains drawn. A year later, I had enough confidence to attend regular classes. I became addicted. I trained to become a personal trainer/instructor, and for many years, the gym and the classes were a huge part of my life. I regularly won the local gym competitions; I modelled in a fitness magazine; I lived for my daily fix; and when I heard the thump-thump-thump beat of a familiar song, I would be transported and lose myself entirely in that class. Exercise is highly addictive. Endorphins are like drugs. You crave them, and you go berserk if you can't get that high they provide.

Unfortunately, my enthusiasm was also my undoing, and I put too much strain on my body, and it rebelled. The valves in the veins of my left leg started to collapse, and one morning after a high-octane spinning class, my leg turned purplish black. It couldn't cope with the strain of my blood pumping around at top speed. I won't bore you all with the details, but it suffices to say that I didn't listen to my surgeon the first time he told me to calm down and a year later was readmitted for exactly the same problem.

Hence, this week, in a bid to try something new but not overdo it, I signed up at the local fitness centre and was about to attend my first Yoga class. Now I know many of you love yoga, but I am used to throwing myself about like a complete loon to get fit; so sitting in a lotus position and focusing on my breathing is a completely alien concept.

Another tiny, serene woman wafted into the waiting room and spoke in soft, almost hushed, tones. The room was ready for us. All the women quietly floated into the room, not even murmuring. I could hear the thump-thump-thump of the music starting up next door. I could feel my legs wanting to start marching and join in. I ached to be there. Instead, I collected a foam pillow, a soft mat, and a blanket from the cupboard, and plonked them down near the instructor, who smiled gently at me.

We warmed up. When I say warmed up, I don't mean the usual sort of marching and arm swinging I used to do. We tapped our arms and breathed in and out several times. We stood upright and then were told to loosely fall forward. Hmmm! My spine is fused. I had a couple of operations on my back when I was younger, and now I don't have the normal range of movement that other people have. I have trouble falling further than my stomach. All the other women seemed to be made of rubber and drooped forwards simultaneously, like a rehearsal of some yoga ballet. Some soothing music was warbling in the background, and the instructor's voice was calming.

Through the wall I could hear their instructor yelling in French at the group, urging them to work those muscles. They would soon be punching and kicking. The beat resonated through the wall. I had a desperate urge to round kick my neighbour, who was now almost propping herself up by her head. I continued to stare at my round stomach.

My instructor's lilting voice dragged me back to the class. We were to follow her lead and get into a tree position. My knee cracked loudly as I bent it to rest on my other inner calf. No one giggled. Position after position followed, always performed very slowly and never forced. We spent ages focusing on breathing in and breathing out. I looked at the clock on the wall. It'd been twenty minutes. Only another hour and forty minutes left.

Through the wall I could hear the women counting loudly back to the instructor as they punched their way to fitness. "Dix, neuf, huit, sept, six…"

My eavesdropping was interrupted by "Et la posture du chien (tête en bas)".

Luckily my French is good enough to translate this one: Downward-facing dog position. I desperately wanted to snort childishly, but everyone was so serious, and I was the foreigner so I resisted the urge.

Another two positions with peculiar names later, I found myself on my mat doing some more breathing, preparing to get into yet another position. Only one hour and twenty minutes to go. The music was soothing. The noise from next door was not as noticeable, and I was starting to feel more relaxed. In fact, I was starting to feel *very* relaxed.

I awoke to a gentle shaking.

"Oh sorry, just getting ready for the next pose," I said to the gentle-faced instructor. "I nearly dozed off then."

"Oh I sink you might 'ave done more zan nearly doze off. Ze class ended fife minutes ago. I sought I better wake you. Zee cleaner will come soon. I'm 'appy you enjoyed ze class. You seem more relaxed now,' she continued smiling. ''Ope to see you next week."

Well, I think I might be a convert. If I need to catch up on my sleep, I can always trundle along to the next class, and as an added bonus, I feel much suppler today. I bent forward and nearly looked at my knees instead of my stomach. I think I can see the attraction—although I'd better make sure I go to the back of the class in case I snore next time.

Posted by Facing50.Blog

8 Comments:

PhillyFilly says…I am a yoga convert. You stick to it, Amanda, and you will feel the benefit. It does wonders for your posture.

SexyFitChick says…It does wonders for more than your posture, Amanda. By the time you next see Phil, you'll be in marvellous shape and will be so supple that you'll be able to surprise him in more ways than one.

QuiteContrary says…I can't see the attraction myself. I'd have fallen asleep, too. Don't those sorts of people who practice yoga live on a diet of bio yogurt and lettuce? No wonder they are so slim. Hope I haven't offended.

Gypsynesters2 says…We're big fans of yoga. We practiced with a guru when we visited India. We took up Tantra yoga and have never looked back. That's not true—we can look back, under, and over!

Facing50 says…I think I'll grow to like it. I need to become more flexible. It's supposed to be very good for older people so that's me then.

Hippyhappyhoppy says…Oh I laughed so much at this post. Hugs x

DonnaKBab says…This is not for me. I would fall asleep, too. I'd like the boxing class. It could come in useful here. I could do with learning a few moves to keep the little man in his place.

Chapter Twenty-Seven

It wasn't fair to use Amanda as her pretend persona now that she was going to be residing in France a little longer. It was frustrating because Bibi had been grateful for her harmless friendship with Richard. Her online relationship wasn't helping the situation with Didier, though. She had carelessly dropped Richard's name into the conversation the other evening, hoping that Didier would pick up on it and ask who Richard was. He hadn't. He'd been more interested in the copy of *Le Figaro* he had brought home from the office.

Bibi was beginning to despair. To the untrained eye, Didier was the model of a good husband. He was courteous and polite towards her. He complimented her on her cooking and her new hairstyle after she had visited the salon. On the surface, there was nothing wrong with their marriage, but Bibi knew that they were in trouble. Didier had not touched her in weeks. When challenged, he pointed out that he was not as young as he used to be, and with all the travelling in the day, plus all the extra responsibility he had taken on at work, it was a miracle he could keep his eyes open after nine o'clock each evening, let alone frolic in bed with her.

Bibi had never been the demonstrative partner in their sexual relationship because Didier had made it so easy for her. He had always wanted her. Never had there been a time when she had not been able to seduce him by looking at him or pouting. She had never needed to make the slightest effort; she only had to turn her smouldering eyes on him, and he would leap on her. He had always putty in her hands. He caressed her frequently at home and even when they went out; he would pounce on her at most inappropriate times, like when she should be serving the dinner. Even when he was having a silly affair, he had still managed to pay her some attention.

It had been some time since he had been so ardent, but since he had begun this latest fling, she had discovered he had no desire left for her. Maybe the tart was wearing him out. One thing was for certain, she would not beg for his attention or for sex. She would not try to interest him by pleading or throwing herself at him. If she could not interest him by being herself, then that was that. He was a ridiculous idiot, and she would not play by his rules any longer.

She clicked onto her messages. Richard had been discussing food and restaurants with her. His favourite place was a charming restaurant—La Taca d'Oli. According to his latest message, it was unassuming and had the best *soupions a la Nicoise* (tiny squid in tomato and basil sauce) in the area. It must be wonderful to live by the coast and eat the catch of the day. The soupions sounded delicious. There wasn't too much fresh fish in the locality. There were river fish caught from the river Aveyron, but mostly the fish in local restaurants was frozen.

Which is your favourite local restaurant?

Le Carré des Gourmets, she typed back without hesitation. Didier had taken her there the year before to celebrate her birthday. They had enjoyed a romantic meal and shared a bottle of fine Gaillac wine. The memory lit her eyes for a moment.

The quality of the food was excellent, and the location is divine. St Antonin is simply delightful. The abbey here was founded in the 9th century. It's a tourist hotspot, and they even filmed Charlotte Grey here. The terrace at Le Carré des Gourmets overlooks the river Aveyron, and if you are fortunate to get an outside table, you can have no nicer view from this beautiful medieval town.

I saw Charlotte Grey at the cinema when it came out. Cate Blanchett, the Australian actress, was in it, wasn't she? asked Richard, having Googled the film and learned something about it. *I shall try your restaurant recommendation if I am ever in the area.*

You should. It is worth a visit. There is a lot of good regional cooking here in the area.

She signed off shortly afterwards. It would be her last message to Richard. She couldn't continue pretending to be Amanda Willson when the real Amanda was still in France.

Richard fisted the air in triumph. He had her—hook, line and sinker. From the piece of information he had just received, he would be able to find her. He would soon be able to work out where she lived and bowl up at her place or at one of her favourite restaurants. He would accidentally bump into her, and then he would be able to woo her. He'd better hurry up because he could only afford two more months of rent on his place. He'd do a little more research into the vicinity and then surprise her. He tapped away, trying to find a bed and breakfast in the area where he could stay while he made his investigations.

Amanda was trying to sketch an apple. It had taken her ages. She'd eaten the two red apples in the bowl, so now she was having a go at a green one. She had placed it on a dish and was sitting, tongue out, trying to capture its shine. She was quite pleased with the result. Not bad for her first attempt. She was almost finished when PlayGirl.77 interrupted her.

"Evening Sweetheart! Just thought I'd let you know that Grego and Spencer are going to the men's fashion show in Paris next June. Are you likely to still be over there then?"

"Hello, Mum. What are you wearing?"

"Don't equivocate, Amanda," she instructed before answering her question. "It's a beret. Very French. I thought you'd feel at home if I wore it."

Her mother looked like a giant mushroom. She resisted the temptation to laugh. "It's quite large, Mum."

"Yes, I think I picked up the wrong size in my haste to come and talk to you. This could be Grego's. So, will you be in France in June?"

"It's not likely. I think I'll go back to England once I finish the book. I'm beginning to miss Phil—"

"Pity. The boys would have liked to meet up with you there. We are all going to the London Fashion week in February. I'm going to put them up at home, and we'll catch the train in to London. Should be a good day. So, what have you been up to since we last chatted?"

"I've taken up yoga and art."

"Yoga? Isn't that where you stand like a tree for hours and chant? Why don't you have a go at that new craze, Zumba? That sounds more like it."

She hummed and rocked from side to side in a sort of shimmy. The effect was disconcerting. The woman looked like a huge, wobbling, mushroom jelly.

"No, yoga is just fine. I get enough exercise walking."

"If you insist. So, how's the art going?"

"I'm just about finished with this," replied Amanda hauling the large drawing up from the table and placing it where her mother could see it.

"Amanda, that is very good. Actually, it's very good, indeed."

Amanda puffed up with pride. Praise from her mother was rare.

"Okay, well, you probably won't see the boys then for a while. We have decided not to show Grego's creations to a fashion house. He's going to become an independent. He'll show them at the fashion show here on Cyprus. It's a major event, and he should do well on his home turf, so to speak. They've been working so hard on the collection. It's impressive, and I've had a kick out of being part of the team. I'll be going to the big event, too. They've asked me to model a couple of the senior ranges that I helped design. Fancy that—me, a 78-year-old catwalk model. I'd rather like it if you could come over for the event. I've told everyone about you, and they are dying to meet you."

"Well, give me the dates, and I'll see what I can do."

"I'll email them over to you. That's very good news. Time to go. I promised Roseanne I'd watch her new routine before she shows it to her husband. Bye. Be good. I really like that picture of the frog that you drew. Keep it up."

Frog? Amanda looked at her picture, tore the page from the sketch book, and took a large bite from the apple. Yoga and art seemed pretty tame compared to her mother's activities. Didn't Jeanette run Zumba classes? Pity her foot was still sore from falling off her roller skates. She hadn't been able to walk as far with Ted in recent weeks. She rubbed it gingerly. It seemed a little better now. She'd check with Jeanette when she returned to Beaulieu next week and see how energetic Zumba was. She was still smarting from the trip she had made to the doctor about her foot. *Blasted man!* He was to blame for her latest feeling of inadequacy. Luckily, Bibi arrived to save her from her misery. Bibi was always good for cheering her up and always provided her with excellent writing material for her blog.

Chapter Twenty-Eight

The physiotherapist had finished checking through the notes for her next patient, who had been injured in a nasty collision during a cycle event. She had read all about the incident in the local newspaper. The patient had suffered a broken shoulder, which had been pinned together in a lengthy operation, and serious leg injuries. He had responded well to surgery but now required physiotherapy, especially on his leg and knee, to ensure he would walk properly.

The physiotherapist knew all about Todd Bradshaw. She knew far more than merely what had been reported in the newspapers. Sitting back in her chair, she chewed on the end of a biro and wondered how she should handle this particular patient. He deserved every ounce of pain that she could inflict on him. He was a love rat and a cheat. He was exactly the sort of man she despised. He sounded just like her ex-husband, who had left her a couple of years ago. He had been a self-centred, low-life cheat. He had left her damaged. He had broken her. The day he left her, taking not only the furniture, ornaments, and shared goods, but also the small amount of money her father had left her in his will, her world had imploded. She had wept for days. She stopped eating. She stopped living. Her colourless world, filled with nothing but emotional pain, drove her to consider suicide. It had taken months and months of therapy and then months and months of intense exercise to get over the anger and regain her self-worth. She had come through it. She was now a strong woman, both physically and mentally; however, she would never let another man hurt her again.

Todd Bradshaw had cheated on Amanda Wilson, not once but twice. The first time had been after they had lived together for almost two years. They had met, fallen in love, and moved in together into an apartment over a bakery in the romantic city of Casablanca. When his teaching contract there ran out, Todd chose to take up an appointment in Kuwait. Kuwait was a strict Muslim country, and Amanda could find no employment there, so she had returned to the UK. The plan had been to each save enough money to enable them to move to Turkey where they would start a language school together. It took Todd less than a month to betray Amanda. He met a diplomat's daughter at a party, and before long, all thoughts of Amanda were forgotten. He eventually confessed to Amanda during a phone call that he had been unfaithful and begged forgiveness, but Amanda had been too distraught to forgive him.

Last year he had schmoozed the bridesmaid at his nephew's wedding and bedded her. He had never contacted the girl again, leaving her sobbing into her pillow every night and crying down the telephone to her cousin. He had not only seduced this lovely young woman, who was half his age, but had done it when he should have been meeting Amanda to make up for his misdemeanours in the past. He had spent all year flirting outrageously with her on Facebook, encouraging her, and leading her to believe they could have a relationship again. He had played on Amanda's vulnerability and her feelings for him, which had never completely left her. It had been his idea to meet up in the UK, and he arranged to do so during a visit to attend the family wedding. He had desperately pleaded with her to meet him. The sly old fox hadn't turned up to the meeting, though. He was too busy frolicking in bed with his latest conquest.

Over the last year, the physiotherapist, known in blogging circles as SexyFitChick, had become one of Amanda Wilson's followers, best online friend and confidante. They had met online, thanks to their blogging.

SexyFitChick wrote a fitness blog. She had immediately felt a sisterly concern for Amanda after reading her posts in her previous blog about her life with Phil and the things that happened with Todd. The woman needed a friend, and SexyFitChick had filled that role. It didn't matter that they lived hundreds of miles apart; they had forged a solid and enjoyable relationship. SexyFitChick also needed the friendship. She was at that time still in shock from her divorce and needed a distraction from her own problems. Amanda had been it. Her stories about her life were hilarious and just the tonic SexyFitChick had needed.

Being almost the same age, she had related to Amanda's posts about getting older and feeling worthless. Amanda's upbeat temperament and witty observations about life had helped her more than she realised, and in return, SexyFitChick had offered Amanda advice and support during her hours of need. She had even encouraged her to leave her husband and start over with this over-sexed buck. She felt responsible for Amanda's let-down. Not only was she useless at choosing men for herself, she clearly couldn't choose them for her friends either.

As for the bridesmaid who had been seduced by Mr Bradshaw, well, she was SexyFitChick's cousin. She had returned to Australia, despondent at having been duped by Todd. SexyFitChick felt it was time to redress the balance. So, how exactly was she going to deal with this super stud?

A knock at the door announced the arrival of the patient. A nurse held the door for him as he hobbled in on crutches. He smiled enigmatically at his new physiotherapist. His piercing, blue eyes held hers in a gaze. He exuded both charm and confidence. This was a man who knew his own mind. Also, he had the physique of an Adonis. SexyFitChick was immediately torn between drooling over him and smacking him in the face. How dare he be so gorgeous! She nodded brusquely at him and motioned for him to sit down. She may not like what he was, but she was a professional, and this man needed her help to get back to full health. She'd make sure he did. She'd put him through his paces all right. She would work him hard every day until he whimpered for her to stop. She would make him hurt so much he would plead with her to stop. Mr Todd Bradshaw had met his match. That boyish charm would never work on her.

BLOG: Fortifying Your Fifties

Day…Whatever!

Rather stupidly, I fell off my roller skates a few weeks ago while trying them out and hurt my foot. I managed to get about on it, but it smarted quite badly. The yoga session I attended made it worse, and so I decided to visit the local doctor as a precaution. He asked me to remove my clothes, checked me over, shrugged a lot (the French are good at that), and suggested I would benefit from losing some weight. I was horrified. I had been walking Ted faithfully four or five times a week (in spite of the pain), and I thought I was looking good. I've lost weight and now only weigh nine stone (approximately 126 pounds). I am hardly obese.

I have been irritated by his suggestion ever since. I was feeling particularly peevish the other day, and when Bibi, my guru and role model, popped round to keep me company, I chuntered to her about it.

"You need super sexy underwear," she announced.

"To seduce the doctor?"

"Non, idiot—to make you look slim. You put your brassiere high like zis, so your boozoms will be high. Not like you—by your waist. You will look slimmer." She sipped on her tiny cup of high-octane coffee.

I took a quick check. My boobs weren't low slung at all.

"Zen when you eat your food you must remember 'ow you look in your sexy underwear."

"Okay, that's one possible solution, but I get hungry. I need to eat, especially after I've walked Ted across all the fields. Do you exercise? Do you cycle?" I asked casually.

She looked at me in horror.

213

"Of course not. I am a French woman. I do not take zee exercise," she said. adding something that sounded like "Pffft!"

"Well how do you stay so slim then?" I continued.

"The secret is to enjoy food."

"Well I already enjoy food. I enjoy my breakfast—"

Bibi tutted. "You should never eat breakfast, only zee black coffee and a little end of a croissant," she announced and pouted.

"—and my lunch, and I adore pasta," I continued, ignoring her.

"No, no, no. Zut!" She wagged her finger at me. "Not enjoy—*enjoy*," she said again with the emphasis on the second *enjoy*.

Seeing my perplexed face, she decided there was only one way to solve the problem and that was to take me for a lesson at a fabulous restaurant in Toulouse. The following day, all dressed up in our best clothes, her in her designer suit and me in my washed jeans, we arrived at a typical gastronomic restaurant where the waiters tried to push and jostle each other out of the way to serve us...well to serve Bibi.

She ordered several courses for us both and a half bottle of Chablis. One waiter poured a glass, and another brought some hot bread rolls. I grabbed my glass, raised it to toast Bibi and quaffed a large mouthful. Bibi raised a perfectly arched eyebrow at me.

"And zat is what I mean," she declared triumphantly. "You must never, ever, ever drink zee wine. You must let it touch your lips and leave a little flavour then put it down." She puckered her mouth as my hand moved towards the bread roll. "Non, never ze bread," and she patted her flat stomach.

"Great, the art to staying slim seems to be to *not* eat," I reflected.

As it happened, it was marginally better than that. Bibi taught me that to enjoy a meal, one must appreciate the flavours.

"What can you taste?" she asked when our carpaccio of salmon was laid before us.

"Salmon," I said. Gosh! I amaze myself with how funny I can be sometimes.

"Non, try again, and zis time, you 'old it in your mouth and tell me what chef has added to zis dish."

Trying not to shovel the tiny portion that was before me into my mouth in one go, I put a teeny weenie amount on my fork, slid it into my mouth, and waited.

"Lemon, and some coriander."

"Correct. Now, let the flavour rest in your mouth a while; savour it. Now, take another small amount on your fork. Do zee flavours taste the same?"

"Uhm no, not quite. It's not so obvious."

"And again?"

"No, I can't taste the coriander."

"Good, bon. Now you must put down your knife and fork. When you can no longer appreciate the flavours you must stop eating straight away. It is simple."

She dramatically pushed away her plate containing half the carpaccio. It was instantly swooped upon by a waiter who whisked it into the kitchen.

And guess what? It works. Admittedly, it only works if you eat very tasty, delicious food and not the sort of muck that I serve up. You have to learn to appreciate and savour the flavours of the food, not just wolf it down.

In France they have a completely different approach to eating, and the women have a different attitude toward staying slim. It is part of their culture. They expect to be slim. Even the men, like Monsieur Doctor, encourage them to stay slim. French women seem to have perfected the art of eating without ever drinking an entire glass of wine or eating a whole meal.

So, ladies and gentlemen, there you have it. You can stay slim if you work at it. Personally, I take the approach that life is short, and a little of what you fancy does you good. So I raise my large glass of Château Plonk to you all. Cheers!

Posted by Facing50.Blog

12 Comments

SexyFitChick says…Can't beat a good, old barbie on the beach and a few tinnies or some Australian Shiraz. Bibi is a freak of nature. (I don't really mean that, Bibi—you probably read this. I'm only a jealous Oz girl.) Blimey Amanda—you have lost a load of weight. Don't worry about the French doctor. He probably needs to get his eyes checked. Does Phil know you have lost all that weight?

Facing50 says…Haha! Bibi stuck her tongue out at you and said you were an Amazon. I think you two would get on really well. No, not heard from Phil for some time now. Out of sight....

PhillyFilly says…I have tried the Atkins Diet, the Blood Diet, the Cabbage Diet, the Boiled Water Diet, in fact, I have tried every diet that has ever come onto the market. I think Bibi should patent her idea and sell it for millions. I'd buy a book entitled *A French Woman's Secret Guide to Staying Slim*.

Facing50 says…I have never really worried about my weight before. It was not a conscious decision to lose any. However, the best way to lose weight seems to be to get stressed. Worrying about life on my own is having an effect, and Ted is helping tone up the rest.

Pandora'sBox says…Bravo, Bibi, for this advice. I shall try it out as soon as I have finished this bottle of Chianti! Cheers, Amanda!

Facing50 says…Way to go. Cheers!

MomofTen says…You would think that running around after the children would keep my weight down. The problem is that when they leave food on their plates, I have to eat it rather than let it go to waste. Eating ten leftover cheeseburgers can only mean one thing...

SexyFitChick says…In response to the comment above from MomofTen - Have you thought about just feeding your kids salad or soup? At least if they left it, you'd eat something healthy.

QuiteContrary says…Diets don't work. None of them. The diet industry is worth billions. Why do you think that is? Because none of them work and people are always looking for the next quick fix. Bibi—healthy eating in moderation is the right course to take. Hope I haven't offended.

YoungFreeSingleandSane says…Hurrah for Bibi! I am going to try and be like her. I have bought a new bra and raised my breasts to staggering, new heights. It works because the workmen who are fixing the heating in our office whistled at me, and Jonathan asked if I would like to go out to dinner with him. Don't worry—I am not going back out with him. There is a quite nice, shy guy in accounts who glanced in my direction today. Who knows what may happen?

Hippyhappyhoppy says…What fun you are having in France. Have a lovely day. Hugs

SexyFitChick says…I cannot believe it. I am on the computer at work because I just had to tell you this. You will never, ever, ever guess who I have just treated. I had to work on a man who was injured recently. His shoulder was broken and his knee needs manipulation. I'll give you a clue....his first name is Todd.

Chapter Twenty-Nine

It was the last day in October, and yet the trees had not given up their foliage. A light breeze rustled leaves of gold, magenta, and burnished copper. Amanda breathed in the crisp air. Ted trampled through leaves at her feet. Mark and Jeanette had returned from Ireland. Jeanette's sister was much better and able to look after the children again. Everyone was glad the ordeal was over. Ted ran about the house with a sock in his mouth, charging up and down stairs, stumbling in his excitement to have his family home again. He whimpered continually and chased after the children like a puppy.

The family was delighted to be back. They had spent a long time in Ireland and were more than happy to resume their life in France. The children had forgotten the few words of French they had learned, and Jeanette was itching to get back to her exercise classes. The night before, they had invited Amanda over to join them in supper and wine to thank her for looking after Ted for such a long time. The evening stretched well into the night, and several bottles of Château Plonk were quaffed. So, it was a sluggish Amanda who now plodded down the leaf strewn track with Ted.

Ted had now decided that he had two homes. When it got too noisy next door, he would wander over and visit Amanda. When it was time for the children to be fed, he would charge back home in case he was required to clean up any leftovers that might have fallen on the floor. Amanda had some company if she needed it and was now spending the cooler nights curled up in front of the toasty log burner with her writing.

Phil had phoned again. He was making quite a habit of it. That was the second time this week. He told her about the new warehouse deal and then went on to explain that he had been flying at the weekend. He had had his first proper lesson and been allowed to take the controls to learn to fly straight and level.

"It's not like driving a car. You have to spend time learning the controls and being briefed on the mechanics of flying," he explained as Amanda sat on the veranda, phone to one ear and stroking Ted's silky coat with her free hand. "I had a ground briefing before my first flight. I had to learn the effects of the controls: the ailerons, the rudders, and the trims. At the briefing, my instructor, Stuart, explained what we were going to do and talked about who would be in control of the aircraft. Stuart flew to start with, and then at about 3000 feet, I took over the controls and was given time to familiarize myself with how they worked. You need to be very smooth with your movements and not make them too large. It's not like a steering wheel. You have to make small adjustments. We were up for a good hour, and then we had a coffee and a debrief. I've got a few books to go through. I have to prepare for exams."

"Exams?"

"Yes, there's a navigation exam, one on Airframes and Engines, Air Law—that's very grueling: and meteorology, you know, clouds and weather. It's very interesting. Next week, I'll learn to do turns, that is, if the weather holds. It's been windy."

"Lovely here," she gloated. "The sun has been shining all day."

Phil hesitated for a moment. "I'd like to be there...with you," he added.

Amanda glowed inside. Phil was not known for romanticism. "It'd be nicer if you were here, too, but I guess you're enjoying doing what you are doing. There's plenty of time for us to return and do this together."

"Yes, I'd like that. I'm definitely coming over in December, though. I've requested some time off, and it's fairly quiet by mid-December with many firms shutting down early for Christmas so it'll be good to catch up. We could go away in Bertie for a few days, maybe go to the mountains."

They parted with fond goodbyes. Amanda felt more at ease than she had for a long time. She was carefree, she was staying in an idyllic spot, and Phil was content. She was secretly proud of his new hobby, too. Not everyone could fly an aeroplane. Crumbs, she had enough difficulty controlling Bertie, and it was on the ground. It must be hugely rewarding for Phil. She wondered idly if he'd start talking like a pilot and come home saying things like, "Hello, old girl, had a spiffing time with Jonty up in the air today." She smiled at the thought of Phil in a flying helmet. She should start calling him *Biggles*, the nickname of the adventurous pilot from the Biggles series that stretched from the 1930s to the '60s.

Smiling, she was pleased to discover that life was infinitely better than the year before.

Recently, she had received a request from an American magazine to write some articles about getting older. Someone had read her entries on her old blog about Phil, and they wanted her to write about how men coped with male menopause. Since she received the query, she'd been researching and working on an article all week. Having read as much as possible about the male menopause or andropause, as it was sometimes called, she now understood exactly why Phil had been such a misery the last few months. Happy with her work, she sent her article entitled "Irritable Male Syndrome – Or How To Deal With A Grumpy Old Man" with a confident click of the Send button.

Todd was online. He was playing on the Scrabble Board again. She had chortled enthusiastically at his description of his new physiotherapist, who he was convinced was trying to break him into little pieces and crush his spirit. SexyFitChick had also sent her emails suggesting that she was trying to make him squeal. It was comical. Amanda loved the idea that two parts of her online world had collided in the real world. Todd would be fine in SexyFitChick's hands; she wouldn't really hurt him. Well, maybe only a little bit.

Ouch, played Todd.

Is that a proper word or are you just looking for sympathy? she typed.

I could do with your cool, healing hands. That masochist has pummelled me and prodded my knee so much I'm surprised it's not black and blue.

Bet it's much better than it was. Amanda couldn't help smiling as she thought of SexyFitChick's email.

She played *caress*.

It's feeling much better now that you played that word. I could do with some gentle caressing.

I thought you were a tough, macho man nowadays. Amanda liked lobbing provocative comments back at Todd.

No, I'm just a softie as far as you are concerned. How's the writing going? Do you need me to help you write the sex scenes?

No, I can manage those. There aren't very many of them in the book, and they're not very exciting.

You should heat them up a bit. Everyone likes a raunchy sex scene. You could have your main character as a hot blonde, who is desperate for the attentions of a hunky, semi-Aussie man. She could corner him in the bathroom, lock him in, push him against the sink, and kiss him passionately. Oh, let me think...that actually happened, didn't it?

He played *aflame*.

The memory shook Amanda more than she wanted. *At least you still remember that first time. I was much younger then. I didn't know how else to get your attention. You'd better get some cold water to dampen your ardour. I thought you hurt too much to be feeling randy,* she typed, hoping to divert the conversation.

Sorry, it was the thought of being caressed. My mind wandered off to those hedonistic days in Casablanca when we canoodled on that perfect, white beach among the dunes with just the sound of the ocean bashing against the shore. They were happy days. I wish I could turn back the clock, Mandy.

Amanda didn't trust herself to continue the game. It was getting too serious for her. She wasn't going to get flirtatious like she did the last time they contacted each other. She needed to remember that she was now in a good relationship with Phil, even if he was in the UK and was now obsessed with work and flying.

I have to go now. I'm going to Bibi's house to meet her family. I'm glad you are making progress, and don't be too hard on that physio of yours. She's doing a brilliant job.

I'm too scared of her to misbehave. Getting better seems to be the only option. Bye for now. I shall get some rest and think of your gentle hands on my.... He signed off with a winking face.

BLOG: Fortifying Your Fifties

November…that's as close as I can get

Last week the trees were resplendent with their hues of yellow, copper browns, and deep reds. Even more colourful are the phenomenal chrysanthemums that are to be found outside every florist you pass or at every market you visit. The colours range from majestic magenta through to passionate pinks and glorious goldens. They are truly breathtaking.

I was about to learn the true significance of these flowers through a genuine gaffe.

My new best friend Bibi, like many traditional French women, lives with her husband, Didier, and her mother-in-law, Mathilde. They all coexist in one enormous house for reasons I have yet to work out. Every time I tackle Bibi about Mathilde, she has been reluctant to tell me too much. All I know is that her mother-in-law is an absolute tyrant. She rules the house with a rod of iron, and her son obeys her every wish or command.

Bibi can't stand the old bat, and she really is an old bat. She uses every trick in the book to ensure that she enjoys a very comfortable existence and is waited upon by Bibi and the gullible Didier, of course. She has her morning coffee brought up to her, claiming she is too old and frail to come downstairs for it. She has a small bell by her bedside that she rings constantly to get Bibi's attention.

Mathilde, of course, is neither old nor frail. Yes, she is elderly, but she enjoys robust enough health. After a morning lounging about in bed and ringing her little bell for Bibi to fetch a glass of water or a magazine to read, she descends in time for lunch—lunch, which, incidentally, Bibi always prepares. Mathilde chomps her way through all the freshly purchased bread and delicious casseroles that have been cooked for her. She even enjoys a glass of red wine with her meal and some cheese to follow.

Every Sunday she insists on joining them for lunch, leaving them no time to be together, Unlike the rest of the week when her son is at work, she picks at her food, claiming to have little appetite and reminding Didier that she has not much longer left on this Earth. She prods and pokes at Bibi's homemade lunch and sighs loudly.

"Ah, iz Maman not being very brave?" Didier will say to Bibi. "She 'as struggled to join us for zee lunch when she is so weak. She told me she had to make much effort today." Then he will fuss after her all afternoon, ensuring she is warm enough or comfortable enough while Bibi clears away the remains of lunch.

Bibi told me all about it. I thought she took it all very well. I would surely have murdered the old battle-axe by now, and she would be buried under the sunflowers in the field outside.

"How do you cope with her?" I asked. "You have so much patience."

"Ah well, one day zee old boot will, 'ow you say? One day, she will actually croak!" she confessed to me. "Zen I will 'av zee peace."

Mathilde is also quite a hypochondriac and is always claiming to have this pain or that ache. She frequently sends Bibi to collect medicine and suppositories—don't even ask about those—to help ease her sufferings. Bibi is convinced she lines them up by the bed to get Didier's sympathy and then flushes them down the toilet. Bibi has seen the evidence floating about.

Anyhow, back to last week. I had been invited to supper at their house on Tuesday evening. It was quite an honour as they do not invite many people to their home. I knew it was important to create the right impression, so I spent a long time buying the right bottle of red wine for Didier. I chose some scented candles for Bibi, which I knew she had admired in a shop window, as chocolates would be a taboo for her. But what could I get Mathilde? Driving past a florist's shop I saw the most gorgeous pots of chrysanthemums. I chose a large pot containing the most wonderful cinnamon-coloured plant. The florist wrapped it beautifully in autumn-coloured paper while I admired the bouquets in the shop, distracted by the gorgeous, bright, shiny paper that they were sitting in. I must have been a jackdaw or a magpie in another life. I adore shiny objects and colour. I was sniffing a huge, pale yellow flower when the florist asked if I would like a card made out to the recipient. I told her the name, and a card made out to Mme Mathilde Chevalier was slipped into a pretty envelope, which matched the plant exactly.

At eight-thirty, I bowled up to the mansion on the hill. I had learned that it was correct etiquette to turn up half an hour after the appointed time. It's a French thing. I crunched through the gravel up to the front door where I was greeted by an effusive Didier, who gave me the traditional three kisses—one to the left cheek, one to the right cheek and back to the left cheek. Then he uttered an "ooh la, la!" of delight when I handed him his bottle of wine. Judging by the sucking in of his breath and the way he raced off to open his bottle, I had chosen well. Bibi appeared, immaculately dressed as always.

"I 'av only just finished in zee kitchen. Zee old witch 'as been very difficult today. I would like to make a voodoo doll of 'er and shove big pins in it!" she whispered.

"Bibi," shrieked an imperious voice. "Shut zee door. I do not want my cold to get worse."

Bibi grabbed me by the hand and rushed me into the house to meet the dreaded Mathilde. In front of the log burner sat a large, rosy-faced woman. She looked the picture of health.

"Excuse me, I am not very well. Zee doctor says it is a miracle I am here at all," she harrumphed and took a slurp of her sherry.

I greeted her in French and handed over my present for her. Her rosy complexion paled. Her hand shook a little. She opened the card and the colour completely drained from her face. She grabbed her glass of sherry and drained it.

Bibi smirked.

"Is everything okay?" I asked as Bibi whisked me away to the kitchen.

"Yes, my clever, leetle Eenglish friend."

"But your mother...the plant...the card?"

"Ah yes, I had better explain to you the significance of zis flower. You see, today is the first of November."

"Yes, I know, and…?"

"In France, we celebrate le Toussaint —All Souls' Day. We go to visit our dead relatives in the graveyards, and we remember them."

Bibi paused for effect, but leaving me even more confused. "We remember zem by putting flowers on their graves." She chuckled, obviously enjoying something I was missing.

"Chrysanthemum flowers to be exact. My mother-in-law was quite surprised to get such a flower and even more surprised to get such a pretty card which said 'In Memory of Mme Mathilde Chevalier'."

Posted by Facing50.Blog

11 Comments

Hippyhoppyhappy says…I am still laughing at this. The poor woman. How funny. You are so funny. Hugs x

MiaFerrari says…It's the same in Italy. If you'd been brought up a Catholic, you'd have known.

Gypsynesters2 says…It's called Day of the Dead–Dia de Muertos—here in Mexico. They have the day as a national holiday, but it lasts three days. Everything is shut, including the banks. Why are you still in France? Why don't you jump in that camper van and explore the world? There is so much to see. We've been all over Mexico the last month.

Facing50 says…Mia Ferrari - I should have done some research, shouldn't I? We only celebrate Halloween back home. Here they have a strong Catholic culture, and All Souls' Day holds much more significance. I feel a right muppet at the moment. I should know better; after all, I can speak French. Gypsynesters – you are far more adventurous than me. I would probably go off if Phil was here, but exploring new places on your own isn't quite the same. Hippyhappyhoppy – glad it made you giggle. At least there are two of you who are laughing. Bibi couldn't keep a straight face all evening after the faux pas.

SexyFitChick says…We celebrate November 1st with the Melbourne Cup Day. It's hugely popular. About 100,000 people go to the race at the Flemington racecourse in Melbourne, and everyone else watches on television or goes to their local races. The old biddy deserved it anyway. Maybe she'll be less of a hypochondriac. I can't stand whiners. Bibi gets my sympathy. My ex-husband was a mummy's Boy, too. She helped turn him against me with her poisoned thoughts. I should try that voodoo doll idea and make an effigy of her, then stick pins in it. On second thought, I can't be bothered anymore. Thumping the punch bag tends to work for me when I feel needled. I just imagine it's his face I am whacking. Don't know why I wrote all of that. I don't normally talk about it. Thanks for the smile, Amanda. I'm off to put you-know-who through his paces. I'm in a better mood now, so he's very fortunate I read this first.

TheMerryDivorcee says…Bibi only has one mom-in-law to make her life a misery, imagine how hard it is for me. I wonder what's the collective word for a large group of ex-Mom-in-laws? It would be a coven of mom-in-laws.

QuiteContrary says…I am surprised that you didn't know this vital piece of information. I had you down as an intelligent woman. It is a Catholic tradition to celebrate the passing of loved ones and indeed a tradition for many countries, even in the United States where they celebrate All Saints' Day on November 1st. In New Orleans, for example, people gather in local cemeteries and decorate the graves with flowers. The descendants of the French Canadian settlers around St. Martinville, Louisiana, observe this day in the traditional French manner. Even the most obscure graces are graced with wreaths and bouquets and candles are lit throughout the cemeteries in anticipation of All Souls' Day on November 2nd. In the UK, All Saints' Day used to be called All Hallows (Hallows being an old word meaning Saint or Holy Person) The feast was actually held the day before, on All Hallows' Eve, which is where we got the word Hallowe'en. In the 19th and 20th centuries, children would go souling, rather like carol singing now, to request soul cakes (like hot cross buns) and alms (money). So, you see, my dear, the day is heaped in tradition, and maybe now you have learned something. We are never too old to learn. Hope I haven't offended.

Facing50 says…QuiteContrary - I feel even more stupid and most humble now. Thank you for the interesting facts. I knew none of this. Before, Halloween just meant dressing up in silly costumes or in Phil's case, refusing to answer the door in case the knocking was from children trick-or-treating. He hates that—calls it begging. I shall now enlighten him as to its origin.

PhillyFilly says…I love dressing up for Halloween. I dressed up as Barbie this year. Of course, I didn't eat any of the candy I got.

YoungFreeSingleandSane says…Another good reason to stay single—no mother-in-law!

MomofTen says…I worked out that when my kids get married, I'll not be losing ten, but gaining ten, which makes twenty. I think I'll be the mom-in-law from Hell, which should keep them away.

Chapter Thirty

The exercises had done him the world of good. His knee was back to normal, and his shoulder was feeling so much better. He was about to be signed off from the old dragon of a physiotherapist he had been seeing. She had made him jump through hoops the last few weeks, but he had her to thank for his emerging even fitter and stronger than before the accident. She had measured out further pain and pleasure in equal doses, providing him with relaxing massages and evil manipulations. Initially, he had wondered if she was deliberately hurting him and twisting his limbs with unnecessary force.

The atmosphere had been frostier than under the North Pole when he first appeared in her office. She had turned her icy, grey eyes on him when he first arrived in her office, looking him up and down coolly. He had tried smiling at her, but that had just made matters worse. Gradually, she had thawed. He assumed it was because he did everything she told him and didn't once question her. This was a woman who wanted to be in control, and he had a grudging respect for her. He knew her track—the more effort he made, the more progress he made; the more progress he made, the more she warmed to him; the more she warmed to him, the more he opened up to her. In fact, he had found himself opening up to her more than he intended recently.

She had coaxed out of him, in-between his grimaces and silent screams of pain, the entire Amanda story. The woman was a taskmaster. She believed in a lot of stretching. She made him extend his leg fully even when it felt like the tendon would snap in two with a loud twang and his knee cap would blow up. She insisted he try harder when they were working in the gym, even when he felt he had nothing left to give and his arms were trembling with fatigue. He gritted his teeth. If this woman thought he could do it, then he would.

Between repetitions or during treatments, he explained all about how he had let Amanda down years ago and how he had stupidly gone off with a harebrained girl half his age. He told her about his life since then and how he had had a succession of beautiful women, but none of them had got under his skin the way Amanda had.

On the last visit, she had him working in the gym for a final assessment. She was certain he was recovered but had advised him to tell her if he felt any pain whatsoever. She didn't want to undo all the good that had been done. As he started off on the treadmill, he had divulged the whole wedding fiasco story where he had managed to become so intoxicated that he had got off with the bridesmaid and missed a vital rendezvous with Amanda the following day.

"It wasn't really my fault," he said as he walked on the treadmill, watched beadily by the physiotherapist.

"I was somewhat worse for wear because I was nervous about seeing Mandy again."

The physio smiled politely and increased the incline slightly.

Todd walked on for several minutes before he felt the need to speak again.

"This Aussie bird threw herself at me at the reception."

"She was a fit bit, too. Guess she just couldn't... resist my good looks... flirty... booze. It was... fun," he puffed as the incline went up another two notches, and the speed was increased.

The physio focused on the machine and let him continue.

234

He began to perspire but struggled on. More minutes lapsed. "Morning... tried to leave... flaming nympho jumped on me again... couldn't get away."

The physiotherapist's eyes darkened. Todd was now running gently. "Ripped off my shirt with her teeth... good thing wasn't... my trousers... those teeth were... sharp." He wheezed as the pace increased. "I... tried... to leave... she started... blubbing... couldn't walk... out... on... her. Didn't... want... her..." His pace had been increased again. "to...feel...used. Wished... I... hadn't... been... drunk.... Can I...stop now?...Please?"

The physio nodded and wound down the machine. Todd's breath came in short rasps.

"I think you are well on the way to recovery, Mr Bradshaw. You'll be back racing in no time. See, your knee didn't even hurt. Just need a little more time for that shoulder, and you'll be back to pulling hot, little chicks."

"No, that is all behind me now. I'm older and wiser now. If Mandy doesn't want me, then I'll probably go to a monastery and become a monk."

The physiotherapist laughed merrily. "Somehow, Mr Bradshaw, I can't picture you in a brown robe sitting in a cell all day."

Todd actually felt more alive than he had recently. Fair play to the woman; she knew her stuff. She was as bonkers about being fit as he was. She was in tremendous shape, too, for a woman her age. If he weren't obsessed with having one last attempt to win Amanda, he might have chatted her up.

It was just as well he hadn't attempted to pull her because SexyFitChick was just waiting for Mr Todd Bradshaw to put one foot wrong, and she would tear his arm off. After all, this was the man who had broken her friend's heart and had managed to seduce her cousin at the aforementioned wedding. Having listened to Todd's side of the story, she had to admit that her cousin had not been exactly holier than thou, and Todd was certainly not the first man to be persuaded to lounge in bed all day with her voluptuous cousin.

The longer she worked with him, the more respect she had for him. He was tenacious and hadn't once complained in spite of all the tortures she had put him through. It soon became apparent that he was not the gigolo she had expected him to be. Time, the accident, or both had transformed Mr Todd Bradshaw into a nice guy. In spite of her crusty exterior, SexyFitChick rather liked Todd and hoped that he could win Amanda's heart because they both deserved a happy ending.

"Have you decided what you are going to do about Amanda?" She asked as they shook hands for the last time.

"Oh, yes, I've thought about nothing else. I'm going to catch a flight to France, hunt her down, and see if she if she would like to spend the rest of her life having fun with me on The Gold Coast or stay with that miserable old husband of hers, who appears to have left her in France and gone back to work. Who, in their right mind, would do that? I don't think I have much competition, do I?"

"It would appear not. I hope Amanda is thrilled to see you. If you come back with her, make sure you drop by here with her. I'd love to meet her. I already feel like I know her."

"Will do. It'd be a pleasure. Thanks for sorting me out. I thought at one point that I'd be stumbling about with a stick like an old man."

They shook hands.

"No, you are one of those people who will never grow old. Good luck. Don't forget that I want to meet Amanda."

Chapter Thirty-One

Richard typed in the name *Amanda Willson* for the sixteenth time and pressed the search button again on his page. *No results found*, it stated. He smacked the keyboard in irritation and growled menacingly at the computer. Where was she? Yesterday they had been messaging each other, and today she had mysteriously disappeared altogether from his friend section on his page, and now he couldn't locate her.

He tried typing her name into the Google search engine and came up with a couple of images of people on Facebook with a similar name. Neither of them could possibly be his Amanda, his wealthy Amanda. One, another Amanda Wilson, but with only one *l* in her surname, appeared to be an ordinary-looking woman in her fifties. From the small image he had found, she seemed to be sitting on a stupid Space Hopper with a glum-looking man next to her. That couldn't be her. Amanda was single. Where was that Aston Martin image?

He had no idea of her appearance. He had wanted to obtain further details about her today. He had also hoped to charm her some more and had spent all morning researching artists who held no interest for him to woo her with his expert knowledge. That had all been a waste of time. He stabbed at the keys and snarled some more.

There was no evidence of Amanda Willson ever existing. How exasperating! He would have to visit the place she mentioned and work on what little information he had about her. He'd book a flight to Toulouse for the weekend and find a small bed and breakfast somewhere close to the town of St-Antonin-Noble-Val. He'd be able to find her. There couldn't be many MGs in the area. From what little he knew about the region, its population consisted mostly of elderly people, Brits and farmers. An MG would stand out a mile.

Damn the woman! Why had she disappeared from Facebook? It never paid to make Richard Montagu-Forbes angry. When angered, he could become an extremely unpleasant character as several woman who had known him before could testify.

Unaware of the irritation she had recently caused Richard, Bibi was sitting beside the river Aveyron, attempting to paint the stone houses with bright blue shutters clustered beside the large river. They were reflected in the calm of the river along which odd branches floated lazily.

She had deleted her Facebook account. It hadn't served the purpose for which it had been created. Bibi had succeeded in finding some interesting people, especially Richard, who had been as passionate about art and literature as she was. Had he lived nearer, she might even have met up with him, but Nice was quite some way away, and life there was considerably different to life in this particular rural part of France. She paused to smile at a harried-looking woman, scuttling across the bridge and grasping a baguette for lunch. The woman nodded at her and murmured a "Bonjour, Madame" at her.

Bibi had run out of ways to interest her husband, it seemed. She had resorted to putting on her most seductive underwear the evening before, ensuring she was caught wearing it and nothing else when he arrived home. She had been hoping to evoke some desire, but he had merely thrown his jacket on the bed and gone to run a shower. She had lost her touch, or worse still, she had lost her man.

If she could find out his mistress's address, she would have to pay her a visit. Woman only had to look at her to feel inferior. This young girl had no sophistication, no class, nothing compared to Bibi. She could make the girl squirm just by raising an eyebrow at her. She would have to consider that possibility. Attempting to make Didier jealous was obviously having no effect.

She had stayed out for three nights last week. Didier hadn't even asked where she had been. One night she had even booked into a motel, telling Didier she would be spending the night with Amanda. She had asked Amanda to phone her at home that night to talk about arrangements for the following day. Amanda had duly phoned. Didier had picked up. Amanda had asked to speak to Bibi. Didier had replied, "I thought she was with you tonight." Flustered, Amanda had conjured up some lie about how she had got the wrong day, and how silly it was of her, of course. Bibi must certainly be en route to her house via the supermarket where she had no doubt gone to buy some cheese. Even to Amanda's ears, it sounded like a blatant lie. She fervently hoped that she hadn't dropped her friend into the *merde*.

Didier had not mentioned the incident, which could only mean that he was not interested enough to worry that his wife might be having an affair. He might even believe that she should have one, since that was exactly what he was doing.

It was now becoming a concern. Even Mathilde was picking up on the subtle shift in the atmosphere back home. She had questioned Bibi that very morning while dipping a croissant into her coffee. "Didier is coming home tonight, isn't he?"

"I'm not sure, Mathilde. He is very busy these days. He is under a lot of pressure from the management."

Mathilde had opened her mouth to reply but had shut it again instantly, her eyes saying more than words could. She had patted the back of Bibi's hand affectionately, bringing a lump to Bibi's throat and sending her rushing to the kitchen to get some more coffee before Mathilde could see the tears, which were beginning to well.

What would she do if Didier left her? The part of her that was strong and independent yelled that it didn't care. If he was dumb enough to run off with a mere child, who would have nothing to offer him other than sex, then he was a fool. A man like that could have a girl as a mistress, but as a wife or partner, ha! He would be laughed out of the region. He would face being ostracized by this community he had grown up in and that he knew so well.

His mother would never forgive him if he embarrassed the family. Didier prized respectability; of course, he would not leave her. He would never leave behind everything he valued, and above all, he would never hurt his mother. Another voice in her head, the timid one, croaked very quietly that life would be dreadful without her mate. She chose to ignore that particular voice and set about refilling the coffee pot. Challenges did not faze her.

Chapter Thirty-Two

The invitation to appear on an American radio show had come completely out of the blue. The *Better Heath Show*, starring Dr Dick Fox, chiropractor to the stars, had requested an interview with her. Her article about male menopause, which had just been featured in an American magazine, had impressed the producer of *The Better Health Show*. She, in turn, had contacted the magazine and begged for Amanda's email address. She had sent her a praiseworthy email, commenting on how much they had enjoyed reading her article and requesting that she be part of a show about growing old disgracefully. They would call her next week, and she would be put on air live if she would like to participate.

With a mother like hers, she was extremely qualified to talk about growing old disgracefully. She was still reeling from the photographs her mother had sent over of the strippers who had entertained them at her birthday party. Amanda felt sorry for the strippers. She bet they'd never been so heckled and wolf-whistled in their entire careers. The audience, although relatively small, had consisted of all of her mother's friends and all of the women from her apartment block, their sisters, and their mothers, and in some cases, their grandmothers. Her mother had been given a bottle of baby oil as a birthday present to rub into the chest of one of the strippers. There were a couple of photos of her with a hunk, rubbing with glee if you judged by the smile on her face.

Erasing the image from her mind, she hurriedly sent a reply stating she would be delighted to be interviewed. What a coup! She couldn't contain her excitement, and in the absence of anyone nearby with whom to share her good news since Mark and Jeanette had gone out with the children, she invited Ted around for a celebratory slice of ham and an exuberant pat. Then she settled down to tell those she knew best about this latest development. Her friends and followers, who had helped her get through last year when she was at a crisis point in her life, would be very happy to share her good fortune.

At last, her life was beginning to take shape. She was about to become a somebody. Her mother, when not attempting to live life like a single thirty-year-old, was busy with Grego's collection; Phil was preoccupied with work and learning to fly; and now she would become a well-known writer. Tom, well, she guessed Tom was just getting on with his life. He had sent a couple of jokes to her mobile that morning, which was rather sweet of him.

Did you know that dolphins are so smart that within a few weeks of captivity, they can train people to stand on the very edge of the pool and throw them fish? he texted. Then: *A computer once beat me at chess, but it was no match for me at kickboxing.*

He had sent a smiley face and lots of kisses along with the message.

Hope you come back home soon. Dad keeps coming round to the house to tell me all about his job and flying. I wish you were here to keep him off my back!

To Amanda the world now seemed a rosier place. She saved Tom's message. He was finally beginning to appreciate her after all this time. It was nice to be missed.

A message announced Todd's arrival on Facebook. *Hello, gorgeous lady*, flashed the message. *Been out celebrating my recovery. Bit tipsy. I'm not used to all this wine. What are you up to at the moment?*

I'm about to do some housework. Amanda didn't want to pick up where they had left off the last time.

Are you dressed in a frilly, white apron and wearing stockings with suspenders?

No. How many women dress like that to clean the house?

Freddy Mercury did in the video for Queen's "I Want to Break Free", rambled Todd.

I love talking to you, but I think you should get some sleep. I've got to vacuum the house, then prepare notes for a radio interview.

Will you be talking about Freddie Mercury?

Shaking her head, she typed, *How much wine have you consumed?*

The Scrabble board flashed to reveal a new word played by her opponent: *Euphoric*

Not drunk so much wine that I can't play Scrabble. I am euphoric because I am feeling well. I am euphoric because I have been signed off as fit again, and I am euphoric because I have devised a secret plan. Shh! No more now. Bed beckons. I think you'd look very sexy in a starched, white pinafore, holding a large, extendable, fluffy duster. I think I might have just the thing somewhere in one of my cupboards. x

Time seemed to be shooting by. It had been several months now since Todd had been injured. The squatters were now a distant memory, and very soon Phil would be coming back to France to visit her. This time it would be different. They wouldn't bicker or fight or sulk. Phil wouldn't be ungracious or aloof. It would be like the old days. He was only able to stay for a few days, but that would give them ample opportunity to enjoy each other's company. In fact, short and sweet would be much better than long, drawn-out, and dull. They might even take Bertie down to the mountains for a couple of days, although as far as Mark and Jeanette were concerned, they could stay in the cottage until next summer.

The more she thought about spending time again with Phil, the more she felt she should ensure that he was occupied the entire time he was here. She didn't want to take any chances that he would morph back into Grumpy Phil. She didn't want him to wish he was back home, at work, or flying. Clicking away at her keyboard, she noticed an advertisement. She had stumbled on just the thing for Phil. She would try to make sure that when he came over, he had the time of his life. Next, she had to write up her fabulous news and tell her friends in blog land about the radio interview. Where would she be without the internet?

BLOG: Fortifying Your Fifties

Early December

Today I want to share my good news with you, my very dear friends, who have been with me through thick and thin the last few months. I am about to appear on radio, and I can't contain my excitement any longer. I did one of those silly little dances in front of the computer when I got the email asking me to be on a show in the States. Yes, some of you who live across the pond will be able to tune in and hear my dulcet British accent. I'll give you all the details when I have them, but today I am posting the article that caught the attention of the radio producer. Watch out, folks! I could be on the *Ellen DeGeneres Show* next!

Irritable Male Syndrome
***or* How to Deal With Grumpy Old Men!**
By
Amanda Wilson

I discovered an article recently called "How to Deal with Grumpy Old Men", which left me flabbergasted. The author listed suggestions that could help everyone cope with their irritable old chap. One of those was to give him a back rub. I had to laugh. I have spent the last few years dealing with the grumpiest of men. He is worse than the television character Victor Meldrew in *One Foot in the Grave*. He complains about everything possible.

I have tried every trick in the book, and quite frankly, nothing works. If the old bugger is going to have a grumpy day or week, then that is what he'll have. The author of the above article also suggested repeating the mantra "he helped me so now it is my turn". Snort! Just how has he helped me? If I'm having a bad day, he hides until it is safe to come out.

Ladies, don't waste your energy. Trust me, when a man suffers from this syndrome, he won't let you near him to rub his back. In Phil's case, a slice of cake is the best solution; however, even that doesn't always work.

One cause of grumpiness the article mentioned was declining testosterone levels, known as male menopause or andropause. I had heard of male menopause, but I had never thought about the connection between what I experience with my own personal, grumpy old man (GOM) and the syndrome caused by declines in males hormones.

I looked into it further and discovered that in fact, I should maybe stop being cross about his attitude and become more understanding. After all, I know all about the female menopause and its horrible side effects. Since hormones are currently the bane of my life, I should pay more attention to the male side of getting older.

It gave me food for thought. What if a "Grumpy" was not merely a grouch but was actually suffering from decreased hormones and the mental side effects the decrease causes? What about if there was a treatment for it? Would men actually seek help?

I brought the subject up with my Mr Grumpy, only to be shot down in flames. He refused to acknowledge that there was a medical reason for his lack of enthusiasm for life. As for considering any treatment for the condition, well, in his opinion, going to the doctor is just not manly. Asking for help with male hormones is completely taboo. He complained about doctors for a full hour following the conversation.

Men need to recognise and deal with their problem in a responsible way, just as women deal with menopause. I know why I am bursting into tears every ten minutes and why I want to rip my husband Phil's head off for no good reason, but I do what I can to remain a functioning human being. I stay out of the way when I feel I am going under. I take supplements and try relaxation techniques. I use aromatic oils to produce positive energy, and above all, I laugh at life. Men also need to recognise and address their issues.

I don't want to be the bearer of bad news, but I also have a word of caution. According to several websites, many men become victims of death by their own hand as a result of this syndrome. For many, my own husband included, retirement can lead to a loss of identity. If you add to this dropping hormone levels and a society that does not recognise male menopause ,you have a potentially worrying situation.

The solution? Well, the only one I can come up with that seems to assist my own personal Grumpy is laughter. One article seemed to corroborate my own findings. It suggested that laughing "promotes good health", but at the same time it also pointed out that "researchers have found that grumpy old men (and women) tend to outlive their happier peers".

All of that leaves me in a quandary. Maybe I should just leave him to be a miserable sod; after all, he could live to a grand old age. Yet, because I am who I am, I try to be as cheerful as possible when Mr Grumpy is having a down day. If I'm lucky, he will come through it and return to normal in a short period. Keeping your own spirits up is fundamental to the whole affair. If you can stay positive, it might well have a positive effect on your GOM. However, I can't promise anything, but I am going to cook dinner next time I'm with my own Grumpy while wearing a red clown's nose to see if it works.

Posted by Facing50.Blog

9 Comments

247

TheMerryDivorcee says…This explains so much. My present husband is a misery at the moment and sits around the house in just his shorts and tee-shirt all the time. I thought it was because he was becoming a slob, or because he knows I am seeing a horny ranch hand I met in a bar; but now I think it could be because he is going through the menopause. I just can't wait to see his face when I tell him. That should secure me a divorce, no problem.

YoungFreeSingleandSane says…Congratulations on the radio show. You will soon be too important to blog any more. The guy I have been going out with is mardy most days. How old do you have to be to go through male menopause? He's thirty.

QuiteContrary says…Given that males have to put up with women who behave like screeching banshees at various times of the month, I would have thought that a little understanding when we are feeling low would be acceptable. Men have to carry so much responsibility in their lives: they support their families, they worry about their jobs, and they have to be good role models to their children. A little understanding is not too much to ask when they want to have a little rant from time to time about the terrible state of the education system today or about how many speed humps the Council has erected in a town. It's bad enough trying to get to places without having to slow down to two miles per hour to go over the ridiculous humps without ripping off your spoiler. Which idiots are allowed to design our city centres? Do they not have brains? I would rather get my four-year-old grandson to design the road system. Whoever sat in a meeting and announced one day, "Oh, we've got all of these spare speed humps; we'll use them up and put fifteen of them along Faffington Crescent," wants their head knocked off. Sorry. Hope I haven't offended. Well done on being on the radio. Hope you will be able to understand their accents.

SexyFitChick says…Who rattled QuiteContrary's cage today? Great news about the interview. Not all men seem to be grumpy. I have been working with one who is very upbeat. I think it's a myth, and Phil is unique. LOL

Hippyhappyhoppy says…I am happy for you. You deserve success because you are always so cheerful. Hugs x

Gypsynesters2 says…We both appeared on *Oprah* talking about our adventures since we took up travelling. Maybe we could give you a few pointers to help you through your interview.

Madasahatter says…Don't forget to smile while you are talking. People can hear it in your voice. I shall be tuning in when you send the information. I love the British accent. It is so cute. Do you sound like that actress Joanna Lumley? Wow! I can't wait to hear you. It means you are a real person and not just a cyberperson like me.

MomofTen says…Way to go! I think my poor hubs has this syndrome, too. Or it could be due to all of these kids hanging around all the time.

FairieQueene says…I am going to have to Super Glue my lips together so I don't spill the beans about this news. Have you told your mother yet? I'll have to pretend to be surprised when she tells me your news. How could you do this to me? Now, I am just dying to tell her and Grego.

Chapter Thirty-Three

You could feel the warmth even at this time of the morning. It might be cold in France, but in Australia, it was a beautiful summer morning. It was a wonderful time of the year. It was Todd's favourite time of the year.

"It was really nice of you to meet me," he said to his companion, seated next to him at the table.

"I couldn't refuse such a charming request for breakfast on such a beautiful morning," replied the tall, striking woman next to him.

Digit, the cattle dog, was sitting with his head resting on her lap, gazing at her with huge, soft eyes.

"Sorry about the dog. He can't resist a pretty woman."

"Like his master then?"

"I guess he learned from his master. He's his own dog, though. He's discerning about whom he follows, whom he lets pat him, and whom he chooses to slobber on. You're lucky. He hasn't slobbered on you at all."

Digit's eyebrows furrowed as if to impress upon her that his master was telling huge, porky pies.

"Will he be all right whilst you are away?"

"Oh, he'll be fine. He's my best friend, but I get the impression he sometimes likes to have time out on his own without being crowded out by me. Jezza is going to look after him for me. I'm going to erect his kennel in Jezza's garden this afternoon. He absolutely adores Jezza's partner, Suzanne. He follows her about all the time, looking lovesick. He's a hopeless case when it comes to women. Again, he's like his master. Also, the Australian Shepherd bitch next door is in heat, I gather. They'd better keep her inside. This dog can leap the tallest fence if he wants to. He's one of the best of his species and faithful," he added gently.

"Perhaps this time his master will find what he has always been looking for."

"I hope so. Hey, did I tell you I finished painting Digit's kennel? I've painted a mural of Tintin and Snowy on it for him. He likes Tintin. He would love to have met Snowy. He's particular about the sort of dog he hangs out with. If he sees a Labrador, he goes for it. Labradors are his arch enemy, but he loves hanging out with fox terriers like Snowy. You're special, aren't you, mate?"

Digit lifted his head briefly and sniffed the air. The waiter was bringing breakfast. He dropped his head back onto SexyFitChick's lap in preparation for the feast he was sure he would receive. No woman alive had been able to eat while he gazed fondly at her. He always succeeded in coaxing tasty morsels from them, and this one didn't look like she ate too much.

"Is he always this affectionate?"

"Yes, when he knows that there is food about," Todd replied as the waiter dropped the fruit salads, toast and juice down for them both. "It's the vegemite he's after. He's addicted to the stuff."

"When are you leaving?"

"New Year's Day. I know, it's a funny day to travel, but it was easy to get tickets then, and I shan't be celebrating the night before. I've seen the fireworks at the harbour loads of times. I'm willing to give them a miss this year to catch that early flight. I'm going to fly to Singapore, stop off for a day or two to break the trip, and then go on to Paris. I'll go from Paris to Toulouse, and from there I'll drive to where she is staying. I have an idea of where it is. I'll send her emails if I need to know more. I really appreciate everything you've done for me," he continued. "You've helped me get my life back on course, and not just physically. Thanks for listening to me. You know everything about me, and I know nothing about you except you are one hell of a physiotherapist. Is there someone in your life?"

She shook her head. "I have my work. That keeps me going, and when I'm not working, I train. Right now I'm training for my second dan in Taekwondo."

He whistled through his teeth before taking a large bite of toast. "You're a black belt. I wouldn't want to piss you off. You'd make mincemeat out of me."

"Funnily enough, I am not as tough as you might think."

"Still pretty formidable, though," he grinned.

Breakfast over, they sat for a while longer. Digit sat obediently by his master, ever watchful.

"You must be serious about her to give up this beaut weather and go to Europe. It's cold there, you know." The look in his eyes told her everything she needed to know. "Right, well, thank you for breakfast. Good luck again. I'll cross my fingers for you. I hope you manage the long flight, too. You have that diagram of those stretches I gave you if you get cramps in your legs and remember to drink plenty of fluids. Your body has been though a lot recently, and a twenty-three hour flight to Paris is not an easy journey to make—even if you do stop for a few days in Singapore."

She bent down to pat Digit, who held her gaze with knowing eyes. He panted comically and then gave her hand a friendly lick.

"Twenty-two hours and fifty minutes to be precise," he grinned boyishly. "Then, of course, the flight to Toulouse. I'll be fine. I'll jog up and down the plane if I get stiff or bored."

"Make sure you do. I don't want all that effort wasted. Have a good trip. Let me know how it goes?"

She stood to shake his hand but at the last minute succumbed to a hug, the intensity of which surprised her. Meeting Todd had been an eye-opener. She was more aware now that there was often another side to the story. She had been wrong about him. He wasn't the snake in the grass she believed him to be. She wondered if she had been too quick to judge other people, too. She was certain that her ex-husband was a slime ball, but he must have left her for a reason. They had never discussed it. She didn't want to go back over that, but Todd had taught her to trust others again. Thanks to Mr Todd Bradshaw, she would now be able to move yet another step forward in the healing process, and who could tell where that would lead her?

BLOG: Fortifying Your Fifties

Still December

Following on from my last post, I have nipped online midweek to tell you about the Big Radio Interview last week.

It was my big moment. I was going to be live on the Mid-Morning Show with Dr Dick Fox. Surprisingly, I was horribly nervous as I am much better with the written word than the spoken unless, of course, I have had several glasses of wine, and then I am hilarious. (Well, *I* think I am hilarious!). I am prone to opening my mouth before my brain engages, so I had to ensure I would not make any faux pas. I knew we were going to be talking about "Irritable Male Syndrome" and "Growing Old Disgracefully", so I spent all week diligently preparing answers to all possible questions. I wrote them all down neatly in my special writer's book so I wouldn't get caught out with nerves and not come across as a professional.

The big day arrived. I showered four times that morning. I checked my notebook a zillion times. *Answers to possible question?* Check. *Had I added a couple of witty anecdotes?* Check. *Did I have all the facts about male menopause?* Check, Wikipedia and numerous websites had done the job. Aha, they would not fool the wily, old Facing50.

I paced around the gite, waiting for the phone call. They were to call me at just before 5:00 p.m. my time. I had warned Mark and Jeanette about the call, and the children had been carted off to visit friends, just in case the little darlings decided to scream and shout outside while I was live on air.

Prepared as I was, the shrill ring of the phone still made me jump. I grabbed the handset.

"Hello," I breezed. "Amanda Wilson here," I added, hoping I sounded professional.

"Hi Amanda," drawled a voice. "Great to talk to you. This is Bev, the producer of *The Better Health Show*. Are you ready for Dr Dick Fox to ask you some questions?"

"Yes," I replied confidently.

"Okay, then. Standby…"

I listened for Dr Dick. Should I say, "Hi Doc"? or "Hello, Doctor"? I waited for the introduction. Nothing. I strained my ears for an American accent or hint that someone was there. I was met with silence. After a few seconds of shuffling the handset from one sticky hand to the other, I had an urge to cough. I put one hand over the mouthpiece and gave a sharp cough to clear my drying throat. That was better. I took my hand away and looked at my papers with all my notes on them. I wiped my sweaty hand on the leg of my jeans while I gazed at my notes again, ready for the first question. Bother! I needed to blow my nose now, thanks to coughing. I blew as quietly as I could, which wasn't quiet at all, and as I finished my elephant impression, I heard:

"So, welcome, Amanda Wilson. What made you write about this fascinating subject?"

Now what did I say? Flummoxed, I did that fish impression. You know the one—where your mouth just opens and closes. I urged my brain to engage gears.

"Good afternoon." Damn! It is morning over there. "Er, Good Morning. Thank you for inviting me to your show," I replied, looking for my notes. I had taken my glasses off to blow my nose and now couldn't find them. I turned my head about in search of the elusive specs but became entangled in the telephone cord.

Everything was in a fog, as is often the case when I don't wear my glasses. I couldn't see and therefore couldn't use my carefully prepared notes. I was stuffed—snookered—done for. I'd have to ad-lib. I did what any experienced writer would do at an interview—I panicked. The more I panicked, the more I sounded like an idiot.

The interview became less chatty and more intense. This man wanted expert answers to serious medical questions, not flippant comments from some jumped-up woman who lived with a grumpy man. I was out of my depth. By now, Dr Fox, the disembodied voice at the other end of the phone, sounded irked and asked me what I thought I should do to help my husband get through bouts of depression. I should have responded "make him laugh", but instead, I tried to win over the interviewer by using his name. I had read that interviewers like you to use their name. Being a Brit, I felt I should address him politely by his surname. I fumbled about in my befuddled state trying to recall his name...Dick...Dick...

"Well, Dr (slight hesitation as I thought about my answer) Fucks," I began. Hearing my voice echoing back at me through the phone, I felt the radiating heat of embarrassment rise up my neck and into my face where the power of speech completely left me.

I cringe every time I think about the entire episode. I don't think I am cut out to be a celebrity. I must apologise to all of you who tuned in. I hope you will still visit this blog and have not been put off.

It's a good thing I am hidden away here in the middle of nowhere. I feel like Greta Garbo— "I want to be alone!"

Posted by Facing50.Blog

Comments

QuiteContrary says… I am sure it did not go as badly as you felt. On a minor point, Greta Gabo never said, "I want to be alone." She said, "I want to be left alone." There is all the difference. I hope that I haven't offended you.

PhillyFilly says… I heard it. It was hilarious. You are even funnier on the radio than on your blog. I think I might now have some laugh lines, thanks to it. Does Dr Fucks do any surgery or is he one of those other sorts of doctors? He sounded a doll.

Hippyhappyhoppy says… It was the funniest thing I have ever heard. You should take up comedy. Hugs x

SexyFitChick says… Sounded like your mind was on something else—Dr Dick Fucks! You have been alone too long. You clearly need a shag.

Gypsynesters2 says… Missed the interview. We were out yachting in the Atlantic Ocean. The radio couldn't pick it up. Practice makes perfect. You'll be much better prepared for your next interview.

DizzyC says… Is there any way us Brits can listen to a podcast of this? I would love to post it on my blog.

FaerieQueene says… It's a jolly good thing you didn't tell your mother about the interview.. She would have had us all tuned in to it. I promise to say nothing. Don't worry about it. Put it down to experience.

Chapter Thirty-Four

The bed and breakfast was adequate at best. The noisy, old crone who ran it, however, was a nuisance, and Richard decided that if he had not tracked down Amanda Willson by this afternoon, he would look for alternative accommodation. The crone had given him a beady look when she gave him his breakfast of croissant and orange juice. He felt she could see right to the centre of his soul. She was one of those ghastly people who always look like they don't trust you.

He had found the small B&B outside the town of St-Antonin-Noble-Val, and today was market day. He would put money on the fact that Amanda Willson would come to the market. Everyone went to their local market, and this would be hers. He had camped outside the café Gazpacho, which was in a prime position. He could spot any car that came in from the Caylus road. Should he not spot an MG, he would wander down to the car park on the other side of the river and wait there for the remainder of the morning.

The night in the stuffy B&B had made him bad-tempered. It was either that or he was missing the anonymity of the French Riviera. Here, people seemed to watch you as you tried to behave without suspicion. He should have dressed less like a tourist. After all, there weren't many tourists here in this part of France in December. That was the problem—everyone knew each other here. A person from another area stood out like the proverbial sore thumb. This would have been easier during the summer months when the town and surrounding area were filled with strangers. Today, attired in his smart black trousers and leather jacket, he looked like a trendy bank manager from Toulouse.

The barmaid came over to his window seat and asked if he would like anything to drink. There were a few citizens seated outside in spite of the cold weather. The weak sun was shining on the tables, and they were making the most of it. Families with baskets of shopping were meeting up to grab a quick pastis before heading off home and to a large lunch.

He ordered a Ricard. He had grown to like the aniseed drink since he moved to France, and by adding water and ice to it, he could make it last a long time. He read the local paper while he waited. More people came into the café, greeting each other with hearty "bonjours" and clustering around the small bar. Finished now with the newspaper, he replaced it on the bar and returned to his seat in time to observe a white MG, slowly making its way down the road. At last! The MG was having difficulty in making progress through the streets. He could only see the back of the head of the woman driving it but she was wearing a noticeably bright, fuchsia scarf.

Gulping back the remainder of his drink, he tossed a few euros on the table and exited the café in time to see the MG turn left at the end of the road. It was searching for a car parking space; something of a rarity here, it would appear. He was no longer in a hurry. He would catch up with her here at the market. There couldn't be many bright fuchsia scarves.

Bibi had arrived later than she intended at the market. There were no spaces left. She should have brought the Peugeot, not the MG. She didn't want to get it marked so she navigated her way with particular care through the thronging masses, who, carrying wicker baskets of vegetables, ambled across the main road, oblivious to the traffic.

She succeeded in finding a space on the far side of the river near the restaurant Festin de Babette. She also discovered her friend Amanda, who was looking less cheerful than usual. Stopping off for a quick coffee at the main square, Amanda told her all about the terrible interview she had given earlier that week. Bibi thought it was a hilarious story once she understood the mistake. She felt sorry for her little English friend, though. Amanda had been trying so hard to be good at her art and her writing. She always made Bibi laugh, and at the moment that was a difficult task.

Amanda was now regaling her with some jokes that her son had sent her. She didn't often speak about Tom. Bibi sensed that although she loved her son, there was some reluctance to chat about him as a mother normally would. Bibi was relieved, though, that Amanda seldom spoke about her son, especially as Bibi had no one to talk about. Amanda's mother was another cause for mirth. No wonder Amanda was so funny. Amanda had pulled out her phone and revealed some photographs on it that should have been X-rated. What was Amanda's mother doing with her arms around a muscular body and a bottle in her hand?

As they stood up to leave the café, Bibi's scarf tumbled to the ground where it lay until Amanda spotted it and handed it back to Bibi.

"This is beautiful, Bibi. You don't want it to get trodden on. What a gorgeous colour it is."

"You like it?"

"Yes, it's cheerful and colourful—just the thing for a December day," replied Amanda holding it up to admire it. The colour looked good against her complexion and brought out the green in her eyes.

"Take it. It is yours. Yes, really. It suits you much better than me. You can have it as a present for doing so well on the radio show and making everyone laugh. One day you will be a great comedienne."

Amanda caressed the pink scarf, placed it around her neck, and asked, "Are you sure?"

"Of course, I am. I have hundreds of scarves. I don't like this one as much as my red or blue or green or yellow and black—"

'"Okay, I get the message," laughed Amanda.

Bibi fussed over Amanda, tying the scarf correctly so it looked stylish. "There, now you look like a French woman."

Richard Montagu-Forbes was hovering near the display of French cheeses on a stall in the middle of the market. He spotted the scarf before he saw the woman. She was with a friend, a sensational brunette. What a pity she wasn't the one. Still, if this was Amanda Willson, she was certainly passable. She was probably late forties or early fifties with blonde hair. Judging by her demeanour, she seemed lively and gregarious. She was laughing hysterically with the dark-haired beauty. He listened carefully to the two women, trying to pick up on their conversation. Straining his ears, he finally heard what he had been waiting for.

"Oh Amanda, I don't know what I would do without your sense of humour. Now, I am going to get some vegetables. Would you like to come to lunch at our house or would you like to eat on your own again at yours?"

He had found the woman he had been looking for. Richard rubbed his hands together, smiled at the cheese seller and hurried off after the dark-haired beauty. She stopped by the vegetable stall near the newsagent where she was now scrutinizing the beans and feeling the tomatoes expertly. He flashed his best smile at her.

"I am so sorry to trouble you, but I noticed you were with someone I think I know. Was that Amanda Willson I saw you talking to?"

The woman relaxed slightly.

"Yes, how do you know Amanda?"

"We, that is to say, my wife used to exercise at the same gym as Amanda. My wife will be tickled pink when I tell her Amanda is here. They used to swim together at the centre and were good friends. I'm just about to meet her for coffee. She'd love to see Amanda again. She moved away some time ago, though. She's living here in St-Antonin-Noble-Val, isn't she?"

"No, not here, she's up the road in a hamlet, Beaulieu. It's not far from Caylus. You should visit her. I'll tell her I met you if you like."

"No, no. Don't do that. I'd like it to be a surprise. Would you mind keeping it a secret for now? I'll tell Fiona, and we'll drop in unexpectedly if we get the chance. We're only here for a couple of days. I wouldn't want Amanda to get excited at the prospect of seeing us and then let down because we don't show."

"I understand. Well, goodbye, and as we say here, *Bonne Vacances, Monsieur...?*"

"Footherley, Simon Footherley. Lovely to have met you Mademoiselle," replied Richard, acting the part of a goofy Brit rather well and shaking her hand firmly. "*Au revoir.*"

Bibi thought no more about her encounter with the bespectacled stranger. If you had asked her to describe him, she would not have been able to pick out any remarkable detail. Richard Montagu-Forbes was a chameleon when he needed to be, and now he hurried away unnoticed to his hire car to check out Beaulieu.

Chapter Thirty-Five

He pulled up in a lay-by on the outskirts of the hamlet. It was one of those places you could walk around without being noticed. On first impression, the hamlet seemed to be abandoned. Every stone house had its external, painted shutters closed. The only sign of life came from the cats, lying on the steps and balefully watching his climb to the church, their half-closed eyes taking in his progress as he crossed to the square in front of the church and stood outside the bakery. A chalked board in the baker's window notified him of opening times. It would not open again until Tuesday. He heard a child's plaintive voice coming from a garden. It was an English voice. The cats stretched lazily and continued to observe through slit eyes.

The only signs of life came from the large farmhouse at one end of the hamlet. There was an aroma of cooked chicken permeating the air. The house stood next to a nicely renovated cottage. Made from the same local grey stone as all the other properties, this one was brighter and cleaner. The house had been sand blasted recently and had freshly-painted, wooden frames. The shutters were pulled to rather than latched. Adjoining the cottage, but separated by a tall hedge, was a gravel parking area. Weeds pushed through the small stones, and brambles covered the far end. This turned out to be the communal car park. There were no vehicles in it. He noted, however, a large camper van standing under an open barn near the cottage, a GB sticker on its rear bumper. It probably belonged to the family in the farmhouse.

There was no sign of Amanda Willson either. She had already left for lunch with that striking woman he had met. Knowing how long French families took to eat, he

265

worked out that she wouldn't return for hours. It was difficult to know which property was hers even though there weren't many to choose from. There were no locals about that he could question. He heard a donkey bray nearby. The cats had lost interest in him and were lazing about, some licking their paws and some dozing. He would have to return the following day. Then he could be more certain.

Amanda had not gone to Bibi's home for lunch as Richard believed. What he hadn't heard, when he had been attempting to eavesdrop, was her excited whisper that although she would love to have lunch with her friend, she was going to the Toulouse airport to collect Phil. He was coming back and would be staying until the New Year.

After she parted from Bibi and before Richard had found his way to Beaulieu, she had shot back to the cottage, grabbed a shower, jumped in Mark's car and headed towards the airport to meet Phil. She sang along to *Nostalgie* Radio as she headed towards the motorway, and the closer she got, the quicker her heart beat. Would Phil be pleased to see her? Would he like the surprise she had arranged?

Phil tumbled out of Departures, carrying a small holdall. Even in December, he had decided to wear a jacket rather than a coat. His tie was askew, and his cheeks flushed. She knew better than to run into his arms. This was Phil. He didn't do romantic reunions. He smiled at her, gave her a quick hug and then moaned about his trip to the airport in the UK.

"Bloody road was crawling with traffic, even on a Sunday. You'd think people would have something better to do than drive about on a weekend. Why don't they do something useful like wash their cars or take their kids to the local park for a walk? I suppose they're all going shopping.

It's the national pastime, flaming shopping," he droned all the way through the airport building.

The airport in the UK had been chock-a-block with travelers, all trying to get away for Christmas. He complained every year about the commercialism of Christmas. He'd be all right here. The French hadn't put Christmas trees up until December the first, and shops were decorated prettily, yet lacked the materialistic push that was so familiar in the UK. He ranted all the way through the car park until he reached the car when he suddenly breathed in deeply, announced he was very happy to be back in France, and gave Amanda a proper hug before jumping in the driver's side.

"I don't want to be scared off back to the UK straight away, thanks to your driving, do I?" he joked and winked at Amanda.

They reached the hamlet where a jet-propelled Ted shot out from the veranda directly into Phil's stomach. Dropping quickly to the floor, he bounced up and down as if on springs.

"Ted!" he exclaimed. "You haven't forgotten me, even after all this time."

"He is a wise, old dog, who doesn't forget his friends or his stepparents, do you Ted? Mark and Jeanette have invited us to supper, but first you might like to unwind with a glass of wine and a bath."

"Just the ticket. Actually, there was one other thing I would really like to do before I have a bath or a glass of wine," he stated, pulling Amanda towards him and dropping his lips onto hers.

The following day Amanda had her surprise all lined up for Phil. It was to be his Christmas present. Mark had given them full use of the Peugeot again, and she had planned a trip to the mountains for just the two of them. They would spend time at Ax-les-Thermes over Christmas and the New Year. Mark and Jeanette could celebrate their family Christmas without worrying about Phil and Amanda, and Phil and Amanda could let someone else serve them Christmas lunch and have a well-deserved holiday in a wintery, romantic resort.

Phil was a new man. They had made love five times in the last 48 hours, which by her reckoning hadn't happened since Tom had been born. If work and being away from her was going to turn him into a new sex fiend, then she was a very happy woman. He was currently engrossed in the details of flying. He was describing how the pedals controlled the ailerons and how the navigation system worked. He had lost her at the word aileron, but she nodded cheerfully as he simultaneously drove and explained the rudiments of flying.

They started a new game en route. Phil had to learn the phonetic alphabet as part of his training. He'd shown her the list the night before. Being quick on the uptake, Amanda now knew most of it, too, and in order to ensure he knew it well enough, they devised a daft game in which they wouldn't say words but would spell out the letters of the word using the phonetic alphabet.

"There's another Romeo, Echo, November, Alpha, Uniform, Lima, Tango," commented Phil as they progressed towards the mountains.

"There are hundreds of those. But you don't see many Bravo, Mike, Whiskeys," replied Amanda.

"Fancy a Sierra, Hotel, Alpha, Golf?"

"Tusk, tusk. Not while you're driving."

"We could always stop off in one of those *aire de repos* places."

"No, families stop there all the time. We'd get spotted by some French child staring through the window of the car while we were at it. Seeing my unfettered backside could give them nightmares."

"Boo. Are you sure because I am feeling a little Romeo, Alpha, November, Delta, Yankee? There is nothing the matter with your bottom as it happens," he added.

Amanda sat back in her seat, admired the view of the mountains which were fast approaching and looked forward to arriving at the hotel. Then she could give Phil his surprise.

BLOG: Fortifying Your Fifties

Late December

So, Phil has managed to come over here for a few weeks of R&R in France. I've been looking forward to this trip because I thought it would relax the dear soul and maybe even give him some different interests. Being so close to the Pyrenees, I saw this as a golden opportunity for Phil to take up a brand new hobby—skiing.

He loves the mountains, fresh air, blue skies, and hot cocoa, so it seemed a natural choice. I didn't exactly inform him completely. He was under the impression we were going for a short trip to the mountains to take photographs, drive into Andorra, slob about at the hotel, and enjoy the beautiful landscape that is still covered in snow this time of year. I, of course, had booked him a surprise—a skiing lesson.

Once I found out that Phil was coming over a few weeks ago, I succeeded in telephoning the resort at Ax-les-Thermes at the foot of the Pyrenees. A helpful Frenchman answered the telephone, and I explained I needed to book a lesson for a beginner on Tuesday morning, the day after we arrived at Ax-les-Thermes.

"E's never skied before?" he asked.

"No, so he'll be very excited when he finds out," I told him with my fingers crossed behind my back.

It was a cracking morning. The sun was rising, and the sky was a wonderful pinkish-orange colour. Phil was already enjoying being in the mountains. Ax-les-Thermes, typically alpine with pretty buildings, was once an old spa town. I subtly suggested that as it was such a magnificent morning, we should continue a short way to the ski station as we would be sure to get a nice, hot chocolate there and a great view of the mountains. Poor old gullible Phil carried on, oblivious to his treat.

Once at the ski station, I was surprised to see so many people. I should have anticipated it with its being Christmas time and all, but I thought the French liked hanging out with their relatives at this time of the year. The place was heaving. Parents and children were marching up to the ski lifts, skis over their shoulders and determination written across their faces. I dragged Phil to the nearest café, and as he breathed a sigh of contentment and drank his mug of hot chocolate, I told him that I had arranged a lesson for him.

The news didn't quite get the reaction I had hoped for. Phil tried to claim he was too old to ski. I pointed out the aged French people who were snowboarding down the slope. He said that he had no equipment. I had thought of that and had arranged a hire at the local ski shop. So, having run out of excuses and having decided that it actually might be fun, Phil and I sauntered over to get him kitted out. I think we should have arrived there a little earlier as there didn't seem to be much choice left. Never mind, Phil was sorted out rapidly and efficiently by a hassled Frenchwoman, who literally threw his garments at him, having cast a cursory look at him and deciding he was *petit* (small).

Looking very fetching in a tight, red ski suit and bright green boots, Phil was marched over to the ski school, although a little late, for his lesson. I explained to the woman on the desk that I had booked a beginner's lesson. She looked somewhat confused and asked if it was for Phil.

"Of course," I replied. Well it wasn't going to be for me dressed in my snug, fake fur coat, was it? The woman looked vaguely amused. Phil's attire must have been slightly more outrageous than I thought. Maybe the orange and pink hat was too much with the red suit and the bright green boots after all. At least he'd stand out in the crowd.

"Are you sure he wants to join this class?" she inquired.

"Well, of course. He's come all the way from the UK to do this."

She looked very surprised.

"It's a sort of present. He's always wanted to learn to ski," I continued, looking at Phil who was checking his clips on his boots in a thorough fashion. "He *is* booked for this lesson, isn't he? It would be awful if you haven't got him down, especially as we drove two and a half hours to get here." I can be very persuasive when I try. She nodded reluctantly.

"Now, shall I leave him here or should he go to a meeting point?"

"He needs to attach his name tag to his coat," she declared thrusting a large luggage type label at me. "Jean-Marie will be his instructor, and you'll find him just outside the back here with the other students in his group. He's wearing a pink hat."

Ah! Phil wouldn't look that outrageous after all then.

I thanked her and dragged Phil outside. Jean-Marie was indeed just outside with his students. He was wearing a pink furry bear costume and a pink hat. His students were all about ten years old. Phil joined the class, looking confused.

"Don't worry. There'll surely be some adults joining in a minute."

I scooted back to reception to check that Phil was in the right place.

"Oh, yes, Madame," the girl assured me. "You see, because it is the holiday week, we only run courses for children. Normally, we don't take adults on these days, but because you have come from so far away just to ski, I put

273

him in the class with the oldest children, and at the end of his lesson, he will earn a certificate and a *flocon* (a small snowflake badge) to prove he can ski. It will be a nice memento," she continued, grinning at me.

I sneaked off out the front before Phil could twig what had happened. He seemed to be listening to Jean-Marie intently. Later I took his photograph as he came down the nursery slope with a half smile on his face, the last in a line of children following a large pink bear, each one performing a snow plough proudly for his *flocon* badge.

P.S. I have disabled the comments section today because I know you will all be honking with laughter at poor Phil, and I feel very guilty about putting him through this. I can imagine what you will all be thinking, and yes, I am being a spoilsport by preventing you from having your say. Sorry! FaerieQueene, if you are reading this, don't you dare tell my mother!

Posted by Facing50.Blog

No Comments Allowed

Chapter Thirty-Six

Red mist descended in front of his eyes. He would have to sit down. When he was like this, he was capable of committing heinous acts, and he really shouldn't draw any more attention to himself. He pummelled the dashboard with clenched fists, his face contorted in rage. How dare she!

According to the child he had just questioned, Amanda Willson had gone away for a few days. He had returned Monday evening and found no MG car. The hamlet was silent. Street lights illuminated the picturesque scene, and light snow fell, drifting casually onto the streets. Richard waited in his car in the communal car park, huddled in a large, dark coat. With the engine off, he got steadily colder and colder. *Where was the damn woman?*

The following day, he returned. Again, he found no sign of life save for a couple of children who were playing near the cottage. One was attempting to ride his large, plastic tractor, struggling to control the wheel with his mittened hands. The other was throwing sticks and twigs for a black dog that sat beside them. The dog wasn't interested in chasing after sticks. He was far too old for that.

"Let me have a go," shouted the smaller one, bored now with the dog.

"In a minute," replied the other, making a throaty, growling noise like the engine of the tractor. "You can have it when I have fetched the hay."

He pedalled the tractor to the end of the path and dismounted to collect a large, green ball, which represented the hay bale.

"Hi," called Richard, casually strolling up to the children.

The first child ignored him, and lifting the ball with a grunt, dropped it into the trailer, which was attached to the tractor. He got back onto his seat and made the same growling noise he had made earlier. He refused to acknowledge Richard.

"He's a farmer," explained the younger child simply.

"Oh, I see. What a smart tractor you have, farmer. Do you need any help on your farm?"

The boy continued with his tractor noise and drove past Richard towards the farmhouse behind the cottage.

Richard tried again to engage him in conversation. "I am a shepherd, and I have lots of sheep. Would you like them for your farm?"

The first child didn't reply.

"Where are your sheep?" demanded the smaller boy, prodding the black dog with a stick. The dog let him tap his rump good-naturedly.

"In a field. Is your dog a sheep dog?"

The boy laughed. "He's not good at running now. He likes sleeping."

"He looks like a good dog. I bet he could be a good sheep dog."

The boy giggled again and shook his head. "I was a sheep at Christmas at nursery. I wanted to be a wise man, but I was a sheep."

"Sheep are just as important as wise men," continued Richard. The first boy looked like he might be going inside the house, probably to tell his mother that there was a strange man loitering outside. He didn't have long.

"Listen," he said to the smaller boy. "I can't find my friend here. She lives here, but I don't know where. Do you know any ladies here?"

The boy nodded wisely, pleased to be considered more important than his older brother. "There is the old lady

276

who lives with the cats, the lady with the donkey, Mummy, Amanda..."

"Amanda, that's her. That's her name, Amanda Willson." Richard looked up to see a woman looking out of a farmhouse window. He waved at her so she didn't think he was too suspicious. "Where does Amanda live?"

"Here," replied the boy, pointing to the cottage in front of them. "But she is not here. She has gone to the mountains. She went yesterday to go skiing. She went with a man. We are going to the mountains, too. Daddy says we can go soon to see the snow. I am going sledging with Daddy."

The man waved again at the woman who was coming out of the house with her elder son.

"Sorry to trouble you. I was looking for a café, but there isn't one here in this hamlet." He shouted affably and shrugged innocently. "Nice children. You should be proud of them."

Jeanette put a protective arm around both the children as the second one ran back to her and hugged her. "What did that man want?"

"He is a farmer. He has sheep. He wanted to know if Ted was a good sheep dog," he giggled.

The red mist swirled around his head some more, then little by little, his vision returned and with it clarity of thought. The anger wouldn't subside. It would remain locked inside until he felt vindicated. She had led him on. She had encouraged his interest. He had wasted precious time on her. She had told him there was no man in her life. She had lied to him. No one, but no one, lied to him. He would take revenge on her. He would make her wish she had never heard of Richard Montagu-Forbes.

Chapter Thirty-Seven

Amanda hadn't been too upset to say goodbye to Phil. They had spent just over a week in the mountains, and it had been one of the nicest times they had had together. Christmas had come and gone without the usual razzmatazz that she had endured for years. This year she hadn't spent weeks searching for appropriate Christmas presents for her family. She hadn't suffered the queues in supermarkets as she attempted to buy traditional Christmas food that no one seemed to enjoy on the day.

Christmas was for children. It was for young families. This year Tom had delighted in being at home with only Alice for company. They had phoned on Christmas Day to say they were just going down to the pub and then were going to spend the afternoon playing a game of Monopoly. They were happy to just be together and not have the pressures of having to visit families.

The conversation had been pleasant. Phil had hogged the phone and spent considerable time reminding Tom to make sure the house got plenty of air and asking if the heating was working properly. He had asked about the condensation on the windows and had checked that Tom had been wiping it off each morning. The windows always got condensation on them during the cold months. If you didn't clean it up, it would turn to mould.

Amanda had managed a few words with them both before they had to go. Tom and Alice had sent her a pair of soft, woollen gloves and a matching hat to wear when she walked Ted. Phil had received a smart leather appointment diary. He had spent all morning filling in his forthcoming meetings with his new Dupont pen that Amanda had given him.

279

Phil had splashed out and ordered some fine, French champagne with their meal at the hotel restaurant on Christmas Day. After lunch, they had walked around Ax-les-Thermes, listening to the river rushing over the stones that made up the river bed and admiring the huge, lit Christmas tree that stood in the square. French families had also been taking afternoon strolls and had been meandering around the town, nodding politely to Phil and Amanda as they passed by. It had been Phil's idea of perfection. No Christmas nonsense. No Christmas repeats on television and no Brussels sprouts!

They had been up to the slopes, which were filled with holiday makers staying in chalets, who had escaped for a few days skiing. The second day after they arrived, she had taken him to Bonascre, the ski slope next to the town, and surprised him with a skiing lesson. It hadn't been what they expected, but it had provided marvellous fodder for her blog. Phil hadn't skied again. He had preferred watching others race down the slopes on snowboards and skis. He would sooner sit at a café with a hot chocolate in front of him.

They had rung in the New Year with the crowd at the hotel. The French families there had made them feel very welcome. The meal had been extremely elaborate with several courses, which stretched over several hours. Amanda had kept the menu as a souvenir. Neither of them had eaten such a feast before. There had been fine egg mousse, raw and cooked green asparagus, and black truffle paste soldiers as a starter. This had been followed by langoustines wrapped in nori with foie gras foam in a crustacean broth. Next, they had been served line-caught sea bass with imperial caviar, green cabbage, and whipped lemon butter. The waiters and waitresses had then come around with Beauce hare à la Royale, celery root, and chestnut-stuffed conchiglioni pasta. Just when they had thought they might explode, aged Brie de

Meaux with walnuts had turned up. They had then been given a light, pink champagne granité, gilt grapefruit, and hibiscus jelly to cleanse the palate. Amanda hadn't been able to eat the soft coconut cream, strawberry, and wild strawberry elixir, so Phil had helped her out with it. Just in case there was anyone still hungry, waiters had deposited trays and dishes of sweets, stuffed fruit, and chocolates on each table.

A group of musicians had played traditional music, and the dancing began. Just before midnight, the waiters had reappeared with silly hats and confetti, which they distributed, and everyone had counted down to the New Year together. After that, there had been considerable commotion as everyone in the room exchanged handshakes or kisses and wished each other a *Bonne Année*.

It had been a thoroughly enjoyable experience, but now that the New Year had begun, Phil was ready and anxious to go home. She felt he was becoming distant again. She spoke to him on several occasions, but he failed to respond—too deep in thought to hear her. He had work on his mind and was refocusing on what he had to do when he returned. She understood. It was best to have had a few fabulous days together. When she got back to the UK, there would be plenty of days to become used to each other again. This had been like a mini-honeymoon.

They drove from the Pyrenees directly to the airport. Phil checked in, collected his ticket for his flight, and suggested she make her way back to Beaulieu. There was no need for her to hang around the airport with him. He'd go through to departures and catch up on some reading for his flying exam. He held her arms briefly and gave her a peck on the cheek. "Romantic Phil" had left the building; "Business Phil" had replaced him. It was time for her to go back to her writing; after all, she had one or two funny tales to tell, and she couldn't wait to see Bibi again.

She'd enjoyed being with Phil, and she recognised the fact that she would soon have to face up to her normal life again. She would need to go home. It was a fresh new year, and she should be making positive plans. It was a different year to last year. She didn't have to worry about her husband, and her son was less of a concern, too. She had far more to look forward to than the previous year.

Phil had requested she find a buyer for Bertie. Mark had plenty of contacts, and Phil didn't want to continue on his trip through Europe now. He would rather sell the camper van and use the money for something else—like learning to fly. Amanda agreed. Bertie would be put up for sale, she would complete her book and a few articles for magazines, and then she would return home. She was probably ready to start over again back in the UK. She just needed a few more weeks of peace and tranquility. Then she would join her family. After all, that was where she belonged.

Chapter Thirty-Eight

Mathilde was talking to Didier on the telephone in hushed tones. Bibi couldn't hear the conversation, but Mathilde often spoke to her son conspiratorially like this so she was not unduly anxious. Besides, she was completely fed up with Didier. She could almost not be bothered with the pretence of their marriage. It left her both furious and paradoxically, deeply upset. When she was feeling vulnerable, she would try to fathom out what she could possibly have done so wrong to chase Didier away into the arms of another woman. Other times she did not care. He was a stupid, old fool who was having a mid-life crisis. He was a cradle-snatching idiot. She had been on an emotional roller coaster now for weeks, and it was time to get off.

After weeks of attempting to win him round and getting nowhere, she had made up her mind to live her life as she wanted and to no longer be tied to Didier and his demanding mother. Her venture had come to her while she was sitting with Amanda. They had been attempting to paint a watercolour each of the old ruin at Penne, a charming castle that had all but fallen down. The location was superb, and if you were in the right position, you could paint the castle perched high on the hill with the river flowing beneath it.

Amanda was pensive. She had daubed light smudges representing trees onto her canvas and was now concentrating on the hillside. She had come a long way in a short time. She was very quick to learn, and assisted by Bibi, she had produced some sweet watercolours that could grace anyone's walls.

"Bibi, you are a genius. I couldn't have managed this without your guidance," squealed Amanda when she finished her painting and sat back to admire it. "You are a fantastic teacher. You could do this for a living, that is, if you ever had to earn a living, which of course you don't because you are fabulously wealthy and live with the delicious Didier," burbled Amanda. "You could display your paintings in a huge studio and teach others how to produce such masterpieces. You'd look fantastic in a smock, wearing glasses."

For one moment, Bibi almost blurted out her problems to Amanda. Amanda would have understood and been sympathetic, but Bibi was not used to revealing her emotions. She was used to getting her own way and not having to try very hard to get it either. Instead, she had smiled graciously, but the thought had been planted; later, when she sat in her small studio at home, she had made the big decision. Since then, she had been looking at shops for rent. She fancied setting up a small gallery—one where she would display works by local talent and of course, some of her own paintings. There were plenty of tourists who would snap up an original painting by a talented French artist. Her work had already commanded interest from those who had viewed it. If Didier expected her to be nothing more than a mere servant for his mother, then he could think again. She had been patient for far too long. It was time for the caged bird to fly.

She had circled some potential rental opportunities in *La Depeche du Midi*—the daily newspaper in Toulouse and intended to visit them today. She would also visit some estate agents to see what they had to offer. She needed more than trips to the salon to get her nails done and cooking for Mathilde to stimulate her. She had been twiddling her thumbs for far too long. As for Didier, she would bide her time for the moment and stay at the house, but as soon as this venture was up and running, she would most certainly rent an apartment near the new studio, or preferably over it, and leave Didier.

She was sorry that she had severed contact with Richard Montagu-Forbes. She could have visited him on the Riviera. They had shared a passion for art and culture that evaded Didier. In fact, the more she thought about it, the more she wondered what she had ever had in common with Didier. If she went to Nice, she could look Richard up but this time as Bibi, not as Amanda Willson.

Mathilde had replaced the receiver and was fiddling uncomfortably with a ball of wool. She had been crocheting when the telephone had rung.

"Didier has to go to Antibes on business again. He'll be back the day after tomorrow." Mathilde's eyes were rheumy, and she seemed fatigued today, which Bibi had not noticed earlier.

Raising her eyebrows dramatically, she responded, "Ah, as always, precious work."

Mathilde didn't defend Didier with her usual fire. It was standard practice for her to support her son's actions by reminding Bibi that without Didier's hard work, there would be no trips to the salon and no fine wines in the cellar. This time she merely nodded.

"Did he say anything else?" Bibi demanded.

Mathilde shook her head again and looked at her ball of wool, which she carefully balanced on the table next to her crochet hook.

"I am going to make a tisane," she replied finally. "Would you like one?"

Unusual as it was that Mathilde had offered to make a drink for her, Bibi had to refuse. Her first appointment was at 11:00 a.m., and she had an hour's drive to get to Toulouse. She declined the offer of a drink and patted Mathilde's hand affectionately. Mathilde was not open to showing displays of

285

affection and offering to make a tisane was as close as she got to it. Bibi appreciated it and at any other time would have gladly joined the old lady. Today was different, though.

"I'm sorry, but I really must go out now," she explained. "I'll make sure I am back by mid-afternoon, though, and maybe we could have one together then. I'll buy us a nice cake or tart to go with it."

Mathilde supported herself against the door frame, and in a voice that was barely above a whisper she said, "I'd like that. Thank you."

Just when did Mathilde suddenly become so old? Bibi pondered as she headed through Montauban. She had always seemed so youthful, so fierce, and full of gumption. It was probably because she was on her own so much at the moment. No doubt she would soon be back to her old self when Didier returned. She missed him when he stayed away. That was probably the reason for her acting strangely. Bibi didn't dwell too long on these thoughts, though, because the open roads of the motorway beckoned, and she opened up the throttle on the MG to enjoy the ride.

Chapter Thirty-Nine

The flight attendant politely addressed the family with the screaming toddler as they finally exited the aircraft, "Thank you for flying with Air France/KLM. Have a nice stay in Toulouse." The child had screeched nonstop from Paris. The parents had tried to ease the wails, but it had continued to scream so loudly that at one point it actually went blue with rage. It must have superb lungs. Todd had decided it would make a great underwater diver someday. He had been unfortunate enough to be seated slap bang next to the family. Since the flight was stuffed full, there was no way he could change his seat.

The air stewardesses had been very grateful that he had not complained, but quite frankly, he had travelled for so many hours now that not even a pneumatic drill piercing his eardrum could have prevented him from dozing off for an hour on the short flight from Paris. Come to think of it, the kid had been almost as noisy as a pneumatic drill.

The child was now cradled in his father's arms, head slumped on his father's shoulder. He had fallen asleep as soon as the plane began its descent. The parents stumbled out of the plane, carrying all that palaver that travelling parents always needed to carry: a large bag containing drinks, snacks, games, books, and toys; plus nappy changing stuff, blanket, extra clothes, wipes to clean up inevitable messes; and of course, the obligatory soft, cuddly toy, which was usually the same size as the child.

"Thank you for flying with Air France/KLM. Have a nice stay in Toulouse," repeated the stewardess. Then seeing it was Todd who was exiting, she treated him to an extra wide smile.

"Thank you. I am sure I'll have a great time," he replied.

The journey had been horrendously lengthy. Even having stopped off in Singapore for a few days and again in Paris, Todd was feeling the effects of being cramped up for hours on end. It wasn't in his nature to sit still for too long. He had upgraded his seat to Business Class from Sydney to Singapore and again from Singapore to Paris, but even then, the journey had been most uncomfortable. He had watched all the movies on his small personal screen instead of sleeping. Dressed in his ultra-soft Qantas pyjamas, or slumber suit as some called it, doled out to Business Class passengers, he attempted to sleep, but it evaded him. He refused the evening meal in case that would keep him awake, but in the end, it was the actual seat that kept him from any shuteye. He couldn't seem to get comfortable enough, even though its position could be controlled, and it could be transformed into a bed. Todd got it as flat as possible but felt it was like a narrow coffin. Once that thought entered his head, sleep evaded him. The discomfort, combined with the hefty snores of the adjacent overweight businessman, gave him no choice other than to watch the offerings on the screen.

He was now "filmed up", and his shoulder was sore. He would try and find a hotel with a gym. He could do with a workout. His leg muscles were seized up from all the sitting around. He had done the stretches he had been shown and had walked about the cabin as much as was physically possible when you have to keep diving off to avoid the trolleys and the other passengers.

His luggage had actually made it all the way to Toulouse without getting lost. Things were looking great. Following the signs, he found his way to the car rental desk and handed over his reservation number. He had booked the car via the internet. It was just a basic Group A car, one small enough to weave about the lanes and roads, but he had added a GPS to his package for good measure. He'd need to find his way about, and navigating French traffic would be bad enough without trying to find towns and villages of which he had never heard.

Before long, he was directed to bay 218 where he discovered he had rented a silver Renault Twingo. It was a far cry from his Cadillac truck. Digit would hate this car. He was used to sitting in the back of the truck with his tongue out, ears flapping in the breeze, barking at other dogs. Good thing he wasn't here. He hoped Digit was behaving and wasn't missing him too much.

The controls on the vehicle took some working out. He sat figuring out what each of them did. Hire cars never come with manuals; you are expected to just leap into them and drive them. After mixing up the indicator and windscreen wiper a few times and attempting to tune the radio into something that had music on it, he was ready to go.

This was it. He would finally catch up with and see Mandy after all these years. What a surprise it would be for her, for him, for both of them. He checked his reflection in the rearview mirror. He still looked jaded from the travelling. He should give it a day or two before he tracked her down. He wanted to be on form when he met her, not look like a wreck. He'd check into a hotel for a couple of days and recover from the jet lag first.

Chapter Forty

"Oh, Celia, must you chew gum? Spit it out immediately."

The sulky-faced model walked to the bin, withdrew the grey blob in one long string and plopped it into the bin. She sauntered back behind the chair, resumed her pose, and stared into the lens.

"Super, sweetie. Now, look at me. Follow the camera. That's it… and…head back. Look over your shoulder. Lovely. Smile…and again. Think of something funny. Think of Spencer dressed in that poncho. There… lovely, that's a super smile. Head back again. Show me that beautiful smile. Lovely, sweetie. These are amazing. I'm happy with these. Thank you."

Amanda's mother was waiting to one side, watching. Grego was standing next to her. She squeezed his hand.

"It's a fantastic collection. You'll be a huge success."

"I couldn't have even got it together without your help and support. Yours and Spencer's," he added as Spencer came into view carrying a floral tray on top of which were perched two china cups and a small plate of biscuits. Looking at her more closely, he asked, "Are you okay? You seem quieter than normal."

"No, I'm absolutely fine. I'm as tough as old boots. I ate too much of Reni's moussaka last night. It lay on my stomach for a while and prevented me from getting a full night's sleep."

Grego laughed. "Reni's moussaka is well known for that. Why do you think I always abstain?" He laughed and patted her fondly on the shoulder.

Part of the collection was being photographed. The rest of the collection would remain under wraps—hush-hush until the day of the show, but these few shots were meant to tantalize the public and the press, who would be attending what had become one of the most important events on Cyprus. If all went to plan, Grego would become a household name overnight.

The idea had been the brainchild of Grace, Amanda's mother. Italian-born Grego had wanted to pitch his creations to a well-known fashion house, but Grace suggested he show them as an individual at the Cyprus fashion week. He had been running his own boutique in Cyprus, selling fashion wear for several years, and was considered a local. He offered all sorts of labels for men and women, and people knew him well but not for this—not for this hidden talent that had been coaxed out of him. Cyprus fashion week was an appropriate time for him to launch himself as a local designer.

Grace had pointed out that Cypriots adore designer labels as much as they love supporting a local name made good. Since Cyprus Fashion Week made its grand entrance in March 2008, it had become a permanent, twice-yearly fixture. The Cypriot dispensation for latching on to anything new made the event an instant success, and the society pages were filled with photos of sharply dressed, fashion industry insiders, editors, and pop stars out in force. Having not been to the event, she spoke to her own friends about it. Some of them had attended the catwalk shows in the exhibition space in the Famagusta Gate Cultural Centre and raved about it. Further research led her to convince Grego that this was exactly where he should reveal his collection *Yesteryear*: centre stage in Nicosia.

Yesteryear had kept them occupied for months. Grego was the actual designer, but he had taken much of his inspiration from some individual patterns that Grace had made in her own youth. On a tight budget and with money better spent on food, she had bought cheap fabrics and fashioned them into clothes for her and for Amanda. She had not wanted to spend money on patterns either so she had not only copied some designs from magazines, but had also used her own imagination to create designs based on the fashion of the day. She had first produced the tracing paper patterns that she would use and then the clothes. Over the years, she had amassed a huge pile of patterns, which she willingly handed over to Grego when she first learned of his passion for sewing. Together they had shared nights together over several glasses of wine while she showed him old photographs of clothes she had made on her Singer sewing machine.

Out of nostalgia, she had kept several items, particularly the matching capes she had made for her and Amanda with caps fabricated from the same material. She had kept quite a few clothes she had made as sets for mother and daughter. They served to remind her of her time as a proud mother and wife. Grego had gushed over the fabrics, the colours and the designs and with her permission, had created designs based on her own. He brought in fabrics from Italy and working with his team, created new textile designs, which would make him stand out from the other designers. The style of the seventies and the new textiles were a fabulous combination, and even Grace had to admit he had an uncanny knack for transforming a tired idea into something vibrant.

She relished being part of the team, too. She may have been seventy-eight, but she had felt half that age since she had come over to Cyprus to assist with the range. She had learned so much, and everyone had fussed over her. You would have thought at times that she was the designer, not

293

Grego. It had done her good. She had somehow managed to fulfill an ambition—one that had not dared reveal itself until now. It would have been Shangri-La to have been a fashion designer when she was younger and been part of this dynamic community, but had she gone in this direction, she would not have been able to enjoy her life with Amanda's father or indeed, to have had Amanda. No, she didn't regret following the path she had chosen. You can, after all, only travel one path at a time, and now she could participate in the fun at a time when there was little else in her life.

She was aware that time was running out. Each morning she woke, relieved to have made it through another night, and although she felt alive when she was working with the boys, she noticed that her health was gradually declining. The night before, she had been unusually tired, bone-weary tired and had gone to bed early instead of staying up until after midnight as was often the case. She had woken at ten o' clock and spent the remainder of the night awake. Night fears had gnawed at her. She had opened her Christmas gift from Amanda—the latest Terry Pratchett, an author who could always raise a smile. Instead of it transporting her to another world where she could forget her anxieties, as was often the case with his books, she had been plagued by terrifying thoughts. She had risen early, unable to lie in bed frightened any longer and had stood by the sink to make a cup of tea. Being alone and old was not for the faint-hearted. She wasn't sure how she had managed to last this length of time on her own. It had been dreadful since she had lost Amanda's father. The emptiness threatened to suffocate her some days, and in spite of what people may say, time would never heal the void left by his departure. Grace mourned him every day, so she had surrounded herself with people and distractions. To the casual observer, she was the light and soul of the party. She adored the company of others, craved it even, but some days, or more accurately, some nights, it was so hard to face old age and solitude.

The sky was just beginning to shake off its dark cloak, and she could hear the first stirrings of the family in the apartment above her when the pain had struck—intense heat followed by a tightness that took her breath away from her. Her chest was being squeezed and crushed in a vice-like grip by an invisible python. It had been worse than the last time she had experienced it. It had descended into her left arm.

The pain had stopped as suddenly as it had begun, leaving her weak and shaken and slightly nauseous. Grace had collapsed onto the kitchen chair, reached for a cigarette and prayed that she would survive until after the Fashion Week.

Chapter Forty-One

She had parked the MG in the airport car park and caught the shuttle bus into town. The car would be safer there and stood less chance of getting a dent from some old jalopy parked next to it by a careless person. The shuttle bus, or *navette,* was an easy way to get to the centre of town, and there were plenty of stop-off points so she could get back on at any one of a number of stops.

She had now seen two potential shops for her gallery, but neither was suitable. She would visit an estate agent and see if they had anything better.

It was a crisp, cold day even though it was spring. The bus had been fusty so she decided to walk for a while. It gave her further opportunity to ponder on the subject of Didier. Apart from the first flames of jealousy that he had experienced when he thought she had been out with a man instead of being with Amanda, he had shown little interest in her. He continued to be polite to her and was still generous with the allowance that he gave her, but he clearly was no longer interested in her physically and spent so much time away from the house that she felt at times that she lived alone with Mathilde.

It seemed that Mathilde was finally warming to her at the same time as Didier was becoming colder towards her. They had whiled away quite a few hours each evening playing cards, watching television together, and even chatting a little about the world and life. She had sketched Mathilde, sitting in her favourite chair. Mathilde had been enchanted with the sketch, and it was now proudly displayed in a frame next to her bed.

Amanda had been to the house on several occasions, which had helped. Since the mistake with the chrysanthemums, she had made every effort to get into Mathilde's good books to make up for it. She was so funny and charming that Mathilde had forgiven her almost immediately. The look of horror on Mathilde's face when she discovered the significance of chrysanthemums had been priceless, and Mathilde, despite being a crusty old lady, could see the funny side of it and now enjoyed Amanda's company.

Amanda had brought over some old games from her childhood to entertain them and had tried to teach them the rules. Mathilde had howled with laughter at one ridiculous game called Ker-Plunk. Amanda had set up a strange cylinder with holes. She then spent considerable time pushing plastic straws though all the holes, then tipped handfuls of glass marbles into the cylinder. They rested on top of the straws. The object of the game was to remove as many plastic straws as possible, which were now supporting the marbles, without letting any marbles drop. It was a game of precision and care. Mathilde concentrated hard with every *go* and withdrew each straw with a dexterity that surprised both Bibi and Amanda. It wasn't long though before marbles gradually began to fall through gaps, and when Amanda let tumble the entire, clattering pile by accidentally jolting her straw, Mathilde nearly choked with laughter.

Amanda's light-hearted approach to life was infectious, and they often enjoyed evenings now laughing together at old *Benny Hill* and *Mr Bean* DVDs that Amanda had brought with her from England or listening to her attempting to tell jokes in French. She knew a few jokes about Belgians, which Mathilde particularly liked. She was quite a mimic, and with her ability to speak French, she soon had Mathilde enchanted.

In some ways, life was certainly more fun than it had been for a long time, but Didier was more distant than she had ever known. This floozy was more than a fling; she was a threat. Didier had never stayed with one woman for this long before. He was no longer the Didier she fell in love with and married. He had changed. Bibi asked herself if she should try to arrange a meeting with this woman. Usually, when a woman saw Bibi, they immediately felt inferior. There were not many women who could match Bibi on style, looks, or intelligence. She could tell this girl to "back off" and leave Didier. The girl would be instantly intimidated by Bibi, and Bibi could have Didier back. She wasn't sure that she wanted him back, however. That was part of the problem.

Deep in thought, she strolled beside one of the many canals. Toulouse, also known as the *Ville Rose* because of its wonderful pink buildings, held many surprises, including a network of canals, which linked to the famous Canal De Midi. There were several canal boats moored to posts, selling the famous Toulouse violets, a delicate, unobtrusive, mauve-blue flower symbolising Toulouse.

Bibi always visited the Violet Festival, which was held each year during the month of February. Being an artist, she was enchanted by all flowers—their colours, intricate designs, and beauty. Toulouse had such beautiful gardens and flowering walkways which interconnected the bandstand of the Grand Rond with Jardin Royal or the Jardins des Plantes. Today, having wandered through the Jardin Royal, Bibi was headed for her favourite café, la Maison Pillon. It served the most sumptuous mouth-watering pastries, ice creams, and chocolates but was best known for Le Pavé du Capitole—a type of chocolate sweet, consisting of orange-flavoured praline ganache covered in 70% chocolate. She wanted to get some for Mathilde. It would cheer her enormously. Amanda would love it, too.

Opening the door and focussing on the display cabinet in front of her, she almost didn't notice the couple seated nearby. She recognised the man instantly even though he had his back to her. He had dressed in that very same blue suit this morning to go to work. She knew that head of thick, dark hair, which tumbled down to his collar because she had caressed it on numerous occasions. The coat that was casually draped on the back of the chair was the same soft cashmere coat she had given him as a present for his birthday only last year. The man was tenderly stroking the hands of a fresh-faced girl, which were clasped in his own, murmuring to her and oblivious to all around. It wasn't the fact that Didier was that man or the fact that the girl, clearly besotted with him and gazing doe-eyed at him, was so young. No, it was the fact that the young girl in question was, without any doubt whatsoever, expecting a baby.

Bibi backed out of the shop in alarm. A dull drumming began in her head, and she felt the world around her fading to grey. She managed a few steps away from the front door, but tears welled in her eyes, blurring her vision. She turned back to the café. The door was now opening, and Didier was emerging. He would almost certainly see her. She turned away wildly in an attempt to flee down the street and bashed into a stranger. He grabbed her with strong arms, steadying her, and looked at her with genuine concern.

"You okay?" he asked in gently in English.

"Husband...lover...here...will see me," she gushed, eyes wide open with panic.

The stranger took in the situation instantly, encircled her with his arms, thus hiding her from the oncoming couple, and pulled her head towards his and kissed her.

Didier walked past without noticing the couple embracing in front of him. He had his own arm around his young lover. He was blind to everything else.

"I'm so sorry," said the stranger. "I couldn't think of what else to do to prevent him from seeing you. I don't normally snog beautiful French women I've never met before."

Bibi smiled in spite of it all. He had very attractive eyes and an easy manner. The kiss had actually been very enjoyable, and she had felt rather comforted by those strong arms. As he spoke, she detected a slight accent. He wasn't English as she had first thought.

"Thank you. Thank you so much. I didn't know what to do," she replied.

"No problem. It was my pleasure. I don't suppose you fancy a tea or a coffee or something to help with the shock? Oh, by the way, how rude of me. I'm forgetting my manners," he continued, extending a hand. "I'm Todd, Todd Bradshaw. How do you do?"

Chapter Forty-Two

"Easterly winds blowing from the Atlantic will cool the coast again today. Inland it will be marginally warmer with temperatures about 8 or 9 degrees."

Richard turned off the radio and clattered about his kitchen. He was still smarting from Amanda Willson's betrayal. He had spent months looking for a mark. He could have chosen someone else and been much closer to having some money in the bank by now. It was all her fault. He had returned to Nice after discovering that she had gone away to the mountains. This wasn't the end of it though, no siree! Having been around his apartment for a week and having demolished almost everything in it, thanks to his temper, he had decided to return to Toulouse to visit her again. He hadn't devised a plan this time. He would think of some just revenge when he got there. He was no longer interested in extracting money from her. He wanted to give her what she deserved, the two-timing slag. He was tempted to steal her precious MG, too. It would fetch some money if he could offload it to some other gullible idiot.

The two-timing slag in question was putting the finishing touches to a sign to sell the camper van. The sooner she could sell it, the sooner she could return to the UK and be with Phil. She had also written several cards advertising the van, which she would put up in various shop windows. There was surely someone who would want to buy a newly repaired, spinky-spanky clean camper van. Bertie sparkled after her efforts with a large, yellow sponge and lots of warm water. She would take some cards to Caylus tomorrow and drop a few more off in Saint-Antonin-Noble-Val when she went to do her shopping.

She had spent the last two weeks working hard on her book. It had taken up almost all of her days and nights, but she was now close to finishing it. She also had to post a funny story on her blog about her friend, Bibi, and someone they had met at a café. Bibi provided her with so much material. All her followers loved Bibi and her tales of how to stay youthful; they'd scream with laughter at this next one.

Checking the clock on the windowsill, she realised PlayGirl.77 would be on Skype any minute. She set up in front of the screen ready to receive the call. Her mother had been texting regularly, telling her about the latest events on the island. There had been messages about nights in tavernas, Sunday evenings at various music and dance events on the seafront at Larnaca, and excited texts about an International Regatta. She had sent photographs of the people who had been working on the fashion collection with her and some great pictures taken at a picnic in the Trodos Mountains. She sent a photograph of her flying a huge, red and white kite. Spencer was helping her hold the strings, and they were both hysterical with laughter. Her mother was more energetic than ever.

The computer rang. Amanda waited for the usual curl of cigarette smoke. Instead, PlayGirl.77 came into view.

"Hello Mum. It's so nice to see you again. That's a lovely blouse. Did you make it?"

"No," replied her mother, looking at it as if she had forgotten which blouse she was wearing. "I got it from Asda, I think. Thank you, though."

There was something odd about the scene in front of her. Her mother looked unusual. Her mouth seemed to be swollen on one side.

"How are you Mum?"

"Fine," replied her mother, sounding not fine at all. "Bit tired, though. I think I'm getting a bit too old to do all-night parties. Monday was okay, but Tuesday night was hard going."

"Have you been partying every night?"

"No, just Monday and half of Tuesday. I'm not as young as I used to be. I used to be able to stay up all week if I wanted to," she chuckled softly.

Amanda became transfixed by the swelling, which seemed to move up and down. Her mother continued, "I've probably got too much blood in my alcohol system." She chuckled again and coughed a little.

Amanda hadn't been able to put her finger on it until that moment. There was definitely something different about her mother; she wasn't holding a cigarette.

"Mum, have you given up smoking?"

"Er, not given up exactly. That would be impossible. I've been a sixty-a-day person for years, but I have cut down." The swelling moved from the left side of her mother's mouth to the right side.

"I've taken up eating chocolate éclairs instead. They keep my mouth busy and glue my teeth together so I can't get a cigarette in. The worst thing, though, is that I have nothing to do with my hands now. They are used to holding a cigarette so I got these." She held up a pair of knitting needles. There was a long, gaudy, yellow object hanging from them. "It keeps my hands occupied, but it doesn't have the same kick as nicotine. Anyway, I've knocked the cigarettes back to about twenty a day now."

"Why have you suddenly decided to cut down? You're not ill, are you?"

"No, no, not at all. It was Grego. It started when he refused to let me smoke near the fabrics because he said it made them smell badly. After a few days working in the room with them, I realised I didn't need the cigarettes all the time. I was so busy with the sewing and the patterns that I forgot I needed a cigarette. I still smoke when I go out with friends, though. I couldn't manage a night out without a few puffs. The rest of the time, I try to behave and eat chocolate éclairs and of course, knit. Dull, isn't it? I've eaten my own bodyweight in sweets since I cut back on the ciggies. I know they'll make me fat. Still, I'll be able to knit myself huge jumpers to cover my vast frame when that happens."

She beamed at Amanda, who laughed out loud. Her mother had a large lump of caramel stuck on her front tooth, so it now looked as if it was missing. She looked like a mischievous urchin. Amanda felt a wave of love wash over her briefly.

"I'm glad you've cut down. I've nagged you for years, decades even, about them. They are no good for you."

"Yes, yes," replied her mother dismissively, waving a knitting needle. "Enough of the lectures again."

"I know I sound like a nag, and I know you know all about the ill effects of smoking. It's just...it's just that I don't want to lose you, Mum," admitted Amanda wishing that the computer screen did not separate them, and she could hold her mother tightly like she used to when she was much younger.

BLOG: Fortifying Your Fifties

January

We were standing in a well-stocked boutique in Montauban. Bibi insisted I try on a pair of smart, woollen shorts over a pair of thick tights, teamed up with a large scarf tossed carelessly over one shoulder. She appraised me as I came out of the fitting room rather self-consciously.

"Ah, now you look more chic," she said approvingly.

"I can't wear this outfit," I replied. "I'm too old to carry this look off. It is an outfit for young women."

She stared as only French people can stare and shrugged her shoulders as only the French can shrug.

"It is a question of confidence," she explained. "We women wear what we like. If we know we look good in it, we wear it with confidence and defy people to say it is not chic. You must learn the way of walking with confidence," and she demonstrated by walking with a haughty air around the boutique.

Bibi has given me huge amounts of valuable advice since I have been here. The other day she caught me rubbing some hand cream onto my face because I had run out of my favourite Vitamin E face cream. She patiently explained how important it was for me to look after my body and face. French women are taught from an early age by their mothers how to look after their skin. She herself has an abundance of pots of cream, which she uses religiously. Each morning she performs facial exercises in front of the mirror for up to an hour followed by a further half hour of treating her skin to a workout with a sort of scouring machine that exfoliates her gently. Next, she massages various creams gently into various parts of her face making sure she pats her eye cream with great care so as not to drag the skin around her eyes which, she informed me, is very delicate.

She lectured me on the importance of getting regular facials, manicures, and obviously haircuts. She wouldn't leave the house unless she was wearing at least lipstick and some mascara, and she, like many French women, spends a fortune at the beauticians. When I asked how Didier, her husband, felt about such expense, she shrugged again and said: "Didier knows it iz important zat I look beautiful. If I look good, zen he looks good. And 'e would not want me to let 'im down ,would 'e?"

Phil would have a fit if I spent as much as Bibi on beauty products. She took me out to meet her beautician in town and insisted that I at least have my eyebrows shaped.

"You 'av 'air growing all over your face. Like 'zis one," she remonstrated, yanking out a long, white, stray hair that she had found somewhere between my eyes. My eyes watered. My eyebrows are beginning to grow haphazardly over my forehead and in various parts of my face. I can't see them without my glasses, and I no longer have my magnifying mirror because it is back in the UK, so I don't see these random hairs. What I can see is a bald patch where they used to grow. What little hair remains is so fine and pale that it doesn't form a noticeable eyebrow, so I have to pencil in a line every day, or I look, well… weird, like an alien extra on Star Trek. Some days I have arched eyebrows; some days thick eyebrows; and some days wacky-shaped eyebrows, depending on how much light filtrates the bathroom and how steady my hand is.

The beautician, who smelt pleasantly of mimosa, scrutinised my eyebrows with the now-familiar French pout. She whisked up a small pot of hot wax, and before I knew what was happening, she had smeared it above my eye area. She removed it expertly without pain and then tinted what was left of my eyebrows. The effect is incredible. For the first time in my life, I have smart, neat, semi-arched eyebrows. I instantly looked chic. She triumphantly held the mirror for me to see the magical transformation. That was it; I was a convert. I will definitely visit her again.

Bibi nodded approvingly, and arm-in-arm, we walked to the nearest café. No sooner had we ordered than Bibi pouted toward the door. A gorgeous woman, elegantly attired in skin-tight jeans, perfectly teamed with a soft, leather jacket was entering the café. She embraced Bibi warmly. They knew each other from the days before Bibi had moved to this area. She gushed over Bibi, saying how wonderful she looked, and Bibi complimented her on her own youthful appearance. After a while, the woman departed, and I questioned Bibi about her.

"Pfft, zat is Michelle. She worked wiz me in Paris a long time ago, and we went out togezer a few times to galleries because we were zee same age. Ten years ago, she ended up 'ere in the same region as me. She is married to an artist. He is a lovely man and sinks ze world of 'er."

"Bibi, you look fantastic, but she can't possibly be the same age as you. She has to be about thirty at a push."

"Pouf," she replied, pouting. Yes, the French say things like *pouf* and shrug their shoulders simultaneously. "Ah, she has discovered the secret of eternal youth," continued Bibi, sipping her small black coffee.

"Like facial exercises, the creams, the little exfoliating machine, and the phials of vitamins, and the regular trips to the salon?"

"No, no. All French women do zat. I have been looking after my face and body all my life. No, Michelle has truly discovered the elixir of youth."

Fascinated, I begged Bibi to reveal all. She leant forward conspiratorially.

"She 'as a young lover," she said enviously. "He is thirty-two."

"What about her husband? Does he know?"

"Of course he does—'e is very pleezed. 'is wife looks fantastic so 'e is very proud to be 'er husband," she said blowing out her cheeks as if I were mad to think otherwise. "The lover, he iz a doctor, a facial expert," she confided knowingly.

I looked a little puzzled.

"Ze lover gives 'er ze injections of Botox and fillers to stop the little laughing lines," she whispered, looking around to ensure no one could hear her. "He 'elps' Michelle for free. So, she has indeed found ze secret to looking youthful," she concluded triumphantly.

So, ladies, and I dare say the same would apply to gentlemen. The secret to looking fabulous is to find yourself a young, generous lover, who is in the medical profession, preferably a facial aesthetic doctor or maybe even a plastic surgeon.

I wonder if I could find one in the telephone directory?

Posted by Facing50.Blog

18 Comments

PhillyFilly says…This is my idea of paradise: a man who can perform his miracles for free. I have spent a fortune on my face and body. Does Bibi's friend know any other surgeons who'd like to meet a gorgeous American lady?

Facing50 says…From what you have told me, there can't be much left for you to have a go at. I bet you look amazing.

QuiteContrary says…This is one of those posts that makes me feel queasy. Unnecessary surgery is to be avoided at all costs. I have undergone several operations vital to my survival, and I cannot understand why women in particular feel the need to go under the knife. They should accept old age. Operations are not always successful. I blame the media and our culture, which is obsessed with celebrities and beauty. Nothing is worse than looking at a plastic face and a crinkly, old neck. I do hope I haven't offended anyone here, but really, is it necessary?

Facing50 says…I have to agree with you on this. I shall let myself get old and wrinkly and hope Phil's eyesight fails before much longer.

MiaFerrari says…I would have considered surgery after my husband walked out on me for a bimbo–not on me, on him! He'd have needed it if I could have got my hands on him.

Facing50 says…I wouldn't want to be him if you ever get to see him again. Mind you, with your new position at the hotel and the detective agency, I am sure you have got those mitts full now.

YoungFreeSingleandSane says…One of the best things about living alone is not having to wear makeup. You don't have to mess about with creams or eye shadow or anything. It might have been better for the postman if I had put some on this morning, though. He looked like he'd seen a ghost when I opened the door to him first thing this morning. Haha!

Facing50 says…Poor man. I'm sure you didn't look scary. I scream when I look in the mirror these mornings. I suppose I should make more effort.

MomOfTen says…I need surgery—but not for my face. I need to get my female bits put back in place.

Facing50 says…I winced when I read that comment. Try Pilates. SexyFitChick recommended it. It should help.

TheMerryDivorcee says…I don't seem to need surgery to attract men. Possibly my natural 38DDs might have something to do with it.

Facing50 says…That explains a lot. ☺

SexyFitChick says…You know my feelings on this subject. Look after your body—it's the most efficient machine you will ever have. As for your face— you can't beat a healthy glow that comes from a good work-out to make you look youthful.

Facing50 says…Well said. I agree, oh, great SexyFitChick.

Gypsynesters2 says…We checked out some of the amenities in Switzerland when we went to a yodeling competition there last week. The clinics are sublime. If we needed surgery, we would go there. Your friend's advice is very good, though. We both moisturize regularly. Men should look after their skin, too. Hans, the masseur at a Clinique la Prairie told me that. We have lots of pots of creams. They retail at about $130 so they must be good, mustn't they?

Facing50 says…You two are incredible. You get about, don't you? Did you take part in the yodelling contest? As for the cream, I read that it contained petrolatum (Vaseline), and that wasn't good for your skin.

Hippyhappyhoppy says…Bibi is lovely. I wish I had a friend like her. I wish I had a friend. Hugs x

Facing50 says…You have got friends. We are here in your computer. I'll send you an email this afternoon, and we can chat properly. x

Gypsynesters3 says…I have just discovered your blog. I was looking on the laptop, and I see that my husband has been following it for some weeks now. Please excuse his comments. He's been like this ever since we moved into the trailer park. He lives in a fantasy land. I read some of his wild stories. The closest we got to Mexico was a deep-fried burrito. As for Switzerland—he has seen the film Heidi twice. You just have to love him. Humor the poor guy, will you? He needs his fantasies.

Chapter Forty-Three

Amanda couldn't shake the feeling she was being watched. It had started a couple of weeks earlier when she was on the balcony hanging out some washing. She had noticed something glinting in the distance, a shaft of light. At the time, she had thought it was peculiar but dismissed it as either a figment of her imagination or the reflected glare from someone's windscreen as they travelled the road in the distance.

At the Sunday market in St Antonin, she had been chatting to Mark and Jeanette at the Gazpacho. The market, as always, was heaving with people, and many had stopped off to grab a coffee, a beer, or a chat with friends at this popular café. She had a superb view of all the stalls opposite and was enjoying the convivial atmosphere. She also had her eye on a stand which was selling homemade honey and had a tiny pig attached to the stand to grab the attention of passersby. She had wanted to go over and pat the pig which was turning a few heads; however, she was absorbed in a discussion with Mark about which was the best cheese to enjoy with a glass of Nouveau Beaujolais.

As Mark was talking, she noticed a figure in the distance standing in a doorway, facing the café. Amanda rarely wore her glasses. Horrid childhood memories meant that unless she desperately needed to put them on, she would not wear them. She had to wear them for reading or typing ,but when she went out, she refused to take them. She was not able to make out the figure very well, but it had seemed odd that anyone would just stand in a doorway for the whole length of time she was sitting at the table. He, for indeed she was certain it was a man, wasn't moving his head to people-watch either. His gaze seemed to be fixed on the café.

Everyone else was bustling about, waving, greeting each other, or chattering in high-pitched voices. The market stalls were swarming with people seeking out fresh produce for lunch or some local delicacy to enjoy. It was a continuous, moving sea of people. Maybe this person was waiting to meet someone. It still seemed peculiar though, and a sixth sense told her that something was amiss. She didn't voice her suspicions to either Mark or Jeanette, and when they left to continue with their weekly shopping, the figure had mysteriously disappeared into the dark streets.

The following Tuesday, Amanda had been in Villefranche, a large town several kilometres away from the cottage. She had plodded around the town, looking for a nice present for Phil. After a fruitless search, she emerged from the cobbled streets to stand and watch the ducks on the river. Sunlight played on the rippling water. She stood lost in her thoughts about her life again. Looking up briefly, she was certain she had glimpsed the same figure she had seen in St Antonin, who was observing her from the bridge. She really should wear her glasses. She was beginning to spook herself. It probably wasn't the same person; after all, everyone looked like a blur from that distance.

She shook the feeling off again but was aware of a silver Twingo with hire car plates on it following her as she drove home. It pulled out behind her as she wound up the hill from Villefranche and kept a comfortable distance behind her all the way to Caylus. There should be nothing peculiar about that, other than it was after 12 o'clock, and every French person in the area would either be seated at the table enjoying lunch with their family or steaming home at full speed to ensure their meal would not be cold. Also, no French person would sit behind Bertie. Without exception, they always overtook her, some waving fists at her, particularly if they had been stuck behind her for some time as Bertie puffed up the inclines at a slow pace.

She slowed down a couple of times to encourage the car to overtake, but the Twingo slowed, too, and remained some distance behind. She accelerated, and the Twingo dutifully followed, maintaining the same distance. She was considering some form of police type manoeuvre, which would be mighty difficult in Bertie. She had decided to slip out of Caylus via the back road to St Antonin and then hide in a large side street when she noticed the car indicate left and pull off the road in the direction of St Project. She breathed a huge sigh of relief. She was getting so tetchy these days. It must be her age. What she needed was a large glass of Château Plonk.

Life back at the cottage was manic. The children were at home and were screaming at each other in the garden. She found Ted sitting by her door. His tail wagged furiously when he saw her.

"Too noisy for you, old chap? Come in," she offered. He bolted into the quiet house and plopped down on the carpet.

She unpacked her few provisions, poured a glass of juice and clicked on to the Scrabble game she and Todd had begun yesterday.

Straddle

Todd must have been rather pleased with that word because he had put a smiley face in the conversation box and written: ☺ *Bet you can't beat that. I was going to play* saddle *but this is better. It would be a great word for an erotic novel. Is your book erotic? If it is, I give you permission to use it, and you must now produce some sentences to prove you can use it appropriately.*

Gamely, she typed: *Tim decided that the best investment strategy would be a long straddle. Then Gertie placed one boot into the stirrup and straddled the large chestnut with ease. "Tally Ho," she yelled and joined the chase.*

Finally, with a wry smile she typed: *The Aston Martin straddled the white line as it cornered the tight bend at over 80mph.* That should make him smile. As for writing erotic literature, well, she would be hopeless at it.

Todd didn't reply immediately, which meant he was busy or asleep. She checked her emails and found one from Phil.

Dear Amanda,

I am not much good at writing emails, but I wanted to let you know that all is well here. I am going to Milton Keynes to look at some new premises on Friday. I won't bore you with the details, but it seems promising.

Gareth is flying to Amsterdam for a "Boy's Weekend" and invited me along. Think I might give it a miss this time. I've got plenty of paperwork to go through. It seems preferable to lots of booze, the red light district, and drugs.

How is the writing going? How are Mark, Jeanette, and Ted? I hope you are still enjoying yourself. I look forward to seeing you soon.
Best wishes
Phil

Amanda read it twice. Phil would be even worse than her at writing erotic literature. It was almost like he was writing to a supplier or business colleague. Phil had never liked computers, though, so it had probably taken him all morning to compose it. She could picture him now—index finger tapping the keys brutally, cussing every time he hit the wrong key. She should be thrilled he had made the effort to send her an email. She sent a detailed reply which she hoped gave him a flavour of France even though he was not here.

It was only after she had finished her epic email to Phil and had gotten up to let Ted out that she noticed the envelope on the mat in front of the door. The note inside was addressed to her. *Amanda—What naughty underwear you wear under those jeans. You are a saucy minx, aren't you?* Her heart hammered against her ribs. This couldn't be! She raced to the outside laundry room. She hadn't put her dry washing away after bringing it in from the balcony that morning. Groping frantically through the items, she realised that her new, seductive, black lace knickers had disappeared from the pile.

Chapter Forty-Four

Dressed in jeans and a sweater under a large black coat, Richard blended in well with the other locals in the café. He was sipping a neat espresso and picking at a croissant. A copy of *Le Figaro* was open on the table in front of him, but he was not focused on the item about the forthcoming presidential election.

He was observing Amanda Willson, who was now coming out of the newsagent's shop, a handful of postcards in one hand, a magazine in the other. She had parked that ridiculous camper van on the square near the café. The woman was deranged. She had spun him a load of fibs. She didn't even own an MG. Her attractive French friend owned the MG he had seen at the market. He had seen her driving it only the other day. Amanda either lived in a fantasy land or had deliberately fed him lie after lie. She didn't own the MG; she wasn't exciting or adventurous from what he had noted; and he doubted very much that she knew one interesting fact about art or culture. She certainly wasn't wealthy. She couldn't be, judging by her attire, or the fact she drove about in either a beat-up old Peugeot or the camper van.

He was furious. The ignominy of the situation was like a red rag to a bull. The woman had had the audacity to attempt to dupe him! He had succeeded in rattling her cage, though. He had taken to following her, and his latest effort of stealing her underwear had been most satisfying. He had watched her through a small pair of binoculars as she scurried to the laundry room, emerging pale-faced when she discovered that her knickers were gone. *Hussy. Tart. Trollop. Slut.* He kicked the table leg in irritation, attracting the attention of a couple of men in blue overalls, who were

321

taking an early cognac. He smiled politely and pointed at the newspaper as if he had read an article which had annoyed him. They acknowledged him, smiled briefly, and returned to their conversation about cattle.

His sharp eyes picked up on a small sign in the window of the motor home. He paid his bill and meandered over to it. She had attached a notice written in French and English to the window offering the vehicle for sale. He rubbed his chin. This was perfect—just perfect. He tucked his folded up newspaper under his arm and whistling tunelessly, he wandered off in the direction of the local supermarket.

Amanda pushed the door handle down with her elbow and tried to get through the door. She was almost instantly knocked down by Ted who careered into her from behind and dashed to the kitchen. He was certain she had bought him some ham. She always bought him ham when she went out. All he had to do was look at her dolefully, and she would surrender a large slice.

True to form, she dropped her bags on the table, took out a packet, and extracted something that looked even more interesting than ham.

"Okay, what do you do for a treat?"

Ted gave a paw. Then he solemnly handed her his other paw. His tail thumped.

"Good boy. Here you are. I have a special treat for you today. It's a chew." She handed over a large bone-shaped chew.

Ted took the tasty treat from her fingers with care and hid under the large, wooden kitchen table to work on it. He didn't often get chews, and so he would make the most of this one. He was concentrating so hard on the chew that he didn't hear the slight cough at the door.

"Sorry to interrupt you. The door was open. I have come about the motor home. It is still for sale, isn't it?"

"Oh gosh! Yes, it is. Right. Sure. No problems," replied Amanda, taken aback for a moment by the stranger at the door. She was particularly wary since the disappearance of her underwear. This chap, however, didn't look the sort to be interested in her underwear. He was nondescript, apart from the round owl-like glasses he wore, which, in fact, made him look a right anorak. She didn't want him in the house though, anorak or not.

"I'll show you around it." she said, grabbing the key to the van from the table and shutting the front door behind her. She couldn't have Ted suddenly rushing out in a frenzy and running off a potential buyer.

"Spiffing," he replied.

Amanda hid a smirk. Who used that sort of language these days?

"So, here it is. This is Bertie. Sorry, that probably sounds very silly, giving it a name and everything. This is the camper van. Obviously, it is the camper van; it's clearly not a Porsche, is it?" she gabbled. "I'm Amanda Wilson, by the way. Pleased to meet you."

She held out her hand. The man extended his. "Delighted to meet you, Ms Willson. I'm Stuart...Stuart Granger."

"Er, sorry, Mrs Wilson, not Ms. I'm married. Mr Wilson isn't here at the moment."

The stranger's eyes darkened.

"So let me show you around the inside of the van."

"I'm quite familiar with *Bürstner* motorhomes. We used to have one like this, only an earlier model. Ours broke down last holiday on the way to Bordeaux, and I've been looking to replace it ever since. It's difficult to find good quality, second-hand camper vans with so few miles on the clock. We usually take the children to the coast during the summer months. It's much easier having a place to sleep than having to stay in a hotel and infinitely more pleasurable. Maisie, my wife, misses the old camper van, so I'd really like to replace it before the family holiday this year. What I'd really like, Mrs Willson, if you don't mind, is a quick trip out in it. Would you mind if I gave it a run? Make sure the engine is sound and all that?"

Amanda hesitated. She had heard of people pretending to come to buy a car, asking to test drive it and never coming back with it. She wished Mark was here, but since Ted had been outside, the chances were that he had gone out with the family. She could tell this man to come back later, but she knew Phil wanted to sell the van. He'd be so proud of her if she could sell it quickly and get a good price for it. She had to decide quickly. He looked a bit odd, but the man must be all right. He'd used the word *spiffing*, had a family and a wife called Maisie, for heaven's sake.

"Of course you can take it for a drive, Mr Granger, but if you don't mind, I'd rather I accompanied you," she answered.

"But, of course. You can't be too careful these days, can you?" replied the man, giving her a thin smile.

Amanda handed over the key to Bertie and jumped into the passenger seat. Strolling round to the driver's side, Richard Montagu-Forbes tightened his grip on the long silk scarf hidden in his pocket. He couldn't wait to use it on Mrs Amanda Willson.

Chapter Forty-Five

They had driven several kilometres from Caylus. Stuart had not spoken one word to her since he had turned the key in the engine.

"Well, what do you think then?" asked Amanda cautiously. He didn't look as if he liked Bertie very much. Come to think about it, he didn't look as if he liked anything or anyone much. His mouth was set in a tight line, eyes fixed ahead on the road. Amanda's sixth sense finally kicked in. This man was trouble.

"I think we should be going back now. My husband will be waiting for me," she coughed nervously.

"No he won't," came the reply.

"Yes, he always gets in about now. He'll come out looking for me if I'm not back soon, and I left a note to say I was with a potential buyer..."

"Shut up. Shut up you lying, cheating...whore!"

Amanda's eyes flew open in surprise. Her brain went into shock.

"You are full of lies and deceit. You led me on. You were unique. You were the one I had been searching for. You made me think we could have something special together, but oh no, you were only stringing me along, laughing behind my back all the time, weren't you?"

Stuart tugged at the steering wheel and pulled the camper van off the road and into a narrow lane with a screech. There was no one about. There wasn't a dwelling or building in sight. With her mouth feeling like it was stuffed full of cotton, Amanda desperately tried to make sense of it all.

"I...I...don't know you, Mr Granger."

"Of course, you don't know me, you harlot. You don't know Mr Stuart Granger because you have never met Mr Stuart Granger—but you have met Richard. You do know Richard Montagu-Forbes, don't you?" Amanda shook her head earnestly.

"No, I've never heard of Richard Forbes Montague." Her mind was spinning, trying to think of a way out of this. Was he nuts? Had he mistaken her for someone else?

"Montagu-Forbes, you thick bimbo, and don't pretend you don't know that name Miss Amanda Willson." He rolled the letter *l* and peered at her with ebony black eyes. "You don't fool me now with that fake look of astonishment. Oh no. Remember, I can see you now. You can't hide behind the screen this time, telling me all your fabrications."

"Look, I really think you have made some dreadful mistake. I honestly don't know you. I have never heard of you, Forbes-Montagu or Montagu-Forbes. I don't know how you think you know me, but I have no recollection of you whatsoever."

Richard whacked the side of the door with the flat of his hand. Amanda squirmed. This man was definitely a lunatic. Heart hammering against her ribs, she sat tight and wondered what on earth she should do next. She remembered an episode of the television drama *Spooks* that she had watched with Phil. In a hostage situation, you should try to get the captor to recognise you are a human being. Find some common ground. Talk to them.

"Okay, let me explain. I am not always good with faces or names. If I have offended you in any way, I would like to make amends," she began, wetting her dry lips with her tongue. "You know my name, but I can't, for some bizarre reason, recall how we have met."

"Let me help you, Mrs Willson, since you now claim to have a case of early-onset dementia. You use Facebook, don't you?"

"Yes, I do have an account with Facebook." She continued to look at him with a blank expression. God! This woman was incredible! She either had acting skills worthy of an Oscar nomination, or she was a complete airhead. He glanced at her, trying to work out which it was. She stared at him, wide-eyed with an air of confusion. You could almost see the cogs in that brain of hers whirring around, conjuring up some new set of lies.

His patience snapped. "You contacted me on Facebook. We chatted about painting."

Amanda looked even more confused. "I like painting, but I have never spoken to anyone other than Bibi and Phil—"

"Shut up! What about the first message about being at the film festival at Cannes—the lady in red?"

Amanda snorted nervously. "Isn't that a Chris De Burgh song? Cannes. I've never been to Cannes."

Richard was now turning red with rage.

"Well, Little Miss Innocent, what about asking me for advice on stock shares? What about all those meetings with your broker that we discussed? What about all those lengthy messages where you told me about yourself, and how, now that you are single, you have the strong desire to have a great adventure and spend time with someone who can appreciate the same fine things in life as you? What about all those cosy chats we had every evening? Artists? Music? Culture? Theatre? Cuisine? You promised to come and dine with me by the coast at Nice. You told me that you lived here, Amanda Willson? Do none of these facts ring a bell with you?" He was spitting as he spoke, which unnerved Amanda, but she shook her head, more confused than ever.

327

"What about the classic MG car you professed to own? I spent an inordinate length of time checking out garages for it. I spent hours researching so I could keep up with you and your intellect. I wasted my time completely!" he screeched, his voice rising to a terrifying crescendo. "And finally, why did you suddenly remove your profile from Facebook? Was it because you had found another man who offered you more than me? Was that what happened? Did this man win your affections and sweep you away on a mountain holiday in the MG, Amanda Willson?"

"I don't have an MG. I would never say I had one if I didn't. My friend, Bibi, has an MG, but she is French and obviously not called Amanda. Look, I am called Amanda Wilson, I have never denied that. I am Amanda Wilson who is married. It states quite clearly on my Facebook profile that I am married. I am going to be completely honest with you now. I am extremely frightened to tell you this, Mr Richard WhoEverYouAre, but I truly believe you have made a mistake. I am not the woman you made friends with on Facebook. My page is still on Facebook. I have not removed it. Would it help if I showed it to you?"

She rummaged around and pulled out the iPhone which was in her pocket. She held it out to him so he didn't think she would try any tricks. "Click on the Facebook application" she requested. Her hand trembled, but she looked him in the eye. He pressed it.

He read the name *Amanda Wilson* and recognised the profile picture that he had seen before. It was of a woman sitting on a large, orange balloon. Standing next to her was a man wearing a tired, grumpy expression. He checked again. This woman was called Amanda Wilson with one *l*. She was not the woman he had been chasing after. Someone, whom he would probably never find, had messed about with him. Someone had set him up and given him some facts to send him on this wild goose chase. Someone had played him like a fish. He could feel the throbbing in his temples mounting. Richard Montagu-Forbes threw the phone against the dashboard with a clatter. The red mist was descending again. He couldn't prevent it. With a menacing look at Amanda, he extracted the silk scarf from his pocket.

"Get out," he said coldly to her. "Get out now."

Chapter Forty-Six

She pushed the door opened and was greeted with a musty smell. The house felt cool, gloomy, and abandoned. In a way it even seemed hostile, as if it resented being woken up from its slumber. She shut the front door and sighed. This house had shared so many joyful memories with her. It had been a place of optimism, exuberance, and gaiety. Now it was devoid of happiness. It served only to remind her that time was running out, and all that had been good in her life had gone.

She dropped the small suitcase down in the entrance, went into the lounge, opened the window to let some air into the house, and slumped on the nearest chair. She hated coming back here after the life and warmth of Cyprus. There she could forget. Over there she could bury herself in parties and trips. She could go dancing and be with other people, other human beings. The sunshine, too, helped lift her mood. Here was just the opposite. Everyone in her street was working and had no time for an old widow. They were young and had their own lives. They didn't want to come over for dinner or a drink.

She loathed being reminded of the fact that now she was alone. Each time she returned home, she felt like she was in a vacuum. She lived in suspended animation. Here she had little to do except some gardening and keeping her home clean and tidy, the home she had once shared with her beloved husband and Amanda. Each day merged into the next without shape or reason. She would get up, clean the house, and go shopping if she could be bothered. Later she would read and maybe watch television. If she was lucky, there would be someone online to chat to. More often than not, they were busy, too. This emptiness would gradually

331

erode any enthusiasm she had for life. There was no joy left here, and yet she couldn't leave it. She couldn't pack up and move lock, stock, and barrel to Cyprus because getting rid of this house would be severing the only link she had to her past—the past she remembered vividly wherever she looked in this house.

The house shared her memories all right; they were in every corner and on every surface. She recalled them each time she used the pottery ashtray on the coffee table. Amanda had made at school. Grace could see her daughter now—one pigtail ribbon coming undone, paint on her fingers, standing proudly, hands open to reveal the blue and white object she had made for Mothering Sunday. She was reminded of the past when she looked at the painting of the leopard cubs on the wall that had been a wedding anniversary present. She had seen it in a shop, loved it instantly, and commented on it. A few weeks later, her smiling, gentle and loving husband had presented it to her. It had been wrapped in light blue tissue paper, the same colour as his eyes.

Her eyes scanned the rest of the room. She could see the three of them—her, Amanda, and her husband—around the dining table, laughing joyously at one of her husband's jokes. He had such a dry sense of humour. She could almost sense his presence in the room. She closed her eyes and pictured a typical Sunday lunchtime. It was a tradition for them all to sit and do the crossword puzzle together with a glass of wine before lunch. The meal would be cooking in the oven, the aroma filling the house. Her husband would be seated next to her on the settee. He was in charge of reading out the clues and filling in the answers. They would all offer suggestions as to the possible answers, and it was Amanda's job to check the answers in a dictionary if they were not sure. There had been much family banter and a lot of laughter, laughter and love. These had been precious times. Then, of course, there were all the photographs which sat on every surface. Each one of them was a captured magical moment in time. There wasn't one object that wasn't precious here because each and every one of them represented her past, their past.

Grace took a deep breath. The trip had tired her. She was becoming tired more easily these days. Even Spencer had commented on the fact that she had not stayed late at the party the other evening. It was getting more and more difficult to keep up with everyone, and although she was still vivacious and energetic, it took every ounce of energy and grit to keep up the front. What alternative did she have? Curl up here in her home and give in? No, she would fight it to the end. Her grandmother had been ninety-nine when she passed away. She had been scrubbing the kitchen floor on her hands and knees when she had suffered the attack and had dropped dead. She'd like to *just go*, too. That would be the best option.

These thoughts were too depressing for her. She needed a cigarette. Instead, she reached for the tube of mints she had bought at the airport. Amanda's mother forced herself out of the chair and into the kitchen to get the house back in order. It needed to be fresh and comfortable for visitors and for Amanda when she next came to visit. She hoped that Amanda would come by again soon. She'd enjoyed the last visit hugely. She'd had a really good catch-up with her. She still had Amanda's old recorder somewhere. It was probably in the attic with all the other bits and pieces she couldn't bear to part with. The recollection of Amanda concentrating hard while playing "Frère Jacques" on the old wooden recorder in front of an audience at school made her smile briefly. She must try and find it for when she next visited. She used to love playing the recorder.

Grace hadn't had any more pains since the last intense pain she'd experienced in Cyprus. They'd come though; it was just a matter of when. The last one had frightened her badly. It was the reason she had chosen to come back early from Cyprus. The boys didn't need her there now. The collection was all decided, and the team had everything in hand. If she felt better, she would make sure she was there for Gregos' big launch. If not, then she would rather be in her home with her memories when the time came.

She picked up a dusty photograph of a smiling schoolgirl taken several decades earlier. She wanted to talk to Amanda, but if she phoned now, Amanda might get cross with her. She would probably be busy. Amanda needed some time to get her writing done and wouldn't want to hear from her miserable, old mother. She'd better leave it until Sunday when Amanda would be expecting to speak to her. She didn't want to upset that fragile relationship so soon after it had been repaired. Grace wiped the dust from the photograph with her sleeve, gazed at the picture, then lifted it to her lips, and kissed it. A tear traced its way down her cheek and landed on the upturned photograph, which she clasped to her chest.

Chapter Forty-Seven

Phil was driving on the M6 headed back to the apartment he was sharing with Gareth. He had just completed his examination on meteorology. There was no question, he would pass it. He had known all of the answers. They had seemed easy. The whole examination had been simple because Phil had delighted in learning about this subject. His head was still buzzing with facts about weather conditions, wind speeds, cloud formations, and weather patterns. Nature was incredible. Who would have thought that there were so many types of clouds for instance? He glanced up through the streaked windscreen. That was stratus above, characterized by horizontal layering with a uniform base. The gray, flat cloud was indicative of drizzle, which was accurate since it was now raining steadily. The weather would clear later, and the cloud would change into stratocumulus. Phil's wiper blades kept up a steady swishing noise as they cleared the screen.

He indicated and pulled out to overtake a truck. It was an enormous vehicle with Lithuanian plates. It was stuck behind another three large vehicles, all trundling along in close convoy, kicking up spray, which blinded the passing motorists. There were far too many trucks on the roads. He opened his mouth to moan about them before remembering he had no passenger to listen to his complaint.

Caro Emeraud was playing on the radio. Phil turned up the volume. He hummed along to the track "A Night Like This". His thoughts turned to Amanda. If she had been sitting next to him, she would have been swaying in time to the music. She often danced or sang to tracks. She seemed to know most of the music on the radio, while he paid little attention to it. He suddenly had an urge to talk to her and tell her all about the exam and about stratus clouds or isotherms. She would be genuinely interested in it all. She loved learning new facts and displayed interested in whatever he talked about. She'd ask him all sorts of crazy questions about the clouds. He'd pretend to look annoyed but would be secretly delighted that she wanted to share his knowledge. She was always pleased when he was happy or content and listened patiently when he banged on about some debacle or other that always seemed to occur on a regular basis.

He wanted to share this moment of contentment with her. In that instant, he realised how much he missed her. He missed her laughter most of all. She could make him laugh even when he wanted to shout at someone. She could make him see the funny side, no matter what it was. She always had a silly joke or two to ease a situation. If that failed, she would pull a ridiculous face at him until he cracked. He wanted to see her do that ridiculous impression of Mick Jagger that always made him chuckle. He wanted to hear her off-key voice singing along to this track. He wished she was sitting next to him now, nodding excitedly about how well he thought the exam had gone and squeezing his hand in enthusiasm. He realised that a part of him was missing. That part was in France writing a book.

Caro Emeraud had finished, and now he was listening to Bill Withers mournfully declaring "Ain't No Sunshine". The lyrics seemed pertinent. There was certainly less sunshine in his life when Amanda wasn't there.

Phil had had enough of the bachelor life. Gareth was a great bloke, but sharing a flat with him certainly wasn't the same as being with Amanda. He had rather hoped that Gareth would have moved out by now, but his divorce was proving very messy; he and his wife couldn't agree on a settlement, which meant for the interim he was staying put in the flat. Phil was tiring of the whole affair. Last night,

Gareth had stunk the place out with an Indian takeaway and left the dirty tin foil trays out on the kitchen top. Phil hated untidiness. He was fastidious about keeping a place tidy. Amanda was, too. He had had to clean the bath yesterday before he could use it because Gareth had been in it and left a dirty tide mark around the sides and a huge puddle of water on the floor. It was like living with Tom, only you couldn't reproach him.

The flying had absorbed him totally at weekends, and work had been gratifying, but deep inside, he was a family man. At the end of a long day, he liked to come home to an understanding partner, open a bottle of cold beer, and eat a cooked meal. Even one of Amanda's cremated offerings would be better than all the ready-made meals he had been eating recently. They played havoc with his digestion, and his stomach kept him awake with gripe-like pains most nights. He missed those home comforts that he used to take for granted. He wanted to get back from work, drop into a clean shower, use one of the nice-smelling, cream towels that Amanda would have put out for him, and relax. He wanted to sit in his own comfortable chair beside the television in his well-worn slippers with his wife next to him.

He would talk to Tom and explain that he needed to return to the house and get back to normality again. Tom would have to take the plunge and rent accommodation in the village as he had first planned. He wouldn't mind. He'd be happy anywhere as long as he could be with Alice. Since the episode with the squatters, Tom had listened much more to Phil's advice and would probably feel relieved to pass the family home back to its owners. It was time to get life back on track and to ask Amanda to come home, too.

The rain pattered against the windscreen, but in spite of the heavy skies above, Phil felt lighthearted. He had plenty to look forward to. He had his flying. He had employment. His life had purpose again, and he would soon be able to enjoy it all with someone who understood him and who would support him no matter what.

His mobile rang. Amanda had put on "The Great Escape" as a ringtone. He didn't recognise the number that was trying to reach him. He didn't answer it. He didn't like taking calls when he was driving, even if his phone was hands-free. Mobile phones—another curse of the twentieth century. You could never get away from people these days.

Chapter Forty-Eight

"Have you seen Amanda?" asked Mark. "I've brought Claude to look at her camper van. He's interested in purchasing it for his sister. I thought she'd have been back by now. It's lunchtime."

"I heard her pull up only a short while ago. Judging by the way Ted belted off to see her, she had been shopping. She can't have gone out again. Has she taken Ted out for a walk? He's not come home since he begged to be let out to see her."

"No, the camper van isn't here. There's no sign of Ted. I thought it was unusual he hadn't come to say *hello* to Claude. He normally does."

Mark wandered around to the cottage. "Have you two seen Amanda?" he yelled up at the large oak tree in the garden. A small face appeared between the leaves. "Hi, Daddy. How did you know we were in the treehouse?"

"Daddies always know everything. Since you weren't in the house and you weren't by the pool, it was sure fact you'd be up here, especially since Mummy made you some cakes to take up there for a picnic."

The boy laughed. "Do you want a cake? Amanda went out in Bertie."

"Did she say how long she would be?"

"No, she didn't see us here. She went out with a man."

"A man? She doesn't know any men, only me and Phil, and he's in England. It wasn't Phil, was it?"

"I don't think so."

Another face appeared at the entrance. "Hello, Daddy. I'm a squirrel." The boy pointed at the piece of rope around his midriff. "This is my tail. I saw 'manda, too. She went out with the farmer, the man who has the sheep. He came before. He is her friend."

Mark ran this piece of information past Jeanette. "If you mean the strange man who was hanging around here talking to Charlie the other day, then I don't think he is a friend. He seemed suspicious to me. Don't ask me why, but it didn't seem right that he was asking Charlie questions. What grown-up asks a two-year-old where to find a café? I thought at the time it was peculiar and worried he was one of those dreadful people who goes after children. I gave the pair of them a right lecture about strangers and how they shouldn't talk to them after he went. Is Ted with her?"

The whining inside the cottage confirmed the fact that Ted was not with Amanda. He raced out when they opened the door. Jeanette went inside, shouting for Amanda. There was no reply.

"Mark, I'm worried. Amanda would never shut Ted inside alone. She knows he hates it. Another thing, there is a pile of shopping dumped on the table—milk and yogurts, you know, the sort of stuff you put in the fridge straight away. It's just sitting there. It's next to her handbag. Mark, I think something bad may have happened."

Mark and Claude had an urgent discussion. Claude got on the phone to rally his friends to search for the camper van. They would all take a main direction. Claude would head south towards the motorway, and Mark would take the more northerly direction out of Caylus. The road in this direction was winding and hilly; Bertie would not be able to travel fast. They just had to hope that Amanda had not left the main road. Jeanette phoned the police and alerted them to her suspicions. She chewed at her nails and fervently hoped that nothing dreadful had happened to Amanda and that one of them would have the good fortune to find her very soon.

Unaware of Amanda's plight, Bibi was sitting on a bench at Le Roc d'Anglars, a popular beauty spot at the top of the gorges, which overlooked the town of St-Antonin-Noble-Val and which had breathtaking views of the countryside around it. Today it was deserted, which suited Bibi. It was almost silent here, too, apart from the calling of a pair of honey buzzards that were circling above her head. She was resting on the bench, her head back against it, eyes closed. It would be ideal if the peace around her could permeate her skin and give her jumbled brain some form of tranquillity.

Bibi had not slept since she had seen Didier with his lover. On her return to the house, she had raced upstairs, ignoring Mathilde, and sobbed for what felt like forever. She hadn't come downstairs for dinner, preferring to sit in the dark in her bedroom. Mathilde tapped quietly on the door at one point.

"Bibi, I have some soup for you. Do you want it?"

"Thank you, Mathilde, no. If you don't mind, I would prefer to be left alone. I have a very bad migraine and would like to rest."

Mathilde had made no further attempt to question her.

Bibi wasn't sure if she was more upset that Didier had chosen to be with someone else or that he was going to be a father. She would have given anything to have been the person who could have offered him that possibility. She had yearned for a child for years. Didier had not seemed unduly worried that they had never had children, though. He had been happy with his work, and he had always appeared to be happy with her. She had been the perfect woman in so many ways save one: she had not given him a child. This could not be the only reason he had tired of her. Why had Didier fooled around? Was it because he was having a mid-life

341

crisis? Was younger flesh the attraction? Had he intended to merely have a fling, but the girl had become pregnant so now he felt duty-bound to stand by her? She didn't know the answers, but what she did know was that Didier did not love her. If he had loved her, he would have confessed to the affair. He would have told her everything. Together they would have decided what to do, and she would probably have forgiven him. She had forgiven his misdemeanours in the past, but this betrayal she could not forgive.

Details that she had hitherto ignored now tumbled into place. Mathilde had known about this girl. She had known about the baby. Those muttered conversations weren't just mother and son conversations, Didier had been asking her advice. That was why she had suddenly become friendlier towards Bibi. She didn't want Bibi to cause a huge fuss. She was protecting her son, as a mother always does, from further upset. She had probably advised him to keep his distance from Bibi in the hope that Bibi would tire of the late nights and trips away. She would have reported that Bibi was staying out, that Bibi was going out to dinner, and that Bibi was always communicating online with a man. Bibi had quite simply misread the situation. Instead of making Didier jealous with her fictitious lover, she had given Didier a "get-out" clause. She had handled it badly, and now it was too late. She was defeated. Didier was lost to her, and she was partly to blame.

She would shed no more tears now. She had decided what she would do. She would not break down in front of Didier when she confronted him. She would ask him simply if he loved this girl. If he said he did, she would walk away from him and their joke of a marriage. The child would need a father. She could not deny this innocent unborn child that. Over the years they had been together, Didier and she had both changed. She recognised that fact now. They had grown

342

apart, and among all the soul searching she had done overnight, she realised that they had grown apart some time ago. They should have talked sooner. It was too late now.

A rustling sound alerted her to the approach of someone. She wiped the tear that had cascaded down her cheek away, picked up her cardigan, which was beside her, and prepared to leave the tourist spot.

"Please don't leave on my account. Wow! It's stunning up here," said a familiar voice. "Well, hello, again. It's a jolly, small world, isn't it?" Todd Bradshaw lifted his sunshades onto his head and seeing her tear-streaked cheeks, sat down beside her. "Fancy a chat?"

Chapter Forty-Nine

She had been pouring out her heart for a long time now. The honey buzzards had long gone. Todd put a friendly, comforting arm around her shoulder. "Sometimes these things happen for a reason. It gives you the opportunity to do something you should have done. If I hadn't had my bike accident, I would probably have carried on being the Todd Bradshaw I have always been—selfish, unfocussed, unappreciative, and did I mention selfish?"

She smiled.

"It made me realise that in life, we don't always do the right thing. We chose a path, and we think we have to follow it all the way. Well, we don't. We can get off that path and chose another one. That's why I came to France. I'm looking for someone whom I hurt badly years ago. She has been on my mind a lot recently. I had the chance to make things up with her last year and an opportunity to start afresh with her when her marriage was breaking down. I messed up. She's here in the area. Her marriage is over, and I am going to tell her exactly how I feel about her now. I'm going to get down on my knees and beg forgiveness. I'm not sure if she'll have me, but at least I can try. If I fail, then I'll have to get over it. At least I'll know that I had a go, that I made an attempt to change my destiny, and that I tried to get off my path.

"If your marriage is truly over, then as painful as it may seem now, you will have to accept it. I don't want to be cruel, but the sooner you do that, the easier it will be for you, and you will be able to move on to the next phase of your life. You must forgive my analytical nature, but I'm a bloke, and a semi-Aussie one at that. You are a stunningly beautiful woman who, if I am not mistaken, is very talented, and you will not fail in anything you decide to do."

Bibi was grateful for his words. He had been with her for some time now, and he had been a huge comfort again. His way of facing facts was refreshing. She didn't want to get over-emotional about the situation. Facts were facts, and deep down, she was relieved that it had come to a head. She was sick of Didier's philandering. Let someone else deal with that.

It seemed strange she had met Todd again. When he had helped her in Toulouse and sat with her after she had seen Didier and his new love, they had only spoken briefly about the circumstances which had thrown them together. He had told her about cycling, his accident, and how he was now grabbing life by the horns. They had discussed France with its diverse culture. Todd had been fascinated by it all. He had made notes about places to visit while he was here and had kept her mind off the shock she had received. He had insisted on taking the shuttle bus back to the car park to make sure she was all right for driving and wished her luck. At no point had she told him where she lived. Now, he had stumbled into her life again. It was fate, or he was a type of guardian angel. He pulled out a bottle of water, a couple of apples, and some biscuits.

"I brought these along in case I got peckish. I needed to get some sun and some exercise, and this seems a wonderful place to get back to nature. It's very green, quite unlike where I live."

He drew out his wallet containing some photographs of his home in Sydney. The first picture was of a cattle dog sitting on top of a fabulously painted kennel. Having laughed at the dog's expression, which was one of utter pride, she admired the artwork. This was superb. Todd revealed he had painted the kennel one weekend for his dog. It was his gift to

Digit to let him know he was unique; a unique kennel for a unique, faithful dog, who never judged him, never let him down, and who never sulked when his master ate the last potato chip in the bowl. It led them on to talk about art and artists.

Bibi showed him her sketchbook, which she had brought with her. He told her about the fantastic collection of art he had seen in New York when he has visited a few years ago. They discussed art galleries, artists, and the works of Paul Cezanne, Georges Braque and William-Adolphe Bouguereau. Todd liked French music and knew songs by Jacques Brel, Serge Gainsbourg, and Édith Piaf. He was easy to talk to. He made you feel comfortable. Time raced by, and Bibi almost forgot her woes. It began to get cooler.

"Gosh, look at the time. You're getting cold; you should consider going back now. Look, I don't want to be forward, but I'm staying at the Residence in town. I'll be here for a few days if you need to talk again."

"I'd like that, but I don't want to spoil your plans. You have come to meet this special person—"

"Mandy. Oh, I'll meet her. I've waited almost a lifetime to see her again; a few extra days won't hurt. Besides, I need to make sure I have rehearsed exactly the right words I need to say, and I want her to see me when I'm looking fit and healthy. I don't want to go limping into her life like an old crumbly. You could do with a friend at the moment. I think that's just as important."

"Thank you. I feel much better, stronger, now that we have spoken. You have been so kind and very good to me. I'll come by and see you tomorrow, but don't let that keep you from Mandy. She is so lucky that you think so much of her that you have travelled from across the world to be with her. It is probably one of the most romantic stories I have heard."

"No, you've got me all wrong. I'm not romantic at all. I'm a mess-up. I'm a dumb guy, who should have grown up years ago, but if Mandy can forgive me and will have me, then I'll be the lucky one."

"All right, we'll meet tomorrow then for a farewell drink and to toast our new futures. I'll come by the Residence at ten."

"Yeah, that'd be great. I'll look forward to it."

Bibi made her way back to her car parked down the slope. Todd's words rang in her ears. He was right. She should chose a new path and walk down it with her head held high. She would confront Didier tonight.

Chapter Fifty

Mark tore along the major route leading out of Caylus and belted towards Villefranche. It was a steep, twisting climb to the top of the hill where it flattened out and you could see for miles. If the camper van was headed in this direction, he would stand a good chance of spotting it. As he charged down the tree-lined road, past the shut petrol station, he noticed a man, dressed in the traditional farmer garb of blue dungarees and shirt, sitting under an oak tree observing his flock of sheep. Mark screeched to a halt and yelled at the man. He asked if he had noticed a large mobile home headed this way. The old man slowly shook his head. No, no one had come by. It was lunch time. There was rarely any traffic passing by at this time of day.

He doubled back along the road and peeled off in the direction of Puylaroque. The road was full of sharp twists and bends, which he hugged tightly as he revved the engine and drove at full speed. If the camper van had come in this direction, he would have caught up with it by now. He sped on a few more kilometres. There was no sign of Bertie. He cursed and headed swiftly back towards Caylus. He would make one last attempt to find it. He tried the road to Limogne. It was another road which wound away from Caylus and snaked in a northerly direction. Mark travelled as far as Limogne itself, then decided he would not be able to find them now. The road divided here and went in several directions. There were just too many possibilities.

He turned the Peugeot around and drove back towards Beaulieu. He hoped that Claude or one of the others might have discovered the camper van and Amanda. If not, then it would have to be up to the police. Jeanette would have alerted them by now. Mark was fond of Amanda. She

349

had a sunny disposition, and he didn't like to think of anyone hurting her. He would have to phone Phil soon and tell him what had happened. It was a complete disaster.

Driving back at a more sedate pace, he passed a gap in the hedgerow which afforded views of the fields adjoining it and the magnificent views beyond. He squinted. He could make out the rear of a mobile home. It appeared to be stationary. He took the next turning, which led into the lane and discovered the camper van positioned halfway along it. The way it had been slung onto the side of the road, you could be forgiven for thinking that it had broken down. He phoned Claude to let him know where he was. Claude and his friends would make their way there, too.

Unsure of how to handle the situation without exacerbating it, he sat in his car for a while and just observed Bertie. He had tucked his car into a verge out of sight because he didn't want it to be spotted. He didn't want to do anything that might cause alarm. There appeared to be no movement in the camper van. He couldn't make out any shapes of people. He couldn't just sit there; he had to investigate it. Exiting his car, he clambered over a gate and walked beside the hedgerow, hidden from view. The hedgerow ran alongside the camper van. If he were cautious, he would be able to get right up to Bertie without being seen. He didn't want to put Amanda in any jeopardy if she was with a maniac or indeed, make a complete fool of her if she was just out on a jaunt with a friend.

He sneaked past the camper van and cocked his head to one side. He couldn't hear anything. He peeped over the hedge and ducked behind again. Bertie appeared to be deserted. He peered again more slowly. There was no sign of life in either the driver's or passenger's seats. He slipped out of the field at the next opening in the hedge and doubled back as quickly as possible towards the front of the van.

Mark tiptoed around to the front window and looked in. There was no one. The keys were in the ignition. He cupped his hands in front of his eyes and looked once more for a clue. There was a phone lying on the floor. The screen on it was cracked. It looked like Amanda's phone. Her iPhone had a multi-coloured shell, black with brightly coloured hearts in rows on it. He could make out blue and pink hearts. There couldn't be many covers like that.

The door was unlocked. Taking a deep breath, he eased it open as quietly as possible. Bertie squeaked in protest.

"Is there someone there?" called a shrill voice from inside.

"Amanda, is that you? It's Mark."

"Oh, thank goodness, you're here! Come round to the side door. Hurry up."

Mark rushed round and opened the door to find Amanda sitting on the floor, bound to the leg of the kitchen table by a silk scarf. On the floor was an unconscious form.

"You okay?"

"Yes, surprisingly calm as it happens. He wasn't going to hurt me. He was going to leave me here, tied up so he could escape without getting into trouble. He became quite upset in the end. Someone had made a fool of him, you see? He told me the whole story. Do you think he'll be all right?"

Mark took in the supine figure on the floor with a bluing bruise to his temple. The man was unconscious but breathing and would come round soon.

"He'll be fine. Let's get you out of here and get this character to the police. I'll take him in my car. Are you all right to drive Bertie home?"

"Yes, of course. I actually felt sorry for him. I was scared of him for a while, especially when he got angry, but after he had shouted for a bit, he just caved in and broke down. He kept saying that someone was out to get him. He thought it was revenge for some reason. I think he needs a shrink, not the police. You haven't told Phil about this, have you?"

"No. We wouldn't worry him unnecessarily."

"It's probably best I don't say anything about it to him just yet. He doesn't need any extra pressure at the moment, and I am absolutely fine. Oh, I can't phone him anyway. Stuart or Richard or whoever broke my phone. I'll have to get a new one tomorrow. You know, one good thing has come out of this. It'll make a great post for my blog."

Mark released her from the silk scarf, which bound her hands. She rubbed her wrists absent-mindedly and explained the whole episode to Mark as they waited for Richard Montagu-Forbes to come round.

BLOG: Fortifying Your Fifties

It's not every day you get kidnapped. I spent all last year moaning about having no excitement in my life and bingo! Now, I can say that I have had enough excitement, thank you. In retrospect, it wasn't a proper kidnap. I didn't get a bag put over my head and thrown into the boot of a car. No one had to pay a ransom to have me released. My mother always used to say as a joke that if I ever got kidnapped, the kidnappers would give me back and pay her to take me because they wouldn't be able to put up with my constant babbling. Do you know, I think she might have been right!

Fortunately, I wasn't frightened. The simple reason for that was I was too confused to be scared. I couldn't work out what was happening and me, being me, talked a lot. I do that when I'm confused or nervous.

The man drove off with me in Bertie. I won't bother you with how we came to be in Bertie, but it was thanks to my stupidity that I had got into the camper van with a complete stranger just because he looked meek and claimed to be married to a woman called Maisie.

We didn't go too far. Luckily, Bertie did not have much fuel, and so we couldn't go too far. It was lunchtime, so the stations were shut. He turned into a lane and started quizzing me.

He insisted I was someone he knew. Of course, I was not. To prove it, I got out my phone and showed him my Facebook page. It has that great photo of me and Phil that my mother took—the one just before we began this trip. The man looked at it and threw my phone down in disgust.

"Get out," he growled. Then he grabbed my arm and hustled me into Bertie from the side entrance and forced me to sit on the floor.

"Listen, Stuart," I began. That was the name he gave me at the cottage before we drove off in Bertie.

"I'm not Stuart."

"Oh yes, sorry. Um, listen Richard—" That was the name he used when he thought he was communicating with me on Facebook. Long story.

"I'm not Richard either."

"Well, that's just plain confusing. If you are not Stuart and you are not Richard, then who the heck are you?"

He glowered at me.

"What's your real name? Does Maisie know your real name?"

"Maisie doesn't exist either," he yelled. "Shut up, will you? You are doing my head in with your irritating questions."

"I don't want to annoy you. It's just that I'm really confused and somewhat nervous. I always talk a lot when I'm nervous. Phil tells me to shut up a lot, too, but he doesn't mean it nastily. That was Phil in the photo with me. We've been married twenty-five years. You'd like Phil. He's always calm and very sensible. Tom, that's my son, isn't like his dad, though. He's more like me. He doesn't talk as much as me, though. He grunts a lot. He'll probably become more sensible as he gets older, but at the moment, he is going through that difficult age."

The man looked at me quizzically.

"You know the one where you don't want to live with your parents, but you can't afford to move out? That time when you wish you were independent? Well, no matter how much we think we are helping Tom, he sees it as interference. He's living in our house at the moment. It's to help him become independent, but so far he has broken most of the furniture, set fire to the curtains, and let squatters in. Actually, it turned out he didn't let the squatters in at all.

Alice's father forgot to lock the door when he went round to clean the windows for Tom. It was his mistake. Tom tries hard. He's a good lad really. I still think he would be better off in a flat. His real name is Thomas, but we have always called him Tom. He never looked like a Thomas. Do you have children? Oh, of course not, how silly of me! That was when you were with Maisie, who doesn't exist. Children bring a lot of hard work but a lot of joy. I've been missing Tom a great deal recently. So, what's your name? What did your mum call you?"

The man let out a soft groan. He sat for some time. He was torn between saying something and probably smacking me in the face. In the end, he let out a deep, sad sigh.

"The last name she called me was Pumpkin. She patted me on the head and said 'Goodbye, Pumpkin. I'll try and come back for you. Be good for your daddy.'"

I shut up instantly. This was a pivotal moment. I looked him straight in the eyes.

"I never knew her. I was only three years old when she walked out. I never saw her again. She went off with another man, and that is all I know."

"She left you when you were only a small, helpless child?"

He nodded.

"Did your dad look after you?"

He crouched down on the floor next to me. He stared absently into space.

"Sort of. In the beginning he did. Then the drink made him sour and bitter. He would go out on benders for hours and collapse into bed when he got back. He hated my mother for leaving me with him. He used to drink every night. When he was completely legless and just before he collapsed, he would tell me what a whoring bitch she was.

355

She must have been because she never did come back for me. He told me all women were the same. They lead you on, and then drop you when you are no use to them anymore."

He spoke at length about his childhood. Then he progressed to an incident at school when a group of girls, led by one he fancied, had ganged up on him and called him *spotty owl* because of his glasses. All the class had laughed at that. It was made worse by the fact that he had let girls call him names. The boys considered him a real weakling and ostracized him for it. I knew how cruel children could be. I shared with him how the name-calling caused me to stop wearing glasses in public and how much I was tormented once the other children discovered that my front teeth were false, like old people's teeth. My teeth had been smashed out in an unfortunate incident when I was younger.

He became quiet after that again. He apologised and told me that he would have to leave me there tied up. He couldn't take a chance that he might get caught. He had been looking for someone whom he had fallen in love with on the internet. They had built up a good relationship, and he had become serious about her. The problem was that she had vanished from Facebook. He had followed the clues she had given him which had led to me. The whole thing was a complete mystery. He wouldn't tell me anymore, only to say that he probably deserved the let-down.

I kept very quiet. I had a dreadful feeling that if I said the wrong thing, he could turn against me very quickly. Yes, me, Facing50, being quiet—there's a first! He shook himself out of his reverie and told me to sit quietly. Someone would eventually find me, and by then, he would be miles away. He tied my hands to the table leg. Caught in his thoughts again, he began to sob quietly. Tears blurred his vision, which was why when he stood up abruptly to leave me, he tumbled over the huge, orange Space Hopper that was right behind him.

The Space Hopper was in Bertie because I had taken it to town that morning. I had intended to donate it to the nursery in town, but I forgot. When I got to the cottage, I propped it up on one of the seats because it had been bumping about in the back. He must have knocked against it when he pulled me into Bertie. He was so busy talking to me and then focusing on tying the scarf that he just didn't notice it. I would have thought it quite difficult to miss a huge, grinning Space Hopper, but hey, he did! He tripped right over it, bashed his head against the cupboard, and went down with a clatter. He was out for the count. I shouted at him, but he didn't wake up. Almost as soon as he went down, I heard a voice outside, and hey, presto, Mark magically appeared to save me.

So, there you have it—an adventure indeed. Although I am writing this with a smile on my face—after all, it is not every day that you catch a kidnapper with a Space Hopper—today's post has a serious message. Be very careful whom you befriend on the internet. I am extremely cautious about who my friends are on Facebook now. I only have a few friends, and they are real people whom I know. They are not cyber friends. Yesterday, I got kidnapped by a man, who thought I was his cyber-girlfriend. He was crazy about this woman. She led him to believe she cared about him and then dumped him, unceremoniously, by disappearing from his cyberworld. The outcome could have been quite different. Well, maybe not. Who in their right mind could put up with my inane ramblings? He'd have given up at some stage. ☺

Posted by Facing50.Blog

Comments

Hippyhappyhoppy says… OMG! Hugs. More hugs and more hugs. So glad you are okay. x

QuiteContrary says… I have no contrary opinion to offer today. I am delighted that you handled the situation so well. You would make an excellent negotiator in hostage situations.

TheMerryDivorcee says… Holy Cow. You sure you don't need counseling after that? I would. None of my husbands were as nutty as that freak. Is he locked away now? You are right about the internet. I met husband number 6 online. That was a mistake.

PhillyFilly says… Goodness gracious. I cannot believe this. So glad you are not traumatized and are able to share this with us. I am not on Facebook. I wouldn't dare put a photo up of myself.

YoungFreeSingleandSane says… I would have freaked out. You are incredible. Well done on talking him round and well done to your mother for giving you the Space Hopper. What a weapon!

SexyFitChick says… Cripes, I almost choked on my muesli this morning when I read this post. I demand you take up self-defence lessons. You need to always be prepared. Of course, you could take the little, fat, orange fellow along with you if you like. He could upgrade to black belt! Relieved to hear you are all right. I'd hate anything to happen to you. Have you told Phil yet, or would he be disappointed that the kidnapper didn't keep you?

Gypsynesters2 says…Wow! This week your life is infinitely more exciting than ours.

DonnaKBab says… I'm closing my Facebook account. I have four hundred friends, and I don't know any of them personally. Thanks for the warning, and I'd like to add my two cents worth, too—I'm very happy that you got through it and are still here to tell the tale.

MiaFerrari said: You got into a vehicle with a stranger because you thought his wife was called Maisie? How crazy are you? Please promise you won't ever do that again. He was suffering from some weird disorder due to his mother leaving him when he was young. He probably hates all women. Good thing you talked him into submission. Your maternal approach no doubt rekindled his memories of being a boy and made him more submissive. Good that you talked about your family. It made you come across as human, which, of course, you are—aren't you? Or are you some odd cyber friend, who isn't who she says she is?

Facing50 says… Thank you all for your good wishes and comments. I shall email you all individually because there isn't enough space to write everything I want to say to each of you. I'll send a photo of me with my new hero—the Space Hopper.

Chapter Fifty-One

Phil was in the shower when the same number that had rung in the car rang for the second time. He didn't hear it because of the warm running water, which cascaded over his head and down his neck, soothing his tired muscles. While he was drying his hair and wondering how long he had before it all fell out and he wouldn't have to worry about drying it at all, the phone rang again. It rang a further three times while he was watching a documentary about polar bears in the Arctic. He didn't hear its muffled ringtone because he had left it in the pocket of his jacket, which was hanging neatly on a coat hanger in the wardrobe.

It had been dark for a long time. A few stars were visible in the night sky, but clouds shrouded the moon. There was a shuffling sound at the front door. The door was unlocked quietly and pushed open. A figure crept into the house and made its way to the staircase, hesitating only to ensure that it did not stand on the first stair which normally creaked badly.

In that instant, the door to the study opened, and a shaft of dim light fell onto the man, illuminating him in a soft red glow. He hesitated, then removed his foot from the stair, his shoulders hunched.

Bibi spoke in resigned tones. "Didier, we need to talk."

He turned around to find his wife silhouetted in the door frame. A small lamp threw a subtle light into the room, revealing the crumpled cushion of a leather chair and a box of tissues on the table next to it. He nodded and followed her retreating shape back into the study. It was time.

After a restless night, Amanda finally got up from the tangle of bed sheets. She stumbled downstairs in the half light. Unsure of how to employ the time, she turned on the computer. It whirred into life. Overnight, several of her friends had left messages for her. That was the beauty of blogging. When you were asleep, someone on the other side of the world was wide awake and reading your posts. They invariably left a comment or message for you, so you always had something to look forward to in the morning. What a supportive bunch of people they were. She could almost picture each and every one of them. She had learned so much about them the last two years that she had been blogging. She would email all of them today. She had nothing else planned other than dropping off the orange Space Hopper and her old toys to the children's nursery as intended and maybe purchasing a new phone.

Her old phone was next to the computer. It no longer worked. She couldn't even get the photographs stored on it to display which upset her because she had several that she valued. She'd try and get it repaired in the first instance. If not, she'd replace it. She needed a phone. She would like to phone Phil and have a chat with him now. The whole ordeal had not fazed her yesterday, but this morning she was aware of how the outcome could have been different. She had not been quite as brave as she indicated on her blog or to Mark. At one point, she had been terrified that Richard/Stuart would lose the plot and harm her. It had taken a huge amount of self-control to not start blubbering, and it was only because she gibbered like a demented baboon when anxious that she had walked away from the whole affair. The internet afforded the chance to make friends and have a social life, albeit online, but this episode had heightened her awareness to its pitfalls.

She checked her Facebook account. She only had twelve friends on it and most of those were Tom's old school friends who stayed in touch with her and occasionally asked about Tom. There was a woman she had met and exercised with at the gym many moons ago when she was younger. She had moved to Spain now but stayed in touch. Her hairdresser was also one of her friends. He often shared funny photographs of cats. Then there was Todd. He hadn't been online for a while now. It was normal for him to be absent from the internet for long spells when he went off on his travels. He had told her that he was going on a trip, but he had not divulged much information about it. He'd no doubt return soon with photographs from some exotic destination and fascinating stories. The Scrabble Board revealed that they hadn't played for almost two weeks. It was his turn. She had played last. The word was highlighted in red: *wicked*.

She wasn't feeling very wicked or very playful at the moment. In fact, even her appetite for adventure had waned. She had reflected on the whole Bertie incident all night. Ironically, Claude had decided that Bertie was just what he was looking for. He was buying the camper van, and now there seemed little point in staying in France any longer. The adventure, if indeed you could call it that, had served to point her in the right direction. She wanted to go home.

She was ready to face Phil's depressed moods, or Tom's lackadaisical attitude, or her mother's lengthy conversations. She didn't mind that she was a middle-aged woman with hormonal outbursts and a tubby stomach. It really wasn't of consequence. It was much more valuable to be with the people you loved. She would be content with days in her home and now that she had written her book, she could try to get it published. She could even write another. The online magazine that had featured her article about

"Irritable Male Syndrome" had requested some more articles. She had found a vocation. Life didn't have to offer spectacular challenges every day. She could create her own personal challenges, and they didn't need to be insurmountable ones. She didn't have to travel the world on a crusade. She could find pleasure and happiness by being at Phil's side and through her writing. Adventures were for other people. She wasn't convinced she was cut out for risks. She wasn't sure she wanted any more surprises either.

Her ruminating was broken by an urgent knocking at the door. Jeanette stood outside, dressed in pyjamas, her hair uncombed.

"Come in!" exclaimed Amanda. "Children got you up early? Fancy a cup of tea? I was just going to make one."

"Amanda…" began Jeanette. "I am so sorry. There's a call for you at the house. It's Phil. He tried to reach you on the mobile, and when it kept ringing out, he phoned us. He didn't know what else to do. Oh, Amanda, I'm really sorry. It's your mother…"

Chapter Fifty-Two

Todd paced back and forth for the umpteenth time. He had rehearsed his speech so often he was beginning to bore himself with it. He had chatted again with Bibi yesterday. She had provided a pleasant distraction to his anxiety. They had shared a pot of coffee at a tearoom in Caussade and talked about their lives.

She had left Didier. The old buffoon had told her that he was going to stand by his new girlfriend. She was expecting his child. He couldn't leave her, and he admitted that he loved her. He had explained to Bibi that although he still had deep feelings for Bibi, he had fallen for the girl who worked in accounts. She had been fresh, vibrant, and amusing company. It had begun as a light affair, but he had gradually fallen for her. He hadn't meant for it to happen. He would rather die than hurt Bibi, but, in his opinion, his relationship with Bibi had become a tired format. Surely, even she had to acknowledge that they had little in common now? He was grateful to her for looking after his mother. He admired her hugely. He even loved her still, but he couldn't imagine spending any of the future with her, and of course, he had a new life to consider—the life of his child.

Bibi was an extraordinary woman. She spoke to Todd about it all in such a matter-of-fact way that he sat almost open-mouthed in astonishment. He assumed it was her very Frenchness that made her capable of understanding her husband's needs. She had accepted it with grace. She hadn't ranted or raved at Didier and thrown pots at his head or screamed at him. She hadn't cursed him or wished him ill. She had quite simply comprehended how it had happened and how he had a duty to his new family. She was a remarkable woman. She was the strongest woman he had ever met, and Todd had met a few. She was now making plans to set up her gallery, and Todd knew she wouldn't be alone for very long. She had a magnetism that would attract any red-blooded male for hundreds of miles.

To his immense surprise, his heart was fluttering. He thought that sort of thing happened to women, not to butch blokes like him. He looked at the enormous bouquet of roses beside him on the seat. No, he wasn't as macho as he thought. He had definitely transformed into an old romantic. Good thing Digit couldn't see him at the moment. He'd be disgusted with his master—all dressed up and smelling of some French aftershave he couldn't pronounce. He was dressed in a white shirt and smart new Levis. He'd scrubbed his teeth four times and worried that his hair was a little too short. He'd been to a hairdresser in the town, and she'd given him an expert cut. He hoped it wasn't too young for him; he was in his fifties, after all.

He pulled the car into Beaulieu. This was it. He'd asked at the local post office and established that an English woman was living alone in the Delfont's cottage. The woman behind the desk had been so charmed by Todd that she had even drawn a map of how to find it. He'd explained that he had come all the way from Australia to see this woman. They were very old friends. The woman had raised an eyebrow, pursed her lips, and immediately pulled out a biro to draw the route out for him. She also pointed him in the direction of the florist's shop. The French knew how to do romance.

So, he was here at last. His epic journey from hospital, to recovery, and now to France was at its end. Behind the door to the cottage was the woman he loved, whom he had always loved. He would have to get it right this time. There would be no more chances after this one.

He checked his breath, looked in the mirror to make sure he hadn't gotten anything stuck in his front teeth, and picked up the flowers. He knocked gingerly on the door. Light footsteps clattered on the stairs, and the door flew open.

Bibi couldn't see the visitor, only an enormous bunch of multi-coloured roses greeting her.

"I know this is going to come as a huge surprise, but I had to come and tell you that no matter what has happened between us in the past, I love you, and I am not leaving this doorstep until you hear me out."

The flowers dropped down to reveal Todd's eager face, which quickly changed to confusion, then embarrassment, then back to confusion.

"Bibi, what are you doing here?"

"I am moving in. Mark and Jeanette have invited me to make use of it until I can find a studio in Toulouse. What are you doing here?"

"I came to see Mandy."

It was Bibi's turn to look confused. Then the proverbial penny dropped.

"Oh mon Dieu! Mandy is what you call a *nickname*. I should have realised sooner. I was too wrapped up in my own misery. You mean Amanda. You are looking for Amanda. Oh, you poor man! You do not know. Amanda has gone. She left first thing yesterday morning. She had some terrible news about her mother and has gone home to England for good. She is not coming back. Jeanette has packed her clothes and is sending them to her." Todd's face turned ashen. "But, Todd," continued Bibi, digesting the facts and attempting to make sense of it all, "why did you think you could ever be with Amanda? She loves her husband. She would never leave him for anyone, not even you."

For the first time in his life, Todd was crestfallen. Bibi took him gently by the arm and led him inside. He sat on the large settee in a daze. She took the flowers from him, placing them tenderly in a large, glass vase filled with water and then uncorked a bottle of chilled Chablis. It was her turn to provide a shoulder for Todd.

Chapter Fifty-Three

The song "Don't Worry, Be Happy" was playing over the speakers. It was the same song that Amanda had as her ringtone for her old phone. The lyrics were about being positive in life. The crowd that had come to celebrate her mother's life were gathering now to watch the firework display. Grego had his arm around Spencer. Spencer's eyes were full to the brim with tears. Amanda picked up her glass of champagne and followed the crowd. There were people here that she had never met, but they were all friends of her mother. Many had travelled all the way from Cyprus to come to this. Some were locals. Amanda observed a small group of elderly ladies, those who went to the races with her mother. They were dressed in their best outfits to do justice to the event. Some people nodded at her. One or two touched her arm affectionately as she walked past. She had spoken to many of them, and they all told her the same thing: her mother was an amazing woman.

The first fireworks exploded with a huge blast—a ricochet of shots. They whizzed up into the dark night with a tremendous bang. The sky filled immediately with brightly coloured confetti, which floated down like giant, sparkling parachutes. More bangs and more whizzing sounds accompanied fireworks that were zigzagging across the dark sky. Others curled and twisted, corkscrewing their way upwards towards the heavens.

The crowd watched with wonder. The display was in time to a classical piece—an aria from Puccini's opera *Turandot*. It was one of her mother's favourite operas and held a special sadness because it was his last opera and remained unfinished at the time of his death in 1924. It was completed in 1926 by Franco Alfano. Her mother's knowledge of classical music and all things Italian was incredible.

The fireworks were magnificent. She had never witnessed such a splendid display. The heavens seemed alive and full of vitality. It was so beautiful, and yet she was so sad. This was an incredible display. Catherine wheels were now hurtling around, sparks flying. There were seven of them, each one representing a decade of her mother's life.

More blasts as fireworks were jettisoned into the sky. The audience was spellbound. Then, the *pièce de résistance*: a special rocket, one that had been specially commissioned for the event. The crowd fell silent as the rocket hurtled towards the heavens. It detonated with a tremendous boom, an enormous cloud of bewitching colours sprayed the sky. Below the massive cloud of twinkling colours, a huge frame sizzled and sprung into life. The colours formed huge letters, which in turn formed words, written in brilliant red and gold:

"Thank you for being my friends—I love you all."

Tears fell then. They were dabbed at by lace handkerchiefs and with soggy sleeves. The lump that had been making swallowing difficult became larger in her throat. The crowd began clapping, then cheering. The noise was almost as deafening as the fireworks. A small figure came to the front of the crowd.

"Thank you. Thank you all for sharing this with me. When I was in hospital, I decided that if I got out alive, I was going to make sure I would have a huge party to celebrate the fact that I am still here. You can call it a wake if you like. I prefer to say it has been a celebration of my life and life in general. Funerals are depressing, so I thought I'd have a pre-funeral party. That way I could enjoy it, too, and we all know how much I like a party."

The crowd laughed as one.

"You have indulged me, and I have had a magnificent time today. I can't express how much you all mean to me. You have helped me through the last few years since my husband and Amanda's father passed away. You have been there when I have felt low, and many of you are the reason I am still here today.

"I hope you have relished it all as much as I have. I must thank you all again for celebrating my life today. I'd also like to thank the fireworks company for this incredible display. The lance work was outstanding. Who would have thought you could write messages in the sky with fireworks? For the more adventurous of you considering a phenomenal send off, they will also fill a rocket with your ashes when you actually depart and shoot it into the sky. What could be better than a final ride on a firework?"

The crowd laughed again.

"Finally, I want to thank my family: Tom and his girlfriend, Alice," she waved at them and they grinned back. "Phil, who has been such a good son-in-law. He has looked after Amanda. What more could a mother ask for than someone who loves her daughter as much as she does?" Phil looked suitably embarrassed and tried to hide behind a large woman, who kept blowing her nose. "And, of course, I want to thank my gorgeous daughter, Amanda. She was by my side all the time I was ill and encouraged me to get better. Her humour got me through the dark hours. So, enough of this. It's time to ask the band to play. Phil, can I have the first dance with you?"

Before her mother could disappear into the crowd again and torment Phil, Amanda shouted out, "I'd like to propose a toast to my mother. *May she be around for many more years and always come up with wild ideas like this one. We all need fun in our lives, and my mother has proved that*

371

she is an expert in that. So please raise your glasses. To my mum."

The band began playing an old 1950s track, and Amanda pushed her way towards her mother.

"You've taken your medicine, haven't you? You're not overdoing it, are you?"

"Amanda, I am not a child. I'm having the best time I have had in ages. The doctor said that as long as I took the medication, I should be able to keep the angina under control. I've got this blessed thing as well now," Grace continued, sucking hungrily on an electronic cigarette. The end of it glowed, emitting an eerie green colour. It emitted smoke like a real cigarette. "I'm getting used to this now. I quite like the taste of menthol or whatever this is supposed to be. It's not quite like the real thing, but it'll help keep me here a little longer. Now, don't fuss. Ah, is that Phil I spy hiding over there? I'm just going to get him on the dance floor. He looks like he could do with some fun. I'll see you later." She blew Amanda a kiss and beetled off in Phil's direction, a determined look on her face.

Grego approached her. "She's quite something. You know she insisted on seeing the video of the fashion show last night? She kept apologising for missing the event, as if that mattered. We were just so happy she was alive. She probably won't be able to travel to Cyprus now, you know. The doctors aren't keen for her to travel so far since the attack. She'll miss out on all of the life there."

"I heard the launch was a massive success. Well done! We're all so happy for you. You deserve the success. I expect you can hardly keep up with orders now. Don't worry about Mum. We're redecorating Tom's old room, and she's going to spend some time with us. I've got a few things lined up for her. Phil booked us tickets to the opera in Birmingham, and I've planned a spa day with her. Tom and

Alice are going to take her to the pub and to a quiz night. She'll love that. We'll sort out other events as and when. She won't have time to be lonely. You'll still come and stay with her, though, won't you?"

"Of course we will. We wouldn't want to miss out on those Twister parties or her demonic wine evenings. She'll be fine. Grace just needs company and friends. She'll be much better now; she's got her best friend back again—you." He hugged Amanda tightly.

She glanced over to the dance floor where her mother was trying to teach Phil to jive. Phil looked like he would rather stick pins in his eyes. She waved over at them. Her mother waved back and gave her the thumbs up sign, then grabbed Phil's hands and tried to get him do an underarm turn, which left him spinning and her convulsing with laughter.

BLOG: Fortifying Your Fifties

Phil is lying in bed with a wicked hangover. It serves him right. He knows better than to drink my mother's homemade wine. Two glasses could knock out an elephant. We came back to her house from the big "Wake Party" that she held at the local centre. You would not have believed how many people came to the event. When she first told me she wanted to have a wake, or as we finally called it, a "celebration of life" party, I thought she was mad. She correctly pointed out that no party in her honour would be complete without her, so she was going to have it before her life was snatched from her. The nasty angina attack had been a close thing. It was very fortunate that she responded to the medication the hospital administered, and she didn't have to undergo bypass surgery.

I just had to write this post today to share a couple of pieces of information. Recently, I have been writing all about my time in France and my wonderful friend, Bibi. She gave me some excellent advice on how to stay youthful and how to keep your man interested in you. Well, dear reader of this blog, you may have been surprised when I told you that she had left her own husband. I certainly was. I had no idea that their marriage was in trouble. It transpires that Bibi is an even darker horse than I thought. Why? Well, I'm going to post some of her last email to me and you will see why.

My dearest Amanda,

I cannot begin to understand life and its complexities or its opportunities. As I explained to you in my last email, your friend Todd came here in search of you. Instead of finding you, he met me. I am not writing to tell you that we have fallen passionately in love, but I thought it was only fair to tell you that I am going to go to Australia and stay there, at least for a while. It will give us time to see if we are right for each other. I expect you will rush out and buy a hat, ready for the wedding at this news. I know what an optimist you are. If nothing else, it will give me a new start and new opportunities. I can set up a gallery there, and who knows what the future may bring?

I cannot tell you how sorry I am for having brought such misfortune to your door in the shape of Richard Montagu-Forbes. That something dreadful could have happened to you because of it is inconceivable. I am grateful every day that you came to no harm. One day I shall make it all up to you. Thank you for forgiving my stupidity. You are a true friend.

I met Didier's new woman yesterday. We met at the Gazpacho, you remember, where you and I often met? The baby is a carbon copy of his father. He is very handsome. I cannot say I am happy about it all, but I am not sad either. I do not profess to understand the complexities of human nature, but I know that in choosing Fabienne and his new son, Didier has freed me and allowed me to find new horizons.

Please send your mother my very best wishes. Give Tom a big hug from his unknown "Auntie" and tell Phil you love him. He may grimace but tell him anyway!

I shall send you a postcard from Australia, in fact, several postcards. Who knows? Maybe you will come over here one day. I would want my "leetle Eenglish friend" to be at my wedding.

Bisous, Bibi xxxx

I have just been onto Facebook. I left Todd a new word on the Scrabble board: *elated*. I added a message, too. *Elated to hear you may have found someone to share your*

"Scrabble-less" evenings with. Make sure you get it right this time. xxx

So, this is quite possibly my last post. I shall be incredibly busy from here on in. My mother will be staying with us for the next few weeks or until Phil has a nervous breakdown. He is going to take me up in the Cessna next weekend, and I have three articles to write for the magazine this month. I don't think I'll have much time for blogging for the moment, so I must take this opportunity to say a huge thank you to you all. You saw me through difficult times last year and have been an imperative part of my life this year. I shall, of course, still come and leave comments on your blogs. As for my book, well, I shall give it to my Mum to read, and if she approves it, I'll send it off to some agents. You may see me yet on the *Ellen DeGeneres Show*.

I have blocked the comments reply form today so you can't leave any comments. I only did it because I hate goodbyes, and this is just *au revoir* for now. Good luck with everything you do and remember that quote: "He who laughs—lasts."

Posted by Facing50

No Comment Form Available

About The Author

A graduate of the University of Keele in Staffordshire, Carol E Wyer is a former teacher, linguist, and physical trainer.

She spent her early working life in Casablanca, Morocco, where she translated for companies and taught English as a Foreign Language. She then returned to work in education back in the UK and set up her own language company in the late eighties.

In her forties, Carol retrained to become a personal trainer to assist people, who, like herself, had undergone major surgery.

Having spent the last decade trying out all sorts of new challenges such as kickboxing, diving, and flying helicopters, she is now ensuring that her fifties are "fab not drab". She has put her time to good use by learning to paint, attempting to teach herself Russian, and writing a series of novels and articles which take a humorous look at getting older.

Named affectionately by her American followers as BOTUK (Bombeck Of the UK) due to her humorous posts, Carol has been a regular blogger and social networking addict.

Having finished *Surfing in Stilettos*, the sequel to her light-hearted debut novel, *Mini Skirts and Laughter Lines*, Carol has assured her husband, who seems to be permanently neglected, that he will no longer have to put up with ready-made meals and a dusty house—at least for a little while.

More information about Carol can be found at
http://www.carolewyer.co.uk

Be sure to read Author Carol E Wyer's debut novel:

Mini Skirts and Laughter Lines

Amanda Wilson can't decide between murder, insanity, or another glass of red wine. Facing 50 and all that it entails is problematic enough. What's the point in minking your eyes, when your husband would rather watch Russia Today than admire you strutting in front of the television in only thigh boots and a thong?

Her son has managed to perform yet another magical disappearing act. Could he actually be buried under the mountain of festering washing strewn on his bedroom floor? He'll certainly be buried somewhere when she next gets her hands on him.

At least her mother knows how to enjoy herself. She's partying her twilight years away in Cyprus. Queen of the Twister mat, she now has a toy boy in tow.

She knows she shouldn't have pressed that Send button. The past always catches up with you sooner or later. Still, her colourful past is a welcome relief to her monochrome present—especially when it comes in the shape of provocative Todd Bradshaw, her first true love.

Soon Mandy has a difficult decision to make—one that will require more than a few glasses of Chianti.

Available here:
http://www.amazon.com/MINI-SKIRTS-AND-LAUGHTER-LINES/dp/1908481811

Lightning Source UK Ltd.
Milton Keynes UK
UKOW051039100712

195746UK00001B/5/P